A Tail for
All Seasons

Volume 2

A Tail for All Seasons

Volume 2

A collection of Manx stories

editor **Linda Mann**

Priory Press

Published by Priory Press Ltd
The Priory, Abbots Way, Abbotswood,
Ballasalla, Isle of Man IM9 3EQ
www.priory-press.co.uk

First published 2009

ISBN 978 0 9551510 4 0

Although this book is set in and around the Isle of Man
some of the characters and locations are purely fictional and
any similarity to anyone living or dead is simply
coincidence and the product of the various authors'
extraordinarily vivid imaginations.

Edited and typeset by
Frances Hackeson Freelance Publishing Services,
Brinscall, Lancs
Printed in Great Britain by
Bell and Bain Ltd, Glasgow

contents

Contents

preface

I am now going to admit to something that maybe I shouldn't admit to, or at least not in public and that is that I like short stories. I especially like short stories with a twist, I like them in any genre and I particularly crave them when I'm visiting a new place and want a little local colour. But unfortunately the art of the short story, with a few notable exceptions, appeared to be fading out – dying on its feet in fact. I'd toddle into a friendly bookshop, clutching my ready money and there would be no new collections of easily digested stories, no creepy tales to have me scurrying around graveyards at dead of night or standing in solitary contemplation outside some Victorian villa, musing upon the stain halfway up the wall. And then to add insult to injury I was told that there was no market for a new anthology, no other sad reader wanted them.

So when Priory Press looked like it wasn't going to be shuffled off into the grimy hands of the Administrators I published my own collection and … it sold so well that I started collecting tales for volume two and here they are, bigger, better and some a lot stranger than the first. All have that element of fact and the rest ... well it may be sheer imagination on the other hand ...

And now I'm going to fill a flask with a hot beverage, grab my copy of *Tails* 2 and my Map of the Island and go stare at a bridge ... well you never know, do you?

Linda Mann

foreword

My tale for all seasons starts in August, late in the evening sitting at home in the warmth of a soft light, in my garret at the top of the house, which I use as an office. I heard a gentle electric pulsing sound and to quote Hollywood "You've got mail" and before checking I knew it was going to be the usual spam, asking in stilted english if I would like to add two inches to my pencil ... but then I realise, it was far worse ... it's an email from MANN ... moving my hand across to the mouse I open the message with trepidation. It starts ... "Bob, I've been at it again ..." consult professional help is my initial response, then I read the first grasping words, gradually being drawn into the document. "I've got another volume of *A Tail for All Seasons* coming out and I thought you could perhaps write the Foreword as last time." After the first shock of the email your whole body relaxes and you find yourself saying Yes!!!

So here is the Foreword to volume 2, and if you're reading this in the bookshop again, I've had the pleasure to read these twelve short stories, so dear reader, now go and buy a copy. I'm always pleasantly surprised that people find the time and have the suffcent talent to entertain us with words. Letting our imaginations wander, allows ourselves to follow in their brain cells, taking us backwards and forwards to wherever they want to go with their vivid minds.

If you were lucky enough to jump on the Manntrain with the first volume this second will not disappoint; dare I suggest without upsetting too many authors that this second volume is just a tad better.

Let us all congratulate the chosen authors and commiserate with the authors whose work was rejected – knowing Linda I imagine the stories will become part of volume 3.

Enjoy these magnificent tales in volume 2, I know you will and if Linda Mann is reading this, I've changed my email address.

Bob Harrison
Evening Extra
Manx Radio

PS   To the author who mentioned Manx Radio in their story, I admire your choice of radio station.

acknowledgements

With many thanks to Frances Hackeson who patiently put up with me and my bright ideas, wove her usual magic on a dozen stories and dealt with all twelve writers, the graphic artist, the printer and still managed to hold on to her sanity.

To Victoria Harrop who managed to pull off yet another wonderfully evocative photograph complete with open book.

To Bob Harrison who patiently read all the manuscripts for the Foreword even though he was on holiday.

To John Kennaugh, Beth Espey, Simon Clarke and Howard Caine for superb vocal renditions which launched the first volume and will hopefully do the same for this one.

To Patricia Foulkes for reading the finished manuscript and for writing some very nice things in the local paper about both volumes.

To Manx Radio, Mannin Media and Isle of Man Newspapers for voluntarily promoting the first volume.

To all the husbands, wives, partners, mothers, fathers, children and friends who had to put up with all twelve authors during the writing process and to all of them for having to put up with me.

Acknowledgements

To David, Moira, Rosemary, Julie, Chris, Spencer, Linda, John, Marion, Philip, Lynne et al. who took a chance on a new collection of short stories and stocked *Tails* – Volume 1.

And lastly to all the people that bought and read our first collection and so enabled us to finance this one ...

✳ January ✳

Alan Lawton was born in the village of Micklehurst in the midst of the Pennines and moved to the Isle of Man in 1962. Alan worked for many years in the farming and construction industries and also served for a time in the armed forces. He has a degree with the Open University and has undertaken research work for the University of Liverpool on the structure of the Manx construction industry.

Alan is a keen historian and writer and achieved first place in the Olive Lamming short story competition in 1979.

His short story 'A Walk Along the North Quay of Douglas' was included as December's tale in the first volume of *A Tail for All Seasons*.

Now retired, Alan lives quietly in Onchan with his long-time partner and concentrates on writing, light gardening and culinary challenges.

Deαth Trαm

Alan Lawton

Caesar Kelly buttoned his overcoat to the neck and picked up a powerful torch from the hallstand before crossing the threshold of his home and stepping out into the gathering darkness. It was a cold and cloudy January evening and he could hardly believe that a whole year had elapsed since he murdered his wife.

Caesar smiled to himself as he picked his way down the badly surfaced lane that led from his tastefully modernised farmhouse to its intersection with the main Laxey to Ramsey road; he felt not the slightest touch of remorse as he dwelt upon the circumstances that had led to his wife's death.

To most of the people who lived in the district, and even within their own circle of friends, Caesar and Helen Kelly appeared to be the perfect middle-aged married couple who never uttered a single word against each other. Few suspected that behind closed doors the pair endured a relationship that was based upon hatred and contempt, rather than love and tenderness. Indeed, there had been love and plenty to spare, when they first joined hands in Lonan Parish Church over twenty years ago, when Caesar was just a junior clerk in a

Douglas law firm. But children had never arrived and Helen had grown ever more domineering once she set about expanding her late father's property empire in Douglas and other Manx towns.

Caesar suddenly lurched as he put his foot into a pothole.

"Damnation!" he cursed aloud, as he fought to recover his balance.

"Keep your wits about you boy, or you'll finish up in Noble's Hospital with a broken leg – and that's the last place you want to be with all of the plans that you've got in mind!"

Yet, despite his best intentions, his mind crept back to the early days of their marriage and he shook his head. The defining moment had arrived when his wife had discovered his affair with a junior secretary at his employer's law practice. It had never amounted to more than a few kisses and a little surreptitious fumbling, but the two lovers had been summarily dismissed after his wife had poured a torrent of complaint upon the head of the chief clerk. Never for a moment had Helen considered divorcing him. Instead, she forced him to become her rent collector. She gained a considerable measure of revenge by requiring him to squeeze the last penny of rent from the cash-strapped residents of her portfolio of run-down flats and rooming houses. He shuddered as he remembered the acrid stale cooking smells and the stench of used nappies that pervaded those miserable dwellings. He kicked savagely at another stone.

"Dammit – she deserved to die!"

The beam of his torch suddenly shone across a tarmac road surface and he knew that he had reached the main highway, near to the point where the lines of the electric railway swept past the entrance to the Dhoon Glen.

He was amazed to see a lighted tram standing alongside the tiny café, but then he remembered Manx Radio broadcasting

Death Tram

an interview with an official from the Department of Transport. The administrator had promised to make better use of the old electric railway system, with more winter services and the hiring-out of trams for special functions, and he realised that this must be one of the latter.

Caesar moved closer and he noticed that the tiny café was brightly lit and open for business.

A man was leaning against the counter and smoking a long clay pipe of antique design. He wore a broad-brimmed hat with a candle fixed to the front and a heavy jacket and working trousers that had definitely seen better days. He gave Caesar a wave.

"Ho there fella!" the man called out. "This tram's heading for Douglas – just as soon as I've knocked the ash from me pipe – but it's stopping at Laxey Junction to collect a bunch of revellers who are all set to enjoy a carnival night in Groudle Glen. You're welcome to jump aboard if you're needin' a lift into town."

Caesar hoisted himself aboard the tram without a moment's hesitation and took a seat in the middle of the saloon, for the offer was far too good to miss. In truth, he had only intended to get a bit of fresh air and then watch television for the rest of the evening – but now he could have a good wet in the Terminus Tavern before taking a taxi home.

Moments later his benefactor boarded the tram and took station alongside the driver. The veteran conveyance then burst into life and plunged into the darkness. Caesar settled down and began enjoying his ride into Douglas. He had been born and raised in Laxey, but he much preferred life in the capital. He loved the glitz and glamour of its nightclubs and the convivial atmosphere in its many public houses. But Helen would have none of it. She had insisted on moving into her late father's converted farmhouse near Ballaragh and

5

constructing a fabulously expensive Finnish sauna, and adding a plunge pool and numerous exercise machines. His wife had loved to sweat like a hog whilst immersed in clouds of steam – but nothing on earth would induce him to enter that damnable place.

He smiled to himself – soon his worries would all be over. The house had already been sold to a London financier who had expressed his intention to demolish and totally reconstruct the dwelling and the scene of his wife's death would conveniently disappear. Helen's property assets had already been quietly transferred to an offshore investment company and the cash was accruing interest in a Wisconsin bank account. In a few days he would board a plane for South America and quit the island of his birth for ever.

He closed his eyes and began falling into a light slumber, but the tram gave a sudden lurch and he looked up to find his host standing over him and looking down with his strange dark eyes.

"You'll be Mister Kelly!" he said. "I've always dwelt in Laxey and I sometimes passed near to your place whenever I felt like takin' a late evening's walk around Ballaragh. I was born Amos Benn a fair long time ago, but people of my acquaintance call me 'The Miner' on account of this get-up that I'm so fond of wearing, whenever I get the chance."

"Like when you're carryin' folks to a festival in Groudle Glen?" Caesar interrupted.

"Aye, it makes a good enough excuse," the miner continued. "But we're just rounding Minorca Hill and I'm going to collect my passengers at Laxey Junction in about five minutes' time."

The miner paused.

"I thought that I'd best give you a quick word of caution. The folks that I'm takin' to the festival don't get about much and they tend to act a bit queer when they do get out – best that you sit tight and say nothing until they alight at the Groudle Glen tram station."

As if to lay emphasis upon his words, the tram gave a sudden jolt and a shower of sparks burst from the overhead power line. The former rent collector nodded in agreement and turned away from his host as the lights of old Laxey began appearing in the valley below.

Soon afterwards, a metallic screech of brakes announced the arrival of the tram at Laxey Junction and a motley group of people crowded into the saloon and occupied all of the available seats. The first thing that Caesar noticed was that his new companions were not attired for any conventional fancy dress outing, but were clad in many of the various fashions that had been in vogue since Queen Victoria had acceded the throne.

The tram had hardly resumed its journey when a stout woman with a fat, over-rouged face, monopolised the far corner of the saloon and began singing Edwardian music hall ballads in a voice that was loud but well out of key. Nearby, two young women wearing 1920s-style flapper outfits attempted to execute the Charleston in a narrow space between the two rows of seats.

One young man even sported a Teddy Boy suit that must have been tailored sometime in the decade of the 1950s, whilst a group of variously clad gentlemen settled down in the rear of the tram and began drinking beer and playing cards. Everyone laughed and chain-smoked, but the merriment had a strange, brittle quality which the ex-clerk found rather disturbing.

Caesar's eyes strayed to a young woman who was seated across the narrow aisle. She was dark haired, sloe-eyed and she wore a post-Second World War sarong-style dress that displayed her magnificent form to perfection. Momentarily, he forgot his host's warning and he leaned over and attempted to strike up a conversation.

"It's a middling good evening for a tram ride!" he essayed. "I expect that you're looking forward to a long night's dancing in the Glen Hotel?"

She stared across at him with a strange puzzled look in her eyes.

"I haven't seen you before," she answered, and before Caesar could frame a reply, the woman had reached over and grasped his wrist – then she sprang back like a recoiling spring and turned her face towards the opposite window.

The former rent collector gasped, for the woman's hand was cold – cold as ice. Caesar turned and stared out of his own window and cursed the woman under his breath. He was now more than eager to get rid of his eccentric fellow travellers and reach the warmth and comfort of the Terminus Tavern.

He stared out of the window and tried to identify some familiar landmarks, but the night was growing darker and the brief glimmering of a few streetlamps was his sole reward. As the journey progressed, Caesar began to wonder if the relationship between time and space was becoming distorted, for he was fully convinced that the tram had taken a full hour to reach the point where the tramlines crossed the main road near Baldrine village. Yet he checked his wristwatch as the tram came abreast of the illuminated traffic signals and was amazed to note that only twelve minutes had elapsed since they had departed from Laxey Junction.

"Get a grip of yourself," Caesar muttered. "You've been under a ton of pressure over the last twelve months and it's not surprising that its beginning to affect your head. But hang on and everything will be OK. Why not take an earlier flight to Rio? You could be lying in the sun with a girl in one hand and a rum and coke in the other within two or three days' time!"

At the front of the tram, the stout female ballad singer had given way to the Teddy Boy as the tram began rattling its way past the lighted houses of Baldrine Park estate, and Caesar calmed down a little as the new performer played his guitar and hammered out a medley of early rock numbers. He was listening intently to a rendition of 'Rock around the Clock' when he failed to notice that a fight had broken out amongst the members of the card school that was situated in the rear of the tram. But he certainly noticed the beer bottle which flew past his ear and hit one of the dancing flappers full in the face – without inflicting any visible damage. His fears returned immediately.

The tram re-crossed the main road near the Liverpool Arms Hotel and started picking up speed as it began descending the long incline that led to the Groudle Glen tram station.

Once again, a shower of sparks burst from the overhead power line and the display created enough light for Caesar to see the hedgerows flying past at a mad pace. Yet time seemed to have regained leaden feet, for an age seemed to elapse before the tram slowed to a halt in Groudle Station.

The guitar immediately fell silent, the two flappers stopped dancing and the revellers exited the tram as quickly as possible. Caesar looked to his left, expecting to see the hotel open and ready to receive its guests, but the building was in complete darkness and there was absolutely no sign of life. However, he could hear the sound of dance music drifting up from the depths of the Glen and his dreadful companions were now hurrying towards the gate which led down to the terminus of the light railway. Caesar heaved yet another sigh of relief. Soon the tram would depart on the last leg of its journey to Douglas and he would be the happiest man in the whole town when he ordered his first pint in the Terminus Tavern. But the tram failed to move. After a while, the miner quit his position at the front of the tram and walked down the saloon to where Caesar was seated.

"I'm just givin' the driver a few minutes to swallow a bottle of Irish porter," he explained, "and then we'll be on our way to Douglas. Yonder man doesn't get to drink porter very often and I'm glad to give him the chance – only fair, you might say!"

The miner paused and began filling his pipe with tobacco.

"I noticed that you had a few words with Phoebe Hall, that smart lookin' woman who was seated opposite you in the tram. She was once charged with pushing her 'Sugar Daddy' of a husband into the sea on a stormy night – but the jury reckoned that the old fool committed suicide and she walked away from the court, scot-free and ten million pounds richer."

The miner's amiable face turned to granite.

"You pair have one thing in common – you both killed your partners by immersing them in water!"

The man casually lit his pipe and walked away to join the driver at the front of the tram.

Caesar Kelly was dumbfounded. The miner must know everything! He knew about the flood of vitriolic abuse that Helen had thrown at him before informing him that she was finally considering a divorce. About the sudden burst of anger that had impelled him to push his wife into the plunge pool and the callous manner in which he watched her drown, after the sudden immersion in the ice cold water had aggravated her recently diagnosed heart condition. The man must also be aware of the straightfaced lies which enabled him to convince the doctors, the police and the coroner that his wife's death was perfectly natural. That damned miner knew everything!

His first instinct was to flee the tram, but the antique

conveyance began moving forward in quite an unnatural manner. There was no longer any vibration or clattering of metal upon metal – instead, the tram sped along as though borne upon a cushion of air. In a trice, the tram was flying past the old Cunningham's Camp bus stop and still gaining speed. Caesar realised he must act quickly if he was to survive this nightmare and he resolved to throw himself out of the speeding tram in the forlorn hope that a patch of soft heather would break his fall. But the miner had stationed himself before the front exit and he appeared to be as immoveable as if built of solid oak.

Then Caesar remembered that the tram had a rear door and he braced himself to flee. To his horror, he found that he was quite unable to move – it seemed as though every muscle in his body was frozen into immobility. His fear turned to numbing terror as he noticed that the tram was mutating into something that had no place in reality, for the body of the vehicle was beginning to stretch like an expanding telescope and sections of the floor and ceiling were becoming first opaque and then transparent. He was nearing mental collapse when he noticed that the tram had parted company with the rail track and was now hurtling over the rooftops of Port Jack. The last thing that his eyes registered was the illuminated crescent of the Douglas promenade, before the projectile of metal and human flesh plunged into the dark waters of Douglas bay.

★ ★ ★

Agnes Kennaugh leaned heavily upon her walking stick and struggled to catch her breath as she stood in the shadow of the great Laxey Wheel. She was almost ninety years of age and the walk from the village, followed by the struggle to circumvent the chain-protected entrance had almost drained her of strength. She recalled the night, over eighty years ago, when her grandmother had brought her here to witness the Promenade of the Dead for the very first time. She also knew that her own granddaughter would stand here in years to come, as other Kennaugh wise-women had done since men had first dug into the solid rock of the mountains. The valley was still shrouded in darkness, but her inner eye told her that the miner was drawing near. Moments later, she spotted the glow from the candle that was burning just above the brim of his hat – then she caught sight of him striding purposefully along the path that led towards the oldest entrance to the mine. Behind their frightful jailer trudged a long file of malefactors, fresh from their night of singing and carousing in the confines of Groudle Glen. Most were still dressed in their chosen finery and a pair of flappers were still attempting to execute a few steps of the Charleston – but most followed behind in dull resignation.

Agnes felt a stab of pity, for she had always known that the shades who follow the miner must spend another year of purgatory suspended in the black, silent depths of the flooded mine – before emerging to enjoy another short night of freedom in the world they had lost.

Agnes brushed away the tears that had welled up from her ancient tear ducts and she noticed a solitary figure bringing up the rear of that terrible promenade. She recognised him immediately.

"Oh Caesar," she said to herself. "I remember the day when I passed by your school and you threw stones at me and called me an auld witch-woman. I warned you then to mend your ways. And now it's too late – far too late!"

The old wise-woman maintained her vigil until a rooster crowed from a nearby farmyard and the first glimmerings of dawn appeared in the sky. At that moment, one of her grandmother's prophesies came to mind as she prepared for the hard trudge home:

When the hills of Mann and the mines beneath
Are ground to dust 'neath nature's heel
Then shades entrapped may seek release
And hope to find redemption.

✠ february ✠

Jacqueline Shirtliff lives in Douglas with her husband and three children. She obtained a B.Ed. Honours degree in Education and Religious Studies at university and now works as a primary school teacher at Marown school.

Jacqueline is a keen writer and has had several articles published by *The Lady* and *Woman Alive* as well as being one of the editors of *Magnet*, a magazine published by the Methodist Church.

Her story 'Perfectly Ruined' was included as August's tale in the first volume.

As well as writing, Jacqueline is also a keen musician and plays the tuba with the Isle of Man Wind Orchestra.

car ny ferrishyn
away with the fairies

Jacqueline Shirtliff

It was going to be a dark, windy night and Emma would much rather have stayed at home. As she got herself ready she glanced out at the line of hills visible from her bedroom window. The sun had only just set and the hills were silhouetted against the deepening blue of the sky, cold and bare and bleak. She drew the curtains across and sighed. She knew she'd enjoy the evening once she got there, but it was freezing tonight and she was worried about ice on the Mountain Road, and about finding her way to the venue. Perhaps she should have gone out to find the place this afternoon? Even better, why hadn't she asked someone else for a lift? Juan and Aalish would willingly have made a detour and picked her up, or Will. Still, it was too late for that now. She said goodbye to Dave and the children, grabbed the car keys, stowed her violin safely on the back seat of her beloved Beetle and drove off into the January night.

She made her way carefully up past the Creg ny Baa and Kate's Cottage. At least there was no fog tonight, and a car in front whose tail lights she could follow, and as she drew closer she recognised the red Mini. Marghaid! Thank goodness! If anyone would know the way it was Marghaid, the band's whistle player. Emma breathed a sigh of relief and settled back into the driver's seat.

Emma had a great evening, as she'd known she would. She wondered if she'd been suffering from a touch of the February blues after all the fun of the festive season. Her mood recently had very much reflected the dull weather and the dreariness of the countryside, and the warmth and sunshine of spring still seemed a long way off. This evening's dance was just what she needed to lift her spirits.

Emma played with enthusiasm and lost herself in the music. She knew these Manx tunes so well now that she needed no music, and one day she determined to learn the language so she could make sense of the words as well. She had played the violin since she was a young girl but had let it drop once she'd left school. It was only fairly recently that she'd picked it up again. A friend had needed a fiddle player in his ceilidh band, and she'd discovered that, without the pressure of exams and scales, she wasn't such a bad player after all! It was a family ceilidh that night so the dances were simple, and the enthusiasm of the youngsters meant more adults were dragged onto the dance floor than was sometimes the case. Emma remembered ruefully one of the first dances she'd played for, a harvest festival at a rural church down south. All the older members of the congregation had turned out, not to dance but to watch … but there'd been nothing to watch! All the younger folk had gone to the Mhellia in the next village!

As the evening drew to a close, the dancers drifted out into the night and the band packed away. Emma glanced at her watch. It was only nine o'clock – she'd be home in time to watch the end of the film with Dave.

"Hey, Emma!" It was Juan. "D'you fancy popping across to

the Sulby Glen for a quick drink? We've certainly earned it, and the night's still young."

Emma smiled. "Not tonight, thanks. It's been a busy day. I think I'll get off home for an early night. Have a good time."

Juan shrugged. "Oh well, suit yourself." He counted out Emma's share of the night's earnings and handed it over. "Here you are then. Don't spend it all at once. Practice next Friday at mine. Drive carefully." And with that he was gone.

Emma placed her bow safely in the case, closed the lid and snapped the locks shut. Behind her, Marghaid and Aalish were deep in conversation.

"No! Did he really? Well I never would have thought it."

"Right, I'm off," Emma interrupted. "See you Friday."

"Oh, Emma. You're not coming over for a drink then?"

"No, I just thought I'd get home. Enjoy yourselves."

Marghaid and Aalish hugged her goodbye. Emma picked up her fiddle, waved to Will who was giving an impromptu bodhran lesson to the vicar and made for her car.

As she drove out of the village Emma was struck once again by how very dark it could be once you were out of the residential areas. She put her headlights on full beam and craned towards the windscreen. As the road ran along the Sulby Glen the naked branches of the trees jostled against each other in the wind and pushed in on either side, making the night seem darker still. Emma shivered and turned the heating up a notch. She wouldn't like to break down out here. No wonder the old Manx folk used to believe in all sorts of ghastly monsters – your imagination could easily run away with itself if you were walking or riding out alone on a night like this. At least in the car she felt cocooned, safe. Nevertheless, a bit of music might not go amiss. She took one hand off the steering wheel and tried to get radio reception.

As the music broke the silence, crackled and distorted,

Emma rounded a bend and her headlamps lit up a group of lads standing in the middle of the road, flagging her down. Emma touched the brakes and dipped the beam, but she was reluctant to stop entirely. Heart beating, hands clenched on the steering wheel, she willed them to move over and let her pass. What did they want anyway? She felt frantically in her coat pocket for her mobile. Damn. She'd left it in her handbag on the back seat. Probably they'd run out of petrol and needed a lift to the nearest garage. Well, she was sorry, but they weren't getting it from her. There'd be another car along in a minute, some butch man who wouldn't bat an eyelid at stopping for three strangely-dressed youths. But not her, a woman all by herself on a deserted road, even if this was the Isle of Man.

She was only yards away from them now, and had slowed to a crawl, but they didn't show much sign of moving. Yet there was an edginess about them, she could sense, as if they weren't quite comfortable about their proximity to the car. Suddenly they leapt from the middle of the road and stood by the hedge. Or, rather more likely, down in the ditch, as Emma couldn't help noticing as she began to pick up speed that their heads barely reached window-level. Lights back on full-beam, Emma breathed a sigh of relief, loosened her grip on the steering wheel and felt her pulse begin to steady.

Suddenly there was a bang and Emma lost control. Wrestling with the steering wheel, she tried to keep the car on the road but was failing dismally. As she careered through the hedge, totally out of control, Emma's thoughts went out to her family. The car rolled down the incline and Emma, who had once been afraid of death, accepted the inevitability of the situation and sheer panic was replaced with a deep peace as everything went into slow motion.

The car came to rest in the middle of the field, just short of the river. Emma opened her eyes, wondering what heaven was like, only to find herself still in the driver's seat and quite definitely in Sulby Glen as opposed to heaven. Cautiously she turned her head from side to side, raised first one arm and then the other, and repeated the exercise with her legs. Well … nothing appeared to be broken. She became aware of a damp trickle running down her hand and held it up to the light still shining out from one headlamp. Hmmm. A slight scratch. She felt in her pocket for a tissue and glanced into the rear-view mirror. Good grief! In the gloom she could just make out the three lads traipsing across the field towards her. She couldn't quite decide whether it was comforting to know that she wasn't totally alone in an obsolete car in the middle of nowhere, or whether being totally alone was preferable to being rescued by three diminutive youths whom she'd heartlessly failed to stop and help three minutes earlier. She decided she'd rather be alone.

Suddenly she remembered her phone. Quickly she unfastened the seatbelt and squirmed around, frantically trying to locate her handbag next to the violin. It wasn't there. She glanced in the mirror and saw the youths now just yards away from the car. Fighting to control a rising feeling of panic, she felt down into the footwell below the back seat. There it was! She grabbed it, turned back into her seat, pushed the lock down on the door and fumbled shakily in her bag for the phone. Snapping it open, she dialled home.

What? No reception? Emma closed her eyes and let her head fall back onto the headrest.

"Miss?" Emma's eyes flew open. Gazing in through the broken windscreen was a grinning face, with two others close behind. It was hard to make out, what with the spider's web effect of the glass, and in the dim light, but …

"Miss? Are you hurt? We're sorry about the flat tyre, but we did need you to stop, and it didn't look like you were going to."

Emma shook her head weakly. "No, I'm not hurt."

"Can we help you out?" One of the lads came round to the door and, despite the lock, yanked it open.

Emma stared up at him. "You don't ... erm ... do any of you have ... could I possibly borrow a phone?" she faltered, not moving from the safety of the car seat.

"Well, you'll not be needing one quite yet. All in good time, all in good time," the young man replied. "Now, we're running a little late so if you could just look sharp a bit and follow us."

Emma shook her head. She was feeling very confused. She still didn't think she'd died in the car accident, but she was pretty sure she'd suffered a moderate amount of concussion and that it would be a good idea if she saw a doctor as soon as possible.

"Now, you're no doubt feeling a wee bit stiff after all that bumping about. Let's be giving you a hand now."

Emma felt both her hands grasped by two smaller, wiry ones and found herself suddenly and effortlessly on her feet.

"Right then, come along, come along."

"But ..." Emma protested.

"Move along now, please."

With one young man leading the way and the two others on either side of her, hanging onto an arm each, Emma found herself moving across the field towards a grassy knoll illuminated by her one remaining headlamp. As they drew closer Emma heard music, pipes and drums, and she felt a strong urge to dance. In fact her companions were indeed doing a sort of step-hop across the grass, and it was all Emma could do to keep in step with their up-and-downing. On reaching the foot of the grassy hummock they stopped beside a large boulder. The young man hanging onto Emma's left arm kicked at the rock and it moved effortlessly to one side.

Emma was struck by a blinding light streaming from the

hole that had appeared in the hillside. She blinked and shook her head, and then, as her eyes refocused, she saw a flight of steps leading down inside the hill. There was a new clarity to the music now, and the sounds of chattering, dancing feet and general merriment drifted up the steps towards them. Suddenly recognition dawned. She'd read about this only the other night: her daughter's bedtime story. It was a fairy knoll, and these young men in their little caps, they must be the Little People. Now there was no doubt about it; she knew she was dreaming. She struggled, as you do sometimes when you know you're sleeping, to swim back up into consciousness, but she couldn't do it. Instead she found herself sinking back into the reality of the dream, following one of her captors gingerly down the steps whilst the other two hurried her along from behind.

"Quickly, quickly please," they urged. "We're late, we're late. Listen to the music. They've started already! Oh, be quick, be quick."

Emma did her best in her dreamlike state to take the stairs as fast as she could, but their tread was so much smaller than what she was used to, and her eyes were still struggling to adjust to the brightness that she stumbled more than once. "Steady now," soothed the leader, catching her. "We don't want any more broken bones this evening."

All of a sudden Emma reached the last step and found herself in a vast underground hall crowded with people, young and old, all dressed in their finery. There were women in flowing gowns in every shade you could possibly imagine, men in fancy waistcoats and breeches and the children were miniature versions of their parents. At the far end was a roaring fire with a spit roast revolving slowly. In front of the fire great tables were laid with the most sumptuous feast, and diminutive gold candlesticks and cutlery glittered as they caught the light. Another table sparkled with goblets filled with fine drink and two young men distributed them amongst the guests from laden trays. At Emma's end of the hall was a dais and it was here that a handful of drummers and pipers were arranged, piping and drumming away. In front of the dais small pockets of dancers jigged and twirled.

As Emma took all this in, a little old man came pushing through the crowd towards her and clasped her left hand firmly in his.

"Miss Emma! Thank to goodness you're here at last. Hom Mooar's the name, and it's your music that we're needing tonight. The first feast of the year, indeed the finest feast of the year, the Snowdrop Ball, and here's Hom Mooar with a broken arm. Would you be crediting it? Now here's the fiddle, and be you playing your finest for the king!"

So saying, Hom Mooar drew a fiddle out from under his right arm and handed it to Emma. And what a fiddle! Emma had never in all her days seen anything like it. Shaped exquisitely out of pale wood, it was intricately inlaid with silver in delicate swirls. The head was carved so that it resembled a fiddler playing, and likewise the head of his tiny fiddle resembled a fiddler playing. The strings, although Emma knew this to be impossible, looked to be spun of the finest gold and the bow, fashioned from the same pale wood as the fiddle itself, was light to the touch and instead of horsehair was threaded with the golden strands of who knew what magical creature.

Cautiously Emma reached out, took the precious instrument and cradled it under her chin. Gently she touched the bow to the strings and instantaneously the music sprang out. Certainly the fiddle seemed to have a life of its own. Emma found herself playing familiar tunes without even thinking about it, and the drums and the pipes immediately fell in with her. Within minutes she was playing new tunes, ones she'd never even heard before, and there was no time to pause or rest, the fiddle just went straight from one tune into the next, and the pipes and drums followed suit.

And the dancing! Never had Emma seen such grace, such coordination, such energy. It seemed that when she played the whole hall erupted in movement, and everyone found themselves dancing whether they chose to or not! Even the waiters with the drinks waltzed gracefully around the hall, proffering their trays to all they passed.

Emma was so caught up in the beauty of the music and the fiddle itself that she lost all sense of time and any shred of reality she may have had left. Some time ago now her three captors had ushered her, still playing away, up onto the dais, from where she had a good view of the whole hall. As she watched the dancers she caught sight once again of Hom Mooar, elbowing his way across the crowded floor towards her. Foot tapping, he reached out and gently took the fiddle from her with his good arm.

"You're doing a grand job, lass, but you'd better stop for a bit and let us have a wee rest. When you play, we can't help but dance!" He smiled at her, handed back the fiddle, and disappeared amongst the crowd. All around Emma the Little People were laughing, panting, leaning back against the walls or collapsing on chairs and swigging drinks. Emma laughed too and helped herself to a sparkling goblet as the waiter sauntered past at a more sedate pace than a minute previously. Her arms ached a little and she could certainly do with a drink. Taking a sip, she savoured the taste on her tongue and felt the liquid slip down, cool and refreshing, like nothing she'd ever tasted before. She drained the glass, tucked the fiddle back under her chin, and let the contagious music flood the hall once more.

★ ★ ★

Juan and Aalish left the Sulby Glen hand in hand and crossed the road to where they'd left the car earlier that evening.

"Ah, that was a good night," sighed Aalish as she went round to the passenger door.

"Don't forget you're driving," replied Juan. "Here, catch."

Aalish missed and dropped the car keys, scrabbling around in the gutter until she found them. "Fool!" she muttered, smiling.

They climbed in and set off along the Sulby Road towards Douglas. They travelled in silence, both lost now in their own thoughts and tired after the busy evening. As they rounded a bend they passed a large hole torn through the hedge.

"Good grief! Look at that! Someone must have come off the road," commented Aalish.

"Hmmm? What did you say?" answered Juan, opening his eyes.

"There was a huge hole in the hedge. I said someone must have come off the road. Hey, look, over there, by the river."

Aalish slowed the car and they both looked over to the left where one solitary headlight shone out over the hillside.

Aalish slammed on the brakes, flicked on the emergency hazard lights and flung open the door.

"What?" Juan cried. "Where're you going?"

"Emma! That's Emma's Beetle. Come on."

Juan leapt out of the car, grabbed the torch from under the seat and followed his wife as she scrambled through the hole in the hedge and stumbled across the tussocky field. Ahead of them the car headlamp flickered and went out. Juan muttered under his breath and trained the torch beam on the wrecked car.

Aalish's heart was beating fast as they approached the car, and her legs had turned to jelly. She could see from here that the car was a write-off. The windscreen was shattered, as were all the windows that she could see. There was a huge dent in the roof and the wing on the driver's side was scratched and somewhat crumpled. She didn't dare go closer but she knew she had to. Taking the torch from Juan she pulled open the mangled driver's door and shone the torch inside.

Aalish gave an involuntary gasp. Emma was lying slumped against the steering wheel, and a trickle of blood was dribbling down her arm. "Quick," she called back to Juan. "Phone for an ambulance." Trembling, she felt for a pulse. There it was! Slow and steady, but definitely there. "She's alive!" she called back to Juan. She dredged her mind for what she had once known so well, and vowed to look up a First Aid course once this was all over.

"There's no signal. I'll have to take the car up out of the glen. Will you be okay?"

Aalish swallowed and hesitated for just a second. "Yeah, I'll be fine. Just leave me with the torch." She turned her attention back to her friend. "Breathing, bleeding, consciousness," she whispered to herself. She reached in her pocket for a clean tissue and wiped away the blood on Emma's hand and arm. At least there was nothing to worry about there, just a tiny scratch. She guessed there might be more bleeding elsewhere but she knew better than to move Emma. The paramedics could do that once they arrived. So now there was nothing to do but wait. And talk. She remembered now. Keep talking to the casualty in case they come round.

"Emma? Emma, it's me, Aalish. You're going to be just fine. We're calling an ambulance and they'll be here soon. It was a good dance this evening, wasn't it? Everyone seemed to be having a whale of a time." Aalish rambled on, talking about everything and nothing. After what seemed an age, a pair of headlights came twisting through the darkness. Aalish heard a car door slam and trained the beam of the torch over towards the road. Slightly irregular running footsteps, and then a panting Juan arrived at her side.

"OK, they're on their way." He paused to catch his breath. "I've phoned Dave too. He's meeting us at the hospital. Poor chap. Couldn't stop saying how he'd told her to drive carefully. I had to put the phone down on him in the end." Juan placed a hand on her shoulder. "You all right? You're shaking all over."

Aalish resisted the temptation to dissolve into tears. "I'm fine. I'm just glad she's still alive. She's not conscious. I decided it was best not to move her. I think we'd better keep talking, just in case she comes round, so she knows someone's here."

"I'm just so glad you spotted the car. Once that headlamp had gone out, she might have been here till the morning. She might have died from hypothermia ..." Juan's voice trailed off as he realised he wasn't helping.

"Anyway, is there anything else ..." He stopped suddenly and listened. "It's OK. They're nearly here."

They listened as the siren drew closer, then the lights of the ambulance came into view. "Thank goodness," breathed Aalish, and began flashing the torch towards the road. "If I talk to them once they get over here and tell them anything they need to know, can you just check the car and take any valuables? Emma wouldn't thank us for leaving her precious violin in a wrecked car!"

★ ★ ★

"Well," said the paramedic as he arranged the stretcher in the ambulance, "she seems fine. No broken bones, and there's no sign of internal bleeding. There are a couple of signs she's regaining consciousness – a bit of movement as we lifted her out of the car, and a few mumbled words of protest. The car's a write-off by the looks of it, but she's been very lucky. I wonder what brought her off the road though? It's icy on the tops tonight, but not down here."

"It was those lads. The Little People."

"Sorry?" The paramedic turned his attention back to the patient. "Did you say something?"

Emma forced herself to open her eyes. She blinked. "You were asking why I came off the road. It was the Little People."

"Emma!" Aalish shrieked with delight and flung her arms around her prostrate friend. "You're awake! How do you feel?"

"I'm fine," Aalish replied. "Totally exhausted, but what can you expect when you've been playing the fiddle half the night …" Emma's voice trailed off as she took in her surroundings. "Where am I? Is this an ambulance? What am I doing here?"

"It's OK," soothed Aalish. "You had a bit of an accident."

"Yes, I know," Emma answered, matter-of-factly. "I told you. It was the Little People. They needed a fiddle player, and so when I wouldn't stop for them they made sure I couldn't get far. I had a blow-out and went through the hedge, then they took me down under the knoll for the dance. The car crash was a pretty scary experience. I was sure I was going to die, but I was fine. And I wouldn't have missed that dance for the world." Emma closed her eyes and smiled to herself as memories of the evening filled her mind.

Aalish stroked her friend's brow and looked up at the paramedic with consternation.

"Don't worry," he whispered, smiling reassuringly. "She's obviously had a blow to the head and been in a deep sleep. She's also suffering from shock. People in her situation can dream all sorts of strange things. She'll be fine after a good rest, you'll see."

To Emma he said, "Sounds like you had a great evening. Now, I just need to ask you a few questions and then we'll get on our way. What's your name?"

"Emma Kennaugh," Emma answered dutifully. The

paramedic glanced at Aalish who nodded.

"Age?"

"Forty last birthday." Aalish nodded again.

"Family?"

"I'm married to Dave. We've got three children. Tom's twelve, Kirree's nine and Breesha's four." Aalish nodded again. "Why do you want to know all this anyway?"

"Oh, it's just routine stuff," the paramedic replied, then turned to Aalish, smiling. "Well, it looks promising. She's certainly *compos mentis*, just a bit muddled between fact and fantasy at the moment. Anyway, let's get off to the hospital and they can check her over properly. I wouldn't be surprised if they kept her in overnight for observation. Seatbelts on please, ladies."

"Wait." Emma sat up suddenly. "My violin's in the back of the car. I can't leave it there. And my handbag. Oh, and Hom Mooar's fiddle too. He said I'd played it so beautifully, that I'd really helped them out, and that he could easily get another. Oh, Aalish, it's a beautiful fiddle, just you wait till you see it. It's inlaid with swirls of silver, the strings are gold, the bow's threaded with golden strands, and the music …When you play, anyone who hears it just has to dance."

Emma's face was shining with excitement.

Aalish smiled and patted her knee. "Well, I'm sure I'll get to see it in due course. And don't worry about your stuff. Juan's getting it."

There was a sudden knock on the rear door of the ambulance. "Hey," came Juan's voice, "does Emma want to take her stuff with her or shall I bring it along in my car? I've got her violin and her handbag, and there's an absolutely exquisite fiddle here, too, it was just lying on the back seat, no case or anything. It's beautiful, all inlaid with silver."

Aalish stared hard at Emma, unfastened her seatbelt and

reached over to open the door. There was Juan, a fiddle cradled carefully in his arms.

"You are a dark horse, Emma. I've never seen anything like this before! Where on earth did you get it? It must be worth a fortune. Have you had it long?"

Emma reached out a hand for the fiddle and smiled at Aalish. "I told you it was beautiful, but that's nothing. Just you wait till you hear it!"

❋ March ❋

Although **Kate Stokes** now lives in London she still retains strong connections to the Island and visits as often as she can. Kate graduated from the Royal Holloway University of London with a BA Hons in English/Theatre Studies and started her theatrical employment appropriately enough at the Gaiety Theatre in Douglas. She has since worked as a Deputy Master Carpenter at the Aldwych and Piccadilly Theatres and also with the RSC during their London seasons. Kate currently works as a freelance theatre technician.

Her first story in the 'Althelbrede' series was included as June's tale in the first volume.

Althelbrede and the Attack of Billy Rhubyn

Kate Stokes

Poyllvill, the pond that Althelbrede had called home for over nine hundred years, was at its bleakest at this time of year – the dead stalks of last year's growth stood stark against a slate-grey sky that turned the waters black and featureless as the wind sent ripples across its surface, so that the pond itself seemed to be shivering in the unrelenting cold. Al pulled his scarf up around his ears and turned up the collar of his coat. It was no use; the chill north-easterly wind that had been scutching around Mull Hill for nearly a week found its way through his defences and sent another shiver through him. Apart from its constant, plaintive whistling, there was silence. Too early in the season for tourists, too early in the day for anyone else, even the birds were quiet; roosting, snugly and smugly, out of sight in the trees and bushes that lined the Darrag.

Al wandered listlessly along the banks of the pond, absent-mindedly tidying as he went; a tumbled clump of briars here, a sprig of gorse snapped by the wind there, but these desultory attempts at activity only served to highlight his melancholy.

He knew what the problem was – he was missing the company of his friends, but this knowledge did not help matters. As a Norse bog sprite, Al had nurtured the marsh woundwort growing in Poyllvill for nearly a millennium, and had never before needed or sought the company of others. Then a chance encounter with a local Manx cat, Sam, had led to an unlikely friendship, and a series of events the previous summer had brought him into contact with several humans from the nearby village of Cregneish, including Jim Quine, the elderly historian with whom Sam lived. Since then, the three of them had spent many happy times together, until one night, after they'd enjoyed a fine meal accompanied by a surfeit of fine wine, Al had announced that he preferred his own company, he was doing perfectly well by himself, thank you very much, and he'd be much obliged if everyone would leave him alone. Then he'd drawn himself up to his full eight inches and lurched off haughtily through the cat flap. That had been over a week ago, and Jim and Sam had taken him at his word, he hadn't seen either of them since.

Al stared moodily at the dark waters of the pond, the now familiar argument running along its well established pathways in his mind. *"You should go and apologise.* Why should I apologise? Contact with humans will only bring trouble. *They're your friends; they'd never knowingly harm you.* Not knowingly, maybe, but a word out of place, a slip of the tongue, that's all it would take to ruin everything. *You should trust them. You need them.* Hah! I haven't needed anyone for all these years, why start now? *Maybe you've been alone for too long? Perhaps it's time to allow yourself the experience of friendship?* Well, if they were really my friends, they'd have been to see if I was OK, wouldn't they? *After the way you behaved? Did you see the look on their faces?* All right, all right, there's no need to rub it in, I feel bad enough already. *Well go and apologise then, you short-arsed pillock.*

Who are you calling a pillock, you Norse git? If you weren't just a manifestation of my own conscience, I'd give you such a thumping. *I'd like to see you try it.* Yeah? *Yeah.* Yeah? *Yeah!*"

Al frowned. He'd only recently started debating things with himself, and he wasn't entirely sure that he'd got the hang of it.

The wind gusted again, and he pulled his scarf a little tighter. The scarf had been a Christmas present from Jim; the finest wool knitted on tiny needles, in a mossy green that matched his ancient, shapeless hat and complemented the lighter green of his ancient suit – it was the first present Al had received for as long as he could remember.

"You should go and apologise."

"Oh will you sod OFF!" shouted Al, and stomped off towards Jim and Sam's house to apologise.

Walking over the brow of the Darrag, it was obvious that spring was at least making an effort; some of the gorse bushes had produced tentative sprays of yellow blossom, and the smallest of knobbly buds were gathering on the branches of trees, waiting for the sun's warmth to usher them into bloom, but the Calf, the great Island barometer of the seasons, still sat hulking in stubborn hibernation across the treacherous waters of the Sound, only the thinnest threads of green discernible amidst the brown vegetation and black mud of its winter coat.

Al scrambled a little way along the verge, pausing only to wrestle his scarf out of the grip of some particularly insistent heather and, checking both ways for signs of early morning activity, darted across the road and through a gap in the whitewashed wall of Jim's garden. He ducked under the Australian holly, dodged past the vast sycamore tree with its long-abandoned swing and slid down the short slope that raised the lawn from the path. Pausing by the back door, he adjusted his jacket, straightened his hat, buffed the toe-caps of his brogues on the back of his trousers and clambered through the cat-flap.

The kitchen was quiet, the range slumbering over the remnants of yesterday's fuel, the kettle silent, empty. The usual jumble of books and papers still cluttered the table and jostled for space on every available surface, but the comforting mustiness of old paper and ever-present cat was overlaid with an unusual scent. Al tensed slightly and crept through the door to the narrow hallway, past the front door to his left, the steep staircase leading up to the bedrooms on his right, past the laden coat hooks on the wall and the umbrella stand, with its assorted walking canes, senses alert, straining for the unfamiliar. The silence seemed to be intensified by the slow ticking of a clock coming from the living room; the door stood slightly ajar in front of him. There it was again! The faintest hint of an almost remembered scent that Al couldn't place but that, in this eerie stillness, awoke in him primeval feelings of trepidation. He pushed at the door and squeezed through the resulting gap. The room beyond was cold, the only movement the hypnotic swinging of the pendulum above the mantelpiece, lifeless ashes in the fireplace below. In front, sprawled and still, lay Sam, his black fur starkly contrasting with the sheepskin hearthrug on which he lay.

"Sam!" Al rushed over to his seemingly stricken friend who leapt up as if he'd been bitten and glared around the room wild-eyed.

"What? What's happening? Get the rabbits!"

Al squeaked a little, faced with this apparent resurrection from the dead, and took a moment to gather himself, and (he told himself gallantly) to allow Sam to wake up fully. When the initial moment of terror had passed for both parties, Al spoke again, this time a little more calmly.

"Sam," he said, "do you know what that smell is?"

Sam looked slightly affronted.

"Well, you startled me, you know."

Al shook his head, relief, as ever in friendships of this kind, being swiftly overtaken by irritation.

"No, Sam," he said patiently, "there's a weird kind of ... scent in the house, like something else is in here. Can you smell it?"

Sam flicked an ear in annoyance, but obligingly lifted his head and opened his mouth slightly, scenting, tasting the air.

"No," he said finally, and a little tersely, "there's nothing unusual at all. Just you, and me, and Jim, and yesterday's dinner and some idiot mouse that must have come in early this morning. Now, what have you – hang on a minute, *what's that*?"

He stalked over to the door and into the hall, Al following. The kitchen received a thorough check, and the passageway beyond, the bathroom and the back door, then back to the hallway and the foot of the stairs.

"It's stronger here," said Sam, looking worried, "but I can't place it at all. I'm going upstairs to see if Jim's all right. You stay here."

With that, he was gone, bounding up stairs that were steep enough to cause Al problems even if he had been invited up. He wondered what Sam was so grumpy about. Then he remembered. He sighed and started on the lowest step. With a jump, he could lay his arms flat on the top of the step, and then an undignified scramble brought the rest of him level. Muttering darkly, he made his way slowly up the stairs, round the curve halfway up, past the window seat overlooking the back garden, until he reached the landing, where Sam sat, calling, outside Jim's firmly closed bedroom door. Hot and winded, Al removed his hat, took a few deep breaths and approached Sam slowly.

"Listen, Sam," he said gently, "I'm really sorry."

Sam turned on him.

"Finally! How long does it take to come and apologise, Al?"

Al was taken aback. Sam was usually so easy-going that he'd presumed a quick apology would suffice. He took refuge in indignation.

"Well I'm apologising now, Sam, I just expected you to be big enough to accept it."

"Oh, so I'm to blame for your behaviour, am I?"

"You didn't even come and see if I was all right."

"You didn't want us! 'Leave me alone,' you said, 'I can do without you.'"

"Well I didn't mean it, did I? I was just being an idiot."

"You got that right!"

The bedroom door was flung open and Jim stood in the curtained twilight beyond, barefoot, in pyjamas, with tousled hair.

"So," his measured tones dropped into the sudden, angry silence. "Apparently I won't be sleeping in this morning. Thank you both. Althelbrede, it's nice to see you, apology accepted. Sam, you're a good fellow, and I'm sure you've made your point eloquently as always. Would you both like some breakfast?"

He reached down and stroked Sam behind one ear. Sam purred, mollified. Al looked down, shamefaced.

"I'm sorry, Jim Quine. Thank you." He turned to Sam. "I really am sorry, Sam."

Sam shrugged.

"Forget it. It's not important. Do you smell it? It's stronger up here."

They both turned back to the bedroom, where Jim was putting on his faded tartan dressing gown and worn moccasin slippers and opening the thick mustard-coloured drapes carefully around the windowsill full of over-wintering geraniums, to flood the room with weak, grey morning light. The unidentified scent was markedly stronger in the room, bitter, almost metallic, but with an echo of something organic and overripe to the point of rottenness. Again, Al was struck by a sense of familiarity, a memory that wouldn't quite surface.

Jim moved towards the stairs, but something about the stillness of the other two halted him.

"Is everything all right? What's the matter?"

Al spoke without looking round.

"There's something here. Something wrong and ... old." He turned to face Jim. "How are you feeling?"

Jim thought for a moment.

"A little under the weather, if I'm honest. I have been for a day or two."

Al frowned. In the daylight he could see that Jim was a little off-colour. Memory tugged at him again.

"Under the weather how, exactly? Aching? Sick?"

Jim looked a little self-conscious about such minute examination of his health but, remembering Althelbrede's origins and great experience, he gave the question serious thought.

"No, not really sick," he ventured finally, "just a little bilious."

Al's eyes widened as the bubble of memory popped. Jim and Sam stared at him as he spun around, searching the corners of the room.

"Rhubyn," he shouted, "Billy Rhubyn! Show yourself."

The smell became stronger, strong enough for Jim to smell it, then strong enough to make him gag. A nasal chuckle, faintly audible at first, grew loud, mocking and insistent, and a yellow haze appeared in front of the window, becoming thicker, like mist, then smog, then smoke, then a solid shape, its blurred outline growing sharper to reveal a figure no more than eighteen inches tall, with sallow skin and hair like straw and a mouth full of wickedly sharp teeth. He wore dark breeches and a dark coat, and as the three of them watched, he swept a wide brimmed hat off his head and gave them a low bow.

"Well, if it isn't the little swamp man," he laughed nastily. "Who'd have thought you'd still be around?"

Al was the first to recover; Sam and Jim still stood, open-mouthed.

"Get away from here, Billy," he spoke in a low, angry voice that made the hairs stand up on the backs of their necks. "I'll kill you this time, you know I can."

"Ah, will you, now?" The stranger seemed unimpressed. "Potions and lotions and it's away with us, is it?" He laughed again, growing more raucous. "Smell the air, little swamp man, taste the water. We're stronger than we've ever been; we're everywhere and anywhere, and we're coming for YOU!" He began to dance from foot to foot, taunting them. "And you too, rumpy, and you too, lanky, but don't you taste so lovely first thing in the morning." He bared his hideous teeth and made a darting motion towards Jim who seemed frozen, a hand pressed absent-mindedly to his right side. Sam hissed and sprang, knocking the creature sideways, and the pair rolled and scratched and pummelled.

"Careful, Sam. Don't let him bite you." Al leapt too, remembering too late that he had no skill in physical fighting. He clung to Billy and tried to pull the wide-brimmed black hat down over his eyes. Billy roared and flung both his assailants off. He spun around, gathering up plant pots and ornaments and anything else he laid hands on, flinging them at the stunned watchers, laughing and making obscene sucking noises. Sam and Al crouched, ready to leap again, but before they could move, Jim had picked them both up and run out of the bedroom, slamming the door behind them.

They could hear Billy Rhubyn's demented laughter and the thud and crash of objects breaking against the door as Jim carried Sam and Al down the stairs, pausing only to lift an overcoat off one of the coat hooks, before piling through the front door. He set them down on the path and they ran through the gate, up the lane, across the close-cropped turf of goose green and a few yards along the Darrag before Jim, out of breath and limping, called for them to stop.

"What was that?" Jim asked, when he had recovered enough breath to speak. "Some kind of Jewish leprechaun?" He shivered in the wind and pulled his heavy overcoat on over his dressing gown, looking ruefully at his slippered feet. Sam was prowling around, ears flattened, tail-stump twitching, clearly spooked. Al was curiously still, staring into the distance, his fists clenched. He seemed to drag his attention back across the ages and when he finally spoke, he seemed infinitely older.

"The Billy Rhubyn," he said dully. "They came here before, a long time ago, but we fought them off."

"What does he want?" Jim shook his head, "I mean, what did he want last time?"

"Last time they wanted revenge." Al frowned in recollection. "The Billy Rhubyn first came here ages ago, before I lived here. Apparently there was a great battle and they were driven into the sea. Then they tried again, by stealth; they'd swept across the mountains like a plague before we even knew they were here. It took all our combined power to defeat them."

"You and all the other … er … bog sprites?" asked Jim, delicately avoiding any swamp references. Al shook his head.

"No, the Mooinjer Veggey. That's what the Billy Rhubyn wanted all along; to defeat the Mooinjer Veggey and take the land from them." Al stared into the past. "Everything sickened; men, cattle, sheep. It was too late to fight, there were thousands

43

of them. We had no choice; we had to find a way to defeat them."

"Althelbrede," Jim spoke quietly, "what did you do?"

Al met Jim's eyes and smiled, humourlessly.

"We poisoned them."

"Brilliant!" Sam spoke so enthusiastically that the others jumped. "Poison them. Great idea. We'll do that again. Come on, let's get your stuff together, we'll mix up one of your specials and shove it right up …"

"It won't work again," said Al softly. "You heard him. The Billy Rhubyn thrive on pollution, infection, disease. Last time we fought them the land was pure, the air was clean. Nowadays …" he shrugged, "we'd probably just make them stronger."

Jim frowned. "So, do you think the rest of them are already here, or have we got some time to prepare for them? If it's just this one, we may be able to send him packing with a message to the others not to try anything."

Al shook his head.

"He is them. They are him. They can be one, or they can be all. Listen, Jim, we have to warn the Mooinjers. That's all the Billy Rhubyn have ever wanted; to take the land. They'll feed here and they'll spread over to Ballaglione in a matter of days."

Jim pressed a hand to his side once more, then started scrabbling at his pyjama jacket, lifting it over his midriff, searching for any bite marks on his torso. Sam coughed,

"Yeah, Jim, you know you just look a bit mad, now."

Jim grimaced, squeamish at the thought of being breakfast for these vile creatures.

"What happens if you are … bitten?"

"Don't worry," Al was reassuring, "he's not been here long enough to do you any permanent damage. You'll be fine in a few days, once we've got rid of them." He spoke with defiance, but seemed unsure.

"Can we defeat them, Althelbrede?"

Al looked a little embarrassed.

"I haven't been to see the Mooinjer Veggey for … a while. I don't know what shape they're in. They may not remember the old ways; they may not even let me see them."

Sam was incredulous. "What? After you helped them last time? Why wouldn't they be glad to see you?"

Al raised his eyebrows. "Sam, you had the hump because I didn't come and see you for a *week*. It's been … well let's just say it's been a bit longer than that." He pursed his lips, thoughtfully. "The Mooinjer Veggey were always concerned with the formalities of behaviour – their customs and rituals were more important than anything. An audience has to be requested with absolute precision or we won't even be able to find them."

"Great," grumbled Sam, sarcastically, "obsessive fairies versus bonkers Billy, and us three in the middle. What can possibly go wrong?"

Al rolled his eyes, testily.

"Have a bit of faith, Sam; I'll remember it once I get there."

"Of course you will," said Jim, generously. "Just like riding a bike, eh, Althelbrede?"

Al looked blank.

"I didn't know you could ride a bike," mumbled Sam out of the corner of his mouth. Jim continued, smoothly.

"Is there anything we can do to help?"

"Do you have any books about the Mooinjer Veggey?" asked Al hopefully. "Their battles and tactics and … things? I only know about my own dealings with them; it would be useful to know more about them."

Jim stroked his chin thoughtfully.

"It's not really my speciality, unfortunately. This would be more in the area of folklore." He brightened, "However, I do know someone who has a great deal of experience in this field of study." He smiled at them both. "Or perhaps I should say, *we* know of someone."

There was a pause.

"Really?" said Al. Sam was avoiding eye contact with anyone. "Do you think she would help?"

"She's a dedicated professional," said Jim. "I'm sure a threat of this magnitude, to a people as important to the Island as the Mooinjer Veggey, would override any … minor personal issues."

They both glanced at Sam, who was carefully observing a nearby clump of grass. Al cleared his throat.

"Do you think we should all go to ask her, or …" he faltered, "… not?"

Jim laughed, and fumbled in his overcoat pocket, bringing out his car keys.

"Don't worry, Althelbrede, you're off the hook." Sam visibly sagged with relief, "I'll go and see her now, and try to persuade her to come back here with me."

Al was about to nod, when a faint sound reached his ears. A steam whistle, far in the distance from the north-east, the shrill call carried on the swirling wind. Al looked towards it, thoughtfully.

"Actually, if Sam and I can get there, will you meet us at the Fairy Bridge later? Sort of mid-afternoon?"

"Of course", Jim shivered and stamped his numbed feet. "We'll bring everything that looks helpful. Will you be OK?"

Al smiled. "I've just remembered how to find them. Thank you, Jim Quine. Come on, Sam."

He bowed low to Jim and then he and Sam started off down the Darrag at a trot. Jim watched them go, then turned and made his way back to the village, past the now ominously quiet house, to his car.

Wendy Caine was sitting in her kitchen, brooding over a mug of coffee, staring unseeing through the window at the gulls wheeling and shrieking over the flat rocks as the wind, a constant companion on this side of Port St Mary, whooped and whistled around the chimney. She was due at work in an hour, and was battling with an unfamiliar sensation: a reluctance to go. In the six years since she had returned to the Island from 'across', she had never regretted leaving her position with the London Arts Council to work with the Manx National Trust. As a child, school trips to the Manx Museum had sparked her desire to learn about her heritage and her enthusiasm had remained undimmed, even as she left the Island for university, informing her choice of studies, and subsequent career decisions. She had returned as an accomplished woman, respected for her experience and her passion for her work.

Wendy smiled ruefully to herself and began to clear away her breakfast things. She had known of the tendency among some Manx people to resent those who returned to the Island after working away, and she had been nervous, at first, of reintegrating with those schoolfriends who had not left their home towns. True, some had shown bitterness, but not many, and she suspected that those who had would have been the friendships less likely to survive the transition from adolescence to adulthood whatever the circumstances. At work, she had tried to cultivate her professional relationships based on her current achievements rather than past ones, and had felt that this approach had been successful. Until last week.

The annual budget recommendations had been working their tortuous way through the bureaucratic strata of the MNT, and some projects from Wendy's department had become hopelessly bogged down. Her initial enquiries had revealed that one or two of the staff were missing opportunities to move things along, through inexperience rather than inability, and Wendy had intervened, through memos and meetings, citing experiences with the London Arts Council to suggest ways of breaking the deadlock. The results had been most satisfying; the budget recommendations were on their way and Wendy had thought no more about it until yesterday afternoon, when she had received an e-mail, copied to her among others, referring to her as 'when I' Wendy. At first, she had dismissed it as a childish joke, the result of a bruised ego, but the list of the e-mail's recipients included some people she considered friends, and she had found herself worrying when nobody mentioned it to her. She had brooded throughout the evening, slept on it, and brooded some more this morning. She knew she was being over-sensitive, but the little, grinning worm of insecurity, always ready for a jaunt around the psyche, had woken, stretched and was now burrowing along, humming show tunes.

Wendy's thoughts were disturbed by the sound of her doorbell. She stacked the final plate on the draining board, dried her hands on the towel hanging next to it, and went through the cosily furnished sitting room to the hallway, opening the front door.

"Good morning, Ms. Caine." Jim's tone suggested that there was nothing unusual about his visit; he'd simply been out in his pyjamas and overcoat and thought he'd drop in, as he happened to be passing. Wendy decided to follow his lead until an alternative course of action presented itself.

"Oh, hello, Mr. Quine. Please come in."

Jim followed her into the sitting room, accepted her offer of a seat and a cup of coffee, and waited until she was sitting opposite him before he spoke.

"Ms. Caine."

"Please, call me Wendy." Although she wasn't quite sure of

the etiquette, Wendy felt that nightwear warranted first names.

"Oh. Thank you. Wendy, I do apologise for turning up unannounced and … um … undressed, but something odd has occurred and I think that you may be … uniquely placed to help."

"Of course, Mr Quine,"

"Jim, please."

"Oh. Thank you. Of course, Jim, anything I can do."

Jim took a moment. He'd rehearsed some of this in the car, but hadn't managed to settle on an opening gambit. He warmed his hands on the coffee mug and decided to start with the most important thing.

"Well, before I go any further, I don't suppose I could borrow a pair of socks?"

★ ★ ★

The bushes at the edge of the playground rustled and two faces peered out. Al and Sam had made good time down the Darrag, racing the sound of the approaching train's whistle, across the bowling green at Breagle Glen and through Athol Park; they could see the railway line through the fence ahead of them and, away to the left, Port Erin station, seemingly deserted. They squeezed through the metal uprights of the fence and, keeping low, ran alongside the retaining wall, feeling horribly exposed. At the end of the tracks was a large stone building, used to house the engines over the winter. The tall, green, wooden doors were open, and a polished maroon engine sat, motionless in front of them, like a dog snoozing outside its kennel. They dived for cover under its great wheels just as two men in overalls emerged from the shed and crossed the tracks to the empty platform. Al peered out from their hiding place, and nearly jumped out of his skin as the steam whistle blew again, this time a nearby shriek, signalling the arrival of the train.

The carriages slid to a halt in front of them, and smoke from the engine at the far end of the train billowed and dispersed, accompanied by the slamming of doors as the few passengers travelling by train so early in the year hurried away about their business.

"So, how's this going to work?" asked Sam, cheerfully. "'One mythical Norse sprite and one cat, please.' 'Certainly sir, single or return?'"

"Shut up, Sam." Al scanned the carriages of the train, finding what he was looking for in the one second from the front. "Look there, someone's left the window open. Let's go!" He darted across the stones until he was alongside the nearest carriage and pressed himself against a wheel. Sam tutted and began to creep after him before remembering that, as no one would think twice about seeing a cat wandering about, he could revert to his more customary swagger. He strolled past Al, who was progressing slowly up the train in a series of darting runs, and pointedly sat down to wait underneath the open window of the second carriage, until Al, slightly out of breath from exertion and adrenalin, arrived next to him.

"Very discreet," Sam remarked drily. "You know you've got grease all down the back of your jacket."

"What?" Al twisted round to look. "Oh bugger," he sighed. "Come on then."

"Come on then, what?"

"Up you get."

"Excuse me?" Sam's eyebrows were almost up between his ears. "Up I get where, exactly?"

"You jump up onto that doorsill," Al began enthusiastically, "then you sort of stretch up to the window," he noticed Sam's expression, "then I ... climb ... up ... over you," Sam blinked, once, "and then ... you sort of ... jump in ... after me."

50

There was a frosty silence.

"Please?" Al added hopefully, if belatedly.

Sam waited until he could trust himself to speak calmly.

"I tell you what," he said, "here's another idea. Why don't you ..."

The whistle sounded, close and deafening, drowning out most of Sam's considerable range of expletives. They stared at each other in the shocked silence that followed, neither of them noticing the clouds of smoke curling around them, until the wheels of the train began to strain towards movement, building momentum until they overcame the inertial friction of the rails and began to turn slowly.

It was Al who noticed that the window was moving away from them. He began to run, calling out desperately.

"Quick, Sam. Please. Please, Sam."

For a moment, Sam's pride kept him rooted to the spot, then he remembered Jim, and Billy Rhubyn's taunts, and he leapt up and onto the moving doorsill, growling determinedly as Al clambered up his back, onto his shoulders, planted one foot in his left ear and swung himself in through the window. He bunched his long hind legs and sprang after his friend, and they landed on the floor of the swaying compartment; Sam, neatly on all fours; Al (he saw to his quiet satisfaction) in an untidy heap.

Sam sat down and began to wash and Al picked himself up, pulled his jacket straight and adjusted his hat.

"See?" he said, re-tying his scarf. "Easy." He climbed up onto the cushioned bench and looked out of the window at the countryside flashing past. The whistle sounded again and the train began to slow as it approached Port St Mary station. Sam cleared his throat.

"So what do you want to do if someone else gets in?"

Al stared at him.

"I hadn't really thought that far ahead" he admitted.
"Huh."

★   ★   ★

Jim turned down the heater and wiped the condensation off
his side window. It had seemed sensible for him to wait in the
car. Although Wendy had many books about the Mooinjer
Veggey and Manx folklore at home, she had thought that
answers might be found in some of the older works kept under
lock and key in the library at the Manx Museum and, as she
said, when sneaking books out of museum libraries it was
inadvisable to bring gentlemen in jim-jams. He had suggested
doing the research in the library itself, but Wendy had argued
that Althelbrede would find the information useful and so the
text should come to him, as he could not come to the text. So,
Jim sat in the museum's staff car park and watched the front
steps, wondering if he should keep the engine running in case
she came charging out, alarm bells sounding, guards in pursuit,
leaping into the passenger seat shouting "Drive!"

He smiled to himself and switched on the radio, letting the
music wash over him. He rubbed a hand over his stubbly chin
and thought about his next shave. What state was his bathroom
in by now? Had Billy moved on, or was he still wrecking the
house? The books and documents in Jim's collection
represented a lifetime's work, a lifetime's pleasure; the thrill
of finding some rare archive in a second-hand shop, the phone
call from a dealer to tell him that a long-awaited manuscript
was available. The thought of that accumulation of knowledge
being so wantonly destroyed was unbearable.

Jim moved the rear-view mirror so that he could study his
reflection. His face was an unhealthy yellowy-grey. He
shuddered at the thought of the Billy Rhubyn feeding off their
victims – their prey, he corrected himself. Hopefully Wendy

could find some information that would help Althelbrede drive them away, permanently this time. Jim wasn't a vengeful man, but the sooner the Island was rid of these grim demons, the better. He shook his head in amazement. Demons and sprites and fairies. Actual fairies! Fairy Bridge fairies! Would he really meet the Mooinjer Veggey? Would he be allowed to?

When he had spoken to Wendy about the morning's events, he had been impressed with how much she seemed to take it all in her stride. Of course, it was possible that she'd simply been humouring him; playing along until she could get the madman out of her house. Maybe she'd gone into the museum to phone Nobles Hospital, and at this very moment men in white coats with butterfly nets were creeping towards the car.

Jim caught himself checking over his shoulder and laughed. Of all the people on the Island, Wendy was someone who had to believe him. The things she'd seen last summer ...

As if on cue, she walked out of the museum and down the steps, looking purely businesslike in a smart suit and tailored coat, her blonde curls bobbing as she approached the car. She was still carrying the briefcase and reusable shopping bag that she had brought from home, neither looking any heavier than they had done when she had taken them inside. Jim leaned over to open the passenger door for her and she sat down, her eyes sparkling, putting her spoils by her feet and shutting the door before allowing an excited laugh to escape.

"That was fun," she exclaimed. "I've never taken part in a heist before."

"Mmm, it's my first one, too," agreed Jim, starting the car and pulling out into the one-way system.

By unspoken consent, they didn't take the Santon road, past Fairy Bridge, but turned towards Union Mills, and drove past dormant fields and wild pastures, through Braaid and St Marks. Wendy opened her briefcase, resting it on her knees.

"So, I picked up some books about the area around Fairy Bridge, general stuff; the original names of the fields and hills and so on, that's all in the bag, but I did think that these might be useful."

Jim looked at the contents of the briefcase and nearly drove off the road.

"That's the Manx Chronicle!" he squawked, trying to divide his attention between the thirteenth-century illuminated Latin manuscript and the road. In the end, he simply gave up and pulled over into a passing place. He took the bound vellum from Wendy and held it reverently, reading the intricate lettering: *Chronica Regum Manniae et Insularum.* "I thought this was in the British Library."

"It's on loan," said Wendy casually. "Don't worry, I'll take it back."

"What else have you got in there?" Jim asked weakly, almost afraid to find out.

"The original manuscript of Bishop Philips's Manx Prayerbook." Wendy brandished it proudly. "I've got one of the translations at home, but this is the *only copy* of the original text – isn't that exciting? The Archdeacon lent it to the museum, it was in the same case, so I thought, why not?"

Jim laughed, a little maniacally.

"Sure, why not? Do you have *any idea* how much trouble we're in if … oh, never mind." He pulled out into the road and they continued on their way for a while in silence. Finally, he pulled over again and turned to her.

"I'm sorry, Wendy, I should have said thank you. You've taken an enormous risk for us and I really do appreciate it."

Wendy shut the treasures back in her briefcase and smiled.

"It was a pleasure."

"Yes, that's what worries me."

"Well, I just thought, if I'm going to be 'when I' Wendy, it might as well be 'when I robbed the Manx Museum'. At least that's got a bit of spice to it."

Jim couldn't help laughing.

"Right, come on then, Raffles, let's get back. I need to stop at my house to pick up some clothes and then we have some serious reading to do."

They drove through Ballabeg, Colby and up the Howe Hill towards Cregneish, approaching Jim's house slowly, craning their necks to see any sign of movement from inside. Jim parked on the road by the entrance to the Darrag, and, overriding Wendy's suggestion that she accompany him, walked back towards the garden wall. Nothing seemed out of place, so he walked round to the front of the house, passing the garden gate and, instead, entering the space where he normally kept his car, between the house and the stone building that acted as his store-room, workshop and garden shed. At the back of this makeshift driveway, a side gate led through to the back door. Jim listened carefully and, hearing nothing, unlocked the door and quietly stepped inside.

Wendy was just beginning to fret by the time she saw Jim approaching the car, carrying a duffel bag. He threw it onto the back seat and sat down, heavily, next to her.

"Is he gone?" she asked. Jim sighed and nodded.

"I think so. It's hard to tell. The place is in a bit of a mess, though, lots of things smashed, dirt thrown around." He was quiet, thinking of plates and ornaments that his wife had liked, that he had kept to remind himself of their time together. Wendy patted him gently on the arm.

"We'll beat him, Jim. We really will."

Jim smiled at her gratefully, started the car and drove back towards Port St Mary.

* * *

"OK, now look for a tree in a field."

"What?" Sam was becoming exasperated; the motion of the carriage was making him feel queasy and smuts from the engine's funnel were flying through the open window and making his eyes sting. "All the fields have got trees in them."

"No, it's a special tree." Al was tense, trying to remember a landscape that had changed dramatically since he'd last seen it. "It's on its own, right in the middle of a field. It marks the boundary." He continued to stare out of the window as the train came out of a long cutting, made dark by overhanging branches, into daylight. He pointed excitedly. "There! Look, Sam."

By the time Sam had looked, the train had plunged behind another bank. He noticed that Al was reaching towards the window, and was struck by a horrible thought.

"Which station are we getting off at, Al?"

"We're not. It curves round to the right and goes over a little embankment thing, and then we jump." Al had climbed onto the top of the sliding window and was bracing himself against the window frame. His scarf streamed in the wind, wisps of white hair had escaped from under his hat and were whipping wildly around his face. Sam thought he looked utterly insane.

"Are you kidding? I'm not jumping off a bloody train. Can't we get off at the next stop and walk back?"

Al shook his head, his eyes never leaving the landscape as it rushed past them, his voice hoarse from shouting over the wind and the noise of the engine.

"It's a magical domain, Sam. It's hidden unless you approach it from just the right angle. You've got to be right over the river."

"*River?*"

"NOW!"

Al leapt.

"*I'm going to kill you!*" Sam howled and leapt through the window after him.

The noise of the train passed, and the only sounds disturbing the peace were two screams, in perfect unison, as Al and Sam fell, landed and rolled through bracken, gorse, brambles, grass and cowpats, down the steep slope of the viaduct, into the Santon Burn.

★　★　★

There were some moments of hectic splashing as Al fought to stay upright against the few inches of icy water rushing over the pebbled riverbed, and Sam fought towards dry land. Eventually, silence descended. Al was submerged to his waist, braced against the current, and watched murderously from a patch of bracken by a bedraggled and seething Sam.

The sun broke through the clouds' haze, creating pockets of shade among the surrounding woodland, shifting and whispering in the soft breeze, reflecting dancing ripples of light from the river onto its overhanging, moss-clad banks, fragrant with wild garlic, so achingly beautiful a scene that it made the soul want to sing with joy. Al opened his mouth, then thought better of it, and began to wade downstream, slipping a little here and there, arms flung wide for balance. Sam growled softly to himself and followed, pausing now and again to shake the water from his fur, soothing himself with dark mutterings of revenge.

As they moved into the cover of the trees, the peacefulness became an oppressive silence. No birds sang, no creatures disturbed the undergrowth, the soft susurration of the wind against the spring leaves was stilled. Even the river was hushed, wider and slower-flowing over silt and mud that sucked noiselessly at Al's shoes. They plodded on, towards the heart of the woodland, disagreements forgotten as they looked to each other for reassurance and the courage to continue, both spotting at once two shadows detaching themselves from the trees ahead and moving, impossibly swiftly, towards them.

The shadows stopped a few feet ahead of them, barring any further progress; just a play of light on the bark of a tree, then in a blink, crouching figures, motionless and watchful, taller than Al, poised to throw the deadly lances that had, seconds earlier, seemed nothing more than briefly illuminated strands of gossamer web. Al and Sam froze, speechless in terror, as voices on the very edge of their hearing spoke in low, chanting unison.

"That's never yourself, is it, yessir?"

In the long, silent moment that followed, Sam looked questioningly at Al, who shrugged slightly before answering, in a small voice, "It is indeed. Who's asking?"

As if a password had been sought and received, the tension left the shadowy figures ahead. Sam blinked, feeling his vision twist slightly, and suddenly the wood was filled with figures, less than a metre tall, painted and camouflaged but still visible in a way they hadn't been moments ago. They looked identical at first, smooth-skinned and wide-eyed, and only on closer inspection could Sam see subtle differences between them; some taller than others, some thinner, some with more prominent features. They moved easily through the tangled undergrowth, as Al waded towards the eastern bank of the burn, until they were grouped together in a clearing. Al took off his hat and bowed to the assembled throng, but as he cleared his throat to introduce himself, a figure emerged from the crowd and spoke.

"Althelbrede of Poyllvill, also called All-Heal, also called Marsh Woundwort. Who's the pussy-cat?"

The figure was dressed similarly to the rest, with the same

ageless, unlined features, but carried an air of authority. Al searched his memory for a name, and smiled.

"Tushtagh of Ballaglione, also called Elder. This is my friend Sam, a warrior like yourselves."

Sam sniffed, modestly. Tushtagh regarded him steadily for a moment, then turned to the others. After a moment of wordless debate, it seemed a consensus was reached, and seven more fairies approached the bank, whilst the rest melted back into the woodland. Sam felt his eyes twist again, and there were just shadows and shafts of sunlight. He breathed out slowly.

"I love the way you guys do that."

Tushtagh smiled at him briefly. "These are the other Elders present at Ballaglione today. You'll remember Stroin and Skibbylt," he indicated two of the fairies, who smiled and waved briefly, "but I don't think you've met Giare,"

"Hello."

"Cruinn."

"Hi there."

"Bouyr. You'll have to speak up a bit."

"HELLO."

"And these are my daughters, Coar and Aalin."

"Pleased to meet you."

The introductions completed, there was the usual awkward moment of silence, and then Stroin burst out "Where have you been, Althelbrede? We haven't seen you for ages. You used to come over all the time."

Sam snorted. "Hah! See, Al? People get annoyed when you drop them." He turned to Stroin. "He did exactly the same to me and Jim. Didn't come round for a week. A week! How long since he last bothered to come and see you guys?"

"About four hundred years."

"Oh."

There was another, frostier silence.

"Thanks, Sam," said Al quietly, "that was very helpful." He turned back to Tushtagh. "The Billy Rhubyn have returned. They were in Cregneish this morning. We came to warn you, and to help you if we can."

There was barely a beat of stillness, as Tushtagh took in the implications of Al's news, then the day was urgent with activity, the Elders swiftly dispersing to carry out his orders.

"Skibbylt, get to Rushen as quick as you can, warn the others. Then warn everyone in the glens, then the mountains. Leave patrols to watch for the Billy Rhubyn, but bring everyone else back here. Stroin, get down to the Scoilt and make sure that the doors are properly sealed, Giare, take Bouyr and watch the bridge. The rest of us will set up perimeter boundaries. Cruinn, the Ballachrink side, Coar, go up to Ballachury, Aalin, up to Cooilcam. We'll meet back here when we're set. All right? Go."

Al and Sam were left alone in the clearing, the movement of the Mooinjer Veggey so swift and silent that the woods might have been deserted. Sam idly scratched an ear.

"Four hundred years?" he ventured finally. Al shrugged.

"You know how it is," he said, "you mean to pop round but other things crop up and before you know it another century has gone by."

"Mmm. So are these fairies as old as you, then?"

"Older, some of them. Tushtagh was an Elder long before I came over. The rumour was that he'd been here with the Ancients."

Sam nodded knowingly.

"Right." There was a pause. "Who are the Ancients?"

"The gods of Mann. You know, Manannan and his crowd. They're supposedly still asleep under the hills, waiting to be woken at the end of the age of something or other. The Scoilt is meant to be the passage that links the two realms." Al leaned across and spoke even more quietly. "Hence the sealed doors. If we wake up the Ancients, Billy will be the least of our problems."

Sam looked around, but all was stillness.

"They're not how I'd imagined. These fairies, I mean. I thought it would be all twinkling lights and wings and stuff."

Al snorted derisively.

"Pah. They're the fiercest warriors you'll ever meet. Even the Vikings left them alone, and we had some right homicidal bastards travelling with us." He smiled nostalgically, "I remember this one time, Hrossketil the Eyebrow challenged ..."

His musings were interrupted by the return of Tushtagh and Aalin. The other Elders followed in ones and twos, some that Sam didn't recognise, presumably returning after being summoned by Skibbylt, until there were over a dozen seated in the clearing, armed with bows and spears, serious-faced and attentive. Tushtagh spoke.

"So now we begin the council of war. Once, we defeated the Billy Rhubyn with our might, the next time with the help of our land's harvest," he nodded towards Al, "and our friends. This time, we haven't the power to beat them by force, and the land is sick from the poisons of men. We must look for a different source of strength." He paused. "Should we wake the Ancients?"

There was uproar as the Elders began speaking all at once, shouting to be heard, interrupting one another.

"Never!"

"The Ancients are the only ones who ..."

"We mustn't wake them. The end of ..."

"... ride the Eagh Taarnagh and drive them into the sea ..."

"... another way. If only..."

"... remember the last time ..."

Sam listened for a while, then stood and shouted over the hubbub until he could be heard.

"Excuse me. You lot are fairies, right?"

All eyes turned to him, including Al's.

"Careful, Sam," he breathed. Sam shook his head and spoke into the silence that had fallen.

"No, I'm not being funny, but you lot *are* fairies, yes? Magical people?"

Tushtagh nodded.

"I see what you mean, Sam. Yes," he hesitated, and spoke the words with obvious distaste "we are ... fairies."

"Right then." Sam was becoming enthusiastic, and Althelbrede groaned inwardly. Some of his friend's brilliant solutions were a little left-field. Sam continued.

"The way you do that appearing and disappearing thing, that's obviously magic, and when we saw Billy Rhubyn this morning, he was all yellow smoke and then he was really there, so he's obviously magic as well, and it seems like a similar sort of magic, with the coming and the going, and I'm sure you can do loads of other magic or else you wouldn't have been around so long and I thought Al was old, but he was saying that you're even older than he is, and Billy Rhubyn's really old as well, so ..." he paused to gather himself for the final onslaught "why don't you see if your other magic will work on him?"

There was a pause as everyone caught up with the end of the sentence, then Cruinn said timidly, "What about the Book of Song?"

Some of the Elders groaned, others looked blank and some brightened. Cruinn explained. "Ages ago, one of the Elders, Gob the Minstrel, thought it would be nice to set some of the old incantations to music, so he wrote them down and made up tunes for them. Very catchy, some of them."

Althelbrede nodded. "I remember him. Fellow with the little harp, used to visit the monks at the Abbey. Where is he?"

"On tour. Doing very well by all accounts, he's had some lovely reviews. He's back in the summer."

A wild-eyed fairy leapt up and shouted, "That Gob's a simpleton. We can't fend off the Billy Rhubyn by singing songs to them. We need to fight. We should saddle the Eagh Taarnagh. Our finest riders on their steeds of thunder will make short work of those Irish imps."

"OK, Brisht, settle down." Tushtagh spoke soothingly. "We'll do both. Take your best riders and prepare the steeds. Cruinn, bring the Book of Song, we'll have a look at it. Everyone else, to your posts. They could be here at any time."

★ ★ ★

The sun didn't reach the lay-by at this time of year, and the car was cold. Wendy shivered and blew on her hands. Jim reached for the ignition.

"I can put the heater on again," he suggested. Wendy shook her head,

"No, your battery will be flat. It's fine, but is there any coffee left?"

They refilled their mugs from one of the array of thermos flasks on the back seat, and Jim bent his head over the Manx Chronicle, adding notes to a small book he held next to it.

"This is amazing" he said, not for the first time. "These could all be references to the Mooinjer Veggey. Especially the miracle of St Mary. Some of the English translations just gloss over anything that doesn't fit in with the prevailing religious ideology."

Wendy nodded, and indicated the several books she had open on her lap and resting on the dashboard.

"I know. There's a whole page of text missing from my copies of this prayerbook. The dialect it's written in is really old, but there's a bit here about the people staying on the land that just seems to have vanished from any of the other translations. Have you found any references to the Billy Rhubyn?"

"I'm not sure." Jim rubbed the condensation from his side window and peered down the road toward the Fairy Bridge. "I need Althelbrede to give me an idea of some of the dates. There's a bit about King Magnus being away in Norway and the Island being under attack, but that could be anything." He looked thoughtful, "I hope they're getting on all right."

★ ★ ★

The search for the Book of Song had not gone well. When Cruinn had first returned to the clearing to say that he was having trouble finding it, Tushtagh had impatiently gone back with him to help him look. Some time had passed, before a rather sheepish Cruinn, his plump face red with exertion and embarrassment, had returned to ask for Al and Sam's help.

They had found the overhanging riverbank, climbed through the opening between two thick, knotted tree roots, and stood in the underground chamber that contained the written wisdom of the Mooinjer Veggey, as well as, it seemed, a thousand years' worth of broken weaponry, discarded clothing and spare furniture. Tottering piles had toppled, neat stacks had slipped sideways and it was only when they'd heard a muffled voice demanding irritatedly if Cruinn had come back that they had realised Tushtagh was still in there, buried in debris. He hadn't been at all pleased to see them in this most private of places, but, when Cruinn had reminded him that time was pressing, had grudgingly given them permission to stay and help with the search.

Cruinn had finally found what they were looking for; a thick sheaf of pages, some paper, some parchment, some like tree bark and dried leaves. They had emerged, dusty but triumphant from the underground chamber, and now sat, once more, in the clearing, poring over the ancient writings.

"There was one that I thought might be useful," said Cruinn, turning over the pages gingerly. "It was about protecting the bridge and keeping us safe. It had a lovely chorus, sort of sad and lilting. If we can keep the Billy Rhubyn away from here, they might leave the rest of the Island alone."

Sam finished cleaning the webs off his whiskers.

"That wasn't quite what I meant," he said. "Don't you have spells for catching fish and hypnotising rabbits so they'll let you eat them, and things like that?"

Cruinn and Tushtagh looked vaguely horrified. Al remembered that Sam had missed his breakfast and was probably thinking with his stomach.

"Why don't you go and get something to eat, Sam?" he said kindly. "I think I heard some pheasants up by the railway."

Sam looked a little affronted.

"All right," he said huffily. "I was just thinking that it's all very well protecting your bridge and all, but the rest of us need protecting too. You need to sort this Billy out for ever, not just hope he goes away."

He wandered off. Al sat up a little straighter.

"Why can't we just write a new incantation, if we can't find one that will do what we want?"

Cruinn and Tushtagh exchanged a glance.

"It doesn't really work like that," explained Tushtagh. "There's no new magic, just old magic. An incantation is ratified over millennia, so it will do today what it did thousands of years ago."

Al frowned.

"But if it has to be the same, then why was it only Gob who bothered writing them down? My friend Jim says …" he screwed up his eyes in an effort to remember Jim's words, from one of their many discussions about Island history. "He says that 'the oral tradition of a pre-literate society accounts for most of the difficulties in maintaining historical continuity'.

Isn't that another way of saying that things change if you don't write them down?"

Tushtagh looked a little nonplussed, but Cruinn brightened up.

"Ah yes, I see what your friend Jim means. Due to the changing dialects of a community, the corruption of language and so on, the meaning and pronunciation of the words would change. Well, that's the beauty of the incantations, see? It's the *sense* of the words that's constant, not the actual words used. So a spell for protecting the oldest tree in the forest can't just be turned into a spell to banish your enemies. We'd be all over the place if people could just invent new incantations on a whim, wouldn't we?"

Al smiled, slowly.

"I think I know what to do. Tushtagh, how long do you think you could fight the Billy Rhubyn for? An all out attack, thunder steeds and massed armies and the whole works?"

"At least a day, although – about the thunder steeds – Brisht is a fine warrior, but it's been a while since ..."

"Never mind, hopefully it won't take that long."

He led them away through the clearing, explaining as he went.

★　★　★

The opaque, grey light of pre-dawn filtered through the trees, and coated the fields in frigid dew. Manannan's cloak, a dense fog, lay draped over the shoulders of the land, pooling in hollows and valleys, softening the outlines of crofts and keels, shrouding events from the eyes of an unknowing world.

Al waited, eyes straining through the fog for any signs of movement. He hadn't fought a battle for many hundreds of years, but he remembered the horror of waiting. Too much time for the futile re-examination of plans long since finalised; hidden ranks of warriors held tense as bowstrings, waiting for the cry of a sighted enemy to release them like arrows into violence and chaos.

Sam was having a quick wash.

Suddenly, the call went up, far away to their left. The Mooinjer Veggey who had been on lookout to the east of the realm came hurtling through the forest, swelling the ranks of fairies along the river, to the west of the realm. Al and Sam kept up as well as they could, but the impossible, sinewy speed of the battle-hungry warriors soon left them behind. By the time they crossed the river, a thick bank of yellow smoke had spread all the way along the railway embankment, and was drifting into the long, empty field in front of them. As they watched, horrified, the smoke solidified; the blurred outlines sharpening to reveal thousands of identical figures, each with the same wickedly sharp teeth. There was no taunting this time, no demented laughter. The Billy Rhubyn formed a single, snarling mass, and sprang forward.

The first wave of Mooinjer Veggey, carrying bows and quivers, ran forward to the shapeless hedge of brambles and bracken that formed their boundary, and let fly volley after volley of arrows. As the first struck and the Billy Rhubyn began to fall, the mass blurred and became smoke once more, the arrows passing harmlessly through them.

"Tricky buggers," remarked Sam. Al nodded.

"It's early yet," he said grimly.

They heard Tushtagh's rallying cry off to their right, and, with an answering cheer, the Mooinjer Veggey swarmed forward, meeting the Billy Rhubyn at the top end of the field. There was no sun to glint off sword and armour, no breath left for battle-cries, just the savage intensity of two armies whirling and thrusting, scratching and biting, the shifting mass of bodies lurching gradually closer across the field.

No matter how many Mooinjer Veggey piled into the fray,

the Billy Rhubyn kept multiplying to match their numbers, and as the fairies became drawn into the rolling morass of bodies, there were fewer between the yellowish ranks of the attackers and their prize. The numbers on the riverbank dwindled until Al and Sam realised they were there alone.

"Quick, Al, the signal!" Sam hissed urgently, and Al unfurled the red cloth he had safely stowed inside his jacket, and waved it frantically in the direction of the railway embankment.

The colour and movement caught the eye of the two armies, and it seemed as though they paused for a moment, hearing perhaps the first, ominous rumblings of thunder, as hooves beat a tattoo on the grassy hillside and the riders of the Eagh Taarnagh swooped spectacularly out of the fog.

Brisht had done his best, and it was a valiant effort. Woolly flanks were covered with plates of gleaming armour; horns were oiled and sharpened. Although some of the Loaghtan sheep were a little elderly and some were a little overweight, the sight of the Mooinjer Veggey crouched low over their backs, steering them with the lower, curved horns caused the Billy Rhubyn to pause in their onslaught. Al was impressed. Sam frowned.

"What's with the sheep?" he asked.

"Specially bred fighting sheep," Al replied. "The Eagh Taarnagh. Steeds of thunder."

Sam opened his mouth to protest, but changed his mind.

"What's Brisht doing? He's going too far up the hill."

Al looked, and realised what Sam meant. The angle at which the mounted fairies were approaching the battle meant that instead of forming a protective flank between the Billy Rhubyn and the river, they would meet them level with the other fairies, leaving an opening.

No sooner had the mistake become apparent to the watchers,

than the Billy Rhubyn gave an exultant cry and swarmed through the gap, racing towards the river, straight for Sam and Al. The Mooinjer Veggey gave chase, but their battle-weary limbs made them sluggish, and it seemed impossible for them to catch the approaching hordes.

"Let's go!" Al and Sam turned and raced alongside the river, scrambling up the sloping bank towards the road, past the lay-by, where Jim stood, alone, by his car. They dived down the bank on the other side of the road, past the cottage and over the shallows of the river, heading due south, hearing the first cackle of triumphant laughter as the Billy Rhubyn poured into the domain of the Mooinjer Veggey, hearing the despairing cry of "Retreat!" first from Tushtagh, then taken up by the rest of the Elders; "Retreat, retreat!" as the fairies scattered in every direction, necessity lending them speed to escape to the boundaries of their lands, leaving the Billy Rhubyn standing alone in the woodland clearing, laughing with the conqueror's joy of total victory.

Al and Sam had reached the southern boundary, and collapsed, panting and exhausted, when they heard the singing. It was not a strong voice, but pleasant, and the lilting tune leant it poignancy. They sat up, and strained to hear the words, repeated as the singer's confidence grew, and the power of old magic carried the incantation across the woodland.

> *"Those who fought to own this land,*
> *from western stream to eastern ridge,*
> *are bound here by the Ancients' hand*
> *And safely kept beneath this bridge."*

When the screaming started, the song was so powerful that it could not be drowned out straight away, and although the screams multiplied until it seemed that thousands of voices were howling in rage, the words still rang inside the minds of the listeners. Eventually, there was just one voice, shrieking the direst threats, and only then did the song begin to fade, not as if the singer had stopped, but as an echo, fading across the mountains. There was silence for a moment and then the everyday sounds crept back into the morning; birdsong in the trees, livestock on the hills and the distant hum of cars and bikes on nearby roads.

Al and Sam looked at each other and wordlessly made their way back towards the road.

Wendy was walking back up the road towards the lay-by, closing the prayerbook that she held. They met at the lay-by, and Jim gave her a brief hug before solemnly shaking Althelbrede's hand and stroking Sam behind the ears.

"Well done, everyone."

Al smiled,

"Shall we go and see Tushtagh and Cruinn? Make sure everything's all right?"

Wendy started.

"Let me lock this in my briefcase first. And the Manx Chronicle."

"I'm sure they'll be safe in the car, Wendy," said Jim. Wendy gave a hollow laugh.

"No, your cat will go to sleep on them, or eat them, or Althelbrede will make them disappear or something. I'm sorry, but just when you think it's all sorted …"

"Oh for crying out loud!" Sam had had enough. "I'm a cat. We eat birds. Get over it."

There was a small silence. Al sniffed.

"Well, now that we've got that off our chests, shall we go and see the Mooinjer Veggey?"

They slithered down the bank and splashed across the river to the clearing, where two small figures sat, waiting for them. Tushtagh looked a little disapproving, but Cruinn stood and greeted them as long-lost friends.

"Oh, that was wonderful. I didn't think it would work at all, I suppose I shouldn't say that after all your hard work, but I never thought you'd manage it." He turned to Althelbrede and continued excitedly, "You saw what I meant about the sense of the words and the actual words and you turned it completely upside-down, so the *actual* words were the same, but the sense of the words was quite different. Oh, I never would have thought that would work."

Al smiled, suddenly shy.

"Well, it was Ms Caine who worked it out really. She translated Gob's song into English and then into modern Manx and realised that you could make it mean anything."

"Hmmph." Tushtagh frowned. "A very dangerous precedent. I mean, thank you all, but you really mustn't do that sort of thing ever again."

"Of course not." Wendy handed Tushtagh a folded piece of paper. "These are the translations that I wrote. I'd like you to have them, so you can destroy them if you think that's for the best." Tushtagh took the proffered page and looked a little less forbidding. Wendy looked a little awkward. "I'm afraid that I can't give you back the original, though."

"Why ever not?"

"Well, it's written on the back of one of the pages of the Bishop Philips's Manx Prayerbook, and I can't start tearing pages out of that. I don't know how it got there. It was only when Cruinn was trying to remember the words of the song that I realised they sounded familiar." She realised that Cruinn and Tushtagh were smiling at each other.

"That Gob," said Cruinn. "You just can't keep him away from the clergy. You're lucky that the Bishop was doing the translation of an earlier work and not the other way round. Gob's songs have turned up in some very odd places."

"Really?" Jim was intrigued. "Where?"

"Well," Cruinn said confidentially, "Once you're familiar with his style, there's one or two of the psalms that …"

"Anyway," Tushtagh interrupted, torn between his gratitude for the intervention of Jim and Wendy and his desire to preserve a millennium of secrecy. "Thank you again, Jim Quine and Wendy Caine. And thank you, Althelbrede. Sam, I salute you as a fellow warrior. You are welcome here any time."

"Oh." Sam was quite overcome. "Cheers, Mr Tushtagh, glad I could help. Um …" he still felt he was missing a key element of the plan. "I understand why we all had to leg it so that the Billy Rhubyn was the only one here when the singing started, and I think I understand about the translating it backwards and forwards so that it meant the same thing but didn't mean the same thing, but … actually, no, that's the bit I don't understand. If it was the same spell, then where's Billy Rhubyn?"

Tushtagh smiled.

"Exactly where he thought he wanted to be. Under the Fairy Bridge for all eternity."

"But, if that's what he wanted, then doesn't that mean he won? Why are we all so happy?"

Al put an arm around his friend's furry shoulders.

"The song said 'below *this* bridge'. Ms Caine was standing on the little white fairy bridge, not the real one."

"What? That's not the real one?"

"No," they chorused, happily.

"So where's the real one?"

"Come on, Sam, let's go home, I'm starving."

They climbed back up to the road and piled into Jim's car. He wound down the window and looked back to where Tushtagh and Cruinn were watching, just visible in the shadows of the undergrowth. He touched his hand to his forelock, solemnly.

"Moghrey mie, fairies."

They touched their hands to their heads in return and nodded, and then the woodland seemed empty, just shadows and light.

"Moghrey mie, Billy," Jim called cheerfully, as they sped over the Fairy Bridge towards home.

"*Bugger off.*"

❧ April ❧

Ellan Moore writes for women's magazines, and sometimes writes as Elaine Aulton. Her stories are true, but embroidered a little.

The Bridge

Ellan Moore

At Silverdale there was no room in the car park, so I double-parked in the lane, leaving the engine running. This was urgent. I had finally worked out the clue: *These old horses have been given a new lease of life.*

I felt stupid. Of *course* it meant the Victorian waterwheel-driven roundabout at Silverdale – and not the Home of Rest for Old Horses. What a detour I'd done. I leapt out of my car and ran for the steps. A woman leaned over the rail.

"Treasure hunter?"

"Yes," I called back.

"You're the last one."

I felt cross with myself for being so slow.

"Shouldn't there be two of you?" the woman asked.

"Yes," I thought. But Tony threw a tantrum when his car wouldn't start and he refused to be seen dead in mine, except when it was dark and he'd had a few. Good start to the treasure hunt. I didn't say this, just smiled and shrugged.

The woman handed me the next envelope. "I thought I'd save you the sprint to the roundabout, seeing as you're the last."

I said, "Thank you," but thought, "why rub it in?" I ran back to my car, grateful that there'd been no other traffic. I drove off, and where the lane was wider I pulled over to read the next clue.

We'd been sent miles – starting at Peel and each car leaving at two-minute intervals, first to St John's, then to Foxdale, then to St Mark's and then to Silverdale – only in my case, via Richmond Hill. Inside the envelope was a typed note: *Fairies can't cross water, so why do they need a bridge?*

I shoved the gearstick into first and headed towards Ballasalla. But surely the Fairy Bridge was too obvious.

As I drove I recalled conversations in the pub, about the present white-painted bridge on the Castletown road being only a tourist attraction. Marion was an 'expert' on folklore. She said things like, "If you see a robin fly from an Alder tree, whatever you dream will come true." She loved the fair folk, as she called them. Where had she said the 'real' Fairy Bridge was? K ... K ... Kewaigue. No. Oak something. Near Kewaigue. I thought I knew where I was headed. I hoped I wouldn't have to trespass.

I slowed to a crawl as I approached where the road crossed the stream and looked around. There. Running parallel to the stream was an almost invisible, overgrown and rutted lane. I stopped the car and peered down the lane. New growth and gold-yellow gorse grew the length of it. The new leaves were lime green and the sun shone palely through them onto the sprinkling of bluebells in the distance, leading my eye further down the dappled 'highway'. I turned off the main road, and changed down to first as the suspension bounced over the stones and ruts.

Gorse branches started to scratch at the car, but what the heck, the paintwork of my old Fiesta was scored with rusty scratch marks anyway. I stopped and turned the engine off. The quiet was peaceful – except it wasn't really quiet; it was the mingling together of running water, birdsong and a breeze soughing in the trees. It was a beautiful Sunday afternoon. Ahead, beneath the overhanging branches, the lane seemed to peter out. On my right, between the trees, like looking down a fairy tunnel through the canopy of spring leaves, was a track to an old stone bridge. I was amazed I'd never noticed it before.

It was ancient – the stones were pale, rough sandstone. Very unusual; everything else in the area was built with Manx stone. Young trees and gorse bushes along its length obscured the left parapet. They encroached on the mossy road across the bridge making it narrow, but passable. The right parapet was pale gold, reflecting the spring sun, and growing its own foliage and miniature flowers. It was wide enough to walk along its top. I drove across, marvelling at nature enhancing its beauty. It struck me that the stream was really wide, here.

On the other side, almost hidden except for its roofs, behind high, unkempt box hedges was a brick and beam house. It was half smothered in two-tone ivy up to the gabled roof; mullioned windows shone in the sun and the huge front door had wisteria hanging from its porch.

I stopped the car in wonder. A man came out of the house and raised a hand in greeting. He was tall and wide-shouldered, and his shirt billowed loosely around him. "Pity he's not my type," I thought. He beckoned for me to get out of the car. I was aware of the almost overpowering, warm, honey-coconut-vanilla scent of the gorse as I opened the door.

"You found the bridge," he said.

There was something about him. He had high cheekbones and shadows starting beneath his sea-green eyes. As he smiled, deep creases ran down his cheeks enhancing his bone structure and framing a wide mouth with eye-teeth that protruded slightly. I was stunned. By his looks, by his smile, by the sheer beauty of the setting. I felt lumpy and unattractive next to him. I stared.

"You found the bridge," he said again.

I held up the last clue; a gust of wind plucked it from my fingers and the man reached out his hand as if to catch it. His fingertips brushed my cheek, causing me to shiver at his touch. My nerve endings weren't expecting anything to be so sensuous. I was able to speak at last. "So, I'm in the right place then? This is where I'm supposed to be?"

"Oh yes." He took hold of my hand and I didn't resist. I walked with him to the house, noting his pale-gold hair tied at the nape of his neck with a brown velvet ribbon. His trousers looked like dark chamois leather, tucked into soft leather boots: his appearance had more than a hint of 'romantic buccaneer' about it, yet he had the panache to carry it off as if it weren't a deliberate image. The organisers of all this had cast him well. To finish the treasure hunt at a house like this was a stroke of genius. Tony had said we'd most likely end up at The Rose and Crown.

The man smiled again and for an instant I felt as though I would follow him anywhere. "Will you stay?" he asked.

I pulled my hand from his and wondered if I'd made a mistake. "Look, this is part of the treasure hunt, isn't it?" He folded his arms and leaned lazily against the huge front door. "I mean ... you seemed to expect me. I thought I'd worked out the clue properly."

"Yes, I have been expecting you." He spoke softly, staring at me without blinking. I found it hard to look away. He wasn't making fun of me, I was sure. He said, "I am Tal."

"Tal?" I didn't recognise the name at all. "Er ... is that short for something?"

"Yes." He smiled, but offered nothing more.

Something occurred to me. "Where's everybody else? Am I the first?"

"The first?" His brow crinkled, but then he smiled and seemed to change the subject. "I saw you come down the track. Then I watched you find the bridge. And at last you arrived, a truly beautiful visitor." He moved away from the wall and stood close to me. I've had lines from men before but I could have sworn this wasn't a line. It may have been his proximity, his grace, his almost-perfect features or the surroundings, but I believed him. His eyes and smile were warm and kind, and I felt like a plain schoolgirl with a crush, being noticed at last.

Again he touched my cheek and I shivered. Common sense told me not to trust a strange man, especially in such a secluded place; naïve confidence assured me I was perfectly safe.

"Let me show you this place," he said. I couldn't speak, so I nodded.

We dawdled along the bank of the stream that was as wide as a river. How odd that I'd been so unobservant. Tal was informative about the wildlife. He directed my attention to a tangle of honeysuckle entwined in the bushes, and a blackbird sitting on her nest in amongst it. We watched her for a long time in silence. Tal finally moved on, and pointed to the water's edge. "Look. There in the spaddowflax."

Spaddowflax? I didn't want to seem ignorant so I just looked where he was pointing. "White throats," he said. There were indeed two tiny birds looking for all the world as if they were playing a form of hopscotch. They made me smile.

Tal linked arms with me and we strolled on. I felt as if I'd known him for ever. From the far end of the tree-edged lawn, through the heavy blossom, I could see the main road that crossed this stream. The quality of light made it appear misty, and though I watched a bus, some cars and a tractor driving across it, I heard nothing except the sound of running water and rustling leaves. I commented on it to Tal.

He raised my hand to his mouth, closing his eyes as if listening. "Yes," he said, and I could feel the movement of his lips on my skin. "It has always been like this. It is always tranquil."

Tranquil wasn't part of my usual vocabulary but it summed up Tal completely – although the effect of his lips on the back of my hand was anything but tranquil. I pulled my hand away. He opened his shadowed eyes and looked sadly into mine.

"I am sorry."

"Well," I laughed, trying to lighten the mood, "I thought for a second that you were trying a seduction routine." It was the wrong thing to say. His face clouded and, to my surprise, he walked away. I watched him stride across the lawn towards the house; his shirt billowing like Errol Flynn's in an old, swashbuckling movie. I was thankful that Tal couldn't see my embarrassment. Tal thumped both fists against the oak door, which swung inwards, and he disappeared into the house.

I remained where I was, taken aback that my comment had caused such a reaction. I was undecided whether to follow him to apologise or just slink back to my car and sneak off. Eventually I retraced my steps and hovered by the car. Car or apology? I veered towards the house.

Tal was inside leaning against a window and I realised he was watching the bridge. For a few seconds he was unaware of my watching him. He looked sad. And lonely. He was certainly an enigma. Then he turned his head and our eyes met and his sudden grin displaced my silly notions.

He opened the front door as I reached it. He disarmed me when he bowed extravagantly then stood and offered his arm – straight out of a period romance – and he escorted me into the gloom of the house. The huge hallway was dominated by the staircase and large paintings and panelling: the dark oak added to the dim silence. There was a Regency chaise longue in front of a massive fireplace, and six upright chairs around an inlaid table. There were four closed doors, patterned with large, black, diamond-shaped studs.

He said, "I wish to start again. May I?" I nodded. He indicated the picture above the fireplace. It was a beautiful landscape, with horses in the foreground and mountains behind. He started telling me about it, but I only half-listened to the words. His voice was hypnotic. He moved on to the next picture. His boots made hardly any sound on the wood-block floor.

I was very aware of his proximity and the woody aftershave he wore: it was more noticeable inside. As he gazed up at the paintings I covertly studied his profile. When he stopped speaking I held my breath and there was nothing but silence. Not a clock ticking, or birds, or any household noises.

As if reading my thoughts he said, "I live here alone."

"What? No telly?" He shook his head, smiling slightly. "No radio? Music?" He shook his head again. "What about books? You must have books."

"Books are important to you?"

"Well, yes."

Tal indicated one of the studded doors. We both moved towards it and our hips bumped, and he slid an arm round my waist. He pressed the palm of his free hand against the massive wooden door, his thumb just touching one of the black studs, and held me a little tighter. Suddenly I felt awkward and large and I didn't know what to do with my arms. He twisted the handle to open the door and a waft of old pages and leather drifted out. The room gleamed with dappled sunlight as the sun streamed through the ivy-edged mullioned windows, and shone on the red-brown spines of the banks of books.

Just as I was about to cross the threshold Tal pulled me to

him. I was both surprised yet expecting it. I was attracted to him, very attracted, and it caught me off guard. Part of me was appalled at my forwardness, but that part was too remote to stop the inclination. Standing there in the golden light from the library I let my arms slide around his waist – he was so slim – and I rested my head on his chest. I could feel and hear his heart, and as he stroked the nape of my neck my nerve endings did a tap dance. I turned my face to his. A smile hovered on his perfect lips and I realised I wanted him to kiss me. I really wanted him to kiss me.

Tal bent his head and I closed my eyes. Every nerve was alive, straining for his touch. I felt his breath on my eyelids, then something like the touch of butterfly wings moving across my cheek. Then he placed his fingertips on my mouth. I opened my eyes, belatedly shocked at my conduct. The touch of his fingers was still on my lips but the spell was broken. I pulled away.

"Please, Penelope, I am sorry." He hung his head. "I should not have done that. I should not have done that."

I felt mortified. What must he think of me? "Hey, look, I'm to blame too. I wanted … never mind what I wanted. I got carried away." I attempted a nonchalant shrug. "I mean, well, for a minute there I thought you found me attractive."

He held my face between his hands and pulled me, unresisting, towards him.

"Penelope, you are beautiful. I want you to stay." Tal tipped my head forwards and kissed my hair.

What must he think of me? Miserably I said, "I think I ought to go."

Shaken at my behaviour, I made my way back to the Fiesta. As I drove slowly across the bridge I looked in the rear view mirror and saw Tal standing, unsmiling, his arms wrapped around himself.

A few minutes later I turned from the rutted, overgrown lane onto the road. As I crossed the stream I slowed, and looked for Tal's bridge. The sparkling stream disappeared around a bend and I could see neither bridge nor house. I was disappointed.

I met the others in the Rose and Crown. "Where've you been?" "Nell!" "We thought you'd gone home." My friends crowded round, handed me a drink, and told me how brilliant they'd been at solving the clues. Dutifully I laughed at their anecdotes and shrugged Tony's arm from my shoulders. I replayed my time at Tal's. He'd called me by my full name yet I couldn't remember telling him, although I must have. I felt suffocated and I wanted to get away.

Marion came out from behind the bar. "You all right Nell? You look a bit peaky." I was grateful for her concern and was about to say so but Tony spoke first.

"She's okay, Marion. She got herself lost, that's all."

Marion frowned at me, and it occurred to me that Tony always spoke for me. Why hadn't I noticed it before?

Marion said, "I think you ought to sit for a bit. You've gone all pale." She indicated the window seat and she sat down with me. She called to George to get me a cup of tea, and then spoke to me in a hushed voice.

"They all got back a couple of hours ago. Where did you get to, Nell?"

"I took a wrong turn and trespassed a bit."

"Has anything happened?" She frowned again. "I couldn't help noticing that when your friends were talking you were as white as a ghost. You weren't with it. Not like you at all."

My cup of tea arrived and I took advantage of it, sipping carefully so I needn't answer. Truth was, I didn't know what the matter was either. I assured Marion I hadn't had an accident or been accosted; yet I felt the tingle of remembered fingertips on my cheek and neck as I spoke. "I did get a bit lost. I – I asked someone if I was in the right place, and he said yes. But it wasn't. The right place, I mean."

She patted my hand. "You watch out for them fair folk, they can lead you a merry dance. Don't you raise your eyebrows at me, missy, I know what I'm telling you." Marion folded her arms. "Never kiss a fairy, they'll steal your heart away. That's what my mother always told me." She must have read my bemused expression well. "All right, love. I'd best get back to my customers." She rose, then said, "Here, you're not on one of them silly diets are you?" Laughing, I shook my head and the tension dissipated.

I made my excuses to Tony, who sulked a little, but to my relief he turned back to our crowd.

I spent the whole week in a dream of sea-green eyes. I kept putting Tony off, which seemed to make him more attentive. I made mistakes at work and got a telling-off from my boss, and on my Thursday and Friday night stints at the Rose and Crown I was clumsy and useless with the customers' change.

Marion was concerned and took me into the back, shooing George out to take our places.

"Now look, love, I know it's none of my business but you're not … you know … pregnant, are you?" I was too shocked to answer. Marion carried on. "I mean, you're always sharp as a pin, but this week you're off with the fairies. I'm serious." I could tell by her face that she was. "If there's anything the matter, and I mean anything, I'll try and help."

I hugged her. "I'm sorry to worry you. No, I'm not pregnant."

She held me at arm's length. "Hmmm." She studied my face. "You're in love, aren't you? And not with Tony. I've always said you were too good for Tony." Marion gave me a rueful smile. It hadn't occurred to me. In love? Obsessed, yes, with the memory of an elegant man with an angelic smile. "I'll need you tomorrow lunchtime, but you can have Saturday night off." She winked. "Okay?"

As I went back out to the bar Tony came in with the usual crowd and because I didn't think quickly enough I told him I wasn't working and ended up agreeing to go out on Saturday evening. But, while pulling pints I made up my mind that I would go back to Tal's.

After clearing the last of the lunchtime debris at the pub, I said my goodbyes and went home shaking with nervousness. I dressed as if for a special date. I did my hair and make-up twice, all the time telling myself aloud how stupid I was being. What if he had someone else there? What if it had been a joke? Even with all the doubts I still found myself driving, only half my mind on the journey. A churning stomach made my driving twitchy, and I almost missed the lane. The day was dull, and thick grey cloud threatened rain. I bounced down the rutted lane, noticing that the gorse was blooming more abundantly than last Sunday.

There it was. Even in the leaden light the bridge glowed a golden brown. There were clusters of tiny purple flowers ruffling in the wind on the right parapet, and the bushes that lined the left side of the bridge were starting to wave pink and white flowers from their buds. I could scarcely believe the change in just one week. The flowing water looked forbidding as it moved darkly beneath the honey-coloured stone arches.

Feeling extremely nervous I started forwards, scraping the right wing on the parapet. "Oh well," I thought, "one more scratch won't be noticed." When I was halfway across Tal stepped out from behind the hedge that hid the house, making my heart leap. He looked just as I'd left him on Sunday, with his arms held around himself, shirt billowing, but this time he was smiling.

"I hoped you would return, Penelope."

"Yes. Well, here I am." I felt self-conscious and girlish again. I'd forgotten how striking his green eyes were. In order to have something to do I studied the scratch on the wing. Tal stood behind me, close enough for me to catch a tinge of his woody scent. My thoughts raced suggestively. This was dreadful; why was I doing this?

He reached out and traced the bright silver scratch with one finger. "Where did this happen?" He sounded worried.

"On the bridge. You know how it is." I straightened and looked at him properly, "Women drivers." As I spoke I realised he looked thinner. The hollow beneath his cheekbones was more accentuated, and the blue shadows under his eye were deeper. "Are you ill?" The question was out before I thought about it. He wagged his finger to indicate "No". Or "Don't ask", perhaps.

I put my hands into my coat pockets and watched the breeze ruffle his thin shirt. "Aren't you cold?" He shook his head without taking his eyes from mine.

"Will you stay?" he asked.

"OK."

His reaction startled me. He grabbed my shoulders and hugged me, hard. "You do not know how much this means," he breathed.

Frankly, as long as he held me like that I didn't care.

We wandered through the gardens on the far side of the house, which were planted with cultivated and wild flowers together. Although the weather was cold and dull, I'd have walked with him anywhere. The gardens were much larger than I'd previously thought, bordered by another stream. I realised that the house and grounds were essentially on an island. Hedges hid private gardens that I hadn't noticed the previous week, reached through archways of stone or boughs.

Through one gated archway was a buttercup-covered lawn. The flowerbeds grew blue flowers, wild hyacinth, speedwell and scilla, Tal said, and behind them were broom bushes covered in yellow blooms. I couldn't get enough of it. I gazed around the garden and noticed in one corner a mound of periwinkle.

"Come away," he said.

"Why is that bit different?" I walked across the buttercup lawn towards the periwinkle with Tal following. The closer I got it dawned on me that the mound was gravelike.

"Blue and yellow were her favourite colours."

"What?" I wasn't sure I'd understood the words.

"Blue and yellow –"

"Is that a grave?" I heard the disbelief in my voice. The wind blew chill across the garden and I moved away from Tal.

"Yes."

"But ...but ... who?" The mound was too big for a pet.

Tal looked at me sadly and said, "Susannah."

The whole garden was blue and yellow. I didn't want to ask, but I heard myself say, "Who was she?"

There was a silence. In among the periwinkle I now saw forget-me-nots. There was a kind of sadness in the air that hadn't been present a minute before. Tal said, "I loved her very much." The way he said it made my stomach take a nosedive. I had to get out of that memorial garden.

I marched down the path to the water but Tal caught up with me and said, "You saw her portrait last time you were here." It took a few seconds but his words finally made sense. But was there an ache in his voice? Who was Susannah? – Mother? Grandmother? No matter. It was someone long gone.

"Why don't we go out and find somewhere to eat?"

He looked alarmed. "I cannot. I must stay here."

"Must?" I looked at him, wondering why I hadn't noticed

the strain before. He was ill. I'd seen that he'd lost weight but I was enjoying his company so much I'd ignored everything: the weather, the cold, his health. "Oh. I – I – shall we rest, then?" He looked grateful. I turned and just then a robin flew out from beneath a small tree that had wide shiny leaves, growing at the water's edge. We sauntered arm in arm to the house. The warmth of him made me feel safe. Marion was right. I was in love. With a tall, thin blond stranger who wore his hair in a ponytail. I've always gone for sporty, muscular men like Tony; not aesthetic, artistic types.

There was a fire burning in the hall so we stayed there. Susannah's portrait hung at the top of the stair. I remembered it now: she was dressed in Edwardian clothes looking wistfully into the distance, and this house was in the background.

We sat on the chaise for a long time in the glow of the fire, me leaning against him, talking. He was so easy to talk to, to relax with. The windows darkened, unnoticed, until the call of nature forced me to move. Tal showed me the bathroom and I was fascinated by it: the claw-footed bathtub, the wide wooden seat that covered the toilet, the enormous gilt mirror and chandelier. In the mirror I looked radiant, flushed by the warmth of the fire and the nearness of Tal.

When I came out of the bathroom Tal was at the foot of the staircase bathed in firelight. I minced down the stairs in best Hollywood fashion and offered my limp hand. I fully expected him to join in the charade, but instead of kissing my hand he rested his cheek against it and stared hungrily into my eyes. Suddenly I was shy again, and I pulled away.

"It's late. It's time I was gone," I said.

He looked dismayed. "But you said you would stay."

The atmosphere was full of mixed messages, from both of us. I felt wrong-footed. "Hey, Tal. Let's not rush things, okay?"

"You said you would stay, Penelope."

"For the day. I thought that's what you meant."

Tal closed his eyes, but not before I saw the disappointment there. "Tal, I'm sorry, but – " Then I remembered Tony. "Oh sod. I should have met someone hours ago. Look, I'm really sorry but I have to go."

He looked stricken. "Do you have a lover?"

I looked down. "Sort of." I felt horribly exposed and I couldn't look at him. "But I don't love him." Tal exhaled with a sound of relief. I said, "I'll come again tomorrow?"

He held me and spoke into my hair. "I do not want you to leave. When you go I am lost."

He sounded sincere. In his embrace I doubted my reading of his motives. He'd not made any untoward advances. Everything between us had been chaste and respectful. And, though I didn't like to admit it, if he *had* tried the come-on I don't think I would have resisted. He still hadn't even kissed me, for goodness sake, except for the top of my head. And possibly my cheek, but I wasn't sure. As if he read my mind he touched his lips to my forehead, so gently I wondered if I was imagining it. I tried to turn my face up to his, but he placed featherlight fingertips on my lips, turning me to jelly.

"You and I have a bond," he murmured. "You found the bridge. But I will not *cheat*. I want you to come to me willingly." He took his fingers from my lips and touched his own.

Walking to the car in the overcast night I couldn't see the bridge at all. "Tal?"

"Look," he said, "bats." I looked up, and when I looked back my eyes must have adjusted to the dark because I could see the pale outline of the bridge against the black of the night. Again, he stood alone with his arms wrapped around himself, looking vulnerable and lost. He didn't smile and didn't wave.

I scraped the left wing and passenger door as I turned off the end of the bridge and on to the track. My driving was awful; it must have been the effect Tal had on me.

On the drive back I had the gnawing pangs of hunger. Not surprising considering I hadn't eaten all day. I pulled up on the Rose and Crown car park at half past ten – more than two hours late. The hungry feeling turned into a tight knot in the pit of my stomach because I knew I had to face Tony. Another car slewed to a stop on the gravel: four youths clambered out and swept me into the loud interior with them. Marion saw me and mouthed something while inclining her head and nodding towards the alcoves. I acknowledged her, and she tut-tutted at me.

Tony was standing with his back to me but some of the others saw me and made "Oh dear" faces, which alerted him. I saw his back stiffen but he didn't turn round. I sighed, joined the group and said my hellos. Tony stared straight ahead and ignored me. I should have apologised but I couldn't have given the reason for my lateness, so I decided to join in the game and act as if nothing was untoward. I knew it would annoy Tony further, but as I no longer wanted to be his girlfriend it made perverse sense to force the issue.

Again I was on the edge of the group, pretending to listen while I remembered the touch of Tal's chaste kiss, and relived the delicate touch of his finger on my mouth. I closed my eyes and I was back there. There was a lull in the jukebox music and conversations, and I was aware that all the gang, including Tony, were looking at me.

"Nell? Hello-o-o-o. Planet Earth to Nell?" I looked at each person in turn and saw they were treating it lightly, except Tony, who looked angry.

"What's the matter with you?" he demanded. "Bloody well smiling to yourself like that. You might just as well be on your own for all the bloody notice you've taken of me. Us. You're acting weird, you are."

"Leave her, Tone. She looks dead tired."

Tony turned on Marcus. "You stay out of this. She's *my* girlfriend."

An awkward pause followed while everyone avoided looking at anyone else. Marion bustled up with a tray for the empties and said, "She's away with the fairies, is Nell. Working in town all week, and working here evenings and weekends. George keeps telling me she does too much and needs to get some sleep." Everyone laughed, gratefully, and the moment passed.

Tony frowned into his lager, and to my surprise mumbled, "I was worried about you. I didn't mean to come at you like a heavy." I didn't know what to say so I stayed silent. He continued, "How about the two of us making a day of it down Port Erin tomorrow?"

"Tomorrow?" I couldn't swallow. The thought of not seeing Tal made me feel panicky. "I can't. I promised …" I couldn't think of what to say to save his feelings. My mind was that horrible blank you get, like when you start to introduce someone and when you say, 'And this is –" and you discover you've forgotten their name.

Marion was still clearing our glasses and she put the tray down with a rattle. "Nell said she'd come for a pamper day with me. Massage, sauna, reflexology and all that. I didn't want to go on my own. Don't mind, do you?"

Tony nodded wisely and slung his arm across my shoulders. "Course I don't, if she promised." I felt as guilty as hell. Marion pointed to the tray so I moved out of Tony's reach, picked the tray up and followed her back to the bar. On the way she said, "George is holding the fort tomorrow because I *am* going for a pamper day, but with my sister. So – *if* you want to see someone – you've got until about teatime. Say, six o'clock. Will that do you?" In spite of myself I smiled, and Marion nonchalantly put her tongue into her cheek and made a mock innocent face.

When I got back to the gang a girl I knew by sight was giving Tony the eye. He was flattered, I could tell, and I found myself hoping he might respond. I waited until the last orders were brought into the alcove before I said goodnight. Tony was torn between leaving his pint so I could take him home, or finishing it and cadging a lift with one of the others. "I'll phone you," I said, and he gave me a quick peck that I deflected by turning my head. He didn't seem to notice.

That night I dreamed about Tal. In the dream I was still me, but willowy and dressed like Susannah. We were riding dark chestnut horses – I've never ridden in my life, yet it felt wonderful – and Tal was laughing, with his head thrown back, and he looked so healthy – no dark shadows – and more solidly built. Then my horse jumped across an impossibly wide river, hooves thudding into rich green grassland on the other side. I turned back to see where Tal had got to. In the dream the horses had gone and he was standing, pale and thin again, with sorrow in his eyes. This was the Tal I wanted. I called, but no sound came. I tried to wade into the river, but it got wider and deeper and fiercer. I looked up. Tal was gone.

I woke with a start, sweating and gasping, feeling like a wound spring. The clock said five-thirty and the birds were starting to increase the volume of their dawn chorus, so I knew I wouldn't get back to sleep again. I ran a deep bath to try and relax, but it didn't work. I couldn't concentrate on my book, or even a magazine. I made breakfast, hoping the smell of toast and Marmite would waken my appetite; it didn't. I couldn't swallow a thing. Breakfast television was banal, so I turned the sound down. From the corner of my eye I thought I saw Tal on the screen and my stomach lurched violently.

I spent the entire morning with a nervy feeling, and the sensation of being on a rollercoaster going over the peak each time I thought of Tal. I'd only felt remotely like this with Tony.

I felt sorry for him – I'd short-changed him.

The clock crept round to ten and then the phone rang. I jumped a mile but it was only Marion to say she was leaving for her pamper session in the next ten minutes, because George wanted her out from under his feet. In the background I heard George telling her to tell me that he'd play darts with Tony. I felt guilty again about being underhand. I put the phone down and my 'spring' unwound. This was only the third time I'd be seeing Tal but it was beginning to dawn on me that perhaps love at first sight is true.

I drove rather recklessly to the hidden lane, and as I turned up the rutted track the sun came out and shone through the canopy of leaves, making mottled patterns on the ruts. There were muddy puddles along the lane so it must have rained in the night – maybe that was where my dream of drumming hooves came from. The turning for the bridge seemed further than I thought, but at last I reached it. It almost glowed in the sunlight, green and gold sprinkled with a confetti of blossom and tiny flowers. Beautiful. I pulled forward, scraping the wing on the end of the bridge. Again. I realised I'd moved too far over because the bushes growing on the left parapet grew so far out. They were ancient, gnarled and intertwined. How had I not noticed before?

I expected him to appear just as he had done twice before. My car jolted off the far end of the bridge and a scream of metal told me I'd done even more damage. What was wrong with me? There was no sign of Tal.

I got out of the car and listened. Only water and birdsong. I walked slowly to the house, still expecting him to appear. When I reached the door I knocked with the heel of my hand. The door opened slowly, and Tal leaned against the jamb.

"Tal." I moved forward instinctively and he held out an arm to enfold me. He felt thinner than ever and his breathing was shallow. "Oh, Tal, I wish I'd stayed, now." I felt him relax and he put his other arm round me too. I don't know how long we stayed like that, but it seemed so natural. He stroked my back, making me shiver with pleasure and melting us closer than ever. When his fingers reached my neck and drew intricate patterns on it I knew I was lost. He hadn't said a word, just held me.

"Tal? Shall we walk?"

We moved from the shadows of the wisteria porch into the sunlight. It was warm and still. I glanced up at him and stopped. "What's happened to you?" He was thinner. Gaunt. His cheekbones too defined and the shadows beneath his eyes were deep and dark. "What's happened to you, Tal?"

"Please do not leave me."

Panic churned in me.

"Tal, please. Tell me what's happening to you."

He turned back to the house and went inside. I followed him, my heart hammering. He lay back on the chaise and I couldn't believe the deterioration in him in just twelve hours.

"Penelope, do not leave me."

I stared. Finally I whispered, "I'm frightened." Frightened? I was petrified – this was so far outside my experience, it was terrifying.

"There is no need to be frightened. All you have to do is stay."

My teeth chattered.

"Penelope, I need you." He smiled, that perfect smile which showed his slightly crooked teeth. He was beautiful. Ethereal. "When you leave you take part of me with you. But I let you go, because you must choose for yourself to stay."

"I don't understand what you're saying."

He shook his head sadly. "Will you stay?"

"For the day?" My brain wasn't working properly; it seemed

as if I were trying to stir mud. I took a step backward. What could possibly do this to a man in such a short time? Was I still dreaming?

"You're not dreaming. Look at me."

He swung his legs down so he was sitting and patted the seat for me to sit next to him. I was aware of the green of his eyes. We held each other like drowning people. I rested my head on his shoulder and he stroked my hair. The firelight was warm and comforting – foolishly I hadn't even noticed the fire was alight.

"Penelope. My beautiful Penelope. I loved one other like you. I kept her here. But she grieved for her family." His voice was liquid, hypnotic. I had a fleeting image of my usual crowd, and Marion and George growing smaller as if being sucked into the distance. Could I give them all up for one man? For Tal? The thoughts swirled but didn't really make sense. Tal's languid voice made me relax. "I should have let her go."

I heard the words, but it didn't connect.

"Of your own free will, Penelope. You must choose to stay of your own free will."

I held him more tightly, then I recalled my dream. The plummeting feeling was back and I had a premonition that I would lose him. "I don't understand what's going on. I think … I'd like to stay."

Tal sighed deeply, contentedly.

I said, "You need to see a doctor."

"That is not possible."

I sat up and studied him carefully in the firelight. He sounded logical but what he said didn't make sense. I looked into his green, green eyes. Then I leaned towards him and kissed him. Properly.

I don't know how long we sat together. Hours. The flames of the fire danced and warmed us, but something seemed wrong. I watched the fire burning through a log, and when it broke a shower of sparks puffed up the chimney and the log settled. But it made no noise. I listened carefully; I could hear nothing except Tal's shallow breathing. The picture above the mantelpiece seemed dull, and as I stared at it I could have sworn it shimmered, brighter colours trying to break through the patina of age. I turned my head so I could see the portrait at the top of the stairs.

"Tal. You loved one other *like me*." I felt him tense. "Who?" I thought I knew already. "Was it Susannah?"

"Of course."

My throat constricted. "When?" He didn't answer. "Tal, you kept her here? When?"

"Susannah was all I wanted, but I was not all she desired."

A wave of nausea swamped me. I leaped up, thrusting Tal's hands away from me and ran upstairs to the bathroom. Bile stung the back of my throat. I spat into the sink and turned the tap, but there was no water. I looked into the dusty, mottled gilt mirror – and my frightened eyes stared back. Yesterday the mirror hadn't looked like this. Yesterday I believed I was falling in love.

Perplexed I ran back downstairs. Tal wasn't there. I was drawn to the library. I tried the door, which was very stiff, but at last it gave. I recoiled. A few mouldering books lay scattered along the mainly bare shelves, and the smell of decay took me by surprise. The ivy almost covered the windows and allowed barely any light into the room, and the whole was festooned with cobwebs.

I backed away. I felt as though I was caught in a nightmare and I didn't know if it was real or not. I ran from the house to my car. It was too surreal to believe. Was I hallucinating? I thought I heard Tal call my name, but there was no sign of him.

I fumbled for my car keys, and couldn't get them in the ignition. The key and steering wheel seemed slippery but I finally managed to start the engine. I slammed into reverse and wrenched the steering wheel round and nearly lost control of the car. I headed for the golden stone and realised, at the last second that I was way too far over.

There was a horrible crunching noise as the stone parapet gouged itself into my side of the car but I kept going. The bushes on my right were being ripped up and it dawned on me that it was like trying to drive through a decreasing space. The momentum of the car was being slowed by the obstructions of the bridge. I forced the accelerator to the floor and the engine roared while the metal shrieked along the stone parapet. The car jounced forward and I could have sworn I saw the bridge actually getting narrower. Sweat dripped into my eyes making them sting. This couldn't be true. It was too horrible, too unreal.

With a shriek of tearing metal the Fiesta met its final resistance. It couldn't move. I tried reverse and first gears like a maniac but the car was held fast. I was trapped inside – the doors were impossible to open. The window mechanism on my door grated and opened only far enough to allow the tangled, spiky branches to spring through and scratch my face. I leaned over to the passenger window and my shaking fingers finally managed to grasp the winder. The car vibrated and groaned. I strained to get out of the window, pulling myself out and onto the roof of the car. Far below the river raged, so far below it made me giddy.

I slithered onto the bonnet, and then onto the parapet. I started to move forwards on shaky legs but the bridge lurched and knocked me to my knees. I clutched the old stone that felt more like sand than stone, and tried to move forwards. I screamed as one hand sank to the wrist into the stonework.

There was another judder and my car gave a grinding screech as it twisted even more.

"Tal!" I sobbed. The bridge grated and narrowed again and the only option I had was to move. I scrambled along the parapet, feeling the solidity of the stone rippling beneath my knees and hands. I fell off the end, smacking my chin against the ground. Blood spurted in my mouth and uncontrollable tears blurred my vision as I lay in a terrified heap at the foot of the bridge.

Through the horrendous, deafening noise of my car being mangled I thought I heard Tal call my name. I looked up – and there was a shimmering haze where the bridge should be. My wrecked car lay upside down, fording … just a shallow stream. Trembling violently, I managed to stand upright, but by the time I did there was no haze. No bridge. No hedges. No house.

I dropped to my knees, shivering, and stared – uncomprehendingly – at where the bridge had been.

"Tal," I wailed. "I want to stay. I want to stay."

❧ MAY ❦

Colin Fleetney was born in Kent and lived there until the 1980s when he moved to the Island to become Vicar of Lezayre. Before being ordained Colin worked as a seagoing engineer and then as a hospital engineer in a large psychiatric hospital. After ordination he continued to work at the hospital as their chaplain and then became Team Vicar for five parishes outside Canterbury.

Now retired and living in Port Erin with his Manx wife Joan he contributes factual articles to magazines in the UK as well as writing short stories and building working steam engines in his garden shed.

He had two short stories included in the first volume, 'The Bracelet' and 'You are standing into danger!'

when children play

Colin Fleetney

I was at the Ballig Bridge Eisteddfod last night – well, until after one this morning – and in the recitation class for 11 and 12 year-olds, out of fourteen children, three chose to say T. E. Brown's 'When Childher Plays' and it got me thinking, well, dreaming, really. I remember when I was that age, and Charlie two years younger, what we could fit into a day …

The wonderful sense of freedom – although at twelve years old I would not have seen it like that. I'm thinking of those quite rare occasions when for some reason or other our parents went to Douglas and left us at home. Oh, by the way, by "us" I mean my brother and me. I'm Robert Mylroie, known as Bertie to just about everyone, and my younger brother is Charlie.

Douglas trips were always on a Saturday. Dad got one week's holiday a year and he was at work all the week from seven thirty in the morning until five thirty in the afternoon. So, for them to go shopping and so on together, we had to go as a family of four and looking back on it, I can see now that very occasionally, once we ceased to be little kids, they had a precious day out together.

We were usually out of bed by seven on Saturday mornings. Neither Mum nor Dad would tolerate us lying in bed "like big hakes". When we came down to breakfast on the day I'm thinking of, there were promising signs; the coat that Mum wore to chapel was draped over the Windsor chair, and her handbag and best shoes were standing on the floor. In the spring Dad would be wearing his grey flannel trousers, white shirt and tie, pullover, tweed sports jacket and trilby hat. If the weather was unsettled, and it usually was, he wore what he called his raglan raincoat. I'm talking about the spring because the incident I'm going to tell you about took place in May. Exactly when in May I'm now not sure, because it was, after all, some sixty years ago.

Anyway, just before they left, Mum showed us our dinner, set out between plates in the larder. "Now don't stay out playing, boys, and forget to eat. You can have half of the rice pudding I made last night, to finish." Finally we got the usual lecture: "Don't get your clothes dirty, don't make nuisances of yourselves, don't go outside St Johns. I'll know if you take any cake, cheese, biscuits, or dip your fingers in the honey or jam, don't go near the river or the railway and keep away from the quarry. Try and act like adults as Walter Corrin would – people envy Mrs Corrin." We both adopted expressions of what we believed to be maturity and humility, nodding thoughtfully as she spoke. If we had seen the day ahead as a blank canvas, Mum's list of prohibitions had provided us with several ideas. Good old Mum!

By now Dad would be getting anxious and say things like, "For God's sake, Mona, the train will have left Peel and we've got to get to the station yet and get the tickets."

Unflappable, Mum would reply, "Well, the Ramsey train'll be late, so our train will have to wait for it, as it always does," and she would be as right as she always was over virtually every aspect of our lives.

Just to be on the safe side, we stayed in the garden cleaning out the rabbit hutch and listening. Sure enough, we heard the whistle of the train in from Ramsey, a few minutes late, as Mum said it would be. A few minutes later we heard the Douglas train's whistle. "They've gone!" Charlie laughed.

Being more cautious, I suggested that we stay in the garden doing worthy things for a few more minutes. Charlie swept the garden path and I thought about doing some watering in the greenhouse but decided against it – Dad tended to be a bit emotional if we did any work in the greenhouse when he wasn't around – so I took over from Charlie, but unfortunately he had almost finished.

Our Dad had a favourite expression, "It's a mercy ..." this or that. I thought what a mercy it would be to eat our dinner now and not chance forgetting it. That would please our Mum. Charlie said that he betted it was what awful Wally Corrin would do, and we'd been told to be more like him. I said I was certain that Mum would have meant us to eat half the rice pudding each, so we did, and gave the dish to the cat to lick. Mum and Dad's train must have got as far as Union Mills by now.

We sauntered off, replete and content, hands in pockets. Dad would have gone wild. So, come to that, would Crabby Costain, our teacher, but he wasn't likely to come biking past, eyes everywhere, because he'd just moved right away – up to Lower Foxdale.

We called in at the Farmer's Arms. Not the front, of course. Anyway, it was still closed. No, round the back. Mr Stanley, the cellarman, would be pleased as he always was for a bit of help. We went down the stairs and the smell of the paraffin lamps mingled with the smell of beer. Mr Stanley was flushing the pipes of the beer engines. He looked up, smiled, and after asking about school and things, he said that if we liked we could clean the men's toilets. It was a job we hated, but it paid well. Charlie got over-enthusiastic with the hose and not only blew water out of the lavatory pans with the jet, he also blew areas of whitewash off the walls and brought down a lot of dust from the roof joists which his hose turned to black mud. We then slopped disinfectant liberally, possibly too liberally, in the urinal and over the lavatory seats. Oh well, it smelt really clean, if a bit overpowering. But as Charlie said, "Just right for tonight – busy night, Saturday, after all."

Mr Stanley gave us sixpence, two packets of crisps each and a bottle of Downwards lemonade between us and told us not to forget to return the bottle or he'd want a penny from us. Fortunately, he hadn't had time to go and see our work first. He had no need to worry about the penny for we drank the whole bottle there and then.

I wanted to get out because Charlie was quite wet and we both smelt a bit, well, quite a bit – strongly, actually – of disinfectant and I wanted the sun to dry Charlie off, and then hopefully the breeze during the next few hours would get rid of the smell. We stood for a minute or two outside the main doors of the Farmer's Arms and I thought of the day the war ended, VE Day. We were little then, and had been to Douglas with Granny Kermeen, Mum's mum. In Douglas everyone, even people who didn't know each other, had been laughing and talking about the war coming to an end, and on the train, coming home, people kept bursting into snatches of song. When we were walking home past the Farmer's Arms, these doors were wide open and the noise from inside really was something. Granny paused and we looked in through the blue haze of cigarette smoke. People were dancing around, cheering and singing 'Roll out the Barrel', and one couple were even dancing on a table. "Look in there, boys and remember this terrible sight," said Granny, "this is what Hell is like." Very keen on religion was Granny Kermeen.

I told Charlie that we should give the quarry the once over. To me it seemed the most attractive of Mum's suggestions. Just by the station yard gates we picked up with Voirrey Kissack and Barbara Forster, both in my class at school. "So where you off to, then?" asked Voirrey.

"Give the quarry a look over," Charlie said. "Want to come?"

The girls exchanged glances. "Might as well, I suppose."

We went down and through the station yard, easily keeping out of sight of the men messing around with the Ramsey engine and some trucks. Then we walked towards the quarry along the Douglas line. After a few minutes the rails started ticking. We knew from previous walks along the railway that the ticking sound meant a train was quite close and sure enough a train from Douglas appeared in the distance. We stood well back, well, quite well back – well, we leaned backwards – and all the time the engine was kicking up a din, whistling. As the engine passed by us with a draught of warm air, the driver, leaning out, shouted "Foolish kids!" Well, I think he said "foolish", but it was a bit noisy at the time. Anyway I know that it started with an "f".

You could just walk into the quarry from the railway, with no need either to climb the fence or to walk up to the top end where there was no fence, and then climb down the rock face. No, it was easiest by way of the railway. There were several railway trucks on the quarry siding, each loaded with about ten tons of crushed stone for railway ballast. As Dad worked in the quarry, we boys always adopted a proprietorial air when we visited. So to be adult and helpful, we checked out the brakes of the trucks, making sure that they were well and truly "on", just in case, over the weekend, the trucks slowly ran down and onto the main line. We checked the brakes by releasing them and then tightening them, one truck at a time. They creaked and stirred slightly each time – just showed how important it was to test them.

Between the quarry faces and the stone-crushing plant was a network of narrow-gauge railway tracks on which ran little trucks called "tipping skips". The skips were filled by the excavator. Dad drove the excavator, then men pushed the skips to the crusher, released a pin and the skip tipped, shooting the big lumps of rock down and into the machine. There were several empty skips standing around so we pushed one up to what Dad called the "deep top end". It was where the quarry face was highest and where Dad's excavator worked. From the top end, the skips would, if allowed, run quite fast, well, very fast if you gave them a good push before jumping in. It was good fun, I can tell you. I suggested that we boys get in, to make sure it was clean enough for the girls, then, when I said the word, they could run and push, finally jumping in when it had gained a good speed. I felt a bit sorry for them because it wasn't the best ground to run on, not like the school playground, for example.

We went a long way on our first trip, almost as far as the crusher. Charlie and Voirrey got a bit intense a couple of times, once when we near as ninepence tipped over when crossing a very poor set of points, and finally when it looked as if we were going to run into the loaded skips waiting at the crusher. But I saved the day. I'd picked a sprag up by the excavator and, thinking it might be handy, I had it with me in the skip. So when the other three started to get a bit excited and I wasn't too happy myself, I suddenly remembered the sprag, well, to tell the truth I caught my foot on it otherwise I wouldn't have thought about it, and I picked it up. A sprag, as everyone knows, is like a cricket bat but is made of oak and is used to stop skips. They've got no brakes, you see. What you do is lunge it at one of the wheels and push it between the spokes. It then jams against the frame of the skip and, providing you run alongside the skip and don't let go of the sprag, the wheels skid along the rails eventually bringing the skip to a halt. Well, thinking of the safety of the other three, I jumped out as soon as I realised we were probably going to have a smash, and I found that I was still holding the sprag. So, having seen the men sprag skips several times, well, once before, I started to run and poked my sprag at a wheel. It really was rough ground, covered in chunks of rock and I felt quite sorry that the girls had had this kind of bother starting us up. Anyway, the others were less than helpful, shouting loudly, well, screaming really, as I poked at the wheel, but the wheel kept throwing the sprag clear. It was a good deal more difficult than I had thought. Then, suddenly the sprag went between two spokes. The wheel stopped, the sprag whipped up and threw me to one side, but the skip skidded to a standstill. I felt a bit battered, but there was really nothing to it. I don't know why the other three were so funny with me. Voirrey was hurtful and even suggested that I had jumped out and left them to it. And after all I had done, too.

We pushed the skip back up the slope to where we had started our trip. The others weren't too keen on a second run to the crusher, so I suggested that we change the direction of the points and so take the old, abandoned track along the ledge between the quarry face and the lake, you'll know where I mean, where they've got those signs "DANGER, VERY DEEP WATER UP TO THE BANK". But although I pointed out that there would be no need to use a sprag to stop the skip because the dense gorse bushes that covered the track at the far end would gently stop it, they weren't interested. I proved how safe it was by climbing in and telling Charlie to start the skip rolling. This he did, and away I trundled. I took the points smoothly and went swaying down past the lake. As I approached the bushes I kept below the rim of the skip. Just as well I did, because the first ten feet or so of gorse bushes didn't stop me and the gorse was thrashing about like a policeman's birch. I climbed out and then had difficulty getting back along the route the skip had taken through the mangled bushes. Needless to say I didn't try to remove the skip. It was best left where it was.

When I got back to the others, Voirrey suggested that we went to the mess hut for a cup of tea. "Good idea," nodded Charlie, "they might have left some food from their afternoon break, yesterday."

Like every other building, except the main office and the concrete explosive store where they kept the dynamite for blasting the quarry face, the mess hut was unlocked. It smelt a bit, of stale cigarettes, old wellington boots and damp clothes. But there were matches by the Primus stove and Voirrey soon got it fired up and the kettle on, which already had enough water in it. There was plenty of tea in the packet and a tin of condensed milk stood open, next to the Primus. We were in luck! For Charlie found some slices of fruit cake on a plate, partially covered by lavatory paper. Barbara looked up from the kettle singing on the Primus to warn Charlie to make sure that there were no mouse droppings on the cake. "They look like caraway seeds," she offered. "Just flick them off. Oh, and if the mice have been at the cake, break that bit off, but go easy, don't be too fussy, don't waste the cake, I'm starving." Charlie muttered his agreement.

Barbara made a nice pot of tea, and the cake was good, a bit dry, well, very dry, and Voirrey found a mouse dropping on her tongue, but all in all it was good, until, that is, Charlie spoiled it. He was sick – not in the hut, thank God – we managed to help him outside, well threw him out, actually.

You see, I had searched around and found two packets of cigarettes. One was Gold Flake, the other Craven A. We took one fag from each packet – it wasn't right actually to steal the men's fags, as I pointed out, and the others totally agreed with me. Anyway, I nipped the two fags in half. I shared a Gold Flake with Voirrey and Charlie shared a Craven A with Barbara. After a couple of drags Charlie turned a kind of lemon colour and muttered, "Oh, I do feel bad," and stood up so fast that he tipped his chair over backwards. As one, the three of us jumped at him and bundled him through the door. He lost everything, poor fellow, dinner, rice pudding, crisps and the fruit cake. He smelt bad afterwards, too, worse than the disinfectant that the girls had named "Ashes of Bog".

While Charlie was recovering outside in the warm sun and the fresh, gentle breeze, we three thumbed through the magazines. They were the usual stuff, you know, old issues of *Picture Post*, *Tit Bits*, even a *Punch* or two, and of course plenty of newspapers, well, not whole newspapers, mainly the sports pages folded to the racing results and football pool listings. There were of course the magazines kept jammed behind the lavatory cistern, which Charlie and I often had a look at. They were what today would be called "adult" magazines. They were several stages further on in stimulating the imagination than the Betty Grable calendar hanging behind the door.

There were also, up on a ledge in the rafters, the wad of twenty or so postcard-size photographs. They were old and well thumbed. Charlie reckoned that they came from Egypt and I reckon he was right, for several of Dad's mates had fought in North Africa.

Anyway, the hut fell silent, except for the fairly heavy breathing as we slowly passed the photographs around. The girls hadn't seen them before, so they were really interested, fascinated you could say. Then, after carefully putting them back up on the rafter, we felt it was time to go.

Voirrey thought that we should tidy up a bit, but we couldn't get the tap on to rinse the cups. "Pull the lavatory chain," I said, "and we'll each hold a cup under the water as it jets out. I'll wash Charlie's, as well. It's only fair to leave things clean for the men." So that was what we did.

Judging by the sound of the trains at the station it had gone midday, so the girls were anxious to get home to dinner and I realised that I was hungry too. Charlie seemed not the slightest bit interested in anything.

As we left the mess hut, Barbara nudged me and pointed up at the crest of the quarry face and there was Walter Corrin – good old Wally. He had his binoculars hanging round his neck because, apart from singing and the chapel, Wally was interested in nothing but birds. He called himself an "ordinarythologist" – whatever that might be.

A minute or two later, as we carefully stepped over the railway signal wires and onto the main line, Barbara, after glancing back, remarked that Wally was starting to climb down the quarry face. "So what?" I said, "There's ducks and so on, on the lake. Let's hope Twinkletoes doesn't fall in." We all laughed, well, three of us did. Charlie was still preoccupied.

Wally – Walter Corrin – was the prize pig of the chapel and school. Serious (humourless), studious (he crawled to the teachers), a sincere boy (he knew just how to get round the teachers, the ladies of the chapel, the local preachers and the minister). Talented he was, he really could sing, and had won the Boys' Solo at the Guild earlier that May. He was a musician in that he slowly and painfully churned out a few hymns on the organ when Miss Kewley, our kindly organist, allowed him to play for the evening service. The result was that at Faith Suppers and such like, the ladies all converged on him, offering extra sandwiches and making sure he got plenty of extra bonnag, drop scones and apple pastry. Remarks like "Walter's destined for the ministry," were heard all the time – yuck.

Anyway, enough of the sainted Wally. We left the girls outside the Farmer's Arms and were faced with a problem – at least I was – of food. Dare not touch anything at home. What to do? Then I thought of dear old Mrs Shimmin, a very old lady who lived alone, just up the road. Charlie suggested caution; the old tabby was no fool and had very little time for the kids in chapel. We'll offer to cut her some firewood, I said. Charlie, still preoccupied, said nothing. Mrs Shimmin listened carefully as I explained that, as part of the group of older chapel children, we were offering to cut firewood, or carry coal in, for, I almost said "older" members of the congregation, but stopped just in time and substituted "infirm" in its place. This was unfortunate because I had forgotten that the old tabby rode a bike all over the village. Anyway, what was said, was said. She considered the offer and, astoundingly said, "Yes, come round the back." In the back yard was a stack of logs waiting to be split into halves. You know, the one smart blow of the axe stuff. "You'll find the chopper in the shed." She nodded at the shed, and went indoors.

The shed was quite large and was in an advanced state of decay. As it rotted so it was tilting to one side. It took some hard tugging and wrenching to get the door open and when we looked inside we saw that it was completely stuffed with junk. It was totally and completely jammed full of all kinds of stuff, apart from a kind of "slot" in the junk where Mrs Shimmin kept her bike.

The axe, a real, full-length woodsman's axe, was just inside the door. I got Charlie to run his thumb down the blade and reckoned that, yes, rusty it might be, but it would split logs. And it did, very well indeed. I suggested that Charlie start off because after his little problem at the mess hut he should have some exercise to get his blood circulating. He did well, very well, to be fair. Split about thirty logs and stacked them. Then the axe-shaft broke, leaving the head embedded in a log. It shook Charlie up and I sympathised with him, but also pointed out to him that he should feel just a bit sorry for me because I was just about to take over from him. We managed to get the axe-head out of the log and put it back in the shed. It was then, as I ran my eyes over the mountain of stuff, that I saw, well back, beyond a pile of coal, a small motorbike. I couldn't quite see what make it was, but from what I could see it seemed to be in a good condition, so I got Charlie very slowly and carefully to move one or two items; a garden roller, an oak bedhead, a commode, a lavatory cistern, a few mildewed books and a grandfather clock case, while I leaned against the door so as to let the light in. How was I to know that the clock case was actually supporting the shed, I ask you? Anyway, there was a kind of creaking groan and over it all went. I just managed to pull Charlie out as the whole lot disintegrated into a pile of junk covered in bits of rotting matchboarding under a big cloud of coal dust. The last thing I saw was Mrs Shimmin's bike kind of folding in half. Well, it was old and not much of a bike really, and anyway, the wicker basket on the handlebars was hardly crushed. I told Charlie that he had been a careless fool and had let me down and he would have to explain the situation to poor Mrs Shimmin.

The back door and the windows of the cottage were open, which didn't help matters, because the coal dust sort of billowed in. Mrs Shimmin, having heard her shed collapse, rushed out of the back door just as the worst of the coal dust kind of surged all round her and into the kitchen.

Rubbing her eyes with the bottom of her apron, she stared at the scene of utter desolation. Then she caught sight of her bike. Under the covering of coal dust I swear her face turned a kind of purple and she started to shake. I thought that she was going to apologise to Charlie for putting him in danger, so to speak. So before she could get started, and while she was kind of gulping in great breaths of air, I said, "Don't worry about Charlie, Mrs Shimmin, he's fine, if a little shook up. You musn't feel it's your fault." I turned to Charlie and shouted, "YOU'RE FINE, AREN'T YOU?"

In order to defuse the situation I said,"Look, don't worry so much, a few biscuits'll set him up. No harm done."

While she was shaking with pent-up emotion – sympathy for us, I assumed – I could see the black shiny grains of coal dust in her hair. Mum had said only recently that Mrs Shimmin was very proud of her thick, silvery-white (well it had been until a minute or two ago) hair. She then kind of grimaced and, through clenched teeth, sort of hissed two words, "Get out."

Well, I could see that there was no doing with her at the moment, and far be it from me to cause the old tabby to lose her dignity, so I took Charlie by the arm and started down the path that ran along the side of the house round to the front door and then on to the front gate. At the corner of the house I suddenly had a thought, the motorbike! So I stopped, turned and called out, "Oh, Mrs Shimmin, what make of motorbike is it, in your, in your – under your shed?" She kind of stiffened – didn't say a word, I give her that – but quick as a flash she picked up the axe-shaft and, would you believe it, hurled it, yes hurled it, at my head! I ducked and it passed over my head. Sadly, Christians' delivery man (the grocers in Peel) chose at that instant to come round the corner, and the axe-shaft smacked him just above the left ear. As he reeled against the house he shouted, "Bless my soul," or words to that effect. The last thing I saw as we pushed past him was Mrs Shimmin rushing to his aid and screaming. I thought that the screaming was a good sign for, as I saw it, it was an emotional release after her being so worried about poor Charlie being hurt in her terrible shed.

Out in the road by Mrs Shimmin's gate I saw the answer to the problem of food. There stood Christians' van, with the back doors wide open and a big tray half pulled out. I remembered that they carried Quirks' cakes – you know, the bakers from Douglas. From the tray there was a gorgeous smell of meat pies and pasties and, yes, YES, they had some! They had vanilla slices, my absolute favourites. I quickly selected, and stuffed into my pockets, two meat pies, but I tenderly carried the two vanilla slices, one in each hand. I left the sixpence we had earned at the Farmer's Arms because I am not, nor ever intended to be, a thief. We then hurried down to the river bank and sat, out of sight, under the Patrick Road bridge to have our picnic.

I was starving and so, to all intents and purposes, was Charlie. I felt, however, that having eaten the top crust of his pie, he had had plenty for his unsettled stomach to cope with. So to be fair to him I gently took the pie from him, forcing myself to eat the two meat pies and both vanilla slices. I always looked after Charlie.

As we, well, I, ate the food, I thought that we should go over to the Forestry Commission's steam sawmill and run our eyes over it, but decided against it. We spent the rest of the afternoon playing around on the river bank.

We were waiting on the station forecourt when Mum and Dad got off the train at five, loaded with bags. They were pleased to see us and Mum's first words were, "Have you had a good day?"

I said, "Oh, it was OK, nothing special." Charlie nodded his agreement.

Dad suggested that we carry Mum's bags. I took the largest

bag which had "T. H. Cowin, Ladies' Outfitter" on it. That was the only shop in Douglas I didn't mind going in, because I liked seeing them send the money on the little overhead rails. I supposed that it would have a summer dress in it, and would therefore require great care, though it was, of course, not heavy. Sadly, that left Charlie to carry the smaller bag containing several tins of paint and two bottles of turps, but it would give him an appetite for tea.

* * *

At teatime on the Monday, Dad mentioned to Mum that there could have been a railway accident over the weekend. It seemed that the four trucks of stone that had been left standing on the quarry siding had slowly inched down, finally stopping just clear of the main line. It was obvious that I alone, by checking the brakes, had avoided a railway smash. I said nothing to Dad. I'm not, and never have been, a boaster.

On Tuesday Mum was full of the news that Mrs Shimmin was unwell – was keeping to the house for a few days and wouldn't be able to help get the chapel ready for the Sunday School Anniversary. It seems that her shed had collapsed, and in so doing had wrecked her bike and hurt a delivery man. I didn't feel the need to comment.

The Sunday School Anniversary was to take place the next Sunday, Whit Sunday. There were about thirty-five children in the Sunday School and we had been preparing for the big day for several Sundays. Wally – sorry – Walter Corrin would be singing once or twice. There would be several duets and Bible readings by us children.

The chapel would be prepared on Saturday afternoon. Extra chairs would be brought in, and the big, tiered benches that would seat all the Sunday School children would be erected to one side of the pulpit by the men. The women would dust the pews, brush the carpet, decorate the windowsills with flowers, and get out of the long cupboard the slightly battered older hymnbooks that were only brought back into use for the Anniversary and the Harvest Festival.

I heard from Mum what I have recorded below. When I write that I "heard" it from Mum, that is not to say that Mum knowingly told me – no, not at all. I had long ago learned that one of the most useful places to sit was next to the garden gnome under the kitchen window which was, during the day, always cracked open. By sitting there, out of sight from the kitchen, one could listen to a conversation taking place in the kitchen. It stands to reason that it was frequently very useful to know, in advance, just what one's parents were planning. Anyway, what follows is what I heard.

Miss Kewley, the chapel organist, being the self-effacing, timid woman that she was, hated playing for special occasions, and for the Anniversary she had arranged, as she had in previous years, for her friend Miss Cain, the deputy organist of the parish church, to cover the Anniversary for her. Miss Cain was one of those aloof, ladylike women who seem to be totally without a trace of humour, who tend to appear detached from the cut and thrust of everyday life and who children instinctively keep away from. She was not able to practice on the chapel organ during the week and had decided to run through the music on Saturday morning when there would be no activity at all in the chapel.

Miss Cain biked up to the Corrins' place – Wally's father, being the Society Steward, was therefore a chapel keyholder. Wally's mother answered the door and said, "You're in luck, Miss Cain, the door to the schoolroom will be unlocked. My boy, Walter, is there at the moment, getting out the extra hymnbooks, dusting them down and setting them out on the porch table. He is a wonderful help to his Dad and me. We really are blessed."

At the chapel, Miss Cain naturally walked straight into the schoolroom. As she did so, she heard a frantic scurrying sort of sound. In the dim light from the high windows it was difficult to see, in that instant of time, exactly what was going on. There were two quite frenzied figures whirling and diving around for clothes. It was a boy and a girl and parts of them were quite bare. That much, so Mum told Dad, Miss Cain could see. Within a matter of a few seconds – twenty at the most – while Miss Cain stood, confused in the doorway, the two partially dressed figures, still pulling on clothes, rushed through the communicating door and out into the chapel, where they were trapped.

Miss Cain eventually found Wally Corrin and Heather Kelly behind the thick red curtain, amid old brooms, half empty tins of beeswax polish, dustpans and dusters up behind the organ, where the pumper stands to work the bellows.

On the school table were the Egyptian postcards from the quarry. I thought no one but me and Charlie knew about them, but how wrong can you be? It seems that Wally and Heather were kind of enacting some of the scenes.

Wally and Heather must have assumed that no one would go near the chapel until Saturday afternoon. A pity for them – I felt really sorry for them. So far as the chapel was concerned, Mum said to Dad that if Wally became a Deemster and lived to be a hundred, someone would still remember. And Heather would always be considered "fast".

There are always one or two kids missing from Sunday School but I, for one, was surprised that Wally didn't show up. After all, he loved singing. I must confess that I didn't realise that Heather wasn't there; why would I? After all, she was not one of our bunch.

One good thing, so far as I was concerned, was that Mum

never again said, "Why aren't you more like Walter? People envy Mrs Corrin."

I got to know Wally during the time he was socially out in the cold. I thought it would help if I sort of found out what exactly, and I mean "exactly", he and Heather had been up to. Eventually he gave me a few pretty broad hints ... anyway, I found that he was no wimp and, given the opportunity, would enter in to all kinds of escapades.

One incident in particular comes to mind. Indeed even after all these years it is occasionally mentioned when we are together. Crabby Costain, our teacher, had been telling us in geography about dams. So we decided to build one. It was late May and the Foxdale stream was low. We picked a place just below the village, where the stream flows between quite high banks (there are houses all along there, now). We sorted around behind the steam sawmill one Saturday afternoon and found a large door. Well, when I say "found" a door, it was leaning against a shed. Anyway, they obviously had no further use for it and it was a simple matter for Charlie, Wally and me to carry it just across the Patrick road and then slide it down the bank to the water. Well, it was a simple matter for Charlie and Wally. Someone was needed to walk in front of them to guide them and I felt it should be me. We had already "borrowed" a wheelbarrow which we filled with bricks. As I say, the stream was shallow, so the work was quite easy for Charlie and Wally. Oh, they both pinched their very cold fingers between bricks and both carelessly got wet feet, but once they had got the door jammed in place by the bricks – and although I told them that it was a pretty rough job when viewed from where I was sitting on the bank – it held back the flow quite well.

We were amazed at how fast the water backed up, although it continually spurted out between the poorly placed bricks. Of course I pointed this poor workmanship out to the lads.

But leaking or not, the dam held. As I say, we were amazed at just how much water was coming down from Foxdale. After perhaps twenty minutes Wally got concerned and the fool wanted us to dismantle the dam. I told him that if he wanted to, he could wade into the quickly forming pool and take a few bricks away – I told him which ones to pull out – but I added a word of warning saying that it might carry him away when the door went. Soon, very soon in fact, the water was backing up beyond the Patrick Road bridge and the door was bowing slightly. Without boasting – I have told you before that I am not, and never have been, a boaster – I think I can say that as a team we made a good job of that dam.

Then, without warning the whole thing collapsed. There was a rattle as the bricks were swept away and the door was carried downstream and out of sight by a huge wave. I didn't like the look of that wave. I felt that it might do some damage. So I suggested that we move away from the area and rest somewhere quiet for a while. The lads saw my point and, moving slowly and casually – you never know who's watching – we sauntered away.

On Monday Crabby Costain told us about an unpleasant experience that Mr Gelling who farms the land just downstream from where we built the dam had had on Saturday afternoon. It was probably caused, so Crabby reckoned, by a shower up on South Barrule. Mr Gelling was installing his portable pump on the river bank in order to pump water for his cattle, when a sudden rise in the stream's level engulfed him. He didn't see the wave coming, so when it hit him he simply sat down. Sat down, that is, in fast-flowing water that, for a few seconds was quite deep. The wave took his pump and carried it the best part of a hundred yards downstream, wrecking it.

Anyway, back to my friendship with Wally. He taught me

about birds and, due to him I developed a passion for birds which has lasted all my life.

Well, they were good days, or at least we tend only to remember the good days – the good times. And now? Well, we're all retired, of course. Charlie did amazingly well. It's strange, but I noticed that after I had left home, and when I was back from sea on leave, he didn't want to come out and around with me like he had done before. I ask you, quiet little Charlie, who'd been so proud to be with me, and whom I had always looked after, preferred to go out with his own friends. He went to Agricultural College, came back to work on a big farm near Port Erin, married the farmer's daughter and is now in the Keys. Funny how things turn out.

Wally retired as the manager of one of the Douglas branches of the Isle of Man Bank. He kept up his singing, thank goodness, and won the Cleveland Medal both in the 1960s and again in the 1970s.

I went to sea with Dalton & Mills, as an engineer cadet. Stayed with the company all my working life and retired as their Fleet Engineer. My wife and I have just bought the cottage that once belonged to poor Mrs Shimmin and we are building an extension where she had her shed. My wife? You'll remember Voirrey from the quarry escapade? Well, actually, all of us would prefer it if you forgot the whole series of incidents.

That's the way with the kids, you know,
And the years do come and the years do go,
And when you look back it's all like a puff,
Happy and over and short enough.

'Betsy Lee' by T. E. Brown

❋ june ❋

Shirley Moore was brought up in Yorkshire where she was educated and trained as a Registered Nurse, moving to the Island in 2000 to take up a nursing position at Nobles Hospital.

Shirley now lives in Douglas with her husband Colin and their three children and spends her free time writing, reading and drawing. This is her first published short story.

The Enchanted Park

Shirley Moore

Phyn, the fenoderee, was perched on the sea wall at the terminus, watching the *Ben* coming into dock at the end of Practice Week, centenary year, 2007. The weather had been unexpectedly good, and it was the first wet day of the festival. Pavements, stone and glass were sleek and shiny with rain; sky and sea were steel grey.

He had never witnessed the Tourist Trophy before, being a country fella. He had not expected the excitement which it generated, both collectively and within himself. It was a spectacle which up until now had been something of a supernatural event to him, with only the odd rumble, sometimes of calamity, reaching him on North Barrule. There, on fine days, he felt that he could almost reach up and touch the sky, with the only noise being that of the gossip of the water sprites and heath elves that dwelt amongst the heather and clefts of the rolling hills.

He had come to love the majesty of the *Ben* docking after performing its famous three-point turn; the bow doors slowly lowering, followed by the staccato roar of a thousand engines coming to life. Then there was this magnificent convoy of vehicles and two-wheeled beasts disembarking in a carefully choreographed pageant of black leather and primary colours. There was a temporary blending of cultures and mother tongues, with the common bond being the engine and the two stroke, spoken through the mutual language of torque and speed.

The unexpected novelty had, at least, temporarily suspended the heartache which he felt at leaving his family and home of echoing hills and constantly unfurling sky. For a great sadness was upon him. Things were just plain wrong at present. Phyn peered dolefully at the restless waves beneath him. He belonged to a large family of fenoderee up north, but there wasn't enough work to go round just now. This was because few humans believed in the fenoderee. They were too busy worshipping the Great Gods – Computers and Money. So there was no "Summoning" to help in the fields or to sweep the hearths as in the old days. Such creeping redundancy and a falling onto hard times were similar to "The Tinkerbell Phenomenon" described by J. M. Barrie in "Peter Pan", where disbelief in the entity led to fairy death. (And none too soon, he thought, disliking "Themselves" – or to those from across the water, F-A-I-R-I-E-S – in general.) And, what was worse, one branch of the family had reverted to the evil ways once more. Those were his larger cousins, hulking and satyr-like. They took delight in jumping out at lonely travellers as they traversed the mountain roads, and ruined honest folk's crops. The Fenoderee Council seemed immune to this and took no action; perhaps they felt intimidated too. Being a particularly timid fenoderee, and teased much about this, but carrying an innate sense of justice in his heart, which he now felt too frightened to express, he had eventually left to find his luck further afield. But so far, nothing had turned up.

And humans had changed too. They were too busy to see the fenoderee, or appreciate their magic and their work anymore. They simply stared at you as if you weren't there. And it was very rare if they left gifts out for you on feast days. Phyn felt invisible, purposeless, displaced. His magic repertoire was at its lowest ebb and the wishing wand in his bag was as miserable as a wet weekend too. The sudden damp chilled him and, today, not even the beauty of the ship coming into harbour could cheer his spirits.

Phyn went into the arrivals lounge and hid behind a soft, ferny plant to watch the foot passengers arrive and collect their belongings. He usually enjoyed working out who belonged to who; tears and joy being etched on the faces of those being reunited. Today, it just made him realise how lonely he was. Amongst the tail-enders were two people who looked as dejected as he felt; a young mother and a boy of about seven. They looked at the ground as they walked along, not speaking. They were close together, and, as hands and clothing contacted, Phyn could see little red sparks coming off them; this was a sign of conflict between the pair. Intrigued, Phyn followed them.

"There is a story here," he said to himself, thoughtfully. "Perhaps somebody needs me."

Bushy's beer tent flapped gently in the breeze, the bins now emptied and the tarmac scrubbed clean of last night's partying. A leather-clad man in a wheelchair came scudding past as the taxi driver, already sweating, his blood pressure rising, manoeuvred his car around bikers who seemed to have forgotten their left from their right. And, he was unintentionally grumpy, which was not the best welcome in the world, to be sure, and fed the fire of the mother's understanding that she was unwanted, an outcast, and would ever be so. Phyn slipped in unnoticed, amongst two battered-looking suitcases. The assortment of carrier bags and rucsacks which followed brought a fresh frown to the cabby's face.

It was a short journey up to an estate of large dwellings in Onchan. Phyn was first out, secreting himself behind some shrubbery. He watched as mother and son walked up the drive, to be met at the door by a neat, grey-haired lady. Again, there was little smiling or exchange of words as the raggle-taggle collection of luggage was passed inside. Finally, the door shut on this dismal looking trio. Phyn crept closer to the house and sat thoughtfully amongst the colourful flower beds, in order to contemplate this new situation and the people who were now within the house.

"At least," said Phyn (he had grown accustomed to talking to himself over recent months) "there is plenty of work for me here in this garden and perhaps I can befriend the little fellow; he looks like he is in need of a friend right now."

With satisfaction, he noted a shed in the far corner of the garden where he could shelter in bad weather. He liked to be outside much of the time, but he could make himself a cosy corner in there, if need be. All about him were large exotic flower beds; beautiful, but blowsy, with the June weather, and much in need of a haircut! There was a vegetable patch to tend, plenty of plant pots and tools to tidy away and a bird table to replenish and keep clean.

"The day is turning out much better than I thought," said Phyn, with a glimmer of contentment beginning to warm his heart.

Meanwhile, inside the house, content was woefully absent, after the usual rhetoric of

"How was the crossing" and "How is your mother?"

"Fine, thank you, aunt." And satisfying one another on the state of everyone else's health, the conversation became dotted with long, embarrassed pauses, despite the best efforts on the part of both adults to accommodate one another. The current weather was discussed in detail, but the reason why Jayne and Charlie had come to stay with Aunt Voirrey was skilfully avoided by both. And, all the while, Charlie was sitting very still and with a very straight back, although Aunt Voirrey strenuously tried to make him feel welcome. Aunt Voirrey finally said that she would freshen the teapot and make more toast, and escaped into the kitchen. This left Charlie free to study Aunt Voirrey's Manx cat with open and undisguised fascination, and Jayne to study her own chaotic thoughts, of which there seemed no escape from, ever.

The kaleidoscope of memories turned inexorably as they had done relentlessly for the last few weeks and months. She had loved her sublimely ugly Glaswegian passionately and with all her heart. Ah! he was a loveable rogue, always getting himself into scrapes but extricating himself with the agility of a gymnast. She allowed herself a rueful smile at some of them. It had been great at the beginning and there were good and precious times. She had done well at school, but ultimately left without qualifications. Her whole world was him and the coming child. That had been at the turn of the millennium. It was now 2007 and her mother had only just forgiven her. They had started speaking again out of necessity as Jayne grew more desperate to escape.

Of course things hadn't worked out. She had tried so hard to get them to function as a family. But the split began, in reality, when Charlie was just a few days old. Her life centred (by necessity) around the flat and Charlie; his was dedicated to hell raising, petty crime, and occasional periods of ineffective contriteness.

Over the next seven years, it became increasingly difficult to sustain a naturally cheerful disposition and to paint a picture of domestic bliss as she became, in effect, although not in name, a single parent. He became just plain ugly; in acts as well as looks, with his roguish activities taking on increasingly dark and sinister forms.

Eventually, she knew she had to get out. There followed the stressful period of laying an intricate plot to leave without raising his suspicions, either to her imminent departure or ultimate destination. In her darkest, most fearful moments, she tried to assess her value to him. Her appeal had long gone; sexually, he acted like the proverbial tomcat. But if she went AWOL he would want her back under his thumb in short order, so that he could enjoy punishing her, with Charlie restored as his most precious possession, although he never had much contact with him, unless it was to cuff him or shout at him, blaming his son for the shortcomings in his own life. Jayne shuddered at the prospect. Her mother, being made aware of the situation, conferred with various relatives. An aunt, who Jayne knew only slightly and residing in the Isle of Man offered a refuge. This was the most secret and safe option and Jayne had no choice but to take it. This was the aunt who, whenever she was mentioned was annotated with "Oh, Aunt Voirrey! You know …", followed by a significant pause.

"She is as Manx as the hills," Jayne's mother would sniff. Jayne's mother felt that Aunt Voirrey had some strange ways and sayings, didn't understand her and disliked her in consequence.

So Jayne was now sat in this reportedly formidable lady's front room. She didn't want to be here but Charlie's safety and future were her priority. The past few years had wrought a defensive but fiercely protective and independent element in her soul and she was determined to pay back the debt which she would owe her aunt as soon as possible. However, expressing this pain, explanation and gratitude left her tongue-tied and she could only do so by agreeing to the suggestion that she and Charlie must be tired and perhaps might like to go to their rooms and catch up on their sleep? Before they went, Jayne was glad to see that Charlie was beginning to unbend a little and was talking animatedly to Aunt Voirrey about why her cat didn't have a tail. Aunt Voirrey looked relieved and said that she would tell him all about Manx cats after his sleep.

Feeling as heavy as lead, Jayne allowed Aunt Voirrey to guide her and Charlie to adjoining rooms, perhaps representing what would be a luxurious prison, but offering them a temporary haven from distress. They curled up in layers of crisp clean linen and surrendered themselves to a period of deep and refreshing sleep.

Mad Sunday 2007

Jayne and Charlie were down on the prom. It had been Voirrey's idea, although she had not accompanied them. Jayne felt a sense of detachment; it was like watching the rest of a celebratory, tumbling humanity from behind a pane of glass. Perhaps she was not the only one; the fishes were wise to keep themselves well out of the way, for June was known as the Herring Month! Yet she did not feel so numb as to overlook the need to distract Charlie from the life which he had been forced to quit. And also to attempt a little bribery. Indeed, she felt a partial success when looking at the reflections in Charlie's wide open eyes as he took in this new world.

There was another spectator; the man in the wheelchair, who, despite his now pedestrian status persisted in wearing full leathers. He had been a talented rider and mechanic. This was still apparent as he could maintain, park and turn his chariot on a sixpence. He had had a spill which cost him his legs and gave him severe concussion. It had given him a different, often uncomfortable, perspective on life as he now saw things which others couldn't. In amongst the vibrant colours and glossy skies of the TT carnival there were images which he didn't understand. He was puzzled – perhaps his injuries led him astray. The man shook his head to clear his sight, but it did no good, the threesome were still there. Against the pastiche of colour were three people who he could only see in monochrome; all grey. The tallest was very grey. Then there was one who looked guilty, acting like he shouldn't be seen. Yet he leapt and jumped, and crouched. He was grey too. The boy was mostly grey, but due to the excitement of the fair and a sudden freedom and room to breathe, he had an odd shimmer of rainbow colours running through him. But, then he would return to his mother and become grey again.

The man had began to question why he returned each year. He had been more or less forgotten; yet he couldn't forget his legs, and, after all, this was the island where he had left them behind! He had grown used to over-lookers and under-lookers. Yet, as the grey woman drew abreast, she held him directly in her eye, not out of pity, for which he was grateful, and he wondered about the tracery of her own pain.

Aunt Voirrey had excused herself from the outing. TT was unbearable and no longer gave her joy since she could no longer share it with her husband. The passion for it had departed with him. Bereavement, she had discovered, like love, could also be a form of possession. She pottered about in their beloved garden, achieving little and growing more frustrated. There was a shabbiness about the once pristine garden; cherished for its scarlet rhododendrons, which had been brought from the Onchan nurseries in the late nineteenth century by her grandfather. The New Zealand Holly, sent by a first cousin who had emigrated years ago was becoming buried in undergrowth, blotting out family ties and remembrances. Only the cabbage plants thrived, and the Monkey Puzzle remained its old, straight-backed and enigmatic self. Not for the first time, she regarded the increasingly knotted and moulded joints of her hands which had began to rob her of the ability to hoe, rake and plant. But it was her Bobby who had been the real magician in the garden. Why had he left her? She could hardly forgive him even now.

She had become brimful of pride and twisted with heartache. In her natural state, she would have welcomed the fugitives without question. It had been a moment of impetuosity; a glimpse of her old self. Bobby would have known what to do. But now there was fear and unease. The previous day had been a strain. How well did she know these people? Hardly at all. And the background which they had come from! Had it tainted them? Only that morning, she had been tempted to snatch one of her precious ornaments from Jayne's hands; Jayne had been attempting to do a bit of tentative dusting as a means of repayment, thinking she was unobserved. But the thought of the intense hurt which would glow in her niece's eyes had stayed Voirrey's hand.

Voirrey was aware of the turning point that she had reached. Now for the conscious decision – whether to retreat and continue to mourn her past or to let it go and embrace change. Here, in the beautiful garden, the colours and perfumes enhanced by sunlight and with the life of birds, plants and a myriad of creatures, thrilling to the warmth of summer and newly established beginnings surrounding her, she shut her eyes, breathed deeply, and let nature inspire her decision.

Yes. She would throw off her protective cloak of austerity and exert herself to be kind; allow her natural self to breathe again. Perhaps circumstances would prove fortuitous and a little workaday magic would come her way.

But fine words cannot change the human condition

overnight. The weather, the crowds and the racing had made the centenary TT magical. However, it was on the last day, carried on the wings of triumph, that tragedy rode in and darker clouds gathered in the heavens. The summer days ticked by as ponderously as the clock on Voirrey's mantelpiece and the household continued in some disharmony. Voirrey stuck to her intentions, yet had her weak moments. Jayne, now the deed was done, and couldn't go back, was fearful, looking over her shoulder – a chance resemblance to him in a passing crowd would throw her into a panic. Her tangled and damaged emotions rendered her uncommunicative, making her appear often withdrawn and uncaring. Then, Charlie would respond with difficult, uncharacteristic behaviour. Phyn would often despair of them all and feel helpless.

Yet a snapshot; a sudden decision and a scrunching up of courage, captured in time, can prove momentous. It was a mid-June day, dull, metallic and lethargic, when Charlie became acquainted with Phyn. The boy had had a bad day and sat on a stone bench in the arbour, sullenly pulling the heads off all the nearby flowers. His mission was to deflower a whole shrub before teatime, hating what he was doing; hating his mum; hating everything. Phyn could sense Charlie's grief and, overcoming his own fear, rested his hand on the boy's shoulder for a moment.

"Why are you destroying the plants, Charlie?" asked Phyn.

The strangeness of the little man now standing before him, and the fact that he knew his name halted Charlie's act of vandalism. The foundations of friendship were quickly laid as Charlie poured out his woes to Phyn. The wound had been lanced and the healing process could begin. Charlie's play grew to be the normal play of childhood, although he still remained cold towards Jayne. She had hurt him too badly.

Voirrey continued to draw inspiration from the garden. At

first, she didn't understand; the garden was beginning to look as wonderful as it had done when her Bobby was alive. It was tidy; the flowers were thriving and the slugs and snails had been put firmly, but kindly, in their place! Then she grew suspicious. First she saw him as a shadow, the tail end of him scuttering out of sight. Soon, she knew that he was real. She had a Fenoderee living in her garden. But she didn't confront him. No, she just carried a bit of a smirk about on her face. A little magic had come her way! She began to leave odds and ends out for him; small plates of food; a thimble or bit of ribbon; a fancy button; things which she thought would amuse him. She smiled more often and more easily.

Phyn and Charlie had great fun decking out the shed in such finery so that it could be a fit house in bad weather. Yet, Jayne remained largely untouched by the gentle healing processes going on around her, causing concern to Voirrey and Phyn.

24th June 2007. St John's Eve. *Trinaid Veg*

"I think Charlie's got an imaginary friend," Jayne stated nonchalantly, disguising her deep concern over her son's erratic behaviour, and opening a conversation on the psychology of childhood.

"I've heard of those," replied Aunt Voirrey, feigning naivety.

There was a meeting of minds as they both enjoyed witnessing Charlie playing "tig" with Sukie, the Manx cat, whom he had made firm friends with. Only Aunt Voirrey could see Phyn playing as well, as all three ducked and dived amongst the trees and plants.

"I can see you, my little man, but I say nothing," she chuckled to herself.

"It is a risky undertaking, relocating a child. But you had

no choice and all will be well," Aunt Voirrey said, displaying one of her bad habits, born out of a life lived alone for several years: to think out loud. Almost before the words were out of her mouth, she knew that Jayne was retreating into her incredibly vulnerable shell.

There was a prolonged silence whilst Aunt Voirrey allowed Jayne to walk the whole length of the terrace, dashing tears away from her cheeks, before returning, composed, to pick up the conversation.

It promised to turn into a rather tense day; Charlie was due to start school in the next week. The uniform had been purchased yesterday; much to Jayne and Charlie's bemusement: at his previous school, they had their own choice of clothing. It was Charlie's birthday at the end of the month and the unexpected expense of the uniform had dented Jayne's plans for the day: she had resolutely refused to allow Voirrey to pay for any of it. This almost caused a row and added another layer of worry on top of the natural anxieties occasioned for them all by starting at a new school.

"It is a feast day today. St John's Eve. There used be a great fair on this day. But that was moved years ago, to Tynwald day. 'Aye they does like to cheat us out of our fairs', the old folks used to say," said Voirrey with a smile of remembrance on her face, at the indignity which the reshuffle, ordered by officialdom, had raised in those who had always looked forward to the fair since early childhood.

"What say you to us having our own bit of a fair today?" asked Voirrey, with enforced brightness. "I've a few ideas in my head so's we can all have a bit of fun, and it'll give Charlie more of an idea about what this island is that he has lighted upon before he starts school next week."

"Oh, that sounds really good," lied Jayne, thinking inwardly, "She's mad!" But she agreed, all the same; anything to make

Charlie feel more at home was OK with her.

It turned out to be a good day for the little household.

"Nice and quiet now the other children are back at school and all that TT craziness is over for another year. Not that it isn't welcome when it comes round again," observed Aunt Voirrey. The weather had become unseasonably cold, in compensation for the lovely first week of the month. But it was warm enough to build sandcastles, which echoed the design of Peel castle fairly faithfully, and to eat ice cream while touring round the actual building, with Aunt Voirrey pointing out all sorts of hidey holes and unexpected corners. The seals put on a fine display and there were gannets and cormorants constantly fishing and wheeling in the sky.

Back home and towards evening, Aunt Voirrey created a wonderful array of traditional fayre, which included battered Queenies, rich fruit Bonnag, shortcake and honey fudge. There was homebrewed wine for the grown ups and ginger beer for Charlie. The lights were turned down and the room illuminated with candles. Aunt Voirrey sat on the sofa with Charlie and Sukie, weaving wonderful tales of mermaids and fishermen, Mannanan Mac Lir, and the Big Black Dog of Peel, until Charlie's eyes began to droop and Jayne, who had been watching, and feeling completely inadequate, but also spellbound by Voirrey's storytelling, carried him to bed, placed a kiss on his head and returned to the warm kitchen where Voirrey was clearing up.

"Of course," said Voirrey, wiping crumbs from the work surface, "there's been sad times associated with feast days too. One St Johns, twenty-one lights were seen dancing up one of the Glens. It was the year of the 'Great Epidemic' and twenty-one souls they lost in the hamlet that year," she added wistfully, making Jayne wonder what her aunt had been thinking about whilst she had been putting Charlie to bed. She had a small plate of food prepared, which she now put outside the porch.

"For Themselves," she explained enigmatically.

"Oh, you mean the fairies?" Jayne said, gradually coming to understand Voirrey's quaint sayings. Phyn, who had rather large, but very sensitive ears, didn't like being referred to as a fairy; nasty creatures they could be if you got on the wrong side of them! But if it meant that he was served a delicious plate of food of an evening, well, then he could forgive anything. He had fallen on his feet and found a wonderful place to dwell, for sure. He made a mental note to send his mother a letter via Rabbit Mail as he wouldn't be heading back up north for a while. But at least he could tell her of his good fortune in securing such a good position, and the rest of his news. But there was one fault about Phyn, and that was that he was terrible at remembering to write and send letters.

30th June 2007: Charlie's birthday

It was very early, still dark, but Jayne couldn't sleep. She often woke about this time. It gave her space to be with her own thoughts. She was grateful to her aunt for the chance which she had been given. Her aunt was very kind in lots of quiet ways and did not pry, but Jayne just felt so uncomfortable, living in someone else's house. And after spending most of her life in cities, the island seemed a bit dull and quiet. But they had no choice. Here they must stay for the present. She kept scanning the papers for suitable jobs but there was nothing.

She turned away from such unsettling thoughts and went through her plans for Charlie's birthday. She was living on the savings that she had managed to scrape together to fund her escape, so there was not much to spare, but she had done her best with the presents. A trip to the park was definitely on the agenda. Charlie loved going to the local park, and it didn't cost anything. She hoped it would be a good birthday. She knew Aunt Voirrey was planning another special feast for the evening.

But the most hurtful thing of all; the knot in the pit of her stomach, which grew tighter by the day, was Charlie's withdrawal from her. They had always been so close, but he was hardly talking to her just now. He resented her for taking him away from his dad. He did not realise that there were other types of dad; neglect and strong language was all that he usually received; but it was his dad, and all he had ever known. Jayne tried hard to understand. She knew that she should explain things better, but couldn't bear to express her feelings and the reasons why they had fled, just now.

The square of grey behind the curtains was visibly lightening now and Jayne could hear the birds beginning to stir in the trees outside. Any chance of sleep had long since vanished; Jayne reached for a book to read to wait out the time until she could shower without disturbing her aunt.

In his bed, Charlie was curled up in a tense little ball. He looked back over the last few weeks. He loved his mum, but at the moment he couldn't forgive her for taking him away from his dad and his meagre circle of schoolfriends, with hardly a word of apology or explanation. He determined that this was going to be the worst birthday he would ever have. So there! He uncurled himself, stretched, then curled back up again in the warm hollow of the sheets.

"What presents will I get?" he wondered in anticipation, forgetting that he was determined not to enjoy his birthday.

"Is it time to get up yet, Phyn?" he whispered. But Phyn was outside in the garden. It was no good. He got up and slipped into his mum's room to ask her if it was time to get up yet.

Phyn was busy at work in the garden, tidying up and feeding

the birds in an attempt to warm himself. It was another un-June-like day! He couldn't help giving a chortle and clapping his hands together.

"It's going to be a great day today," he explained to Mr Robin, who had been sitting on Phyn's shoulder, but had now flown up in alarm. Phyn spun himself round and did a little jig.

"It's the young fella's birthday and I've got lots of plans, just lots!" Phyn exclaimed.

"How wonderful is that?" he asked Mr Robin, who had perched cautiously on Phyn's shoulder again. Mr Robin looked at Phyn quizzically with his bright black eyes, and accepted a titbit of cake, before nodding his understanding.

"What fun we shall have," continued Phyn. "We will have games all day, and I am going to conjure up some magic especially for the little lad."

Then he sobered up a bit

"I hope I can cheer up the sad little lady, his mother, too," he told Mr Robin, who chirped in agreement.

By ten o'clock, Jayne and Charlie were heading for the park, accompanied by an excited Phyn.

"Onchan Park is wonderful for the children," said Aunt Voirrey, describing what it was like on high days and holidays. During the festival, the park had buzzed with excitement and life. It was almost claustrophobic at times as it was so popular. It was hard to imagine the park being packed today; it was deserted. Charlie loved all the different climbing frames, but his favourite feature was the wooden train parked at its station. Jayne looked back at her previous life. She and Charlie had almost lived under house arrest for the last couple of years. Parks where they lived were no go areas, ruled by gangs. A park like Onchan would be wrecked within days back home. It was a smothering, sad and restrictive environment to bring a child up.

It was liberating to be able to go to a park and feel safe, although Jayne still couldn't shake off a wariness of being alone when it was quiet. Aunt Voirrey had laughed at this.

"You are in the Isle Of Man, now, my pet: quite safe."

"You don't know him," Jayne had countered.

Charlie went off to play with his imaginary friend, Phyn, Jayne was very sceptical and a little anxious about this playmate, dismissing it as a symptom of Charlie's recent traumatic dislocation from his normal world. She sat down and was soon so absorbed in the cobweb of her own thoughts that she did not notice Phyn and Charlie playing hide and seek and catch amongst the swings and slides.

Jayne shivered – it did feel cold today.

"Hey, what am I on about?" Jayne asked herself, with a smile, remembering the northern winters which she had been accustomed to, with ice on the inside of the window pane when you woke in the morning. But the refreshment of the ice and cold, the clear harshness of a frosty night still held a wonderful quality for her.

"Stop playing Desert Island Discs," she reprimanded herself sternly, choking down a sudden homesickness. "That life has been left far behind."

The flow of the Gulf Stream kept the island relatively mild, yet against the exotic Manx palms, she felt like a useless weed; anonymous, unwanted, displaced. Her life was changing direction, and it gave her a bittersweet feeling to know that she was coming to a crossroads, and hopefully she would make the right turning this time.

Shaking herself out of her reverie, which she had become increasingly prone to falling into, Jayne sought out Charlie, and smiled to see him happy again. She could almost swear that she saw a little brown man peering at her from the top of the slide. She shut her eyes, opened them; no, Charlie was playing on his own.

There seemed to be no one else in the park, which made her feel a little anxious; even the attendants seemed to have gone on an extended coffee break. In fact, somehow the atmosphere felt different today. It had an eerie quality about it, but Jayne put this down to her paranoia. She stole a glance at the Lourdes Grotto. She found the tableau of frozen statues beyond somehow unsettling. The sky couldn't make up its mind whether to laugh with the sun or cry with the rain that threatened to come. The wind moaned fitfully and clouds scudded across the sky. The trees rustled conspiratorially and the rooks mocked and laughed and gossiped, swinging blissfully to and fro on the high branches. They reminded Jayne of witches' familiars.

The wind sighed, huffed and puffed, chasing reluctant rose petals to mulch along the paths. The wind fell silent, then gave a sudden roar, giving a hint of things to come. Jayne shuddered again.

"We better not be long, Charlie, it's getting cold," Jayne called. Charlie did not appear unduly perturbed by the coldness of the day, in the robust way of childhood, and ignored her.

"Come on, Mum, let's have a ride on the train," Charlie called.

Charlie was driving the train and Jayne had just purchased a ticket to ride to Douglas from him, when, out of the corner of her eye, she saw a swing begin to swing. She was surprised. This must be a very quiet parent and child as she had not heard anyone coming into the park. Charlie distracted her.

"Come on, mum. Climb aboard, we're setting off."

The swing still swung, with only a creak of the chain. Jayne stole a glance behind her and got a heartstopping shock as she realised that there was no one there, but the swing was following its usual trajectory under its own steam, without the aid of any human hand! A few yards away, Phyn was conducting with his wishing wand and dancing his quirky jig.

"The magic is starting," he sang gleefully.

"Charlie, I think we should go," said Jayne urgently, turning back to her son. But to her horror both Charlie and the train had disappeared. There was the smell of sulphur in the air and a hint of smoke dissipating into the trees. Train tracks scorched across the grass and in front of her there lay ten empty blocks of paving slabs, with their metal anchoring hooks twisted and torn asunder. A feeling of unreality took hold of Jayne.

"This is it. I'm having a nervous breakdown," she gasped, as, with a mother's instinct, she ran after the train tracks. But they swerved unnervingly across the boating lake and into the sky, cutting an arc across the bay towards Douglas.

Jayne hared around the boating lake, and the golf course, before finding herself back in the playground, playing hide and seek for Charlie although she knew he wouldn't be there. What corner could he be hiding in? In between the green gloss of summer leaves she strained for a sight of Charlie in his bright blue coat. To add to her discomfort, the roundabout began to turn, methodically at first, then faster, faster, faster, until no child could hang on; no human child, that is.

The swings swung, the chains creaked under the weight of invisible children. Bobby Bright-Eyes, that traditional and aged horse rocked backwards and forwards with his mocking, child-friendly smile. The seesaw seesawed maniacally up and down. The increasingly raucous wind brought the sound of children's voices, calling, laughing and crying. But there was no Charlie and the rooks continued to mock and gossip and caw and scrabble in their rookery. The white metal figures down below in the grotto continued to stare steadfastly into space, frozen in expression and form; impassive and unmoved by her distress. Or were they?

Christ yawned, stretched his arms and hefted down his cross, whilst Mary Magdalene wiped her tears away with the sleeve of her gown and gave a conspiratorial grin.

"Party time," she announced gleefully.

Jayne felt the paralysis of hysteria creeping upon her, combined with the eternal and harrowing anxiety of – where was her child? At the same time ,she desired to dissolve into invisibility, to curl up into a ball and hide, as she had done and felt many times since her foolish marriage when himself was in an ungovernable temper. Jayne, following this now familiar instinct, crushed herself into the ticket office at Onchan Holt, as one, by one, each white figure abandoned its plinth and began walking, rather than drifting, across the grass. Jayne almost coldly assessed, "why they didn't leave entrails of mist in their wake. Surely that was what supernatural beings did?"

"Good races this year," commented a sad faced soldier to his companion.

"Yes. They topped 130 miles an hour. That's faster than Apollo on horseback that time he was late picking up the Manx Independent," came the reply.

Jayne gibbered quietly to herself in a corner, frantically trying to work out what had happened to Charlie.

"I'm going to have a severe mental illness now and go into a decline," she moaned as she cradled her head in her hands.

Suddenly, there was a great whooshing and grinding noise in the sky and a big, black, comet-shaped blob hurtled into the park before it swooshed and chugga-chugged back to the platform. The sulphur and dust settled, and, with a sigh, the train relaxed gratefully back onto its platform, shuddered, shrugged and settled itself back into its usual sedate and sensible form, with only the slightest of indignant puffs from its funnel. A very excited Charlie descended from the footplate and ran to Jayne, forgetting his resolve to sulk, wrapping his arms around her in a bear hug, closely followed by Phyn.

"That was fantastic, Mam. We went right over the bay to Ireland. It was like the biggest rollercoaster in the world. It's great in the park today. Can we stay a bit longer? Can we? I've never been on a flying train before. Now I know what that Harry Potter bloke felt like!"

"I think we should go home," stammered Jayne, "It's not natural here today."

"Wow! Look at the statues," Charlie shouted, "they've come alive. See you later, Mam." Jayne looked into the intensely brown face of Phyn, silently asking for help; then Phyn was gone too. Charlie was making a bee-line for the sinister white figures that were making their way stealthily along the park borders and paths. Jayne went to sprint after Charlie, but it felt like she was running in treacle. Charlie met the white figures joyfully.

"Ah, here is the young man whose birthday it is!" exclaimed the sad faced soldier.

"Happy birthday, Charlie," said Jesus, "would you care for a game of bowls?"

Jayne felt utterly powerless so she eventually sat on a bench and watched whilst Charlie had a game of bowls with Jesus and an intense conversation on the state of the world and politics, which ended in some original and startling conclusions. The pair also chatted, with much gravity, about why his mum had taken him away from his old life and his dad. Mary Magdalene came over to Jayne and bemoaned the price of fish and how it never seemed to go far these days and a group of soldiers had a game of golf and hotly disputed the merits and controversies surrounding the TT.

And all the while, the ghost voices of children called and sang and laughed in the park, for Phyn had summoned many spirit children from the past and the future to help Charlie celebrate his birthday. Charlie and Phyn and the statues then played on the slides and the swings. If it hadn't been so alarming to Jayne, it would have appeared quite funny, to see Jesus coming down the slide backwards with his gown flapping about him and whooping away. But finally Jayne decided that she had had enough; and an aggravated mother can be more than a match for Jesus.

"Charlie," she said, in her Serious Voice."It's time to go home."

Charlie came over to her very reluctantly.

"OK Mam," he said, slipping his hand in hers. "Sorry I've been a long time. But it has been great. I've been feeling so lonely without my friends, but now I've met lots. And Phyn is staying with us, aren't you Phyn?" But Phyn had slipped out of view, so with a final goodbye to his friends, the statues, Charlie and Jayne left the park. Jayne's last view of the statues was of them trailing rather dejectedly back to their grotto, climbing back onto their plinths and resettling their crosses; Phyn's magical treat had ended.

A woman emerging from a house in the nearby close saw Jayne's shocked appearance and called the police, fearing that she had been mugged. Jayne felt too weak to protest. She had grown fearful of such figures of authority over the years, but tried to explain what had happened. Her tale fell on deaf and sceptical ears. The policeman looked serious and asked Jayne if she had been visiting the Kennedy Lounge by any chance?

"Disgraceful!" stated the interfering woman from the close. "Disgraceful behaviour. I've never heard such nonsense in my life. I've lived next to that park for fifteen years and I've never seen any of them statues move, and I've never seen a flying

146

train either."

"That's 'cos you've no imagination, Missus," Charlie stated solidly.

"Yes, well, thanks for your help," interrupted the policeman, hastily, sensing that a dispute wasn't far away.

"Whatever has happened, you certainly look as if you have had a shock, miss. Would you like me to drive you home?"

"Wow, a trip in a police car too. What a day!" exclaimed Charlie.

"This is the end," thought Jayne as the police car drew up outside Aunt Voirrey's house. "Aunt Voirrey won't want me staying with her now."

However, Voirrey was so laid back as to be practically horizontal at times, and she took nieces in police cars in her stride. The policeman talked to her very seriously and mentioned social services, to which Aunt Voirrey replied, "Nonsense, young man. My niece is as sane as you or I. This island is a magical place where such things are entirely possible."

When the policeman had departed, shaking his head over the madness of women, Aunt Voirrey poured Jayne and herself a large brandy and they had a very long talk, while Charlie played quietly with his toys. Afterwards Jayne felt much better and no longer questioned her sanity. Voirrey talked about the nature of the Island.

"Up until now you haven't seen the magic around you as your imagination has been stilted, not surprisingly, by your experiences. It is a magical place, this Isle O' Man. Let its peace and beauty heal you. Most Manx magic is not wicked. Don't be frightened by what happened in the park today. I think we have a resident fenoderee in the garden who arranged that particular piece of theatre to help Charlie celebrate his birthday, with much success, I gather. It would certainly take something very special to bring the statues to life like that. Our fenoderee must be a gifted magician. I wonder if he is aware of that. It is also a charmed headland. And as for the statues, you've no need to be scared of them. A Father McGrath once saw an ugly patch of wasteland sheltering above Douglas bay, but could see it had potential beauty. He bought the land and created Calvary Glen, in which were placed the statues, the Stations of the Cross. It was a lovely glen, illuminated at night. I used to go there often with my husband." Voirrey paused, as she looked back into her own past life for a minute, then smiled. "It puts me in mind of how people often see, or don't see, other people." Jayne didn't really know what she meant by that but the long discussion seemed to have finally broken the ice between Jayne and her aunt. Jayne was able to unburden herself to a placid and wise counsellor and listener, which had the positive effect of melting her recent anxieties down to half their size. Aunt Voirrey called Charlie over.

"Tell me about your friend Phyn," she asked Charlie. Which he did. At length.

"Fenoderee tend to be more common up north, but with our better public transport system, they seem to travel further afield these days; they have to adapt to modernity like the rest of us. The fenoderee will be a good friend to you Charlie, especially if you begin to plant and help in my garden. But never criticise him; they don't like being criticised."

As for Jayne, her world had had a whole new dimension added to it. She was prepared to accept many more things that she would previously have dismissed as impossible and, at the end of a day which she had somewhat dreaded, she felt a glow of contentment, despite the shock of earlier in the day. And, what was more important, was something she hadn't felt for years: a hope for the future. The Island was weaving its spell for her and Charlie. Charlie's birthday was rounded off with another traditional feast. A separate plate was prepared for Phyn, which Jayne insisted on taking outside. She stood for several minutes in the blackness of the garden, finishing off her own meal and waiting. She felt a small hand slip into hers and give it a gentle squeeze, and Jayne found herself looking down into Phyn's brown, wizened face once more.

"Sorry. I didn't mean to scare you today, missus," said Phyn, in a reedy voice, like the sighing of the wind in the trees. "I just wanted Charlie to have a good day."

"That's all right," Jayne smiled down at the eager but anxious little face. "Thank you for Charlie's special day and for showing me some spectacular magic. I'm going in to Charlie now. Eat your supper whilst it's still hot. Oh, and something for you; the nights are chilly at the moment, and she handed him a thick blanket. Phyn's face almost split with delight at the sight.

"Oh thanks, missus. this will be great altogether for keeping me warm. Goodnight, missus."

"Good night, Phyn," Jayne whispered to his retreating back. She watched him scurrying away to his shelter, smiled gently and turned to go inside.

It was then that it happened. Her sublimely ugly Glaswegian pounced on her with the stealth and agility of a cat. Dropping her plate, Jayne found herself pushed cruelly up against a wall, her head being ground into sharp stone and quartz. His hand crushed her mouth and with gathering fear, her breath came in short panicky gasps beneath the force of his claws upon her.

"Hello, Hen. Long time, no see, eh. Eh?" he smiled; toothless empty gum sockets grinning down at her like a jack-a-lantern.

Jayne knew that to struggle with him might result in a snapped neck, but instinct moved her limbs to try and escape

149

those claws, which to her had long been repulsive. In one slick move, he had cuffed her wrists and shifted his weight to still her body. He brought his mouth close up to her ear, and she could feel his hot breath against her cheek.

"Been over watchin' the bikes before I came to get you. Saw youse in the park today, all on your lonesomes, looking like a right pair of saddos. That's where we is going shortly. Your use is over see? I've another blonde bitch now and she's waiting to drive you to your final destination. I allus liked a good climax, dinna?" He started laughing in that mirthless tone of his, which inevitably meant business. With a conjuror's skill and before she knew what was happening, he had taped her mouth shut.

"Talking about climaxes, what about one for auld time's sake, eh? Fancy that do you? Used to lie there like a dead body. Well you'll be one soon enough. But don't worry, mi chick, I've got a wheelie bin with your name on it." He dropped his voice a notch, which was even more chilling, spinning it out like an actor; the cat tormenting its mouse. Talk and threat temporarily spent, Jayne was now dragged, to start with on her feet, but by the time they were at the gate, she was on her back, the unforgiving gravel ripping into her skin. With all hope slipping through her fingers and inevitability dragging her, in turmoil, to hell, the sensation of calmness began to run parallel to her desperation; the unique effect of being in an extreme and life-threatening situation.

"At least I'm leaving a DNA trail" she thought, ludicrously; logically as she tried to focus on what her last thoughts on earth would be – her son. All the things that she hadn't been able to tell him lately; things you mean to get round to but don't.

A sleek black car was pulled discreetly down a side street. Jayne got a final couple of bumps against the car, then she was put into the boot, with only the slightest of views of her usurper; a dirty look from under the blonde crash helmet of hair.

"You're going to need the crash helmet," she thought, leaving a bitter legacy for her replacement. The boot was carefully lowered, but not without a parting shot, before she was plunged into icy darkness.

"Don't you fret ma pet, I'm coming back for me lad and that interfering cow tomorrow."

It was the sound of the plate falling and smashing on the path and Phyn's preternatural hearing that alerted him to danger as he made his way to his garden shed. He turned back and as he drew nearer, stifled gasps and gloating vicious whispers became audible. He crept towards the huddled shadows pressed up against the wall. He hesitated and pulled back into the shadow of a bush, anguished as Jayne fell to her knees and was then involuntarily dragged towards the gates and lifted bodily, but professionally, into a waiting car, which purred into life and then slunk away. Trying to quench a rising panic, Phyn tried to calm himself.

"Thank Mannanan! At least I know where they are going." he reassured himself, having heard much of the one-sided conversation.

"Their way is barred by traffic lights, but mine is not," and with that he headed for the gate.

Phyn ran with a fleetness known only to the fenoderee. In the end it was almost a dead heat. He got there just before the car did. The park lay sinister before him; the pitch black dome of the stadium looming above him, for once quiet and devoid of noise and commotion. There were no little boys summiting trees to get a free view of the famous demolition derbies or the purple helmets. The trees formed linear silhouettes in front of a blue-black sky, broken only by a star feeling sorry for itself and a sulky moon swaying slowly backwards and forwards on the trapeze of the now gently blowing wind. Phyn made his way around to the back of the stadium, where the bins were kept. As he crept nearer, he heard a slight commotion, a gate being muffled from clanging shut and he could see the gleaming wing of the car which was pulled up close to the trees. Phyn hid behind a bush, trying to gather his scattered wits as he tried to think what to do. He could try to raise the alarm, but that would take too long. The evil emanating from the creature he contemplated stole away his magical powers, yet he must act – and quickly! Sounds of violence began to thrill on his ear. He took a hesitant step forward towards the noise, but could go no further. It was no good: he could do nothing. Head hanging down, he turned to walk away. But then he saw a slight movement, white shadows taking an airing about the boating lake. He had done that. He had promised them life until midnight. Now that was power. A sudden shaft of bravery pierced his heart and soul, and Phyn made a rush towards the statues.

"Just borrowing your cross, Jesus!" Phyn called as he picked it up from where Christ had rested it temporarily. He charged towards the place where the last gasps of someone desperate to hang onto life could just be heard.

Jayne had felt utterly degraded; he had started touching her in the old ways that had long made her flesh crawl. Then, deciding he was pressed for time, he went for her throat. She knew the grip would be tough and forced herself to create a picture of her son in her mind's eye; her last, loving view of him; the only comfort she could now cling to. Then there was an almighty crack and he slumped forwards on top of her. Phyn raised the cross again, the sudden spurt of adrenalin heightening his aim and strength.

"Can I have my cross back, Phyn?" gasped Jesus, looking

rather white faced. There was a momentary struggle, but Jesus was successful, gently prising the cross from Phyn's grasp and laying a paternal hand upon his shoulder.

"Can't abide wickedness," he said prosaically, looking down at the unconscious man "But I don't want blood on my hands and neither do you, Phyn."

Mary Magdalene and Phyn held Jayne whilst her silent tears fell and when she was ready they helped her to her feet. After the sad faced soldier had dispatched the handcuffs with one skilful blow of his sword and the thug had been shoved into the recovery position, there was leisure for explanations and some strategic planning. And whilst Christ and Phyn did that, the sad faced soldier, who had been spoiling for mischief all day, began to act.

Later, as the evening wore on, he began to look a bit sheepish and said gloomily," I think we'll have to send a few prayers upstairs after today."

"Speak for yourself," said Mary Magdalene."I was shaped for sin."

"But you don't know what I've done," he squirmed, twisting his tunic about.

"Well. What did you do? Confess, you booby." Mary said as she soothed Jayne.

"Well, you know we aren't supposed to be seen. Close up. Direct, like?"

"Yes."

"That interfering woman from the close, who doesn't believe in us. I ... er ... I jumped out at her when she was bringing her washing in. Hopefully she'll think I'm just a ... well ... a ghost."

"And?"

"Then I stole some booze and fags for me and the lads. After all, we don't come to life often. Its usually only on feast days. And then I splashed some of it – it was Manx Mist – but

153

not much mind, over that ugly ... Bast ..."

"Mind yer language. And then what?"

"I tucked the empty bottle into his jacket – he was still out cold. That'll explain the bump on his head. See? They'll think he was drunk."

"Soldier," remarked Jesus, sternly, "I suggest that you 'Call the cops' as they say in the movies so that that misled man can be discovered whilst he is still breathing and before you are compelled back to your station – EARLY."

"OK boss," said the sad faced soldier, scurrying away, looking rather relieved.

After various sirens had come and gone and twelve o'clock tolled, the statues climbed wearily back onto their plinths, saying a heartfelt goodbye to Phyn and Jayne, who had sheltered in the surprisingly warm arms of the Marys as she recovered.

"Don't worry," said Phyn. "We will visit you in your loneliness. Often. Come on, missus. Time to go home. It was a slow journey back. They were both numb with emotion and shock. Charlie's birthday was over for another year; the tension had snapped and the magic had melted away like Mannanan's cloak. Jayne knocked sheepishly at the door, feeling like the criminal, which she thought she was.

"Come in, child, where it is warm," said Voirrey. "You too, little man." She settled them on sofas by the fire and gave them hot, spiced drinks, which brought them to sleep, despite their anguish. And all night, Voirrey watched over them and over Charlie.

Senior Race Day, TT Festival 2008 – Letter From Phyn To His Mum. Via R. Mail

Greetings, Ma, from the coast.

Lots to tell you since my last letters telling you of grievous, but also heartening events.

Following that night, Jayne was cast very low. Charlie, however, was very resilient. He had talked to J. and this helped him to understand her reasons for doing what she did and was again loving towards her, although she would often sit silent and unresponsive. But time went on and things improved and softened.

I think, Ma, that the pattern of daily, uneventful life; small joys and comforts, chip away at the horror and peace is gradually restored. My position as head gardener is now permanent; Charlie, of course, is my second in command, and he is catching on very quick, so I hope to be able to visit you soon. Jayne has started a college course at the friendliest of colleges; has refound something and that is called FUN.

Onchan Park and the Grotto have become special, almost hallowed places to us all, providing a marker for the acute changes which transformed us from being displaced souls into souls that belong, and therein lies its enchantment. We often go there to reflect. In fact we are there now. Charlie has gone off to play with his physical playmates, so that gives us three a bit of time with our own thoughts.

Earlier in the day, we were down on the promenade. Wonderful racing it was. The sun was shining and warm, like good June weather should be. You will have to come and see for yourself, although I know you swear that you shall never leave Barrule and are busy with the clan. And Charlie – his eyes are like dinner plates watching those bikes. He can roll the names of makes and riders off his tongue like a seasoned biker. Voirrey has had a long cush with her friends. We thought she'd never stop!

Oh, and that man who has the wheels for legs, he was there too. He has abandoned his leathers and his sadness and was wearing what they call a H-A-W-A-I-I-A-N shirt and shorts. Charlie says he is a real D-U-D-E. He had some friends with him. When Jayne and he saw one another, it was like looking at the horizon, where the sea and the sky unite. I think they have a common bond; they have both come out of shadows and into the light. He told us how he is making a fine living and a good reputation as a medium, with his own TV show. Says it's daunting, challenging, sad and heartening. Interesting man, he was. Said he was glad that we were no longer grey. Not sure what he meant. Glad to hear that you are all well and that the Fenoderee Council have caught up with that rascal, Finbar. We shall all sleep easier in our beds now. That's two scoundrels banished for seven years. Perhaps they'll be reformed characters when they return, you never know.

Well, must close now, Ma; you know what a poor letter writer I am. Say hello to Barrule for me, I still yearn for those slopes at times.

Your loving son.

Phyn.

Phyn looked up, content, and gave Christ a wink; after all, even statues should be allowed a bit of fun now and again. And Christ winked boldly back for he knew the kernel of courage which had lain in Phyn's heart, undiscovered for so long.

july

Peter Carlé was born in London and worked in various parts of the world before moving to the Island to train as a Manx Advocate. Prior to taking and passing his Manx Bar exams Peter worked as a police officer in England and abroad and later qualified as an English barrister.

Peter is married with two children and since his recent retirement now finds time to pursue his many interests of fishing, travelling, writing and hunting down pubs that sell real ale.

His story 'The Ghost Walk' was October's tale in volume 1 of *A Tail for All Seasons*.

Manx Molehills

Peter Carlé

It was my first day at secondary school and another boy was also hesitating outside the entrance doors of Castle Rushen High School. He was short, wore thick round glasses, had blinking eyes, a pink scalp showing through his thin hair, and wide shoulders. He held out a surprisingly large hand and spoke with a strong Manx accent,

"Moyhrey mie. Bonjour. Good morning … My name is Philip. My friends call me Phil."

We walked into the building: it was the start of our lifelong friendship, and together we would share magical, wonderful and amazing things. The attempted assassination of the school Games teacher was to be just one of our many escapades.

Phil lived on a small farm with his parents. I loved the place as soon as I saw it – a low stone building with a gentle sloping grey roof. It nestled in a dip, surrounded by some oak, ash and chestnut trees giving shelter from the prevailing strong south-west winds. The doorway was narrow and low, made of massive stone. At the front there were just two small windows on the ground floor and three windows upstairs. Inside, the rooms were small, dark but cosy, with thin carpet over the stone-flagged floor.

Phil's father was a big-boned Manxman, with wide shoulders, a quiff of black hair and a large round weatherbeaten face.

"Ay lad, yurr the English boy, best friend of our Phil ... we heard a lot about you, welcome to us farm."

His head almost touched the ceiling as he got up from his fireside chair. A black iron firebasket held burning coals and some smouldering pieces of log, the smoke drifted lazily up the to the top of the fireplace and into the huge chimney. By the fire there was a brass coalscuttle that looked like an upturned Roman soldier's helmet, full of chunks of wood. High up on the chimney breast hung a sword with a wide blade.

He showed me round the farm,

"Ay lad, see that inscription above us front door?" I looked at a roughly hewn stone that read *JOHN KINRADE 1735*. 'He was my great great ... many times great ... granddaddy. He built this farmhouse, on the site of a previous building that burnt down."

It was wonderful; he spoke to me as though I were an adult, and he had time for me and had a hoard of stories about his family. I had always lived in new houses, and my father had no family history to tell; my father was just a tired-looking pale man who did boring things in an insurance company. As for my mum, I hardly saw her, she worked all hours in a lawyer's office, she employed a daily cleaning lady and left us to survive on microwaved ready meals.

The amazing Mr Kinrade told me a lot about the farm, and how his family had been farming there for at least a thousand years! He continued: "My granddaddy tried digging up a corner of the kitchen to install the water pipes but he came across a huge granite slab that fair puzzled him. Ay, that Juan

Kewley, who knew a fair few things, said it was a cornerstone for a Viking Longhouse."

As the big man showed me the fields, the outbuildings, the wonderful dry stone walls, and the awesome view of the Irish Sea in the distance, I walked slowly round the farm, eying his son Phil with envy. Suddenly words tumbled out of my mouth: "I want to be a vet. I want to look after animals. At our last house in England I had my own shed in the garden. I had two rabbits, four guinea pigs, two pet rats and a blackbird with a broken wing. I found an injured baby mole on the road. He was my favourite animal. I had to dig up 50 or 60 worms every day for him to eat!" I gulped several times and coughed. "My dad made me leave the animals behind when we moved here, I hope the mole is all right."

Mr Kinrade smiled, "I'm thinking, lad, you'll like us black-faced sheep."

He was right; they were wonderful happy creatures and I came to love spending time with them in the fields.

We walked round the back of the farmhouse and there I received the biggest shock of the day. A tiny elegant lady drifted towards me; in her left hand was an open gardening basket containing beautiful flowers, a hand trowel and some freshly pulled vegetables. She extended her right arm round my shoulders and proceeded to kiss me on the left cheek, then the right cheek and a second time on the left cheek. While I stood burning with embarrassment and horror she grabbed my hand and led me to the house.

"You eez Philip's new friend. It eez good you eez so kind to im."

She had the same long pointed nose as Phil, the same thin hair covering a pink scalp, even the same thick round glasses and blinking eyes. She always had her hands either covered in flour (from mixing ingredients for cooking) or grimy with soil (from working in the garden). She had turned the ground behind the farmhouse into a mass of billowing colours, with shrubs, bushes, flowers and plants of every type. The high stone walls around the garden protected it from the constant chilly wind. In the middle of it all was a grassy area carpeted with wild flowers and small pretty shrubs. To one side was a vegetable plot with potatoes, onions, cabbages, parsnips, beans and carrots, and also exotic foods growing under glass against the wall.

Her cooking was superb: fresh ingredients cooked to perfection, thin tarts with exquisite vegetables that melted on the tongue, stews and casseroles full of tasty meat, floury pastries oozing with delicious tasting fruit. I dined there regularly with Phil and his parents. It opened my eyes and my brain to a whole new world of exciting things. Mr Kinrade would explain the latest problems with his sheep, the recent news and prices from the Manx Fatstock Commission, strange decisions by the Department of Agriculture, the "daft politicos" – his description of the members of Tynwald; all the time Madame Kinrade filled my plate with morsels from heaven while singing bursts of French folksongs. Most of the time she sang, and she could also play the piano and accordion. Phil inherited her gift for music, he had a good clear voice as a treble and later as a powerful bass. We spoke about Edith Piaf.

"La Mome Piaf," said Mrs Kinrade, "the little sparrow."

She pointed to her own sparse hair, pink scalp, and then blinked her weak eyes, "At school I eez called, 'Une Taipe raivelle'."

I learnt later it was the French for a female mole.

Their unusual marriage came about when Mr Kinrade was a young man wanting to see the world. He joined the British navy and spent several years based in the Mediterranean where he met a French girl from Provence and despite the language barrier they fell in love. It was a shock to his parents.

"Lad, it's right worrying you wanting to marry a girl who's not local – and what is wrong with a good strong Manx girl?"

On his return from the navy Mr Kinrade took over the running of the run-down farm while his wife took charge of the sparse kitchen and the neglected garden. There was only one thing in the farmhouse that revealed his life in the navy – it was the sword hanging on the chimney breast.

One day Mr Kinrade explained to me the significance of the sword. It was a cutlass, and he had been amongst the last in the Royal Navy to learn to use it. The naval officers still had swords for ceremonial occasions but the junior ranks never had swords, he explained, "Just old- fashioned cutlasses for boarding them enemy ships. Cutlasses were used in the Second World War when the great man Churchill ordered the Royal Navy to board and seize naval ships from the Danish, the Norwegian, and the French navy rather than let them Germans have the ships. Ay lad, strange to believe but yessir, cutlasses were issued to us when we were patrolling the coast of north Africa – searching native boats for guns and contraband. It werr grand to feel cold steel in us hands. No one crossed us. Never used it in anger."

I learnt that the Kinrades were childless for many years then had one child – Philip – who became the centre of his mother's world. He was devoted to her. It was a pleasure to be with them as they talked animatedly in French. My French improved enormously and Madame Kinrade loved to help us with French homework.

The farm had a fierce cat. He was a ginger tom who had been a stray living on the farm but was adopted by Madame Kinrade. The cat was called "Roget de Lisle" and he had eyes for one person only – his mistress Madame Kinrade. She explained about the name,

"Roget de Lisle, ee was a 'ero, he write our French song 'La Marseillais'."

The cat would march around the house, his head held high, and every 14th July (French Bastille Day) he would be dressed by Madame Kinrade in a French tricolore. We could never touch Roget, he would spit and snarl at us, but for her, he would purr and put up with anything she wanted to do. His favourite occupation was being out in the garden with his mistress, watching her cutting flowers, weeding, digging up vegetables. He would try to help her – and could often be seen following her around the garden, holding some carrots or parsnips in his mouth that he had dug up. He was a good digger.

*   *   *

We were 15 years old, full of life, and feeling very restricted at school. At that age we were starting to feel the hormones jumping around inside us, making us awkward and clumsy. Phil and I did some mad things together – our most famous escapade was the assassination attempt on the Games teacher. He did not like us two boys. He believed that Phil had the right build to be the perfect hooker in the rugby scrum – but, "That Phil Kinrade boy is so blind without his glasses he cannot throw straight."

He suggested that Phil got contact lenses so that he could see clearly when playing rugby – but the immediate answer was "No!" As for me, I was tall, skinny and fast, perfect for the threequarters line, but the only problem was that I preferred to be at the farm helping Mr Kinrade with his black faced sheep or being in the garden with Madame Kinrade rather than practicing with the school rugby team on a hard windswept pitch. The Games teacher was English and proud of it. I was also English but I had committed the most terrible sin in his eyes: I supported the French rugby team!

It was strange to watch international rugby on the television in that Manx farmhouse, munch apple and almond tarts, drink glasses of wine, and cheer every French try and conversion. Mr Kinrade had played a lot of rugby when he was young, and he knew much about the game. It was amazing to listen to this farmer with his broad Manx accent as he cheered on the French players, discussed their game tactics, and criticised the French manager for his team selections, all the time sipping at his brimming glass of red wine. On one occasion when the game was slow he explained to me "When I werr young I used to drink lots of vitamin G."

I must have looked very confused because he gave an explanation: "Pints of Guinness, used to drink lots of it. But now," he raised his wine glass, "I've learnt to love the grape." He clinked his glass with mine, "Slaynt!"

★　★　★

One day the Games Teacher was told to step in and take our General Studies class because the usual teacher had gone to hospital with a serious illness. He was very reluctant to take over the class, as he did not like teaching non-sport subjects. He was usually able to get out of this type of work by using the excuse of: "Urgent arrangements needed for the big school match," or, "Must plan for sports day."

On this occasion though, the headteacher managed to overrule him and so it was that a very grouchy Games teacher ordered us to prepare a five-minute talk on the subject of our choice. I remember how Bridget Caine talked about keeping budgerigars – while the Games master sat yawning and glaring at us. John Corlett spoke to us about driving a tractor, Ben Kewley stuttered his way through a description of how to catch mackerel. Cameron Clague tried to teach us mapreading.

Meanwhile Phil and I hatched a plan. We could see that the Games master was fed up with the whole thing so we offered to shorten matters by having our two speeches merged into one. He listened impatiently to our request but then to our surprise he agreed: "It had better be good though," was his parting remark.

The following week the five-minute talks resumed. Phil and I were to be the last ones. We took the class into the empty school hall and started by explaining that we were going to give a practical demonstration. Phil disappeared for two minutes while I introduced the topic of "French Foot Chariots". There was a stunned silence as I weaved a story of how Napoleon had conquered vast areas of the world as a result of using these special foot chariots.

"The original foot chariot," I explained, "was made by Philip Kinrade's great, many times great, grandfather on his mother's side. One of these had been kept by the family and passed down from generation to generation."

I then left the hall to help with the next part of our demonstration.

Twenty seconds later a French soldier shot into the hall, complete with a sword, a brass helmet, and a vast tricolore worn like a cloak. He was speeding across the polished wood floor yet his legs were not moving. The members of the class stood staring, with mouths open, and big intakes of breath. The soldier waved his sword and shouted, "Vive la revolution, vive la republique!"

He began to sing the Marseillaise. At this point the Games teacher walked back into the hall, head down, reading a letter. While I had been outside one door of the school hall getting Phil ready for his speedy entrance, the Games teacher had stepped out of the door at the other end of the hall to collect a letter from Reception.

The French soldier waved his sword in front of him to warn the Games teacher to move out of the way but to no avail. The teacher looked up and saw a soldier speeding towards him threatening him with a sword. The Games teacher turned pale, screamed and tried to flee but was sent flying against the wall. Cries and shouts rent the air, as the soldier crashed hard into the teacher, and to the horror of everyone we saw the sword handle sticking out of the teacher's chest.

Amazing rumours were quickly flying around the school. A teacher had been murdered, a soldier had entered the building and attacked people with a sword, Phil Kinrade had gone mad and killed the Games teacher, dozens of ambulances had taken the injured to hospital.

That night I travelled to Douglas town to visit Phil in Nobles Hospital. He was concussed, bruised, and had two broken fingers. He told me that the Games teacher was being treated for a broken ankle, cracked ribs, and a wound to the chest where the sword had nicked the skin then bounced off the ribs and stuck into the wooden wall of the hall.

There was an enquiry at the school of course. I spent an uncomfortable hour in the Head's office explaining how Phil and I had made the chariots from two pieces of timber, each about three feet long, plus four rollerskates. We had fitted two rollerskates underneath each piece of wood with a Wellington boot fitted on the top of each piece. Phil had put his feet inside the boots and I had pushed him into the hall. Phil had his dad's cutlass in his hand and the brass coalscuttle on his head.

Unfortunately for us, four problems had arisen: the polished wooden floor was slippery and fast, the Games teacher had put himself directly in the path of Phil, Phil did not know how to stop the foot chariots once they were rolling at speed, and the cutlass had been sharper than we thought. The Head's very thorough enquiry ended with the finding that the injuries were accidental – the result of "a silly and stupid prank". The Games teacher never recovered from the shock and humiliation of that day, and he left for a job back in England. Everyone at school was pleased to see him go.

When Phil was out of hospital I went over to see him but was swept up by Madame Kinrade. She was tearful and I found my face was wet after she kissed me the obligatory three times.

"We must av a talkie walkie," she began.

I soon learnt what she meant – a walk around the garden while she talked to me.

"You must look after Philip. Eez a good gentle boy. No more trouble please."

I promised her then I would always look after him whatever happened.

My future life was already sorted in my mind: I loved animals, had learned how to deal with them, and all I wanted was to be a vet. Phil was unclear what he wanted to do. His father wanted him to take over the farm, and although Phil loved people and got on well with all types, he was not a great one for animals. He could never tell the difference between individual sheep in his father's flock and was uneasy when holding a lamb for his father to examine; even the farm cat Roget de Lisle would snarl and spit at him.

One winter Madame Kinrade suddenly became pale, tired, and weak. Instead of being her usual erect and elegant self she was now bent over and moved with difficulty. She needed help gardening or cooking, she was distracted and forgetful. Mr Kinrade took her to Nobles Hospital for a variety of tests. One day Phil came to school tearful,

"Mum is very ill. She has to go away to a hospital in England. Dad is going over with her."

While his mother was away in hospital Phil came to stay in my house and I did my best to look after him. He was never comfortable in our brand new house and it felt odd to eat microwaved meals with him instead of his mother's homecooked food. One of Mr Kinrade's neighbours looked after the sheep. Phil and I went to the farmhouse every two days to check on everything. Roget de Lisle bristled with anger directed at us; marching around the farm he would check the kitchen and the garden every few minutes, constantly looking for his mistress.

Madame Kinrade came back to the farmhouse just once before she died. She was just a walking skeleton, unable to garden or cook, but us two boys would cook things under her instruction, or we would weed and hoe the garden as she looked on. The cat never left her side except to help by digging up vegetables and carrying them in his mouth to his beloved mistress. Mr Kinrade was distraught by his wife's illness. He lost interest in his beloved sheep – he sold them all at market – and rented out his fields to the neighbouring farmer. He was unhappy with the hospital consultant's diagnosis and so he paid for private treatment and sought the opinion of the medical experts. It was all in vain – she died in hospital.

It was her last wish that her ashes be spread over the garden area. Mr Kinrade could not face doing it. Instead he buried an urn containing her ashes in the middle of the grassy area. He would sit in the garden by himself for hours, sad and unhappy; he was mentally exhausted and had no energy for anything. The doctor prescribed various pills to cheer him up but Mr Kinrade preferred to sit in the garden partaking of a glass of wine and some French pastries that we had cooked for him.

I made sure that Phil kept up with his schoolwork. I was fulfilling the promise made to his mother. It was not just me that pushed Phil to work hard – the day Mrs Kinrade died there was a major change in Roget de Lisle's behaviour. He suddenly took up residence in Phil's room, lying across the doorway at night. During the evenings when Phil was working on his homework, the cat would purr and watch over him. Not only did Phil do well in the exams that summer, he also decided on his future career.

"I want to be a doctor," he proudly declared.

We both got good A level results and both were accepted at Leeds University. Mr Kinrade drove us to the hall of residence with our bags. It was like being back at Castle Rushen School again, only much bigger and more intimidating. There were tears in his eyes as he said goodbye to Phil. I felt very sad for him: he had lost his sheep, his wife, and now he was losing his son. Only Roget de Lisle remained at home with him.

We were in our third year at university when the terrible news of Mr Kinrade's death came to us. Neighbours found him; they had checked the house and had gone into the garden to look for him. There he sat in a garden chair, at peace, with Roget de Lisle loyally curled up on his lap.

After the funeral, held in the overflowing Arbory church, Phil went to Douglas and spent time closeted with the Manx advocate who had always handled the Kinrades' legal matters. The bank manager was also there. Phil came out pale and shaking. I took him to the Market pub where we sat in a small room supping our pints. Finally he broke the silence.

"The farm is mortgaged up to the hilt, there are loans, overdrafts and bank charges. And there is no money coming in apart from a tiny sum from renting our fields for the neighbour to graze his sheep. The bank will force a sale unless I can come up with a barnload of money. Us farm, looked after by us family for a thousand years will be gone forever."

I put my arm round his shoulders like his mother had done to me years before. He was now an orphan and was likely to lose the only home he had ever known.

Throughout the next week we ransacked our brains and we

searched the house, opening cupboards, emptying drawers, flicking through papers.

"Keep searching," I demanded, "maybe something of value is in the house, an old forgotten savings account, some jewellery, an old work of art."

Roget de Lisle took up the challenge and with great difficulty dug up the vegetable plot, slowly bringing Phil carrots, beetroot and spring onions.

"Thanks Roget, at least we have us dinner sorted, thanks to your hard work. Wish you could find the missing bank account with lots of money in it though."

It was Bastille Day. That special day had always been celebrated by Mrs Kinrade so we decided to keep up the tradition. We dressed up Roget in his tricolore coat, we cooked French food, we played a tape of the Marsellaise, and finally Phil produced a strange-shaped dusty bottle that was almost full.

"Bottle of absinthe – found in the back of the pantry. A very special French liquor that was banned in France for a while because it sent some people blind or mad. Van Gogh drank it before cutting his ear off. Come on boy, let's drink some and go really mad!"

* * *

I was crying, I was looking for the baby mole I had left behind in England when I was eleven. I knew he was in the garden but I could not find him, even though I was lying on the ground scrutinising the grass in front of me. Phil was lying next to me banging the ground with his fists and sobbing, "Mama, where are you? I need you! I want to keep the farm, help me."

Roget de Lisle joined us on the grass. He was an old cat now, moving slowly and creakily. The vet had examined him a few days before and had offered to put him to sleep but Phil had refused. Roget made a feeble scrabble at the ground and tried to dig up something for us, but he soon gave up and crept over to where Phil was lying on the grass. He licked a few drops of absinthe that Phil gave him, purred happily, grinned then fell asleep looking the very picture of a happy cat.

Phil and I woke up feeling cold, stiff and with the biggest headaches imaginable, and with the world spinning around us we dragged ourselves across the lawn. Roget de Lisle was lying in the same position; he was grinning and looked extremely happy but he was dead. Tears of pure absinthe rolled down our cheeks as we discussed what to do.

"We could bury him in the garden," I shouted. It was an effort to get the words out. Phil was not happy with that idea. He spoke slowly and very precisely. "This place is going to be sold. The next owners might dig up the garden and disturb his grave. Oh no ... Oh no ... mum's ashes are in the urn ... buried in the middle of the garden for ever."

He paused then spoke in a sombre, quiet way. "She wanted the ashes spread over the garden. Us Dad refused to do it."

We reached a drunken agreement. Roget de Lisle was placed on a small funeral pyre and set alight. It was a memorable picture as the flames roared high in the air and Roget's face continued to smile at us till it was hidden by a burst of smoke. When the ashes were cold we collected them up and placed them in a jar. Then we dug up the urn containing Madame Kinrade's ashes and walked around the garden sprinkling the remains of cat and mistress over the ground. Finally we poured two glasses of red wine over the grass plus the last reluctant drops from the absinthe bottle. I was completely exhausted and lay down on the ground. Phil lay next to me. We banged the ground and called out like madmen:

"I want my mole!"

"I want my mother!"

The grass was tall; it was not green grass, it was a jungle made up of hundreds of tiny bursts of colour, it was moving … not the wind, an insect perhaps, no, something bigger … inches away from my face I could see the loose earth being thrown up in a pile that was constantly increasing in height.

"Hello, are you my mole from England?" I asked dreamily.

We both watched fascinated as the molehill grew up next to us.

I stretched out a hand to the black earth. I could see that there were some lumps of stone also being pushed out of the ground. I picked up one. It was smooth and very dark.

"Not a stone," I murmured, "pottery. Pieces of old pottery. It is the rim of an old rough pot."

Something gleamed in the molehill. I gingerly picked up the gleaming object and examined it. It was brassy and very heavy, on it was embossed a head.

"Coin … gold!" I was up and shouting.

Phil put his hands over his eyes. "Please, not so loud," he moaned.

Another coin was being pushed up through the earth.

★   ★   ★

The Manx Museum took possession of our find – there were over two hundred gold coins, some gold jewellery, silver jewellery and over one hundred silver coins. Phil was paid a lot of money for the find. He used the money to pay off the farm debts. The hoard had been buried in a pot about a thousand years ago. The pot must have been breaking up and the coins trickling out. A mole had been digging its tunnel and had pushed the bits of pottery out of the way of the tunnel and up into its molehill along with the surplus soil.

One problem though – there are no moles on the Isle of

Man. The Department of Agriculture visited the farm and set traps but they caught nothing.

If you are in Colby on 14th July come to Phil's farm. Every year, Dr Phil Kinrade, his wife and children put on a special Bastille Day party. I always close down my veterinary practice for the day and take my wife and children. We eat French food, drink red wine and sing the praises of Roget de Lisle and of his beautiful French mistress. We also put out 50 or 60 worms on the grass in case the mole is hungry, two glasses of red wine and a few drops of absinthe are also poured on the grass in case the mole is thirsty.

❧ August ❧

Aidan Alemson lived in Australia and Italy before settling in the Isle of Man, where he currently works as a property manager. Aidan achieved a B.A. from the University of Queensland, Brisbane and then studied the history of art and painting in Florence, Italy. He also completed courses in screenwriting and has contributed to various short films and documentaries.

Aidan has also written a novel entitled *The Point However Is To Change It*, a double-novella *Wolfhound the Troubleshooter* and a stage play *The Mesopotamian Legacy*, all published by Artisan Productions, Brisbane, Australia. His most recent poetry was included in the anthology *Whispers on the Breeze* published by United Press, London, and his short story 'Hommy-Beg' was included in the first volume of *A Tail for All Seasons*.

The Third Eye

Aidan Alemson

"Neil – quick!"

Alerted by the evident fear in his wife's sudden cry, Neil Tolland turned back to face her. She was just visible in the dust-speckled shaft of natural light which beamed down in the manner of a teleporter. The effect spotlighted her honey-blonde halo of curls and hollowed out her cheeks with chiaroscuro shadows. She stood transfixed.

"Lea! What's wrong?"

"Look!"

She pointed at the tilted viewing table in front of her. All the while her emerald eyes stared unblinkingly downwards.

It was a quasi-photographic image of a grass-covered headland. The entire vista was perspectively flattened, with the foreground and background optically merged by the depth of field usually achieved through a telephoto camera lens. The edges of the frame were slightly blurred like an old cinematic flashback.

This was no ordinary 'Instamatic' snap: the blades of grass were constantly billowing while seagulls were circling relentlessly like maritime vultures stuck in holding patterns.

"Looks the same to me. What's the problem?"

"She's gone, Neil. Gone over the cliff!"

"Who, love? Who did you see?"

Lea stuttered slightly; not a usual affliction.

"I … I saw a dark-haired woman in an old-fashioned purple dress. She … she toppled over the cliff below that bench. There was a blond man in front of her. I only saw him from the back … It happened so quickly."

She turned to face her husband. Worry lines ramified across her brow.

"I … I think he might have pushed her. Then he ducked down."

Neil squeezed Lea's right arm. "Och. You're not joking now? Tell me, Lea."

"Of course not! I'm deadly serious."

They both looked back down at the projected image of the cliff's edge on the tapered table. Neil traced a finger across the surface. It caused a shadow to cut a swath through the luminous landscape. Then Lea pinpointed a particular spot near a bench. There was no one there now – no living thing, except the occasional swooping herring gull.

"We'd better go outside to check. Come, darling." Neil grabbed Lea's hand and led her quickly around the curved narrow corridor. The timber floorboards creaked in arthritic agony, mingling with their footfalls echoing in the dark confined space. On their left were similar viewing tables arranged in a circle – eleven in all. High above each partitioned table was a lens and an angled mirror installed in its own paneless window. A ring of stationary periscopes watched the capital of the Isle of Man, its namesake bay and surrounding topography.

The frantic couple burst through the twin exit doors which

banged behind them. A brisk westerly wind greeted them outside. They were dressed in summery polo shirts, jeans and trainers.

The green and white wooden building looked like a big garden gazebo, with a white conical roof incorporating a dozen small dormer windows decorated with carved crested eaves, capped on its apex by a ventilation lantern shaped like a Prussian helmet. "Great Union Camera Obscura" was emblazoned across the base. A small board detailed its Easter till September, weekend-only opening times.

Neil checked his digital wristwatch: 3.33 p.m. They hurried the few steps past a red signal flag to the ticket window inside the entrance door. A wispy white-haired old lady, who had sold them their entry tickets barely five minutes before, lowered her library book in surprise. She was wearing glasses with thick lenses.

"My goodness. You two didn't take long, did you."

"I need to contact Emergency Services. Do you have a mobile? We didn't bring ours," Neil asked in his excitable Ulster accent.

"Why ever? Did you have an accident inside?"

"Nothing like that." Lea faltered, "I ... I think I witnessed someone falling off the cliff over there." She pointed to the right of a lighthouse. Still no one in sight.

"Oh! How dreadful! Here, you use it," the elderly custodian exclaimed, handing Neil her mobile phone. "I haven't seen anyone but you for a quarter of an hour. But then, I was engrossed in this thriller." She held up an enlarged-print edition of *The Lanternist*.

Neil dialled 999 and moments later handed back the mobile. "Emergency services are on their way. Lea, I'll look over the edge to see if anyone's down there."

"Take care, darling."

Neil rushed up the path, across the grass towards where his wife had last seen the mysterious couple.

Lea waited anxiously. She thought how pleasant and uncomplicated life had seemed a short while ago. She and Neil, both in their mid-twenties from Ballymoney, a town twinned with Douglas, had chosen the stylish Sefton Hotel on the seafront for their honeymoon. Lea admired nineteenth-century buildings and was elated on first viewing the architectural sweep of the bay reminiscent of Cannes's *La Croisette*.

Reaching the cliff top near a bench seat, Neil looked down the long drop towards the base. No one was visible. From here at the top, only part of the area below could be seen. He noticed a boat ramp by the lighthouse, but saw no boat either at the landing or out to sea. He'd previously seen steps to the left of the Camera Obscura going down to a small pebbly cove.

Neil ran back to Lea. "Can't see enough. I'll go down and look around. Wait here till the police arrive. Explain what happened, love."

"Neil, don't go! It could be dangerous."

Dismissing Lea's concerns, Neil rushed down the steps to Port Skillion cove. He wondered whether this was for real or whether Lea had imagined the event. Feeling guilty, he suppressed the suspicion; focusing instead on the thought of finding an injured or dying woman. A killer could be there too. He was oblivious to the faintly sinister sound of dripping water constantly oozing down through the eroding cliffs and menacing ridges of compacted slate like an open-cut wound.

* * *

Lea Tolland looked down at her husband. She gazed at his tousled black hair crushed on the pillow. His lean face had a high forehead underlined by two thick dark eyebrows permanently arched in quizzical emphasis. Some people back home in Northern Ireland assumed he had Spanish blood going back to a sixteenth-century shipwrecked survivor of the Armada.

"After last night's exhilaration, better to let him wake naturally," Lea thought. It was almost eight o'clock on Monday morning. She lay back on the crisp linen pillows, admiring the tasteful décor of The Sefton Hotel's Bayview Room. Her mind soon returned to the disquieting event of yesterday afternoon.

"Could the mystery woman have been a ghost?" Lea wondered. She was trying her best to cover up her anxiety so as not to worry Neil. On Saturday evening, before their Sunday trip to the Camera Obscura, they had been so carefree: laughing together while watching a show ('Blowup: The Musical') at the Gaiety Theatre next door. She recalled how before the curtain rose she'd had the feeling of being watched, though non-threateningly. Gazing upward she had been amazed to see a giant rose window ceiling with a central 'sunburner'. Its stained-glass patterns radiated out like an all-seeing 'Eye of God'.

During the interval, while exploring the gallery, she and Neil had viewed a display cabinet containing nineteenth-century stage clothes worn by faceless mannequins. Now the memory of one of those dresses – a woman's full-length Victorian gown – made her shudder.

"The woman I saw from the Camera Obscura wasn't dissimilar. Her face wasn't blank but her features were indistinct. I hope my mind isn't playing tricks on me," she whispered to herself.

Neil's topaz-brown eyes slowly opened. He tried to figure out in that first waking moment exactly where he was.

His young wife draped her slim body across him, dressed in an ivory silk negligée. She kissed her husband so exuberantly that she grazed her face on the stubble of his chin.

"Ow! That feels like glasspaper."

"Let that be a lesson, barmbrack."

"How's that?"

"Allow your man to make the first move."

She drowned out her man's laughter with her pillow lying close at hand.

"And let that be yours, sweetums," she stressed before releasing him. "Now the lessons are over, let's hear the news."

Lea leaned across to the king-size headboard and turned a dial. Hissing white noise was soon replaced by the dulcet tones of a female voice:

"Broadcasting from the Isle of Man, *shoh Radio Vannin*. This is Manx Radio. The news at eight o'clock. *Moghrey mie*. Manx Radio has learnt that tourists on Douglas Head witnessed an attack yesterday afternoon involving a couple near the Camera Obscura. The alleged female victim was wearing a Victorian-style gown. As yet, no one bearing a likeness to the mystery couple has been found ... Onto other news now: a red squirrel illegally smuggled onto the island as a pet has been recaptured after escaping captivity. Its owner, Abel Cain of Knock y Doonee, and the squirrel, Thorleif, are both behind bars – though not in the same cell ..."

Neil fell back from his leaning position, chortling.

Lea, worried by the first news report, switched off the radio.

"I don't understand how the mystery couple simply disappeared."

"Manx magic. Even their cats' tails disappear."

"You don't believe what I saw, do you!"

"Of course, my love," Neil replied, wiping the tears of mirth from his eyes.

"Of course you do, or of course you don't?"

"Och, of course ... I love you."

Neil sprang up, throwing off the russet bedspread. Disentangled from the bedclothes, he entangled himself in his beloved's body once more. They kissed again passionately.

★   ★   ★

Mr and Mrs Tolland exited the hotel lift hand in hand. They strolled across the buff tiles to the ground floor front desk where the male receptionist greeted them:

"Good morning. There's a lady just arrived who wants to see you. I rang your room a minute ago, but you were obviously on the way down. Her name is Ms Brew. She's waiting next door in 'Sir Norman's'."

Thanking him, they followed his directions through the connecting doorway to the adjoining bar-restaurant. It was part of The Sefton complex, but open to the public.

Lea admired the viridian carpet with gold *fleurs-de-lis*. A grand piano was parked on it, amidst the tables.

"This place is like a showbiz shrine," observed Neil.

The walls were as cluttered as an art gallery, with framed signed photographs of the iconic comic actor Sir Norman Wisdom (a much-loved, long-term Manx resident).

At this time of day, late morning, there was more memorabilia than actual customers. However there was one patron who sat at a central table on her own, eating crème brûlée with evident gusto. Lea couldn't help but smile. The woman resembled a romantic foil from one of Sir Norman's innumerable comedy films.

The instant she noticed them entering from the lobby, Ms Brew's face lit up in welcome. She was pleasantly plump, which had the desirable effect of banishing most wrinkles from her round face. She appeared to be in her mid-fifties, yet her bright cornflower-blue eyes glowed with childlike *joie de vivre*. She wore a stylish Manx national tartan outfit with matching tamo'-shanter hat. Its twill weave integrated seven colours – each symbolising a different natural aspect of the island.

Despite being complete strangers, Brew greeted the newlyweds like long-lost friends.

"Ah! Mr and Mrs Tolland, I presume. I'm so glad to meet you, m'dears. I'm Orla Brew. If you have a little time to spare, please be my guests for elevenses. Ha. Waiter!"

Neil wanted to spin around and out of The Sefton's revolving door. Too late. His gracious wife was leading him forward instead.

The trio were soon huddled around cream teas. The local lady was the most at ease.

"I was intrigued by the brief report on Manx Radio last night. I learnt of your whereabouts by way of a good mate at a taxi base. It's a relatively small island you know."

"Are you a journalist, Ms Brew?"

"No, Mr Tolland. I'm a freelance researcher of Manx culture with a particular interest in psychical phenomena. That's why I want to discuss your experience involving the Camera Obscura. I've brought along some relevant things to show you. You don't mind, do you?"

Lea shook her blonde curls in affirmation. Neil, munching a cream-filled scone, simply shook his head.

"I've copies of authentic documents and recorded conversations with elderly Manx folk recalling earlier days. Ah yes m'dears, there once were times when women wore red flannel for curing coughs – believing the magic to be in the colour not the cloth itself – and when our forebears combed the hills in search of the *luss-yn-aacheoid,* the purple meadow-button, to ward off the evil eye."

"As an interior designer, I'm fascinated by the role of colour. I already knew of the 'evil eye' – a global superstition," remarked Lea.

"Yessir. My interviewees often recalled it when referring to the old *skeeal* – stories of the oral tradition. But mind, there were written records as well. The UK's motherless parliament lagged sadly behind ours. Back in the fifteenth century we benefited from women's input: there was Cristina the formidable Prioress of Douglas, an official Member of our Manx Tynwald, and also the Jury of Matrons consisting of six mature ladies."

Neil felt irked. He'd planned to take Lea on the steam railway to Port Erin to get her mind off the 'obscure incident'.

"Sure we'll miss the train now. This eccentric has wafted out of the blue and into our lives as effectively as her perfume has permeated my nostrils," he thought.

"So, you're for full Manx independence," Neil said.

Orla, perceiving Neil's directness, offered him more strawberry jam.

"Oh, don't get me started. All I'll say is '*Shass er e chione hene*': a man should stand on his own head. And a woman too! Don't get me wrong; I may be as Manx as the hills, but I'm not anti-English. I'm a member of the British Society for Psychical Research. Which brings me to the nitty-gritty, m'dears. Were you actually inside or outside the Camera Obscura when you witnessed that mystery couple?"

"I saw them from inside only," replied Lea. "There was a young, hatless woman dressed in a late-Victorian purple gown with lilac trim. Her dark hair was rolled up. A blond man was facing her; he didn't seem old. He struggled with her. She toppled off the edge of the cliff. I'm fairly certain he pushed her."

Lea's teacup shook slightly.

"Take your time, m'dear ... So you viewed them from the third eye, the third table, and the male was wearing a fawn jacket?"

185

"But ... How could you possibly know?"

"You told the police: that Sergeant ... MacGuffin. Word could've leaked out."

Orla Brew sighed, "Oh. Mr Tolland, is your first name 'Thomas'?"

"No, it's Neil."

"Well Neil, your lovely wife is one of several people who've experienced paranormal phenomena within the Camera Obscura. The last incident was witnessed by the voyeuristic Rector of Cronk y Watch in 1990, just before it was bought up, closed down and boxed up by the Government – reportedly for repairs. It only opened again in 2005. In fact there were some who thought ..."

Neil interrupted, "Och, sure you're not suggesting the Manx Government closed it down to undertake a 15-year investigation into ghostly ghoulies? If anything, it would have been a great tourist money-spinner. Naw, it probably just needed repairing."

Embarrassed by his forthrightness, Lea gently tapped Neil's shin.

"Orla, my husband is a science teacher so he questions things. I'm ... well, I'm just glad I'm not the only person who saw ghosts."

Orla smiled kindly. "What is a ghost? Some think a ghostly sighting is merely a re-enactment of an earlier, emotionally charged event which has left an imprint on a receptive surface. And mind, alleged sightings have been of the living as well as the dead. Don't fret, m'dear. I agree with Neil's questioning. When he spoke, I was just about to say some thought the closure had sinister connotations but I wasn't one of them. Some mysteries can be rationally explained. In the 1840s, a local Manxman worked out that sad moaning sounds at Gob ny Scuit, mouth of the spout, were caused by wind effects.

Case solved."

The Manxwoman bent down to open the carpetbag beside her chair. Neil was intrigued. Orla pulled out an accordion-style file and placed it on her lap. She removed a clutch of cards from the 'P' section.

"Take a look at these antique postcards, Neil. They're originals from the late nineteenth century, a time when the Isle of Man was an exotic overseas holiday destination."

"To us, it still is," enthused Lea. "That's why we're here on our honeymoon."

"Well bless the pair of you, m'dears. I mind well my own honeymoon spent with my late husband Barry at Portmeirion in Wales. 'Prisoners of love' he said we were. He was a promising architect. Seems like a lifetime ago..."

For a moment, Orla became lost in her reminiscences. Lea looked on sympathetically. Neil studied a hand-tinted postcard of Douglas's Loch Promenade bustling with horse-drawn carriages of every type (including the surviving 'toast rack' trams) and pedestrians milling about en masse like ants on a sugar-coated croissant.

The remaining cards depicted Victorian thrill seekers swarming around entertainment and refreshment stalls on Douglas Head and queuing to access the familiar Camera Obscura.

"They liked to spy on courting couples in the grass without being seen themselves," commented Orla, snapping out of her wistful reverie.

"They seem easily amused," observed Neil wryly. "The kids of today have virtual reality and they're still bored."

"Yessir. Those were exhilarating island days. Douglas enjoyed what was Europe's largest ballroom and Britain's first open-sea swimming pool at Port Skillion. These multitudes are the ghosts of the past. Yet in one sense they're still with us

– here's the proof."

Neil and Lea handed back the old postcards. Lea looked regretful. "It's a pity there wasn't time to photograph my mystery couple. So I guess we'll never know who they are."

Orla Brew smiled. "Oh, I think I know who they are ... or rather, were."

"Really?!" Both Lea and Neil were astonished.

"The young woman's name was Clara Quayle. She assisted a stage magician known as 'Enrico the Enigma' who performed at The Grand Theatre in Victoria Street. She lived close by at Almshouse Lane. Here's a playbill and photograph from the early 1890s."

Orla showed them a sepia print featuring a petite brunette dressed in tights and a tasselled diamanté costume. She was posed in front of a painted backdrop, holding up her arms to present the man standing beside her: a swarthy bearded gent dressed in typical magician's garb. Lea was intrigued. Her husband was fascinated.

"Well, well. She's certainly a looker. I can see why he used her to draw in the punters. Was Enrico the man who assaulted her?"

Orla shook her head. "No. Enrico had an alibi: he was auditioning replacement showgirls in his demon trap."

"He's taller, with darker hair than the man I saw," commented Lea.

Orla continued, "Her young lover was the assailant. His name was Athol Kelly, aged nineteen, a tailor's assistant from Ramsey. Clara Quayle was still only seventeen, despite her worldly experience entertaining holidaymakers. That was precisely the problem."

"Jealous resentment."

"No Neil. She had eyes only for him. It was the Kelly family who refused to accept Clara. Athol's parents denounced the orphaned Clara for displaying herself for the 'lurid amusement of come-overs in Douglas Town's blood-and-thunder house, The Grand'. Clara gave up her job hoping to win their approval but they threatened to disinherit their son unless he dropped her. To avoid attention, the lovers started to meet at the newly built Marine Drive Gateway."

Lea felt sad for the lovers. She recalled the initial coolness of Neil's parents towards her. She guessed it was because of her mother's different faith. Neil was blind to it and Lea loved him too much to make it an issue.

The Manxwoman continued with her explanation. By now Neil was hooked.

"The pressure mounted. Clara was in dire financial straits. Friends noticed them drinking and arguing more than usual. By the summer of 1892 their relationship looked doomed. They took to joining the crowds up on the headland, including those visiting the Camera Obscura. It had just been constructed with a sensational 360-degree view, replacing the 1887 original which had burnt down."

"It must have been like a magic show in itself, in those days; just three years before they introduced the first paying cinema in Paris," interjected Neil.

"'Twas indeed, my learned friend," agreed Orla, nibbling at the last crumbs on her plate. "I've not heard tell of a better surviving Victorian example ... Now for the tragic outcome. These are reports from the official inquiry. On 7th August 1892, Clara and Athol were seen wandering down past the Camera Obscura just before 3.30 p.m. A few witnesses noticed them at the cliff top near the lighthouse, exchanging heated words. There weren't many people in the immediate vicinity at that time, apart from those inside the Camera Obscura. They saw their altercation becoming more physical. The lovers shook each other. Athol appeared to snap. He pushed Clara off the headland. She fell, screaming. In instant despair, Athol leapt after her to their mutual doom. Their bodies were never found. It was presumed that he'd somehow survived the fall to the rock ledge at the cliff base; grabbed Clara dead or alive and, holding her, jumped off the rocks to be sucked underwater by the strong currents of the Irish Sea."

Orla Brew's contact lenses were swamped by her own salty tears. As if to imitate the waves crashing on the coastal rocks, the Manxwoman poured the last dregs of 'Fairy Bridge' tea into the couple's cups.

"How terrible!" exclaimed Lea with empathy, mindful also of Orla's widowhood.

"There's more," added Orla, looking up towards the restaurant entrance, "there's the incredible twist in the tale I discovered when I ..."

Suddenly she stopped in mid-sentence, staring at the front windows of 'Sir Norman's' as though she'd just seen a ghost herself.

* * *

Orla, Lea and Neil walked together out the front door of 'Sir Norman's', beneath a canopied portico that extended onto Harris Promenade.

At the eatery's entrance, a bronze statue of Sir Norman Wisdom had been positioned on a bench seat as a kind of totem-cum-photo opportunity for customers and tourists alike.

Sitting right beside the statue was a man in his mid-fifties, of stocky build with a noticeable beer belly. He was dressed in a petrol blue suit with a smoky kipper tie. His most striking feature was his bright red hair which was receding on top leaving an unfortunate minge-fringe, compensated for by sideburns that linked up to a fiery Zapata moustache. His looks were a potent celebration of the Viking heritage which had fused so effectively with that of the Manx Celts.

"Well, if it isn't Red Herring! *Kys t'ou*? How are you? I thought I saw you lurking outside."

The red-haired man looked up from the bench with a sardonic smile.

"Witches' Brew! I should have known you'd involve yourself in this palaver."

"I see you've made yourself a new friend, Vince."

Vince Herring rose to his full six-foot height.

"Norm's been cheering me up after my divorce. I still think they should've called the joint 'Wisdom's'. I guess they had neither the wit nor the wisdom. Good morning. I take it you two are Mr and Mrs Tolland."

Neil and Lea were dumbfounded by the colourful character.

"I'm Detective Inspector Herring of the Isle of Man Constabulary. The Sefton receptionist said you were here. I just noticed you leaving."

"There's no need to show them your warrant card, Vince," advised Orla, enthusiastically sticking her bib in, "I can vouch for you. Known one another since we were sprogs at Willaston Infants."

The inspector laughed. "Too long ago, Orla ... Now, Mrs Tolland, my sergeant interviewed you yesterday afternoon regarding the incident you claim to have witnessed on Douglas Head."

Lea tensed immediately. Noticing this, Neil put his arm around her waist.

"Yes ... I ... I gave him all the facts."

Neil lashed out verbally in his strident Ulster tone: "Listen Herring, we told it as we saw it!"

Inspector Herring fixed Mr Tolland with a riveting stare; made all the more rigid by one of his grey eyes – the right one – being made of glass. It was the result of an accident chopping firewood with an axe, when a large chunk had sprung up into his face.

"There's been a development in the case, Mr Tolland. I'd like you both to accompany me up Head Road."

Lea and Neil looked uneasy. Orla was by contrast greatly animated. She excitedly grabbed her old friend's suit sleeve.

"Can I tag along, Vince? I've got my car. Always love seeing you in action."

Red Herring's stern expression drooped like his moustache.

★ ★ ★

The bright red Peel P50 (the world's smallest road-legal car) inched up Douglas Head Road in a cloud of exhaust smoke, squealing like an indignant piglet. Orla Brew sat squashed behind the wheel of the one-seater three-wheeler, determined to make it solo to the summit.

Inspector Herring and the Tollands were already there, waiting beside an unmarked police car. All three gently applauded as the classic Manx microcar finally made it.

"I offered her a lift but she's a proud woman," remarked Orla's old friend. "Since her late husband Barry died in a building site accident, she's chosen an independent life. Unfortunately that's when she got involved in this supernatural malarkey."

Once Orla joined them, the group walked up steps to the front grounds of the former Douglas Head Hotel, since converted into apartments. There they saw an eerily empty open-air amphitheatre. Looming behind it was the Marine Drive Gateway; its castellated stone towers were worthy of an epic film set. It was where Clara and Athol once used to meet. Beyond lay the broad sweep of the north Irish Sea.

"Let's go test the acoustics, shall we?"

The group arranged themselves at the detective's behest on

the amphitheatre's tiered concrete seating. "If I'd known, I'd have brought a cushion," grumbled Orla. She'd brought her carpetbag instead.

The small audience faced the bare, elevated stage which had a central wooden door. It was sheltered by a whitewashed brick box with a slanted roof.

Inspector Herring announced, "Let the matinée performance begin."

The white door opened immediately. A young woman and a young man walked out one after the other. They were both dressed in late-Victorian apparel.

Lea was stunned. Orla clutched her arm.

The inspector asked, "Mrs Tolland, can you confirm that these are the people you saw from the Camera Obscura?"

"They … they're similar to the ghosts …"

Neil snapped, "Och, they're not ghosts! It's a police line-up in fancy dress."

"Vince! You wouldn't?"

Vince Herring winked at Orla with his good eye. He declaimed to the two 'ghosts': "Apparitions! Step forward and identify yourselves!"

The pretty brunette in the long mauve gown advanced downstage.

"Hello. I'm Helen Cannell. I'm an actor in the Ellan Vannin Theatre Group. I play the role of Clara Quayle."

She turned to present her tow-haired partner in a fawn jacket.

"Hi. I'm Jim Gelling. I play the part of Clara's boyfriend Athol in our production of the nineteenth-century Manx tragedy: *The Lost Lovers*."

★ ★ ★

The entire group walked back together towards the Camera

Obscura building.

"Our show premieres at the amphitheatre on the August Bank Holiday weekend. We finished our dress rehearsal at about 3 o'clock on Sunday," explained Helen.

Jim continued, "Then we met up with a professional photographer. She'd been booked to take publicity stills of us in costume. So she took several shots of us posing here, pretending to struggle."

"When we heard the news about an attack near the Camera Obscura in Victorian clothing, we contacted the police. Sergeant MacGuffin organised this mummery."

The group was on the grass slope about thirty yards above the Camera Obscura. Between them and the structure was a spinney of small trees, bushes and brambles.

Lea was about to comment on Helen's dress colour when Inspector Herring spoke.

"So where exactly were you two thespians posing for the snapper?"

"Right here, near these bushes," replied Jim.

Inspector Herring held the palm of one hand up straight as a makeshift sight. He stared hard at the angle and the distance from where the group stood to the dormer windows of the Camera Obscura building.

"So Miss Cannell, Mr Gelling, you can state with certainty that this is as far as you went. You definitely didn't approach the Camera Obscura any closer or move off towards the cliff top?"

"Definitely not," Jim answered. "The photographer said it was too risky. She had 'health and safety' concerns."

"We got in our van and drove home to Crosby where we live together."

"Yes, Miss. We picked you up on CCTV footage driving down past the inner harbour. Unfortunately, there aren't any such cameras near the Camera Obscura – ironic, isn't it."

Red Herring appeared somewhat crestfallen. The Manx bloodhound had just lost the scent.

"Well then, you two couldn't have been the oddly dressed couple Mrs Tolland claims to have glimpsed. So you can go home and practise your lines. Thanks for taking part in the fancy-dress parade."

The attractive actors looked surprised.

"You see," Herring explained, "from where we're gathered, the only lens 'eye' capable of clearly seeing us is the twelfth one. Yet it's been permanently sealed since the 1890s when they introduced a separate exit. Furthermore, even if it had been open, this foliage would have obstructed the view."

The others peered at the wooden structure. It was difficult to see the wood for the trees.

"That's right, Vince," Orla confirmed, "the operator was losing income because visitors kept going around in circles, crowding the viewing tables."

"Sergeant MacGuffin questioned the custodian. She noticed neither you nor the 'other Victorian couple'. What's more, both those coast-watcher cabins farther up are locked, so they couldn't have hidden in there. Add to that the fact that no one has been reported missing and no bodies found ... Well, until something else pops up, I'll just have to shove this case in the freezer."

Lea's anxiety re-surfaced. "Where does that place me, Inspector?"

Inspector Herring half smiled.

"I'm a good judge of character, Mrs Tolland. You and your husband are free to go. We've got your home address. If we solve the case we'll let you know. But for now ... that's all. I've got a mountain of paperwork the size of Snaefell to do because of this palaver! Cop you later, Orla."

"It's been quite an eye opener, Vince. A real red herring. See you. *Hee'm oo.*"

Inspector Herring and the actors returned to their vehicles. The other three remained on the grass slope near the Camera Obscura.

"Look, m'dears," said Orla Brew, rummaging in her carpetbag, "here's a verified transcript from my oral history project. The gentleman concerned is now dead. Let's sit on that bench over there to discuss it."

Lea hid her reluctance to go. That was the general area where she'd first seen the ghostly couple.

Once they reached the bench seat overlooking the sea, Orla sat heavily with a sigh. She regained her breath before explaining: "In the summer of 1985, as a social volunteer, I helped an old Irishman named Fintan Kelly who lived in a cottage near Scarlett. He couldn't move about much, so I brought his provisions. He claimed that his father Rory had told him in 1954 on his deathbed in Dublin that his real name was Athol Kelly and that his late wife, Fintan's mother, had been Clara Quayle. Sadly, she had died from Spanish flu in 1919. Fintan asserted that his parents had faked their deaths from this very spot in 1892. It was an elaborate elopement designed to set them free. Athol, knowing that eloping would result in disinheritance, took proof of his identity hoping to make a future claim. Nothing came of it. His parents lost everything in the crash of Dumbell's Bank in 1900. They died shortly afterwards."

"The more things change ..." Neil opined.

"Sadly true. Late in life, Fintan visited the Isle of Man and settled here. He was a private man. However, learning of my project, he wanted to set the record straight and trusted me to keep it confidential until after his death and until those who had known him were gone. He told me that Athol and Clara had only feigned hostility to give a false impression. Clara had chosen a 'fox day', one seemingly fine but with unpredictable weather, thinking there'd be fewer people up here. They waited until there were no boats at sea and only a few witnesses, though none close enough to intervene. They'd picked a Sunday when there'd be no workers on the lighthouse being rebuilt below. It was recommissioned in October of that same year. The temporarily relocated keeper didn't visit till before twilight fell."

"Foxy all right," commented Lea.

"Using stage magic tricks gleaned from Enrico the Enigma, the pair toppled only a short way down this escarpment, just below the sightline of the Douglas Head pathways. They gripped the bracken as they clambered down sideways. They were young and foolhardy, mind. Once they reached the base but still hidden by rocks, Athol stripped to a bathing costume. Simultaneously, Clara reversed her dual-colour stage skirt with overlaid bodice geared for quick switching. Fintan remembered her having had years of wear out of it – purple on one side, lilac on the other. She then pulled out a blonde wig and bonnet from a string bag which she'd pinned to her petticoat and placed Athol's clothes in them after donning the headwear. From there they separated. Athol reached the bathing pool at Port Skillion wearing spectacles and a cloth cap, having earlier deposited a travel bag and clothes in a lockable changing hut there. Clara, with the string bag and wearing a sprig of purple meadow-button to ward off the evil eye, made her way to Peel by steam train. Each blended in with the crowds. Athol later caught the next boat to Ireland from Peel. Clara was already on board. They had booked separately under false names. Once the dust had settled, Athol and Clara made a new life for themselves in Dublin: he as a tailor and she as a happy housewife. He called himself Rory.

Kelly, as you know, is as common across westward as it is here."

"A persuasive story, but did he show you the proof of identity he claimed Athol possessed?" queried Neil.

Orla shook her head. "No. The 'lost lovers' tragedy was local knowledge, so I kept his story to myself. I suspected he may have been fantasising … until today, when Lea said that Clara's purple dress had lilac trim. All of the inquiry witnesses confirmed Clara's purple dress, but only Fintan and now Lea mentioned the colour lilac."

"It is a crucial fact that only Fintan and I mentioned lilac, but he claimed Clara switched to the lilac side of the reversible ensemble *after* the descent – while making her escape."

"Yes, m'dear, but a gust of the strong headland wind could have billowed up the hemline. With your professionally trained eye for colour and detail, you'd have detected things easily missed by others. You'd have perceived it as a lilac trim."

Lea nodded, though Neil looked incredulous.

"Brilliant deduction Orla, but based on one flawed assumption: Fintan's story may be true but Lea couldn't have seen Clara and Athol. Sure they're long dead."

Orla bit her lip. All three were quiet, thinking of the Victorian lovers in their own way. Lea felt threatened by the sound of the remorseless waves crashing on the rocks below, seemingly determined to consume every fibre of the island. At that moment a Steam Packet vessel came into view, approaching from the south and heading towards Douglas harbour. Judging by its course, it was most likely the summer sailing from Dublin.

Neil's ever-questioning voice broke the silence.

"I'm still not convinced it wasn't the actors. We've only their word for it. After the publicity shots they could've fooled around here, then walked back up along the cliff's edge, out of sight beyond those cabins."

"Why would they come forward and then lie?" asked Orla, unconvinced.

"Perhaps they feared they'd be charged with wasting police time. They knew the photographs would prove they were already up here. They are actors, after all."

"The dress colour bothers me though," stated Lea. "Helen was wearing a pale mauve costume. The woman I saw falling from here was dressed in purple – a darker hue. I know my colours."

"Yes you do, love. It's your job," replied Neil. He looked up at the summer sky – like the day before, it was sunny and blue but a persistent westerly wind constantly blew clouds across the sun.

"Hey, I reckon the changing light conditions must have affected the colour; especially when viewed through that basic projector inside the Camera Obscura. In shadow, mauve could appear as purple. That must be it. There's a scientific explanation for everything."

Neither of the women responded to his done-and-dusted deduction. Orla squinted up at the sun for a second, before watching the Sea Cat sailing in past the lighthouse.

Lea's attention was drawn back towards the Victorian observatory of actuality; the 'dark chamber' of real-life motion pictures. From where they sat, they were indeed in line with the third eye. Its symbolic significance had not been lost on her.

"But it doesn't really matter which 'eye' has been involved. Like superimposed cubistic perspectives, each angle, each view, is as significant as the other. It reminds me of a single eye with multiple pupils: an all-seeing 'Eye of Providence' keeping the watch from its alabaster pyramid," mused Lea.

At that time, however, all the lids on the small dormer windows had been shut in keeping with the twelfth one. The

Manx triskelion flag was no longer flying on the external barrier; the entry gate had been locked, as were the doors. The elderly custodian had gone home till next weekend.

Lea felt her usual sense of wellbeing gradually returning. She too wanted to question the unknown and, like the Camera Obscura, embrace different viewpoints simultaneously.

"I wonder whether the energy generated by the actors reliving Clara's and Athol's passionate act could have somehow triggered a repeat of the original image on the same viewing table? Could the acuteness of my perception at that instant have been reinforced by the intense love which Neil and I share? If Orla is right, and keenly felt emotions can leave an imprint on receptive surfaces, then perhaps similar states of mind can receive similar types of transmissions on the same psychical wavelength? That could mean then that Clara's and Athol's plunge off this headland was an act of love not hatred. The version revealed by Fintan Kelly would be the truth."

She turned back to face her husband and Orla on the bench seat. The cliff's edge no longer felt threatening. The Irish Sea below was glistening in the August sunshine with the mesmeric sparkle of one of Clara Quayle's diamanté stage costumes.

Neil noticed his wife smiling at him. He was touched by her change of mood.

"So barmbrack, you've finally come around to my way of thinking. Och, sure that bodes well for the future."

Neil put his arm around Lea, giving her a kiss and a cuddle.

Orla put the transcript back in her carpetbag. She took care that the downdraught didn't whip Fintan's testimony down the cliff face. The headland was laced with flowering heather; colourfully represented by the purple yarn in her tartan outfit.

"Well m'dears, I'd best let you carry on with your honeymoon. I'm sure this isn't the kind of excitement you had in mind when you came here."

"That's putting it mildly, Orla," giggled Lea.

"Let's stay in touch though ... Perhaps exchanging addresses for Christmas cards?"

Lea steeled herself for one of Neil's schoolmasterly ripostes, but his own mood had lightened as well. Instead, he patted Orla's arm.

"Of course, Orla. We'll be here till Friday – fortunately missing the re-opening of yon Camera Obscura – but Lea and I'd planned a day trip by hire car around the island. Would you like to come with us as our guest?"

"Oh, how sweet," murmured the Manxwoman with a catch in her voice. "Are you sure you want the likes of me chaperoning you around? If my Peel P50 had more than one seat, I'd have loved to chauffeur the pair of you."

The Tollands chuckled. "Ha. Well, perhaps we can hire a three-seater flying a wee three-legged banner from its roof," quipped Neil.

"Well thank you, m'dears," replied Orla. "You never really know a place till you know its people. I'll do my bit by our Manx flag, by putting my best foot forward."

"She's one step ahead of us all," thought Lea, noticing the twinkle in Orla's eye. "I'd like to know more about this magical isle, though I sense that part of its charm may lie in it remaining an enigma."

september

Angie Greenhalgh has lived in Africa, Germany, the Far East and mainland UK until settling on the Isle of Man with her husband and two sons. She graduated from London University with a B.Sc. in Economics and Geography and in 1973 was awarded a scholarship to study for her MA in Canada where she worked afterwards as an economic development planner, spending time with the Ojibway people and the Innuit.

Angie enjoys many country pursuits including fishing. She is a keen walker, amateur artist and is interested in the archaeology, mythology and folklore of the British Isles. She is also the author of various published works in the UK and abroad and her book *Forgotten Magic of an Enchanted Isle* is available from the Shearwater Press and all good local bookshops.

Her short story 'Laa'l Breeshey' was the first story in volume 1 of *A Tail for All Seasons*.

Home Run

Angie Greenhalgh

She lay in secret darkness beside a large rock. Safe in the water. Hidden from the prying eyes of predators. A gnawing hunger to be home consumed her being. An instinctive need she was powerless to resist.

She had not eaten for many weeks, but there was no need for food. The urge to return to where she had been born removed any other need from her gut.

Not far now. Only the wall of stone that shimmered above her, a challenging roar to be surmounted in the river ahead.

She could scent the intricate aromas of freshness streaming past. The smell of home waters. The taste of salt was already a stored memory.

She flexed the tired muscles of her back in preparation for a leap that would launch her into the suffocating light, onward, up and over this obstacle of stone.

She arched her lower body and with a mighty flick soared skyward into a dazzling blindness, trusting only in the deep pulse of direction.

But it was not enough. She crashed downwards against the

rocks and was swept back into the pool, pain searing her side where jagged cruelness had gouged her flesh.

For a moment the current pushed her backwards until she regained her position, once again, in the shadows of the large rock. Anger and frustration at her failure flooded through her body.

Suddenly, she was acutely aware that something had entered the water above her head. Something strange. Something she had never encountered before. Something small and brightly coloured. She moved towards it.

Her initial curiosity changed to rage at this alien invasion of her space. She lunged, at the colours, grabbing them with her mouth, coming into contact with a sharp hardness lying within. And then there was a deep burning sensation; hooking her to some unseen force.

She opened her mouth to rid herself of it. But it wouldn't let go. She tried to move away, but it was relentless in its terrible attachment. Struggling, her heart pounded with terror as she strained to tear herself away.

Panic grew as she thrashed to escape ... the agony ... She couldn't breathe ...

Ginny fought to wake from the terror of the vivid dream.

The cotton sheets were wound relentlessly around her clammy body entrapping her like a netted fish. As consciousness seeped back, she opened her eyes.

It was very dark. She was alone. At first she couldn't remember where she was. The bed felt strange, the room unfamiliar. Then, the distant, acrid smell of paint triggered total recollection.

Of course! She had moved into the spare bedroom at the back of the house because her landlord had, at last, sent painters to redecorate the front bedroom where she normally slept.

She took a deep breath, fighting to regain her equilibrium.

She rationalised that the dream was just a reaction by her subconscious to the events of the past day. A weird interpretation that struck a resonating chord within herself.

She was acutely aware of what had triggered the nightmare's images ... she had been driving from Douglas to see her first case of the day, a lady in her seventies who'd fallen, breaking her wrist whilst suffering a stroke. She also had some degree of paralysis in her left leg. This was Ginny's follow-up visit since the patient's recent discharge from Nobles Hospital.

The notes indicated that Mrs Faragher was a widow, who normally lived alone. Her daughter had temporarily returned to the Island to care for her whilst she convalesced.

Ginny had been on the Isle of Man for only six weeks. The place seemed to get bigger, rather than smaller, and apart from her ignorance of localities, she frequently misjudged required travelling times. So, that morning Ginny had allowed herself an extra half an hour to find her patient's house.

As a Canadian, she found the Island's roads very narrow and the route from the bottom of Bray Hill to Tromode Park was no exception. As she drove along Tromode Road she'd noticed a small group of people, their backs to the traffic, all staring down at something on the other side of the low stone wall.

There was no footpath on that side of the road and she'd reduced her speed as she'd crawled cautiously past them. What was so interesting, she wondered. Perhaps it was something to do with the river?

Ginny's appointment lasted less than an hour. Mrs Faragher was a sensible woman and open to any suggestions that Ginny had made regarding helpful modifications to her home environment.

She reminded Ginny of her own mother who had died many years ago.

It was because of the pain her parents had suffered in their old age that after doing her initial nursing course she had completed an Occupational Therapy degree, specialising in the care of the elderly.

They had been in their early fifties at the time they had adopted Ginny. She'd been left on the doorstep of a hospital in Belleville, Ontario. Another abandoned, newborn baby. Her adoptive parents had no relatives so there'd been nobody else after they'd died that Ginny could call family.

She drove back onto Tromode Road retracing her earlier route. She'd noticed that the crowd of people, mainly men and boys were still there. Still staring down at the river.

Ginny glanced at her watch; not quite enough time to return to her office and too much time before her next appointment in Douglas. On the spur of the moment she decided to stop and see what was attracting their attention. She'd parked her car and walked over to where they were leaning over the low, ivy-covered stone wall.

One of the men, a tall, quite good looking guy of about forty-five, wearing a flat cap, had turned towards her and smiled. "Come to see the September run?"

She'd smiled back, not understanding what he meant until she spotted silver flashing movement in the waters below.

"Oh … so it's fish?" she replied.

"Not just fish. Salmon!" he admonished. "Atlantic Salmon returning to spawn. We've not had numbers like this before."

She could see several fish circling in the pool before the first weir. But her memories of salmon rivers in Canada were of British Columbia, where vast expanses of wild water were thick with hundreds of fish heading in from the Pacific. This little river seemed scarcely more than a stream.

"I didn't think you'd get salmon on the Island," she replied.

"There's always been salmon here!" retorted the man

somewhat belligerently. "There were plenty of salmon in the past. Historically, even the Norse must have had good catches; their word for salmon river was 'Laxa', that's how Laxey got its name. Over-fishing by netting and poaching has decimated the breeding population but recently they're increasing, thanks to more enlightened management ... and heavy fines."

"What's the river called?" she asked, without taking her eyes from following the progress of one quite large salmon that had leaped from the pool up the first weir and now was swimming strongly towards the second one.

"It's the Glass, Manx for green. It joins the river Dhoo further down. Douglas derives its name from their confluence. Our club's got the fishing along this stretch. Up to there ..."

Ginny had become almost mesmerised watching the water and movement of fish. She realised that the man must be pointing at something, but was deeply reluctant to destroy this intense feeling of relaxation. She couldn't drag her gaze away to focus in his direction. "How do they know where they have to go? After years at sea, how do they know where their home is and where they were spawned?"

"Some say it's olfactory – they smell it. Another theory is that, as with all migratory species, there's something similar to a magnetic global positioning within them, something genetically imprinted within them to guide them all the way back across the Atlantic to their home, in the Isle of Man; to spawn in the upper reaches of the river, in the Baldwin valley, completing the cycle and producing offspring."

A motorbike slowed to pass them, the noise of its engine shattering the spell that had held Ginny entranced. She glanced at her watch "Oh my God – I'm going to have to go. I'll be late for my next appointment," she gasped.

She turned quickly. "Nice talking to you. Goodbye. Have a nice day."

As she hurried back to the car she missed seeing his wry smile and the words muttered to the others, "Americans! All the same ... always in a rush and always telling everybody else to have a nice day! Why?"

Ginny sighed in the darkness of her bedroom as she recalled that morning; seeing the salmon leaping up the river had certainly struck a chord. How she envied the fish for that inner knowledge of its origin.

She'd never bothered about her origin whilst her adoptive parents were alive, and after they'd died she'd met Rob, moved to London and been happy during seven years of marriage.

Only after Rob had traded her in for the young Russian girl who'd been his translator in some property deal, leaving her marooned in the apartment in Hampstead, had she'd finally wondered about who she really was and where she'd come from.

She glanced at the bedside clock. God, 3.15 a.m.! Must sleep, she thought, rolling onto her right side. She noticed the square of glass, a navy blue gleam in the dark wall.

"Damn!" She'd forgotten to draw the curtains.

The window was east facing and if the dawn chorus didn't wake her, then the first rays of sunshine certainly would! Hell's bells! If she didn't draw those curtains she'd regret it in a few hours.

She dragged herself from her bed and was about to grasp the fabric when she saw it. An orange-yellow light. It seemed to be suspended in the distant blackness outside. Intermittent. Flickering. Was it hovering in the air? She moved closer to the glass and peered into the night. The surrounding countryside was devoid of any other light.

As her eyes became accustomed to the darkness she could make out branches of trees across the fields moving in the wind. That accounted for the flickering. The light condensed into a square at times – window-shaped?

Yes, she thought, it must be light in a window. Funny, she thought, returning to the warmth of her bed, she'd never noticed a house there before, during the daylight.

The insistence of the door bell woke her.

Saturday? 8 a.m.? She had hoped for a bit of a lie-in. It had been an exhausting week and her sleep had been so disturbed last night. "Who the hell could it be?" she wondered, grabbing her dressing gown. She clattered down the old pine stairs to open the front door.

Oh, the painters.

"Morning, Missm" said the elder of the two, glancing at her dressing gown and uncombed hair. "Hope we didn't disturb you. Just come back to finish off. Only a few hours should see us out of here."

"Oh well," she thought, "there goes any chance of a lie in ..."

Less than an hour later, she was wondering how two men could work in such close proximity and listen to two different radios at the same time. One blaring pop music, the other a continuous monotone commentary on local football teams.

If one of the painters didn't go mad and kill the other, she thought she might be tempted to homicide herself! "I could blame it on the paint fumes!" she snorted.

"Have to get outta here," she thought, reaching for her jacket.

"I'm going for a walk," she shouted to the older guy, who was now contemplating the ceiling, a mug of coffee in his hand. "If I'm not back when you go, leave the door on the latch. OK?"

She marched out of the garden and down the lane, turning for a moment to look back at the house.

It was so ugly. "'Grim' might be a good description," she thought. Two-storey, covered in horrid grey pebble dash, with no redeeming features to soften its austerity, except for four windows painted red and a front porch that was rotten. It would have looked different if it was stone – softer, more natural, but then she supposed that render and pebble dash helped to weatherproof the old damp house from the worst of the Manx weather.

The isolation hadn't bothered her. The rent was lower than others on offer in town but more importantly, she had been strangely drawn to the beautiful Baldwin valley. There seemed to be a secret hanging in the air that made her feel that she had stepped back into a different world where time and space were uniquely separate from any other reality she'd experienced. Hard to explain, let alone understand, but it was as if she were meant to be there.

Funny, she thought, contemplating the soft green outline of the surrounding hills against the bright blue sky, how quickly her life had changed.

One moment she'd been feeling sorry for herself in a coffee shop in Hampstead, casually reading 'Situations Vacant' in a daily paper when she'd spotted the advertisement that was to be her new job. And then less than two months later there she was in the middle of the Isle of Man. A country she was ashamed to say she'd never known anything about until consulting Google.

Her house was at the very end of a long lane, the rutted tarmac already invaded by a central spine of grass and weed due to lack of use. No immediate neighbours.

She stared eastwards.

There was a farm, several fields away on top of a slope, and below it and lower down the hillside was a small clump of trees. Tall, thin, straggling specimens, planted very close together. One or two appeared to have fallen but were still half supported by adjacent timber. Several were dead and raised their branches skyward, silhouettes of silent supplication, sentinels of decay.

And then she remembered last night. That light. Perhaps it had come from a house in those trees, she wondered. But they were so close together and from here she couldn't see any sign of one. And there was no other house to be seen.

She decided to take advantage of the lovely morning to walk the footpath signposted at the end of the lane. The recent heavy rain meant that she had to pick her way carefully alongside the massive hedge banks covered with gorse, through fields muddied and pocked by cattle tracks.

She approached a ramshackle gate and could hear dogs barking ahead. Rounding the bend in the track she realised that she had reached the farm that she had seen silhouetted on the skyline. A collection of farm buildings tumbled around a square, weed-covered yard.

The barn roof was patched with blue plastic sheets and old rusting farm machinery from another era was piled haphazardly in the field in front of the house, which judging from its derelict appearance looked abandoned. But there seemed to be at least two dogs barking angrily behind the ancient front door.

There was no indication of where the footpath went next. She presumed it must run straight across the yard but was reluctant to trespass. However, as nobody was about she began to walk in that direction, hoping that she would soon be able to find the next signpost. She resolved to buy a map next week.

She'd crossed the yard and was about to open the gate when she heard a man shouting angrily behind her "Clear off. This is private property – don't want no contamination here!"

She swung round to see a very old man wearing a battered brown trilby and a frayed, mud-spattered black suit complete with matching waistcoat. He was waving a shepherd's crook

213

at her as he hobbled across the uneven cobbles. To her trained eye, she could see that he had pretty bad hip joints and scoliosis of the spine. Poor old guy, she thought compassionately, he must be in real pain.

"Clear off with yer!" he snarled as he came closer. She noted that his thick grey beard was in total contrast to his very black bushy eyebrows.

"Oh, I'm so sorry. It's a mistake – I was just looking for the path." Ginny was shocked by his anger.

"Well it's not here. Round the front. Can't yer follow the signs? I'm sick to death of you people coming in and leaving gates open. Noseying around other folk's property. Are yer on yer own or are yer with one of them damned walking groups all out for a skeet?"

"No. I'm your new neighbour from down there at Croit Veg. I've just moved to the Island."

"Don't care who yer are – yer can clear off. Sick of damn come-overs and foreign types who've only been here for a few minutes and thinks they can do what they likes. Don't want yer type here."

"OK. Look I'm really sorry to have upset you. I'll be on my way. Perhaps you could tell me where the path continues? Does the footpath go uphill afterwards or down past the house in the trees?"

Whatever she'd said, it seemed to stop him in his tracks.

"What … did yer say?" His voice suddenly drained of everything except surprise.

"Which way afterwards? Uphill, or down, past the house in the trees?"

"There ain't no house in the trees," he said emphatically.

Ginny sensed something was wrong. "Oh, I thought that there was one. I'm sure I saw the lights last night," she said.

"Well, yer wrong. There's no house there and the land ain't

fer sale either! Now clear off or I'll call fer the police!" He turned and stomped painfully away.

Ginny was convinced that there was something that he was hiding. Strange old guy. Most people she'd met on the Island were very friendly. But he was a real grouch.

She walked out of the yard and round the front of the buildings and to her relief she soon found the next signpost which led her down a narrow, rutted path towards a stone stile, slippery with moss.

She climbed the three slate steps and stared at the view. It was … she searched for a word to describe the feeling the landscape inspired, it was so … so … satisfying. Yes, completely satisfying. Nothing more, nothing less, was needed to make her feel so satisfied.

And just below she noticed that clump of trees. It seemed that the old man hadn't been hiding anything. He was right after all. She could see no house in the trees.

It was mid-afternoon when she'd returned to Croit Veg. The painters had gone, leaving only another noxious smell. "It's the spare room again tonight," she thought, picking up two letters from the hallway floor.

One looked interesting. With a Canadian stamp but redirected from her previous London address. She opened it eagerly as she waited for her soup to heat on the stove.

It was from the lady at the Toronto agency whom she'd contacted at least two months ago. She'd almost given up hope of receiving an answer. Legislation had changed a while ago enabling adopted children to trace their parents, but in Ginny's case it was almost impossible because she had not been put up for adoption, but abandoned.

So she'd enlisted a private investigator who specialised in such cases. Donna O'Sullivan had a good track record and hopefully she'd uncover something, even if all clues were long cold by now.

And according to what she read with mounting excitement, her researcher had unearthed some interesting stuff which would provide a reliable lead. "There's love, there's sex, but give me Rock and Roll," breathed Ginny.

Although opened windows had somewhat diluted the paint fumes, by 10.30 that night they were still unpleasantly strong and Ginny decided to use the second bedroom again. She mulled over Donna O'Sullivan's information as she undressed for bed.

The investigator had put adverts in all the major Ontario newspapers offering substantial rewards for any information that would lead to the discovery of the true identity of the abandoned baby. But as she felt Ginny's mother must have come from either Belleville or somewhere close by, she'd concentrated her primary search in that area. There had been a number of replies, two of which Donna indicated were promising and worth following up if Ginny agreed.

Ginny had partially drawn the curtains of the eastern window when she noticed the light again. She scrutinised the dark countryside around the square of orange-yellow. There was no doubt that it came from within that clump of trees she'd seen during the day.

Determined to discover what it was, she went into the other bedroom to fetch her pair of binoculars.

She kneeled on the floor, resting her elbows on the wooden sill in an attempt to steady them as she focused on the light. "I was right first time," she thought. It was a window. The light illuminated a four-paned window. The increased magnification also revealed something else that she'd not seen before, another similar window to the right, for it too emitted an extremely pale glow. So, there was a house there after all!

Why hadn't she been able to see it that afternoon from the

footpath? Perhaps her angle of vision from the stile had been wrong, she surmised, but deep down she knew this to be false, because she remembered with crystal clarity the image of the trees clustered around a small clearing ... and it had been empty.

The following day Ginny emailed Donna O'Sullivan, giving her permission to continue with the investigation in any way she thought fit. She spent the rest of the day writing up case notes from work. It was late afternoon by the time she'd finished but still light enough for a quick walk before supper.

Soon she was striding along the footpath in an easterly direction towards the little wood. She'd brought her binoculars and soon found a stretch of tall hedge bank, devoid of gorse, where she was able to scramble to the top.

"Now," she thought, focusing the binoculars on the wood, "let the mystery be revealed."

The trees had been planted within a rectangular enclosure, a mixture of stone walls and hedge banks. There was a lot of shrubby undergrowth covering the ground at the base of the trees but no sign of a house, except for an area which at first had looked like shrubs but in fact was a high stone wall covered with ivy and bramble. But nothing else. Nothing with windows. "Must have been an optical illusion," she muttered to herself.

That night she moved back into her own bedroom, but was unable to fall asleep as she pondered the light. "There'll be nothing there – what's the point of going to check it out now? There is no house ... trick of the light." But eventually she succumbed to her inner debate and went into the back bedroom to look.

And the light was there. Just as before. Orange-yellow. And it definitely was shining from a window.

"I give up," she thought, going back to bed. "This just

doesn't make sense."

The next week at work was manic.

And on Tuesday, she'd received the most exciting news imaginable. It came in the form of an email from Donna, informing her that she'd struck gold with one of the leads. She warned Ginny she had both good and bad news.

Good news was that she'd discovered the identity of Ginny's birth mother. She was Ellen Carmichael and originally from Winnipeg. It transpired that the person who had taken Ginny as a baby to the Belleville hospital in 1964 had been her mother's flatmate from Picton, a small town not far from Belleville. She was called Edith Svenson.

She'd helped 17-year-old Ellen through her unmarried pregnancy and had been under oath not to tell anyone about the baby girl's birth. When Edith returned from the hospital the flat was deserted. She never saw Ginny's mother again.

The bad news was that Ginny's mother had died of cancer two years ago. However, she'd left instructions in her will for her lawyer to find Edith and give her a letter and a gold watch.

Donna reported that Edith, relieved that the truth could finally be told, didn't want any of the reward money. She'd simply requested Ginny's address in order to dispatch the letter and the gold watch to her as soon as possible.

Donna had wanted confirmation that she could give it and of course Ginny did, by return email.

That Saturday morning at 8.30 a.m., Ginny's mobile kept signalling insistently that she had a text message.

"Oh my God!" she thought, as she reached for the phone on her bedside table, "another Saturday lie- in terminated!"

"No way!" she screeched, squinting at the message. And then the doorbell rang.

"Yep! It's Groundhog Day. Is it to be the painters again?" she growled, pulling on her dressing gown before she unlocked

218

the door.

She was wrong. It was a man from DHL with a package to sign for.

She ripped open the outer envelope. A letter, and in a pouch of reinforced wrapping, an old gold watch, the sort that men used to keep in waistcoat pockets on a chain.

She put on the kettle. She knew she'd need a drink in a minute and it was too early for alcohol, especially now she'd had that text from work.

It was impossible not to cry when she knew she was holding a piece of paper that her mother had once held and that after all these years she was looking at her mother's handwriting. "This is worse than 'Gone with the Wind'," she thought.

But there was no earth-shattering message, just a grammatically poor apology from a dying woman to someone from her past who'd helped her and been deserted without a thank you after the Fat Lady had finished singing – or screaming? No mention of who the father was or anything else, just a reference to the gold watch saying: "*It was given to me by my grandfather who had it from his father, and it had been his father's too. So I guess it is pretty old and as it had been special to Gramps I've hung onto it all these years. But now I'm about to meet my maker and there is no more need of a timepiece that never worked anyhow, so perhaps you could try to find the baby now she's growed up and give it to her. And say I'm sorry, about the way things turned out. I've not been a good mother and I regret it, especially as she's the only child I ever had. If I'd knowed then what I know now, I'd never have let her go.*"

Ginny heaved a deep breath. Perhaps it was better this way.

Ginny was the person she was because of everything in the past. She couldn't change it. Who or what would she have been if Ellen Carmichael *had* kept her?

"Just go with the flow, Honey." That was what her adoptive

father had always said … and the image of salmon suddenly came into her thoughts, going with the flow of the river at one point but against it when they had to fight their way home against the water. Which 'flow' mattered the most, she wondered?

The telephone rang. It was Ruth, her department head. "Ginny, did you get the text message? I'm sorry, I know Marilyn's on call, but she was rushed into hospital last night. It is quite urgent and you live so close. I'm in Andreas at the moment, due in Ramsey in half an hour. I don't know when I could get there …"

"No worries. I'll do it … just don't know how he'll react when he sees it's me!"

Ginny dressed quickly and whilst she drank her coffee she examined the old gold watch. It was rose gold, solid and time-worn around the edges. She opened the front case.

The watch face was a creamy colour with the words 'R. M. Adam, Douglas' in black, with simple Roman Numerals and gold filigree fingers engraved in a Celtic design. The interior of the case front was inscribed, '*To My Beloved Son, William, August 1st 1820*'.

"It's beautiful," she thought. "I'll see if I can find somebody to get it working again and then I'll use it all the time." She hastily rewrapped it and stuffed it into her handbag.

She dashed to her car and drove as quickly as she could to where she'd been directed by the text from work. It seemed that the neighbouring farm was not derelict after all; it was inhabited by that grouchy old man.

"Come in. They told me yer was on yer way." Ginny recognised his voice, but remembering last week ,was reluctant to enter.

"Get in here. The dogs are in the back."

She cautiously entered the dark room. He was lying on an

old sofa in front of the fireplace. There were only ashes in the grate. The room was cold. And filthy.

His face was pale, contorted with pain, but his feistiness returned upon sight of her.

"What are yer doing back here? Clear off!" he gasped.

"No, don't worry. I'm here in a professional capacity. Nobles OT unit have sent me."

"Oh," he growled suspiciously, "suppose yer'd better come in then." He arched convulsively, grabbing at his throat and the front of his chest.

"Not a heart attack as well?" Ginny wondered, rushing to his side.

"So … tell me where you're hurting" she asked.

"All over – but worse in my jaw and the front of my chest."

"Let's get your jacket off, and that waistcoat." She tried to help him remove the jacket, but he was the most cantankerous old man she'd ever had to deal with.

"Keep yer thieving hands off me, you pickpocket!" he shouted.

"Mr Kinvig, I'm not a pickpocket. I'm just trying to help you."

"Nonsense!" he screeched. "Yer a thief! Yer after my watch. But yer not going to get it. I'll set the dogs on yer first!"

"Mr Kinvig, I don't need your watch," exclaimed Ginny and in a moment of inspiration, produced her gold watch from her bag, waggling it in front of his face. "See, I've got a beautiful one of my own."

"That's mine!" he shouted.

"No. This is mine. It came from my great grandfather, might be great great, but I've not had time to work that one out yet!"

He fumbled anxiously in one of his waistcoat pockets and produced a gold watch. Relieved that he still had it, he began to look rather avariciously at Ginny's.

A Tail for All Seasons

"Let me see that!" he grabbed at it and flicked it open. His expression froze and his eyes stared in disbelief. "It's William's …" he slumped back against the sofa, staring at her in amazement.

"How've yer got William's watch?"

"It's a long story. But the abbreviated form goes something like this: it only arrived this morning, sent to me by somebody I've never met, from a mother I've never known. I am led to believe that William is my ancestor. But how many great greats are involved I just do not know! But more to the point, who is William to you?" hissed Ginny, who was by now at the end of her emotional tether.

Mr Benjamin Kinvig straightened his shoulders, cleared his throat and sniffed deeply. "William Kinvig was the twin brother of my great great grandfather, Henry Kinvig. There were two identical watches made by Mr R. A. Adam of Douglas for their twenty-first birthday presents on 1st August 1820, commissioned by their father Ezekiah. The three legs of Mann are engraved on the inside of the case back. Look!"

She'd missed that and stooped forwards to study it. Sure enough, hers also had the Manx triskelion, the national three-legged symbol, and around it the Latin words '*Quocunque Jeceris Stabit*', which she knew translated as 'Wherever you throw it, it stands'.

"So how did William's watch get to be in Canada?" asked Ginny, sitting down beside the old man.

"According to the family Bible over there," he indicated an enormous leather-bound tome currently adding extra support to a table leg, "on the inside page recording the family births, marriages and deaths, William's widow, Ellen, gave the watch to her eldest son Juan on 12th August 1867 when he left for the colonies because there wasn't enough land to support two brothers. He left his share to Edgar, his younger brother. Juan

222

must have been a good man; it were usually the other way round. I know all the entries off by heart – I learned to read from that Bible. Edgar, Juan's younger brother was killed in a nasty accident in 1869, leaving his mother Ellen alone for the rest of her life. She was looked after by her brother-in-law, William's brother, Henry. If yer wish to read the notes in the Bible yer'll see that she lived in Crot na Cushag, the place yer asked about last week. But the house has fallen down now. Only a few rough walls left, though the land is still sweet. The family have farmed it all these years because Ellen wanted the place left for Juan's children. She said they'd come home – one day. Read it … it's all written in the Family Bible … and legal paperwork lodged with a firm of advocates in Douglas."

"Which means …" breathed Ginny with disbelief, "that we are related."

The two looked at each other in horror.

But what Ben Kinvig couldn't tell Ginny, because he didn't know, was that very early on that morning of 12th August 1867, Juan Kinvig had left to walk to Douglas, to catch the ferry to Liverpool.

He did not know where he was headed after that, just the first ship from Liverpool that would let him work his passage to Canada or Australia, where new land offered hope and opportunity.

As he kissed his mother goodbye, she pressed a small leather watch pouch into his hand. "Your father, God rest his soul, would have wanted you to take this," she said, her voice breaking with emotion.

The young man's excitement at the prospect of his imminent departure was as great as his mother's grief at his going. "Don't worry, mother," he said fervently, holding her in his arms. "I'll be back with bags of gold to warm you in your old age and childer to rock upon your knee at the hearth."

"And I'll be waiting, my son. Until that time comes, Juan, there'll always be a lighted lamp set upon the window sill. I'll keep it burning every night to guide you and your childer safely home. I'll be waiting … for all of you."

❧ october ❧

Paul Quaggan was born on the Isle of Man and lives in the north of the Island with his wife Angela. Before retirement he had his own decorating and sign-writing business and was at one time the proprietor of two local hostelries and a private hotel.

Since retiring Paul has had time to concentrate on his two main loves, writing and watercolour painting.

His story 'One Day in May' was included in the first volume of *A Tail for All Seasons*.

The state of
pandemonium

Paul Quaggan

"There we are now, dear." Ruth pointed to a white plastic bag sitting on the kitchen worktop. "I've filled a Thermos with boiling water and I've included a couple of tea bags, a small bottle of milk and a teaspoon. Also, there's a sachet of your favourite mushroom soup. All you have to do is add water. Oh, and as an added treat I've thrown in two or three of Gladys Convery's fairy cakes for afters."

"Fairy cakes!" I exclaimed. "You know I can't abide Gladys Convery's fairy cakes!"

"But it was *you* who bought them at the church coffee morning last Saturday."

"What choice did I have? The vicar is always expected to buy something and it was a choice between Gladys's stale fairy cakes or one of Emily Quine's sponges, and as a rule, they're as flat as a pancake!" I glanced briefly into the bag. "You do realise I'm only planning to ride as far as Castletown and back. I'm not spending the night on the Calf!" There was no response, so, with a peck on the cheek and a fond farewell, I made my way into the garage and proceeded to extricate my sturdy old Raleigh bicycle from beneath a pile of empty potato sacks. With its three-speed Sturmey-Archer hub gears and dynamo lights, I must admit it wasn't the most sophisticated machine around. The large wicker basket attached to the front of the handlebars didn't do much for its street credibility either, but it had served me well over the years and so it was that after giving it a quick dust down and a check of the tyre pressures, we were ready for the off. That was when Ruth came hurrying down the drive.

"After lunch, I may catch the bus into town and do a spot of window shopping. OK?" She stared at my ankles and smiled. "You don't see many people wearing cycle clips these days, do you?"

With a half hidden sneer and a casual wave, I was on my way, grateful that I didn't have to drive her into town in the car.

Although approaching mid-October, it was an extremely warm and pleasant autumn day. The recent rain and high winds had turned the leaves to a mixture of creamy yellow and rusty orange as they slowly began to fall from the tall trees that lined the road leading south. Rounding the bends at Ballalonna, the Fairy Bridge came into view. This, I thought, was as good a place as any to rest my weary legs. Propping my bicycle up against the trunk of a conveniently placed sycamore, I gently picked my way down the sloping bank beneath the bridge. Finding a large boulder to sit on, I proceeded to open the sachet of powdered soup and shake it into the plastic cup belonging to the Thermos flask. All that was needed now was to add some boiling water …

I hesitated. Strange though it may seem, I was certain that a fairly large round boulder, no more than a few feet further down the slope, was slowly moving sideways. Could it be that my eyesight was playing tricks with me? Maybe Ruth had been right after all. Perhaps I should have gone to that well-known firm of opticians in town. But no, there it was again. This was definitely no illusion. Hesitantly at first but then as if on well-oiled runners, the boulder glided gently to one side. Suddenly, it came to an abrupt halt. At first, nothing. All was quiet. Then, after some huffing and puffing, not to mention more than a little choice language, they came into view. Climbing up out of a hole in the ground and barely visible through the tall tussocks of couch grass, were a man and a woman. Albeit a very tiny man and an even tinier woman.

"How's it goin', yessir?" With shoulder-length silver-grey hair and standing no more than nine or ten inches in height, the little man struggled to make his way towards me through the long undergrowth. Without as much as a glance at the little woman, he shouted, "Are yer alright, gal?" It was as if he already knew the answer and within seconds, it became perfectly obvious why. With her long blonde hair, flowing in waves behind her and crowned with a chain of small white daisies, she took off and only then did I realise that, unlike her male companion, she sported the most gorgeously delicate pair of gossamer wings. As she landed with expert precision beside me, it was easy to imagine that for the first time in my life, I had come face to face with a real live fairy. If there was any doubt in my mind, it wasn't so much the intricately woven white lace leotard or the matching silk tights that she wore. It was the frilly, pastel pink tutu, the deep blue woollen legwarmers and the bright red ballet shoes that really threw me.

Finally, reaching the foot of the boulder, the little man held out a hand, "Gawd damn missus! Are yer goin' t' give me a hand up or not?"

"Here," she replied and with that, reached out to help him. "It's a good job one of us has got wings, otherwise we'd never get anywhere!"

Now I could see him more clearly. He was smartly dressed in a white shirt and trousers which in turn were tucked inside an equally sparkling pair of white, knee-length stockings. An emerald green sleeveless tunic was complimented by a wide black leather belt complete with a large brass buckle which matched those that adorned his black ankle boots.

"That's better," he sighed, dusting the grass seeds from the front of his tunic. "It's about time the Department got some sheep over here to eat this grass down a lil' bit."

"Sheep!" the woman laughed, at the same time fluttering her wings. "They won't bother me but *you'll* have t' watch where yer walkin'."

"All right woman," he sneered. "We all know yer can fly!" With that, he clambered over my left thigh, stood directly in front of me, held out his right hand and proclaimed, "Allow me to introduce myself. I'm Digby Cormode and this is my wife, Yelena." He shook my hand and she, in turn, gave a deep curtsey. Acknowledging her with a brief nod, I couldn't help thinking that for all the world, she reminded me of one of those ballerinas that used to be popular on the top of musical boxes. Apart from the leg-warmers, that is.

"Er ... pleased to meet you," I stuttered, still somewhat taken aback by what I was witnessing. "I'm the Reverend Bertram Handley-Stowell. I'm just taking a breather on my journey south."

The strange little man appeared to sense my acute fear and trepidation although just why I was feeling that way was a complete mystery. Neither Digby nor his wife could be described as frightening. Odd, yes. Even weird perhaps, but most definitely not frightening.

"It's all right, boy. Yer not trespassin' or anythin' like that." He cast an eye in the direction of Yelena who offered the faintest of smiles, at the same time attempting to push her husband even closer to me. "Oh, aye," he muttered. "Almost forgot to ask. Would yer like us t' show yer around?"

"Around what?" I asked.

"Our humble abode, that's what." Digby half turned and pointed in the direction of the opening in the ground that had been left by the sliding boulder. "Down there."

I looked myself up and down. "I think that would be well nigh impossible, don't you?" There was no response. He was too busy struggling to extract something from one of the deep pockets in his tunic. Eventually, the little man pulled out what looked suspiciously like a sachet of instant soup.

Pointing to my plastic cup, he asked. "What have yer got in there, then?"

"Mushroom soup," I replied.

"Now there's a coincidence, yessir." He shook the sachet in front of my eyes. "This here's mushroom soup but with a difference. It's magic mushroom." He reached out to take my cup. "Let's tip yours away Reverend, an' fill her up with this, instead."

Quickly, I pulled the cup away. "I'd rather not if you don't mind. Magic mushrooms and the like have never been my ..."

"No! No!" interrupted Digby. "This is *magical* mushroom soup. One or two swigs o' this stuff an' when yer step down into the hole, yer'll be the same height as us, give or take the odd half inch. More than that. Yer'll move forward into our era."

"*Your* era!"

"Oh, aye. Yer see, usually when strange mythical things like this happen, folk always end up goin' back in time." The little man gave a nod and a wink. "Not with us Bertie, yer don't. No ancient fairy stories with us, at all. We're twenty years ahead o' yer, down here. Come below ground with us an' yer'll travel

231

a couple o' decades into the future."

"Oh dear!" I said. "I'm not sure I like the sound of that."

"Don't worry," he said, reassuringly. "Once yer come back up, things will return t' normal. They always do." Slowly, he stroked his forehead. "Mind you, there was that fella from up Foxdale way. Never did find out what became o' him!"

My first reaction was to look to the heavens for guidance but decided I would be extremely lucky to get any sort of response from that quarter and so it was that somewhat reluctantly, I allowed myself to partake of my new-found friend's magical mushroom potion. Suddenly, for no apparent reason, Yelena took off, landed on a nearby rock and with arms fully outstretched above her head and fingertips barely touching, balanced on the points of her toes and performed two perfect pirouettes. Then, following a deep curtsey, flew back alongside her husband.

Digby spotted the startled expression on my face. "Take no notice, boy. Yer'll get used t' the wife's antics after a while."

"Tell me," I enquired. "What type of community do you have here?"

"Well now." The little man ran his fingers through what was, for someone of such diminutive size, a rather fine head of hair and glanced across at Yelena, but once more she ignored him completely. "You'll understan' better than most, Reverend. We're what they call the 'Middle World People'. When the day o' judgement finally arrives, we're not good enough t' go up t' Heaven. Yet, at the same time, not bad enough t' end up in that place where the heat makes global warmin' seem like a return t' the Ice Age!"

"Sorry, but I'm still not clear …"

"Don't yer see? We're a sort o' halfway house. A place to accommodate those who may not be angels yet at the same time aren't lil' devils, either."

Yelena, having now fluttered to the ground, held out a helping hand to her husband as he gently slid down off the boulder.

On landing, Digby pointed to my ankles. "Before we go down, would yer mind removin' those cycle clips an' yer watch as well, if yer've got one. This here soup doesn't work too well on metal and it might restrict yer shrinkage – and yer time warp!" He gestured towards my plastic bag. "Why don't yer put everythin' in there an' hang the lot over a branch o' that sycamore?" He stretched to a full twelve inches in an attempt to peer into the bag. "Nothin' valuable at yer, is there?"

"No," I replied quite innocently. "Only some fairy cakes."

"*What!*" he bawled. "Whoever gave yer permission t' use the word *fairy*?"

"Sorry, I hadn't realised. I'm afraid it was one of my parishioners, Gladys Convery who actually baked them."

"They really do get up me nose, these people." By the colour of his cheeks, which had now turned a deep shade of puce, Digby Cormode was not a happy little man. "Fairy cakes, fairy lights, fairy stories. I'll tell yer what, if this Gladys what's her name ends up down here, she'll be on a charge, straight away!"

By now we had reached the entrance to what turned out to be quite a large hole in the ground. "Climb down that ladder a lil' way an' hol' on tight. Before yer know it, yer'll be no bigger than me and the missus."

Somewhat reluctantly, I did as I was told and lo and behold, I could feel my body decreasing rapidly. One thing about these magic mushrooms, they sure were guaranteed to produce instant results. The little man held out his hand to steady me as I stepped off the bottom rung of the bright yellow ladder. Now, I was the same height as my hosts, give or take the odd half inch or two.

"Tell the man! Tell him what yer do!" Yelena grabbed his

arm and shook it vigorously.

"*All right, all right, woman!* Keep yer leg-warmers on!"

"Tell me what?" I enquired.

Digby carefully placed a thumb in each of the deep pockets of his tunic, stuck out his chest and declared, "As Minister of Information an' Dancin', may I welcome yer t' the State of Pandemonium."

"*Pandemonium!*" I exclaimed. "That seems a rather unusual name for a place like this."

"Ah, yer wouldn' be sayin' that if yer was down here on a clear, starry night with a full moon shinin', I can tell yer." He smiled and shook his head. "What with all them young ones fightin' t' get up through that hole an' do their dancin' an' creatin' fairy rings an' what have yer, pandemonium's not the word for it, yessir!"

I struggled to keep a straight face. "How many of you fairies live down here in … ahem … Pandemonium?"

Digby stared at me with a stern expression on his face. "Let's get one thing straight, boy."

"Pardon?"

"Mooinjer veggey. It's Manx for lil' fellas but if that's too hard t' say, yer can call me a phynnodderee." He looked across at his wife. "Now the missus couldn' care less what yer call her but let me tell yer – I'm no *fairy!*"

I was about to apologise when my eyes were drawn to Yelena who once more, with arms outstretched above her head and balancing on the tips of her toes, was in the process of executing two perfect pirouettes. On completing the task, she came 'back down to earth', curtseyed and then continued as if nothing had happened.

"Sorry," I said, at the same time attempting to show little or no surprise. "It's just that most people refer to you as …"

"Oh, I know the ones yer mean. Them, what's goin' past in

cars an' buses, shoutin' 'Hello fairies', 'How yer doin' fairies', 'Ta-ta lil' fairies' an' all because they're worried we might give them a puncture." The little man gave a loud 'tut'. "Don't they know we've got better things t' do than go gallivantin' about the countryside strugglin' t' stick nails in their tyres?"

I smiled and gave a brief nod of agreement.

Suddenly, Digby looked me straight in the eye and exclaimed. "*My Gawd*, I know that face o' yours from somewhere!"

"Hardly," I replied. "I wouldn't think so."

He thought for a second or two. "Yer not that fella with the double-barrelled name that used t' take off Elvis over at the Balqueen Hotel in the early seventies, are yer?"

"Afraid not. Pop music was never my scene. Besides, I couldn't possibly know you, I've never been down here in Ballalonna Glen before today."

"Hol' on now, boy. I haven't always been down here meself. In fact, if it hadn' been for the wife here an' Dolores, I might not be ..."

"*Dolores?*"

"Aye. She used to be me PA amongst other things. I had a bit of a thingy goin' with her but unfortunately Yelena found out an' when I came home one night, she was waitin' for me on the landin'. There was a bit of a scuffle an' she ended up pushin' me down the stairs! Finished me off right away and because I'd been a naughty boy so t' speak, I ended up down here."

"But what about Yelena?"

"Ah, well now." He gently rubbed his fingers across the back of his neck. "About ten days later the Registrar told me that I would be joined that afternoon by the love o' me life. I have to be honest, yessir, but I had hoped it would be Dolores. Then, waitin' at the bottom o' the ladder, I spotted a pair of unmistakeable Queen Anne table legs startin' t' descend an' I knew straight away, it was the missus!"

"Obviously she couldn't go on without you."

Digby gave a hearty laugh. "Yer mus' be jokin'! Unknowns t' me, in the struggle Yelena got her chiffon scarf caught up in me braces an' inadvertently, I dragged her down the stairs behind me. She held out for a few days but then, when she finally did succumb it was down here that she came. Although the Coroner reckoned she'd committed manslaughter, he decided that she'd had every justification, as they say!"

"Nice place you have here," I remarked, quickly trying to change the subject. Looking around, I could make out a network of long, narrow passages. The ceilings and walls were decorated in what appeared to be one continuous length of very delicate apple-green lace, complimented by a considerable number of doors coated in a sparkling shade of diamond white. But it was the floors that really caught my eye.

"What d' yer think of it, then." Digby smiled with pride as he witnessed the look of awe written across my face.

"Very smart. Especially the floors!"

"Yer lookin' at the best quality glueless spruce laminate that money can buy." He tapped the highly polished surface gently with the sole of his boot as if to prove the point. "Got a job lot of it from a group o' mooinjer veggey over at Chibbanagh. Did most o' the work meself an' I think yer'll agree I've made a fair t' middlin' job of it?"

"Yes, excellent."

"The wife's not very keen but then, nothin' ever satisfies her."

I glanced at Yelena to gauge her reaction but there was none.

Digby laughed. "It's all right. She's a bit hard o' hearin', especially on her left han' side."

As it happened, it wouldn't have mattered which side we

were on as by now, this wannabe ballerina had once more gone into her 'Nutcracker' routine and was totally oblivious to everything around her. Curiosity really was beginning to get the better of me by now, the problem being how to broach the subject without causing offence. It's not that simple, having to ask a man to explain why his wife breaks into a ballet dance every few minutes, even if she is a fairy. Fortunately the little man must have spotted the puzzled expression on my face.

"I know what's buggin' yer, boy."

"Pardon?"

"It's the missus, isn't it?"

"Well," I confessed. "I am slightly puzzled …"

"All my fault. I hold me hands up," and he did just that, in a gesture of exasperation. "Went and bought this video one Christmas, didn't I? A late forties film *The Red Shoes*, starrin' that ballet dancin' woman, Moira Shearer. Biggest mistake I ever made."

"Oh, I rather enjoyed …"

"Yelena wouldn' leave it alone. Playin' it and playin' it and forever practisin' in front o' the telly until she ended up with OCD." Digby gave a deep sigh. "Obsessive … Compulsive … Disorder, that's what's wrong with her. Every five bleedin' minutes!"

"Are you trying to tell me that your wife performs this double pirouette routine every five minutes or so throughout the day?"

"There's no 'or so' about it, yessir!" He rubbed a hand across his brow. "After four minutes and fifty nine seconds precisely, she's on the startin' blocks an' rarin' t' go. Hells bells, yer could set yer ruddy watch by her!"

"I suppose it's all that Russian blood in her veins."

"Well spotted, boy! She's a Rushen gal, alright. One o' the Corteens from Ballakilpheric."

He hesitated for a second or two. "How did yer work that

out?"

"*No! No!*" I exclaimed. "I meant Russia, the country. Moscow, Siberia ..."

Digby burst out laughing. "Oh dear. Yer a bit of a hard man on the quiet. Whatever gave yer the idea she came from Russia?"

"Surely, with a name like Yelena, she must come from some part of Eastern Europe?"

"Glory be! That's only a handle she's given herself. Her real name's Elsie. Tell yer what," he laughed, "Yer don't get many gals called Yelena comin' from Ballakilpheric, that's for sure!"

As we strode along the narrow passageways, I couldn't help noticing something rather odd about the majority of Pandemonium's residents. Their sole form of transport appeared to be skateboards and although most people seemed to own one, none were actually being ridden. Without exception, everyone was carrying them under their arms!

"Anyway, enough o' the missus." Digby took hold of my arm and ushered me into what had the overall appearance of a tiny chapel. "This should be right up your street, Reverend."

"Very nice indeed," I remarked, admiring the pure white walls, the half dozen or so dark oak pews, the highly carved decorative altar and the spruce laminate flooring. "Tell me, what denomination are you folk?"

"Oh, we don't go in for anythin' like that. We have what they call a secular society. Less trouble that way."

"Well, yes," I said. "Although I seem to remember that Saddam Hussein used to boast that he ..."

"I went t' school with his brother, Caesar!"

Like a pair of synchronised swimmers emerging from the water, feet first and in perfect harmony, both Digby and I turned and stared at his other half. For a second or two there was complete silence. Then the little man spoke. "No, no, dear. *Saddam Hussein!*"

Yelena scowled and stamped her foot on the floor. *"Ouch!"* she squealed, suddenly realizing that ballet shoes offer little or no protection against stubbing one's toe on a hard laminate surface. "Gawd damn, Digby! Yer really can be a cussard oul' beggar when yer want t' be."

"Why? What have I said now?"

"I'm tellin' yer and I should know. I was at school with *Caesar* Costain!" She bent down and gave her stubbed toe a gentle rub. "His brother, Sammy Costain was *years* older than me!"

The little man looked at me, shook his head and mumbled something about his other half being 'away to the hills'. "Mind yer back, boy," he said, at the same time, guiding me closer to the wall. "Don't want yer gettin' run over now, do we?"

"No, but I haven't seen any traffic apart from skateboards and even then, everyone is carrying ..." Momentarily, I was distracted by Yelena, commencing another round of her antics.

"That's correct. We only allow skateboards but my goodness, there's a heck of a lot o' them about."

"Maybe," I queried. "But why are all ...?"

Digby smiled. "Why are they all carryin' them?" Once more, the little phynnodderee placed a thumb in each pocket of his tunic and stuck out his chest, even further than before. "All down t' me, I'm pleased t' say. As yer can imagine, a lot o' people down here, includin' the Chief Minister, sleep durin' the day an' the sound of all those skateboards on the hard floor was drivin' them mad. So the Minister o' Passageways decided t' ban them altogether." He hesitated just long enough to clear his throat. "That's when most o' the residents objected an' got up a petition. They asked me t' mediate an' after long discussions, we came to a compromise. Everybody was allowed t' keep their skateboards."

"So it was a victory for the people, then?"

"Well, yes an' no. They were only permitted t' keep them provided they carried them under their arms!" He gave a deep sigh. "Still, everybody's happy an' that's all that matters."

I was sorely tempted to ask the obvious but by now Digby was pointing to a sign on one of the many doors which stated

CHRISTMAS FAIRY DEPT.
ADVANCED TRAINING CENTRE
Closed Until Further Notice

"Not worth lookin' in here, yessir. Hasn't been used for years."

"Oh," I said. "Why is that?"

"Times have changed. I can remember when it was big business hirin' out fairies for the top o' Christmas trees. Give them a good dose o' that magical mushroom soup an' they'd shrink t' three or four inches in no time!"

"But Christmas is just as popular as ever, surely?"

"Too popular, that's the trouble." The Minister of Information and Dancing shook his head. "Years ago, Christmas used t' last for about twelve days or so but then everythin' changed. Now, it all starts at the beginnin' o' December an' goes right through t' the middle o' January. That's when we said 'enough's enough'. It's no joke bein' perched on the top of a Christmas tree for six weeks, what with all them lights scorchin' yer, dogs growlin' at yer, cats tryin' t' climb up and claw yer an' worst of all, cheeky kids tryin' t' pop balloons on the point o' yer star!"

As we moved along the corridor, keeping well out of the way of the many residents who scurried past, I could see a woman struggling towards us with a skateboard under each arm.

"Yer've got yer hands full there, Lena," remarked Digby.

"Yes," said the woman, panting heavily and nodding in the direction of the large skateboard under her left arm. "This one's Charlie's. One of the rollers developed a squeak on his way home from work this morning. It's been in Performance Boards workshop getting fixed!" With that, she took a deep breath and continued on her way.

Digby, with not even an element of surprise on his rosy-cheeked face, carried on walking. Eventually, we arrived at a door displaying a large plastic sign which read

TOOTH FAIRY
Please Knock

"Now," said Digby with a slight sense of pride. "I think yer'll find this lil' room very interestin'." He bent down and attempted to take a peep through the large keyhole. "I hope she's awake."

"Regularly sleeps during the day, does she?"

"Oh, my word, yes!" he exclaimed. "A lot o' night work involved in her job, boy." The little man gave a loud knock on the door and immediately, took two paces back. "She can be a funny oul devil when she wants to be," he whispered rather timidly.

There was a short interval then slowly, the door opened. Standing there with a face like thunder, was an elderly woman with prune-like skin, drooping wings and long, bedraggled white hair that looked as if it hadn't seen a brush or comb for months. *"Huh!"* she snarled. "I might have guessed it would be you." She rubbed the sleep from her eyes. "What are *you* after?"

Digby hurriedly took another pace back. "Sorry t' disturb yer Peg but I'm givin' this fella a bit of a conducted tour."

"Well," she groaned, half turning and pointing into the

room. "He's not goin' t' see much in here Digby, is he now?" She couldn't have spoken a truer word. From wall to wall and floor to ceiling, the room was stacked with cardboard cartons. "Boxes! Boxes! Yer can't move for boxes an' what's in them all – kids teeth!" She swung round sharply. "I thought yer were goin' t' knock through into nex' door an' give me the extra space?"

"I am! I am!" pleaded Digby. "But yer know what it's like tryin' t' get hold of a builder."

"Ah, well. Yer goin' t' have t' do somethin'. I'm gettin' snowed under in here with teeth." She pointed a long crooked finger at the tiny phynnodderee. "An' before yer ask … no, the binmen *won't* take them!"

Digby started to move on but not before the old lady shouted, "That's another thing, Digby Cormode. I'm puttin' in for a subsidy. The days when kids were happy with a 6d piece are long gone. Now they're lookin' for at least a fiver!" She must have noticed my expression of surprise. "You forget, yessir! We're twenty years ahead o' you." The Tooth Fairy shook her head. "I never thought I'd live t' see the day when it would cost yer £1.20 for a local stamp!"

"I'll see what I can do, Peg."

"Aye, well. Yer'd better do somethin' quick or otherwise I'll have t' ask for a move t' the Department of Agriculture an' Fairy Rings."

"Agriculture! Whatever have Tooth Fairies got t' do with agriculture?"

"Well, at least I'll get a subsidy. Them farmers only have t' sneeze an' they get money for a box o' Kleenex!"

"Point taken. I'll see what I can do."

"By the way Digby," she shouted. "I see the wife's not gettin' any better!"

We turned, just in time to witness Yelena performing

242

another of her dances from the roof of what was obviously a green telephone kiosk, judging by the word 'PHYNNODDERCOM' emblazoned above the door.

"My Gawd!" exclaimed Peg. "Yer deserve a bleedin' medal havin' t' put up with that one, twenty-four hours a day!" With that, she stepped back inside and slammed the door.

The tiny phynnodderee ushered me forward and the fairy ballerina, having completed her pirouettes and curtsey, flew down alongside us, totally ignorant of the unfavourable comments that Peg, the Tooth Fairy had made about her.

Arriving at a crossroads, Digby stuck his hand out in front of me. "Watch yer step, boy. It can get quite busy here at times." He pointed to a small circular groove in the laminate flooring. "Tried a roundabout here once but it was a waste o' time. They jus' kept on goin' straight over the top of it!" Momentarily, the Minister of Information and Dancing stopped and looked me straight in the eye. "That name o' yours is buggin' me. I'm sure I've heard it before, somewhere."

I gave the faintest of smiles and changed the subject. "What goes on up these side roads?"

"Nothin' much," he replied, pointing to the passageway on his left. "That's the residential area but apart from those yer see whizzin' aroun' with skateboards, the majority will be asleep durin' the day." He pointed in the opposite direction. "This side houses the Government buildin's but them fellas only surface at night, as well. Even then, they spend most o' the time drinkin' coffee and warmin' their backsides on the radiators!" He tapped me on the shoulder and smiled. "Nothin' new there then, boy!"

Continuing on our tour, I could make out the bright yellow ladder at the end of the passage.

"I'll jus' let yer have a lil' skeet in here before yer go." Digby pointed to a large illuminated sign above a pair of double doors which said

WELCOME TO
THE PANDEMONIUM
PALAIS de DANSE

Swinging open the doors, the little man declared. "This is our *piece de resistance!*"

In front of me was a large room, decorated and furnished in the same restful style as the rest of this tiny State. A considerable area in the centre of the 'job-lot' laminate floor was clear, with tables and chairs arranged down each side. At the far end stood a small stage, flanked either side by gold-trimmed, moss-green velvet curtains.

"C'mon in." He gave a broad grin. "Plenty o' seats an' not a red an' white polka-dotted toadstool anywhere!"

Walking into the room, I couldn't help but notice a door on my right, clearly marked 'CLOAKROOM'. Opposite was an open space. Fixed to the wall alongside was a blue sign with a large white letter 'P' on it. Underneath were the words

SKATEBOARDS ONLY *(No Wings)*

Digby outstretched both arms and swung round in a half circle. "We meet here for a cup o' nectar tea an' a bit of a natter. Most of all, this is where we run our monthly dances."

"Dances?"

"Oh aye, an' very popular they are too." He glanced at Yelena who responded with just the faintest suggestion of a curtsey. "We get a wide an' varied selection o' fairies an' phynnodderees on dance nights. Even get a few elves turnin' up occasionally. Mind yer, most o' *them* come from 'across' an' can get a lil' bit mischievous at times but … we keep a close eye on them!"

"They're not just from this area, then?"

"Oh no, no, Ballasalla, Kewaigue. You name it, we get them

all down here." The little man put a hand on my shoulder. "Yer won't believe this, yessir but one night las' summer, we had a coach load o' gnomes turn up from Laxey."

"Laxey!"

"Aye. Apparently, they're well-known out Lonan way as the 'Afdags'."

"My word," I said. "Now that *does* sound rather Manx."

Digby roared with laughter. "Good grief, no! Nothin' like that. It stands for the Agneash Formation Dance Association o' Gnomes."

"Strange you should mention dancing," I remarked. "At last month's meeting of our Church Council, a suggestion was put forward that we should consider organising dances in the Church Hall. Perhaps you could offer me some advice?"

"Nothin' to it really." Digby thought for a moment or two. "There is one thing, though."

"Yes?"

"Whatever yer do, don't invite any gnomes! Don't get me wrong, they're nice enough lil' folk. The only trouble is, there's no 'go' in any o' them. That crowd that came down from Laxey jus' wanted t' sit there all night, starin' straight ahead. Excep' for the three that brought their fishin' rods with them. Insisted on spendin' the whole night sittin' down by the river." He shrugged his shoulders. "Wouldn' mind, but them fellas couldn' catch a cold, let alone a trout!"

By now, I was beginning to develop the knack of keeping one eye on the phynnodderee and the other on his performing wife. But on this occasion, judging by the startled look on his face, even Digby was taken by surprise as Yelena, without as much as an 'excuse me', flew between us, made a perfect landing on the stage and performed two perfect pirouettes, both worthy of at least an 8 or, if pushed, even a 9.5! A quick curtsey and she landed quite nonchalantly beside us once more.

"My Gawd, *yessir*! The wife certainly *has* took a fancy t' you!"

"But surely," I remarked. "Doesn't she do her ballet thingy every five minutes, regardless of who is watching?"

"But that's what I'm tryin' t' tell yer. It's only three minutes an' forty five seconds since she did the las' one!"

It really was time to go. Before making my way to the ladder, I turned and shook hands with the little man. "Thank you for everything and I pray that Yelena can rid herself of this most unfortunate obsession."

"Not t' worry. It could be worse."

"Really?"

Digby stroked his chin. "Let me see, now. It would be about a year ago." He pointed to a table by the door. "We were comin' in here one night when I spotted this DVD. One look an' I was horrified!"

"Good Heaven's. Was it that bad?"

"Bad enough for me t' grab hol' of it and stuff it up me tunic before the wife spotted it. Put the fear o' Gawd up me!"

"But what could be that frightening?" I thought for a moment before continuing. "Jaws? The Exorcist? Not the Texas Chainsaw Massacres?"

"Far worse than any o' them, Reverend!" He leant forward and whispered in my ear. "It was called 'The Best of ... *Riverdance*'!"

"Riverdance!" I exclaimed. "Frightening? But my wife loves to watch ..."

"Hol' on now, Bertie! Yer've seen what's happened t' Yelena with that *Red Shoes* film. Jus' think what could have occurred if she'd have got hooked on Riverdance!" Digby held up his hands in despair. "Picture the scene, yessir. Wednesday night. Champions League footy on the box. Feet up, remote control in one hand, a can o' Bobtail's Strong Mead in the other an' suddenly, without any warnin', the missus with her nose in the air, straightened back, hands down by her sides, bringin' her knees up so high they're almost catchin' her chin, comes chargin' through from the hall, rattatatat, rattatatat, rattatatat in those Cuban heels o' hers. Straight across the laminate floor o' the livin' room an' into the kitchen. Turns, wipes the sweat from her brow and then rattatatat, rattatatat, rattatatats her way back across the room and out into the hall again!" He shook his head from side to side. "Every five bleedin' minutes! Hell's bell's! Man United would never seem the same again!"

As he finished speaking, Yelena stepped forward and with both hands gripped the hem of her tutu and gave a deep curtsey.

"Thank you *very* much," I said, whereupon she stood on the points of her toes and gave a perfect performance, followed by three encores.

"Jus' hol' on, there." The little phynnodderee ignored his wife and walked over to an alcove alongside the ladder. Putting his right eye to something which bore a strong resemblance to a periscope, he shouted, "All clear! Safe t' surface."

"My word," I remarked. "That's a very useful piece of equipment."

"Oh, aye. Comes up through the stump of an oul' willow down by the river." He gave a deep sigh. "It's not ideal but it serves the purpose. One year, we had it comin' up through the stem of a big yella plastic cushag we got on the Internet but then some fella in a high-vis jacket came along with a strimmer an' chopped it down!"

"Oh, dear. Most unfortunate."

"Aye," replied Digby, "an' the final straw came when he went an' poured weedkiller down the hole. Me right eye was stingin' for a fortnight!"

Slowly, I climbed the ladder and on reaching the top … *whoosh*! I was back to my normal size.

"Hey, boy!" shouted Digby. "Yer'd better go an' sit down

on that boulder for a minute or two. Jus' to acclimatise an' get back t' the right era, like."

I nodded and made my way up the bank. Sitting down, I reflected on all that had occurred. It must have been a dream. One long, unbelievable dream. Without doubt, it was time to head for home. That's when it struck me. Where were my cycle clips? At first, I couldn't bring myself to look but then, ever so slowly, my eyes wandered towards the sycamore tree. Hanging on a low branch, was my white plastic bag. I made my way over and peered inside. They were all there. Wristwatch, Thermos, Gladys Convery's fairy cakes and down at the bottom, my cycle clips. I pressed the date mode on my watch only to realise that, although it showed the day and the month, it didn't register the year. Still, for some unknown reason, I trusted Digby, implicitly. Having thrown Gladys' fairy cakes to the birds, I put on my bicycle clips and was just about to leave when out of the corner of my eye, I spotted Digby and Yelena, barely visible above the entrance to Pandemonium, frantically waving goodbye. I returned the compliment and was riding away when I distinctly heard Yelena remark, "Yer don't see many people wearin' cycle clips these days, do yer!"

★ ★ ★

"Had a nice day, dear?" shouted Ruth from the kitchen.

"Er, yes thanks." Stretching out on the big leather sofa in the lounge, I promised myself that the next time I travelled past the Fairy Bridge, I would have to think long and hard before stopping.

"I had a stroke of luck this afternoon," she remarked.

"Oh?"

"Yes. I was waiting for the bus at the top of the road when a couple in a big black limousine pulled up. The lady passenger lowered the window and very kindly offered me a lift into town."

"Very kind indeed."

"Yes. The driver was a smartly dressed gentleman and as it turned out, the lady was his PA." Ruth gave a slight snigger. "Well actually, she was a little bit more than that!"

"Oh?"

"Oh yes. Sitting in the back, I had a perfect view through the gap between the front seats."

"View of what?"

"Every now and again, she would reach out with her right hand and gently stroke the outside of his left thigh." She began to laugh. "Mind you, what else could you expect from a PA with a name like Dolores!"

"*Dolores!* How do you know that?"

"They introduced themselves, that's how." Suddenly, Ruth appeared in the doorway. "That's a thing, now. When I told them our surname, he seemed to think that he knew *you*."

"Knew me? What was his name?"

"Digby something or other." Ruth began to giggle. "Then he said something rather funny."

"Why do I get a strange feeling that this involves me?"

"You're right. It does. He asked if you were the same Handley-Stowell that used to do summer seasons at the Balqueen Hotel during the early seventies." By now, Ruth was in fits of laughter. "He was convinced that you were the one who used to go on stage sporting a black wig with a ridiculously large quiff, wearing a skin-tight white jumpsuit smothered in sequins and do impersonations of that rock star chap – Elvis Presley!"

❧ november ❧

Prizewinning novelist **Elaine Aulton** lives in the Isle of Man and when she isn't pursuing her first love, writing, can be found patiently teaching the Island's youth. She has been a finalist and winner of the *Mail on Sunday* novel-writing competition. Elaine has short stories and articles published in various women's magazines under her own name and her pen-name of Ellan Moore. She is a member of the Douglas-based writers' group Skeealleyderyn.

Her short story 'The Carrasdhoo' was included in the first volume of *A Tail for All Seasons*

Dennis Turner is Elaine's dad. He too used to teach the Island's youth until he retired. Dennis has a keen interest in Manx history and folklore and the stories he finds there, he retells in 'rhyming verse' (as opposed to 'poetry'). Two of his continually-selling books are *Manx Myths and More …* and *More Manx Myths*. He is also regularly published in anthologies and weekly magazines.

This story is the first collaboration between Dennis and Elaine.

The Monks' Treasure

Dennis Turner and Elaine Aulton

O'Connell smiled and in a loud Irish brogue said to his companion, "Let us raise a glass, Mackenzie."

The two men stood shoulder to shoulder at the cramped bar. The room was warm, full of people, conversation and laughter. No one appeared to be paying the men any heed, but as they clinked glasses O'Connell said, "To a prosperous 1951," then he bent his head and murmured, "and to the gullible. Superstitious eejits. They deserve everything they get."

"Aye," Mackenzie answered with a chuckle. "I'll drink to that."

They drained their glasses, put them on the counter and called good night to the barman. They put their trilby hats on and edged their way to the door, but were stopped when one of the village men laid a heavy arm around Mackenzie's shoulders.

He breathed beery fumes at them. "Are yez off tomorrow, then?" he asked.

"Day after," Mackenzie said.

"And – and ma money?"

"Don't you be worrying about that, now, Mr Quilliam," O'Connell said, removing the man's arm. "We'll not take a penny until tomorrow. To be sure, we're coming back next month. And when we do, you'll see just how fine your investment is."

"Aye. Solid as rock," Mackenzie added.

Juan Quilliam grinned and opened the door for them. "Thankee, gentlemen. Tha's what I want to know, hey?"

Outside O'Connell and Mackenzie pulled up their mackintosh collars against the biting November wind. The light from the pub window made latticed patterns on the road, and lit up the two men. Mackenzie started sniggering. "He thanked us. He only went and thanked us."

"Watch your mouth, you fool," O'Connell snapped, roughly pulling his friend into the road, away from the pub. "Don't let your accent drop."

Mackenzie put a hand over his mouth and mumbled an apology. "It's the whisky."

"Then don't drink. We need our wits about us, man. C'mon, let's clear our heads and talk."

They trudged into the cold, clear night, and turned along the lane towards Sulby Glen, away from their lodgings. The moon was three-quarters and bright, and stars filled the sky. Their breath puffed out in clouds as they walked.

O'Connell broke the silence. "Everything is set. Church hall at half past five tomorrow – "

"Course. I booked it, didn't I?"

O'Connell spun to a stop and grabbed hold of Mackenzie's lapels. "Eejit. What's wrong with you? You're supposed to be Scottish. We've gone over this. I'll batter you if you don't keep in character."

Mackenzie hung his head. O'Connell let go in disgust and marched off; Mackenzie followed, and they walked in silence.

At the little crossroads they went straight on towards Monks' Farm and the looming hills.

"Right," O'Connell finally continued. "Half past five. You sign the receipts, *and* sign the poor fools' documents."

"But – "

"Not what we agreed, I know. But think about it. I'll be free to answer any questions and spin the yarns to stop them worrying, and you will look every inch the legal. See?"

Mackenzie chewed his lip and nodded slowly. "Aye," he said, after a pause. "I ken what you're telling me. And the rubber stamp? Best if I do it all, hmm?"

O'Connell grinned, his teeth showing white in the moonlight. "Good man. Shall we be turning back now?"

"Wait," Mackenzie said, and stopped, tilting his head to listen. "Shhh. Hear that?" He swayed towards his friend, finger held to his lips.

There was a rhythmic, rasping sound, then a faint thump. It came again and again.

O'Connell held his breath. The sounds seemed to grow clearer. "It's further up the lane. Beyond the hedge." There was a deliberate, slow rhythm that reminded him of something... he tried to grasp the faint memory...

"It's digging," Mackenzie whispered. "Someone is digging."

O'Connell nodded. He recognised it now. He whispered in reply, "At this time of night? Do you think we should take a look?" He could see Mackenzie's face clearly in the moonlight, and he raised his eyebrows and smiled in anticipation. He didn't need to say anything else. Their feet crunched on stones. The two men stepped quietly onto the grassy verge so their footfall would be almost silent. They walked single-file, hunched over so that they couldn't be seen above the hedge. They came to a very narrow pathway that left the lane, skirting the big field at the foot of the hill. They were forced to go slowly; the tangled hedge clutched at their raincoats, and they were both aware that the noise of snagging the branches might be heard by whoever was digging in the moonlight.

They heard a rustling as well as the digging as they stealthily got closer. The light suddenly dimmed as a cloud slid in front of the moon. The two men stopped. So did the sounds. It was as if everyone was listening. As the moonlight came flooding back, the sounds started again and the two men crept on.

Where their narrow path petered out, they were able to see through the sparse hedge into the field. They glanced at each other, puzzled.

Mackenzie's whisper was so faint as to be almost inaudible. "Are they – are they monks?"

O'Connell looked back at the circle of hooded people, wearing robes that reached the floor. He nodded, very slowly. He put a finger to his lips, then pointed towards the circle of men. Mackenzie looked where he was pointing. Just past the circle was something like a dark cloth on the ground. Heaped on the cloth were goblets, plates, and what looked like coins. The moonlight gleamed on the pile. Mackenzie's eyes grew large and he mouthed, "Silver?" O'Connell pressed his finger to his lips again. O'Connell squinted at the hoard, and as the moonlight shimmered on some of the plates he gasped. "Could be gold," he breathed.

They watched the spectacle, dumbfounded. Two of the hooded monks were digging, slowly and methodically. The mound of earth next to them showed that the hole must be deep.

One of the monks raised a hand, and the two diggers laid down their shovels.

Four monks left the circle and moved silently to the shining mound of silver on the cloth. They bent and grasped the cloth, lifting everything with some difficulty, and carried it to the hole. They did it all silently, and their silence was such that O'Connell and Mackenzie held their breath as they stared. The treasure was lowered into the hole, then the two diggers picked up their shovels.

O'Connell started looking about him as the sound of each spadeful of soil thumping down on the silver seemed to fill the air. Mackenzie poked him, frowning a question. O'Connell pointed to the naked branches of a towering oak, and then to a small copse of trees, and then to himself. He drew a triangle in the air. Mackenzie tapped his nose and nodded. He too peered at the oak, and then took in the distance to the copse. The sound of shovels being slapped onto soil made both men stare back through the hedge. The monks made a sombre sight, dark and hooded and silent. One of the diggers gave the earth a last slap with his shovel. From where Mackenzie and O'Connell crouched, the site appeared flat. The monks had done a good job.

Then one monk, who had had his back toward them throughout their spying, turned to face the hedge.

Mackenzie gripped his friend's arm in sudden fear. They'd been discovered. The monk's face remained hidden because of the cowl's shadow, but as they watched through the branching hedge the monk slowly shook his head. At them? Mackenzie's grip tightened.

Still in silence, all the monks turned as one to face their hiding place.

"Run!" O'Connell commanded, pulling his arm free. He stumbled and swore, thrashing through the clinging branches, aiming for the lane. Mackenzie followed. Another random cloud obscured the moon's light forcing them to plunge forward, arms outstretched against the branches. When the moonlight returned, they'd reached the end of the field. O'Connell glanced back, over the hedge. The field was empty.

Where were the monks?

The two men gained the lane and sprinted back past the little crossroads towards the main road and their lodgings, breath rasping in their lungs. At the main road Mackenzie stopped and spun round, facing the way they'd come. He leaned forward, resting his hands on his shaking knees, gasping for breath. "They've not followed. We're all right."

"I keep telling you," O'Connell panted. "Don't let your accent drop. Not until we get off this accursed island."

"I'm sorry. But I thought ... no, I'm sorry, man."

They walked thoughtfully back to their lodgings. "Guid night, O'Connell," Mackenzie said with a fine Scots burr. O'Connell touched a finger to his forehead in acknowledgement and went up to his room.

Next morning they met at their table in the breakfast room. O'Connell raised a quizzical eyebrow and nodded towards the door. Mackenzie shook his head. "Nae. I havenae seen her yet."

O'Connell smiled lazily and smoothed back his glossy, brylcreemed hair. "I think she's ripe for the picking, now."

"Aye, I cannae agree with ye more." The sound of the train whistle interrupted them, and they listened to the eight o'clock wheezing into the station. "That'll be our train to Douglas in the morning." He leaned across the table and in an undertone added, "And a few hours after that we'll be away with our real names, in England."

A clattering came from the hallway, and then the door was pushed open. Mrs Christian backed into the room with two pots of tea on a tray. She blew a lock of white hair out of her eyes before saying, "Good morning, gentleman. I trust you did sleep well."

"Aye."

"To be sure."

Mrs Christian laid the tray down and rubbed the small of her back.

O'Connell stood immediately, the picture of concern. "My dear lady. You have looked after us so well. You work so very hard, and for a lady of your … *experience*, to be sure you should be thinking to take some time to rest."

Mrs Christian used the back of her hand to move her hair back from her forehead, and her lined face creased into a wide smile. "That is something I can't afford to do, no matter how much I would like to."

O'Connell remained standing, concern oozing from his expression and his posture. Although he looked Mrs Christian in the eye, when he spoke, he addressed his companion. "Mackenzie? We can't … can we? I mean … our business here is almost concluded."

Mackenzie made a polite cough behind his hand, and Mrs Christian looked at him. "Madam, you know of our business, of course. Everyone is sad about the demise of the Douglas Ferry Company this year. But with the increasing number of visitors who come to holiday on these shores, you can see why our ferry company is needed."

Mrs Christian said, "Yes, I've heard from some of the others who are investing. Juan Quilliam explained it all. It sounds very promising. Black cloud, silver lining, as they say."

"Indeed. Well, we are sure your friends and neighbours will be more than happy with the returns they'll be getting."

Mrs Christian leaned towards O'Connell, who was still standing. She lowered her voice and said, "You are the financial man, aren't you?" Without waiting for his answer she continued, "Juan explained about you taking the money in cash, so we don't have to pay the extra tax."

O'Connell noted the 'we'. He pursed his lips and looked into her eyes. "We wouldn't dream of putting any pressure on you. But if you did decide you'd be wanting to take advantage of investing in 'The Celtic Ferry Company'... well, it could help towards a comfortable retirement." O'Connell put on his concerned look again. "But Mrs Christian, are you in a position to do this? We could not be taking your money, especially with you not having a man to provide, what with you being a widow."

She looked down, her cheeks turning pink, and said, "As it happens, I already have the cash available."

Mackenzie reached for a teapot and she cried out, "Oh, you're all scratched."

Mackenzie held his hands out. "Aye, a wee bit too much of the Manx hospitality, I'm afraid. Lost my balance outside the public house."

"You must let me get something for your hands." She hurried out of the room.

When the door closed behind her, O'Connell winked at him and in a low voice said, "Reluctant salesman works again. Another one on the hook. Well done."

Mackenzie poured strong tea into his cup. "Perhaps a ferry company would be a guid idea, after all," he murmured. Both men chuckled quietly at the joke.

After breakfast they went out. The day was sunny but cold, and they pulled their collars up and their trilbies down against the cutting breeze, hands pushed deep into their pockets. They walked thoughtfully along the lane that wound towards the mountain, the hedges shielding them from the worst of the cold wind. They retraced their path to where they'd seen the odd spectacle of the night before. Both men were surprised at how far they'd walked, perhaps a mile and a half. Mackenzie cleared his throat, "Did we really run all that distance back to the main road?"

"We were being chased – or so we thought."

"I've been thinking," Mackenzie said.

"That we should recover what we witnessed being buried?"

Mackenzie gave a short bark of a laugh. "We think alike. But I was thinking that we wait until dark. It will still be early. We could dig up the silver –"

"It could have been gold. The light of the moon plays tricks with colours."

"I'm nae fussy. We'll pack anything worth taking in our cases. I'd have nae problem about leaving some of my clothes behind. Along with my name."

The men laughed. A short while later they were pacing back and forth rather puzzled. "Sure, we ought to be reaching that other path by now. If we go any further we'll be walking right up the hill."

"Aye, and we should be able to see over the hedge. I could have sworn it wasnae this tall last night."

"Too many whiskies, my friend. We bent down so we wouldn't be seen. Perhaps we didn't have the need to do it."

Mackenzie pulled aside some brambles using the arm of his coat. "Here it is. No wonder I got so scratched. The path's all overgrown."

O'Connell whistled between his teeth. "It's amazing what a dark night and a few glasses can do to a man, eh? It looked quite different last night." He tried to push his way down the path, but it was too overgrown. "Did we fit down here?" he asked, puzzled.

"Possibly we made it worse when we charged down here to the lane? I recall the branches hanging on to me."

O'Connell frowned. "I don't know. I suppose you could be right."

"Getting to the treasure is going to be difficult."

O'Connell grinned and slapped Mackenzie on the back. "Eejit. We don't have to come this way. We can just walk through the gate into the field."

At the sensible solution, both men laughed and sauntered back into the village of Sulby. In Mrs Christian's back garden they saw a shovel and a gardening fork that most likely once belonged to Mr Christian. They noted it, and exchanged a look of complicity, moving away from the fence when a Morris Minor roared past, leaving a large plume of exhaust in its wake.

After a leisurely lunch in the pub, they went back to Mrs Christian's and got everything ready for their church hall meeting. They met on the landing, smartly groomed, Mackenzie with a black briefcase, and O'Connell carrying a locked, tin cash-box. They nodded approval to one another.

As they descended the stairs, the sitting room door opened. Mrs Christian beckoned to them. She looked worried. O'Connell was speaking as he reached the hallway. "Mrs Christian, please don't feel obliged. We'd feel guilty if we thought we'd pressed you …"

"Oh no, not at all. But I wondered if you could do me a favour?"

The two men exchanged a glance.

"Only the thing is, could we do my paperwork here? And not in the church hall? I was thinking about what you said, about me being a widow. It might be frowned on if I was seen to be doing business with all the men."

Mackenzie held up a hand to stop her. "Aye, dear lady, we ken your worries. Have nae fear. As soon as we finish at the hall, we will come back here and talk with you."

Mrs Christian sighed and her shoulders relaxed. "You're so kind. Thank you."

Everything went smoothly at the church hall. Two of the investors surprised Mackenzie by producing more than double the amount they had originally planned to invest. Mackenzie had done his 'legal' act beautifully, signing and stamping each fake document with furrowed brow and rapt concentration. And O'Connell prided himself on his smooth talking and his accurate counting of other people's money.

At Mrs Christian's, they were surprised when she produced an unopened bottle of sherry. "I've been keeping it for a special occasion," she said. They raised their glasses, and toasted the future of 'The Celtic Ferry Company'.

After dinner, O'Connell went up to his room. Mackenzie tapped on his door a few minutes later. "Weel? How much?"

O'Connell licked his lips. "With *her* stash as well, twenty quid short of two thousand."

Mackenzie's eyes narrowed in disbelief and he whispered, "But that's much more ..." He whistled. "Can you believe it? Them having that sort of money so soon after the war?" He shook his head slowly, and then held up his brown pressed-cardboard suitcase. "It's empty. I've hidden my clothes behind the wardrobe," he muttered. "She will nae find them. Are you ready?"

By the moonlight they were able to see and 'borrow' Mrs Christian's garden tools. They put the shovel and fork inside their raincoats, then pulled their belts tight to hold the tools in place. They stayed in the shadow of the trees, and crossed the road once they were satisfied that no one had seen them, the empty case bumping against Mackenzie's leg.

The field seemed even further away than earlier in the day. Mackenzie was sweating by the time they reached the little crossroads, and undid his coat, choosing to carry the shovel over one shoulder. Wrapped up in their own thoughts, they didn't say much. They tramped on, the tools getting heavier. Mackenzie swapped the case from hand to hand, and the shovel from shoulder to shoulder. O'Connell occasionally tutted, but he too shifted the weight of the fork.

When they finally reached the field O'Connell stopped and

Mackenzie's suitcase finished its swing and hit O'Connell in the back of his knees. He cursed, snatched it from Mackenzie's hand and threw it over the gate.

"What is the matter with you?" Mackenzie demanded. His fist tightened on the shovel and he pushed the gate, which wasn't fastened. In the field, both men took their bearings from the copse and the oak. They stepped carefully, the ruts and lumps of earth threw odd shadows in the moonlight and they didn't want to fall. When they reached where they thought what was the right spot, they faltered and gazed at each other.

"I'm after thinking that this is the place?"

"Aye. But it disnae look disturbed. At all."

O'Connell made his way to where they'd been hiding the previous night. "This must be the place. We looked through there and saw that copse. Lined up with the oak … it *must* be right." The moon seemed to cast odd shadows, but he was sure this was the place they'd witnessed.

"Aye, weel, get over here and let's dig."

They shook off their coats and folded them, putting their hats on top. They stretched their shoulders and hefted the garden tools, testing the weight and balance of them.

O'Connell nodded. "Let's find out." They began to attack the hardened earth with the spade and fork, ripping soil from tangled roots.

It was very hard going. Within a minute they'd taken off their jackets and ties. The ground resisted their efforts, and they started to sweat. Mackenzie thrust the blade of the shovel into the unyielding earth and stamped down on it, hurting his foot through the sole of his shoe. He leaned his weight hard against the handle, and finally it sank further in, and he was able to lever out a clod. O'Connell thrust the fork deep into the soil and twisted with all his might to break the tight hold it took of the tines. Both men were breathing heavily, using

264

their forearms to wipe sweat from their faces. The wind picked up.

O'Connell lifted the fork high and stabbed at the ground, letting the weight of the fork do most of the work. As it hit the earth the moon's light dimmed as a cloud scudded in front of it. O'Connell shrieked and jumped backwards, tripping over a rut and sprawling on his back.

"What? What is it?"

O'Connell shook his head. "I thought ... I saw ... The cloud ... made shadows. I thought ..."

Mackenzie turned back to his digging; they were starting to make an impression. He dug in a frenzy for a minute, throwing earth onto the mound he was making. When O'Connell finally started work at his elbow Mackenzie paused, and wiped his sweating palms down his thighs. He carried on. The heavy thud of the shovel in soil slowed as he tired.

O'Connell said, "Change over?" and held out the fork. Mackenzie took it, gratefully.

O'Connell's pace was slower, but he cut deeper with the blade. He threw himself onto the handle to force it further into the cloying soil. Then, there was a different sound – a clang. "We've done it," he said. He pierced the ground again, and was rewarded by another clang amid the scrape of soil and stone.

Mackenzie went at the same place using the fork. As another clod of soil was dug away, both men saw a glint in the moonlight that was definitely metal. O'Connell scraped with the shovel and dislodged a goblet. The men stared at each other, and then another cloud obscured the moon, casting them into dark.

"What are we waiting for?" demanded O'Connell. As the cloud passed both men shivered suddenly, and both looked nervously around.

"Who's there?" Mackenzie croaked. Then he whispered,

"Did you see them?"

O'Connell gave an uneasy laugh. "Moon and shadows. Playing tricks on our eyes, to be sure." Then he grinned, and spat on both palms. He grabbed the shovel and set about widening their hole. "To 1951: it will surely be a good year for us. The gullible eejits, handing over their money like that. And them others, showing us where they buried their pot of gold." He snorted with laughter.

They worked manically, putting their whole weight behind their tools. Then, as O'Connell rammed the shovel deeper there was a resounding 'crack' and the handle snapped off, leaving a jagged spike. The momentum of his body forced his torso onto it.

O'Connell speared himself. He opened his mouth, but could only gargle before he fell limp.

It took Mackenzie a few seconds before the horror he'd witnessed made sense. The light of the moon leached the colour from the scene, making it appear unreal. O'Connell hung there, right in front of his eyes. Impaled on the spike of the shovel, knees bent, head hanging forwards.

Mackenzie screamed. At the edge of his vision there seemed to be dark shadows. Tall, dark shadows. Surrounding them.

Mackenzie fell to his knees. "No. It can't be. No!" he pleaded. He heaved, and bile stung his throat. He looked around. There was nothing else there. Just him and O'Connell. O'Connell twitched. Mackenzie scrambled up, but as he reached his friend the ground let go of the shovel blade. In slow motion O'Connell slumped sideways and slid to the ground. His hip landed on the mound of soil they'd dug out, forcing him to roll onto his back. As he did, the protruding shovel was pushed further out from his chest.

Mackenzie was almost paralysed with shock. O'Connell's mouth was moving, and Mackenzie sobbed with relief. The shovel tilted. He touched it, and it fell away, leaving a dark mess on the front of his friend's shirt. As he watched, aghast, he realised dark blood was welling copiously from the wound. O'Connell would bleed to death.

"I'm sorry, mate. I'm sorry," he mumbled. The other man was silent, except for horrible, bubbly breathing. Mackenzie wiped tears from his eyes. He struggled to lift O'Connell, but he finally managed to carry him. He staggered forwards, hampered by the uneven ground. The bubbly breathing was interspersed with a kind of whistle. Mackenzie kept his eye on the gate, the unbidden tears stinging and blurring his vision.

At the gate he realised with dismay that he couldn't carry O'Connell any further. His legs were starting to turn rubbery, and the slick of blood and his friend's weight meant that O'Connell was sliding out of his grasp. Mackenzie lay him down at the entrance to the field as gently as he could. He ran along the road trying to shout for help, but could only manage breathless wheezing and little whimpers.

Before he reached the houses at the little crossroads a dark shadow peeled away from a gate. "Hey!" called a man's voice. "What you after?"

Mackenzie stumbled to a stop in front of Juan Quilliam, crying, gabbling and pointing back to where he'd left his injured friend.

Juan asked, "What's that? Are you hurt?"

Mackenzie looked down. In the moonlight he could see that the front of his shirt was covered in O'Connell's blood. "No. Not me. O'Connell. Need help. Need help."

Juan frowned deeply. "Where is he?"

"Don't know. Back there."

Juan's frown grew even deeper. "Thought yez was Scottish?"

"Yes. No. Help O'Connell," Mackenzie pleaded, sobbing now.

Another cottage door opened and light shone down the path. Juan called something, and Mackenzie was conscious of other folk, and felt himself being led into one of the cottages. He was dimly aware that men were running up the lane to where he'd left O'Connell.

Mackenzie was taken to the police station. He tried to explain what had happened but the sequence became fragmented, especially when he tried to explain why he now had a Liverpudlian accent, interrupting his description of the monks.

"Where is he? You killed him," one policeman stated. "Thought you'd take the lot. A fight perhaps?" Mackenzie tried to refute the accusations, but his brain wouldn't work. He faltered to a stop, shaking his head at each question, unable to put anything into words. Finally, the policemen shrugged and left the room, leaving the door ajar. Through the door Mackenzie saw Mrs Christian in profile, with the tin cash-box and his incriminating briefcase open on the table before her. She was counting the money.

More people arrived at the police station. He heard Juan Quilliam's voice say, "The body was at the entrance of the Monks' Field. Stabbed."

A man's voice said, "No sign of a murder weapon. No matter, though, he's guilty as sin. He'll hang, that one." There was another low voice, but Mackenzie couldn't hear what was being said. The unseen man's voice spoke again. "We did. There was no digging. Not anywhere." The low voice came again. Then Juan's. "We had torches. Nothing. Thez found thez coats and hats. But no. No digging."

Someone else arrived, and Mackenzie heard a deep voice. "No sign of the earth being touched. We'll have a thorough search in the morning."

Mrs Christian's voice sounded shocked. "There's nearly two

268

thousand pounds here!" There came a clamour of voices. Then Mrs Christian's, "You know what they say, the monks from Rushen Abbey buried their dead and their treasure on Monks' Farm."

A man laughed.

"You can mock," said Mrs Christian, "but it's true. They put a curse on the field so that the treasure can never be found."

Juan backed her up. "Yes sir, thez hid the treasure hundreds o' years ago in the orchard, wherever that were, and there's a curse on it. Pity the poor devils who happen upon it, hey?"

✸ December ✸

Steve Westcott lives in Sulby on the Isle of Man with his wife, Carole and two children, Samantha and Michael. His first book, *Reluctant Heroes*, originally published in 2003, has recently been reprinted by Frontlist Books, with the second in the Black Dragon series *Cronan the Librarian*, also published by Frontlist, launched in 2008. His short story 'April's Fool' was included in volume 1 of *A Tail for All Seasons*.

Steve has recently signed contracts with Priory Press for *Of Light and Shadow*, a modern-day thriller set against the background of Christianity, and his first novel-length foray outside the humour market. It's scheduled for publication in August 2010.

Gaining a growing reputation amongst sci-fi fans in the UK and USA, Steve has contributed to two other print anthologies, *Deeper Magic* and *A Twist of Fate*. He has also sold a number of short stories to net-based e-zines.

Lily

Steve Westcott

It was the intricate scrollwork that caught Lily's attention. Shaped in the style of two interconnecting hearts with an amethyst in the centre, the morning sunlight reflected off the complicated knotwork as though the piece blazed with an inner fire. Mid-stride, Lily took a double-take and halted, turning to gaze at the necklace in the shop window. Nestled on a red cloth in its wooden box, it was stunning. Then again, it would have to be for her to notice it.

Never one to act on impulse – it took two months of deliberation to buy her apartment, for heaven's sake – she knew she must have it. The feeling caught her by surprise, and she almost walked on. But the lure of the necklace was strong, calling to her in a voice both seductive and enticing. Barely aware of having moved toward the entrance, the bell above the door to Allom's tinkled as she pushed it open. The girl behind the counter looked up, and smiled in recognition.

"Hi Lily, how's the new apartment?"

Lily paused inside the threshold and gave a wry grin.

"Fine thanks. Be better still when I finish the decorating. I'm just off to Felton's for yet more paint." She looked down and tugged at the chest of her paint-stained coveralls to emphasise the point.

Zoe laughed, and folded closed the paper she had been reading. "So you thought you'd pop in for a chat on the way?" Although the question was leading, the half-smile on Zoe's face indicated she had long given up on Lily ever buying anything from the shop.

Lily winced. "Not exactly."

Brow arched, Zoe said, "You don't mean you're actually going to buy something?"

Although spoken in jest, the question caused Lily to redden. Raising a hand, she brushed aside a stray lock of black hair that had escaped her ponytail, and looked to the floor.

With a roll of her eyes, Zoe moved from behind the counter and wrapped an arm around her shoulder. Grinning, she said, "Come now girl, don't go getting all self-conscious on me. It's just that, you buying jewellery is something … unexpected. A shovel, some nails, or a set of spanners – yes." She gave Lily's shoulder a squeeze. "Jewellery, no. Now, which piece is it you're interested in?"

The heat of embarrassment faded, and Lily grinned.

"It's a necklace." She glanced to the window display to the left of the door. "In the shape of two interlocking hearts."

With a last squeeze of encouragement, Zoe released her grip and walked over to the display to peer into the window.

Joining her, Lily's heart beat faster, and her breathing quickened. Raising a hand, she pointed to the box containing the necklace. "That's the one."

Zoe reached in and grasped the wooden box. Raising it, her eyes narrowed. "I don't remember buying this in. It's beautiful. I can see why it caught your eye. But it looks more like an antique, and we only deal with new stuff. Usually."

She examined the box more closely, lifting it to gaze at the base. "Even the box looks old." She sighed. Turning to Lily, she gave a wry smile. "And there's no price on it. I bet Dad bought it when we went across sourcing new stock."

Making her way to the counter, she said, "I'd better ring him to find out how much it is."

Without realising, Lily found herself half a pace behind, peering over Zoe's shoulder as they walked. Now that she had found her 'impulse' buy she was reluctant to let it out of her sight.

When Zoe halted to open the gate leading to the till area, she and Lily almost collided.

Zoe laughed. "I'm not going to run off with it, you know." Handing her the box, she said, "Here. Have a closer look while I speak to Dad. That's if I can get hold of him. You know what he's like for disappearing right when you need him."

Lily's hands trembled as she took the proffered box, her eyes drawn to the amethyst surrounded by its golden web. With unaccustomed reverence, she reached in and raised the heart. A warm glow permeated her being as soon as she touched the gold, filling her with a sense of love and belonging. The feeling was so intense she almost gasped aloud in pleasure. Instead, she closed her eyes, calmed herself and savoured the moment. Never in her twenty-three years had she felt so ... so ... feminine. As Zoe had said, hammers, spanners, lawnmowers and spades were more her line of purchases, not frivolous decoration.

In her heart, she knew that this was not a frivolous decoration. It was something that called to her; that belonged to her; that needed her as much as she now needed it. The feeling was both alien and exhilarating.

A curse from Zoe intruded, and Lily opened her eyes to stare once again at the necklace and box. An indentation in the red fabric beneath where the necklace had lain indicated it had rested in that position for some time. Also, the red of the cloth was a much deeper shade in the hollow.

"He's not in and he's not answering his mobile," said Zoe. "Typical!"

Lily placed the necklace in its indentation and tugged at a small slip of card she'd spotted to the side. On reading it, she looked up, handed it to Zoe, and said, "Two hundred and forty-six pounds?"

With practised ease, Zoe rolled her eyes and shook her head. "Men!"

It was at that moment Lily realised she hadn't got enough cash with her, and probably insufficient funds in her account to cover the purchase until she received payment from the last gardening job she'd done. Although loathe to do so, she pulled clear a plastic card from her purse and waggled it in the air.

"Visa?"

★   ★   ★

The smell of the sea was in Will's blood, as it had been in his father's and his father before him. Standing on the sand at South Beach, breathing deeply of the salt air, he closed his eyes and inhaled, the cry of gulls and lap of waves helping to soothe away the excesses of the previous evening. There was nothing like the clear, crisp, sharp smell that came with living on an island to clear the mind – and the head. Why would anyone want to give this up for a life spent in the smog and fumes of the mainland?

Work, was the honest answer. If it were not for the fact he had work aplenty on old Billy Teare's farm, he may well have joined John and left the Isle of Man for good.

Will took another deep breath. His head was starting to clear.

"What's the matter with yer, boy?" A deep, booming voice yelled. "Can't handle yer ale, or something?" The question was followed by a deep, rich laugh.

The gulls appeared to shriek louder at the intrusion. Will winced; the pain in his head exacerbated by the raucous din. Turning, he risked one eye to peer back to the roadway, and spotted Henry Gale leaning against the door jamb to his cottage across the road. Henry was a big brute of a man, all wild hair and matted beard, but the best fishing skipper to run out of Ramsey. And one of the least law-abiding with it. It was not always fish that filled the hold of Henry's boat, according to local gossip.

"Offer's still open, young 'un, if yer fancy it," said Henry, his baritone easily heard over the din the gulls insisted on making.

Will shook his head, and then wished he hadn't. It felt like the gulls had landed and were in the process of pecking their way into his skull.

Henry shrugged. "Well, if yer get fed up shovelling shit give me a call. There's more money in fish than farming, don't yer know? Especially fer the likes of a good un' like you. From good stock, you are, lad."

Managing a weak smile, Will raised a hand, and then turned his attention back to the sea. Eyes closed, back straight, breathing deeply, he ignored the amused chuckle from behind.

He knew he could make more working for Henry, but he preferred the smell of animals to that of fish. Ever since his father had gone missing at sea, along with his boat and crew, Will had turned his back on the ocean. Not that he was scared of the water; he actually quite liked sailing, he just found it hard to forgive the sea for taking away his only living relative.

With his concentration broken, Will decided to head home and risk some breakfast. Maybe some food would settle him down for the day. His stomach roiled at the thought, giving lie to the intention. Sighing, he decided to risk it anyway. The last thing he needed was to spend his one day off lying in his bed feeling sorry for himself.

Will's home was the smallest cottage in Bark Lane. It was just up from the tannery and, although sparsely furnished, was his own piece of the Island, left to him after his father had drowned.

Although it was early summer, the fire in the hearth glowed brightly and the pot Will had left suspended over the flames steamed. His nose wrinkled. The smell of burned oatmeal filled the air of the small room. Cursing, he ran across the earth floor, grabbed a rag from beside the wash basin and made an attempt to rescue his breakfast, but he needn't have bothered: it was ruined.

In spite of the rag, the heat from the handle penetrated and Will's fingers started to burn. The pot dropped to the floor with a dull clang, and his fingers rose to his mouth. He could feel blisters beginning to form, and cursed.

In sympathy, his stomach ceased to roil, and settled for rumbling instead.

★ ★ ★

The key slid into the lock and Lily pushed the door open with her shoulder before picking up the two cans of paint and the bag containing a roller and tray. Heeling the door closed behind her, she made her way along the short hallway to the lounge. Her nose wrinkled as she walked.

There was a strange smell in the apartment, like burning porridge. But she hadn't left anything on the stove, and she didn't even like porridge. She'd never noticed a smell about the place before, so assumed it must be entering from one of the neighbouring apartments. King's Court appeared well-built but, as her father used to say, "They don't build them like they used to. Throw them up now, they do."

The door to the lounge was open, the room devoid of any furniture in preparation for decorating. The thought made her snort. As if she had any furniture to put in it. Her last place was a furnished let, 'furnished' being a loose description for the moth-eaten specimens that the landlord considered fine furnishings, so she had little, if anything, to bring with her.

After placing her purchases on the floor she put her hands on her hips and gazed around the room. She had filled all the cracks, sanded the walls and prepared them for painting. A couple of coats should do it and then she could go and visit charity shops, of which Ramsey had many, to see what bargains she could pick up.

Her thoughts turned to the necklace she'd bought, and she fumbled in the pocket of her overalls for the package containing the box. After what seemed like an age, her fingers feeling like sausages in her haste to extract the necklace, she pulled the small paper bag free. In a very short time the bag was on the floor and the old, time-worn wooden box was in her hands. She studied it, amazed to see that the sides had been dove-tailed. It had been made by a craftsman. For some reason that made her purchase even more special.

Clasped in two hands, she used her thumbs to ease up the lid, her eyes widening as the necklace came into view. In the back of her mind she had half expected it to be a cheap copy made to look old, but seeing it again she knew it was indeed an antique.

With the box still clasped in her hands she settled, cross-legged on the floor, and placed it on the tiled surface before her. After a moment's pause to settle her nerves, she reached in and pulled the necklace clear.

As she did so, a dull thud sounded beside her and she

flinched. The wooden box clattered to the floor. Heart racing, the necklace clasped in one hand, the other clutching her chest, Lily's eyes flicked around the room. The smell of burned porridge grew stronger, and her grasp on the necklace tightened. A sharp edge dug into her palm, breaking flesh, and the smell disappeared.

Shaken, Lily scrambled to her feet. Then, feeling a pain in her palm, she looked down. A drop of scarlet nestled on the flesh beneath where the pendant lay. With one last glance around the room, she made her way down the hallway to the bathroom, there to wash away the blood and clean the puncture.

Detached by the movement, the small card Zoe had attached to the gold chain of the necklace fell to the floor. It landed plain side down. Staring up at the freshly prepared ceiling were a series of marks. If Lily had still been there she would have read £2 4s 6d, before the characters faded and the card disappeared.

⋆   ⋆   ⋆

Weary beyond belief, Will opened the door to his cottage and stumbled inside, heeling the door closed behind him. He shivered, dropped his bag of dirty clothes on the floor and wrapped his arms around his chest. Whether it was the coldness of a stone cottage that had not been heated for days or the after effects of a week spent lambing in foul weather, Will was not sure, but he suddenly felt dog-tired and in need of warmth. Even though it was summer, the nights were cold, and the stone of the cottage demanded to be heated, which was why he'd left the makings of a fire in the hearth before leaving.

Within minutes, Will had the carefully prepared kindling ablaze and was squatting in front of the fire, hands held out to make the most of the heat. With the fire banked, he made his way up to the bedroom, there to sleep the sleep of the exhausted.

The sun was high in the sky by the time he eventually roused and tossed aside the blankets. Bleary-eyed, he made his way to the wash bowl in the corner of the room and filled it with water from the pitcher. Leaning over, he reached into the bowl with cupped hands and scooped cold water over his face before repeating the exercise and soaking his hair. The shock drove away the last vestiges of sleep, and any thoughts of climbing back into bed. Water ran in rivulets down his bare back to spot the unadorned floorboards as he made his way across the room and down the stairs. With any luck the fire would still be smouldering.

It did not take Will long to rekindle the embers. After a couple of minutes kneeling in front of the hearth, gently nursing the glowing coals and adding more kindling, the fire blazed, and Will rose to his feet, groaning as his knees creaked at the movement. He grimaced. Twenty-five and already falling apart.

What he needed was a good woman to look after him. His lips curled into a wry grin. With Billy's growing infirmity and lack of kids to share the workload, he spent more time at the farm than in the cottage. What chance had he of meeting anyone, let alone finding time for a relationship? But most of the other lads he knew had managed, so perhaps it was time to get himself sorted. There must be some lonely girl in Ramsey who was looking for a good catch. The thought had him chuckling. Well, at least he had his own house, a full set of teeth and was the right side of good-looking to not be classed as ugly, which was a good start, in his opinion.

Still chuckling, he scanned the room for his canvas bag. His dirty clothing would be mouldering in the bottom by now.

Not spotting it, he frowned. He could not remember taking it upstairs, but perhaps in his tiredness he had.

His bedroom proved to be devoid of anything resembling his bag. Confused, he made his way back down the stairs. He remembered dropping it on the floor before lighting the fire, so where had it gone?

The front door opened as Will reached the bottom of the stairs and the wild tangle of hair that was Henry Gale's head popped into view.

"Yer decent, lad?"

Will halted, the light of understanding shining brightly, and folded his arms across his chest. He had not put the catch on the door the previous evening. Meeting Henry's twinkling gaze, he said, "All right. What've you done with it?"

Henry's brows pulled into a frown, and his beard bristled. "Done with what, lad?"

★　★　★

Lilly woke with a start to the sound of 'DOA' by the Foo Fighters, and reached out of the duvet to fumble for the snooze button. Seven a.m. was far too early to rise, even during July when the sun rose well before she did. Snuggling back beneath the duvet, she drifted into a light doze, only to be woken by the strains of 'Mandy' by Barry Manilow some ten minutes later. She groaned, and fumbled for the snooze button again, only to knock the offending radio-alarm on to the floor. Unfortunately, the battering was not sufficient to shut down the racket, so she tossed the duvet aside and rose. Judging by the way curtain-filtered sunlight permeated the room, the day promised to be fine, which was just as well seeing as she had Mrs Clague's garden to run the mower over, and a couple more small jobs she needed to catch up on.

Once out of bed she righted the radio and thumbed the off

button, cutting Barry off in his prime. Nodding in satisfaction, she wandered through to the bathroom to prepare for the day. Within twenty minutes she was showered, had her hair pulled back into a ponytail and was dressed for work in tee-shirt and green overalls, her necklace – a permanent adornment since she'd bought it – nestled safely beneath the tee-shirt; the kettle was boiling and the smell of grilled bacon hung heavy in the kitchen. For once, it looked as though she would start the day ahead of schedule and actually have chance to enjoy an hour's relaxation before setting out to earn the month's mortgage.

With a mug of coffee in one hand and a bacon sandwich in the other, Lily made her way down the hallway to her newly decorated lounge. Although it had no furniture yet and the carpet was not due to be fitted for a week, she loved the room, and had set an upturned crate on the floor to sit on while she watched TV on the second-hand set Mr Watterson had been about to throw away. Until she suggested she dispose of it for him, that is. All right, the picture wasn't great and she could only get Border TV, but at least she had something to watch during the evening.

Humming the latest Leona Lewis song to herself, she balanced the plate containing her sandwich on top of the steaming mug whilst using her free hand to open the door. Once inside the lounge she walked over to the crate to place the plate and the mug on top before moving toward the TV.

She never made it.

An old canvas bag she had never seen before sat on the floor mid-way between the crate and the TV, halting her in her tracks. Her eyes widened. How had it got there? The windows were closed and she remembered locking the front door the previous evening. So where had it come from? She stepped closer, and her nose twitched. There was a strange, fusty smell coming from the bag, as though something had died and been dumped in it.

Lily felt the colour drain from her face, and fled the room. Once in the perceived safety of her kitchen she grabbed her mobile from the side and thumbed the number for Ramsey's police station. Her call was answered in moments, and within a further five minutes a patrol car pulled up outside her apartment, tyres screeching, sirens wailing, blue lights blazing and headlights on. A police officer jumped out and ran to the door.

In the short time it took Lily to get to the door a crowd had begun to gather outside. Never one to enjoy being the centre of attention, her face burned with embarrassment as she opened it, despite her fear at what the bag in her lounge may contain. In an attempt to hide herself from view, she used the door as a shield when ushering the policeman inside.

"Did you really have to come in all guns blazing?" she snapped, as Juan Cubbon halted on the threshold.

Juan grinned, and took off his helmet. "Dead bodies in bags? What did you expect?"

Lily growled, deep in her throat, and shook her head. Juan had always been the same, even at school. He could make a drama out of any situation, and the more show in dealing with it the better. She noticed the three stripes on the arm of his jacket, and rolled her eyes.

"Didn't know, hey?" Juan grinned and patted the stripes. "Last week." He winked. "And not before time, if you ask me. Right! Now where's this body bag?" He glanced up and down the hall, and rubbed his hands together, as though in expectation.

The arrival of Juan settled Lily's nerves and she was pleased to note her arm didn't shake when she raised it to point toward the lounge.

"In there. In the middle of the floor."

Juan glanced down the hallway. "And you've never seen it before?"

Lily shook her head, and stole a glance around the door. A sizable crowd had gathered in the parking bays opposite her apartment. The murmur of voices drifted on the breeze and more than a few faces stared her way. To her dismay, she realised she knew most of them, and groaned.

"Were all your windows and doors locked last night?"

Grabbing Juan's sleeve, she yanked him further into the apartment before shoving him toward the lounge. Then she slammed the door closed and leaned back against it, eyes closed.

The sound of a throat being cleared grabbed her attention, and she looked up.

"Assault is a criminal offence, you know?"

Lily shook her head and pushed away from the door, rubbing at her temple, which had started to pound. She could feel a migraine coming on. "Just, just – just go and see what it is. Please?"

Juan shrugged. "Just doing my job, Lily. That's all."

Lily hoped the weak smile that formed on her face did not come out more like a grimace.

With a nod of acknowledgement, Juan straightened his lapels and then turned to enter the lounge. By the time Lily edged to the doorway Juan was already at the bag. He stooped over it and had begun to open the ties that held the top flap in place. "Looks like a kit bag to me," he murmured, easing the ties open.

Gently, he raised the flap and peered inside. The smell grew stronger, and Juan quickly leaned away, his nose wrinkling as he groaned in disgust. "That's putrid," he murmured, clamping the end of his nose between a thumb and forefinger.

"Wh – wh – what is it?" asked Lily.

Juan looked over. "Some toe-rag's dirty kit, is what it is. Farmer, by the smell of things." He met her querying gaze. "Are you sure you locked up last night?"

Lily nodded.

"Well, heaven knows how it ended up in here."

Leaning forward, one hand still clamping his nose, Juan began to pull out dirty socks, leggings, shirts and underwear, to pile them in a mouldering heap on the floor. When most of the bag had been emptied he grunted in satisfaction and looked toward Lily.

"Know anyone called Will Taubman?"

Lily shook her head.

"Well, that's whose bag it is." He shook his head. "Bloody toe-rag. Wait till I get hold of him." Standing, Juan asked, "Have you got a bin bag?" He glanced at the pile of clothing on the floor. "Or two?"

Juan had been gone for over an hour and still Lily hadn't moved from her apartment. Leaning against the work surface in her kitchen, she was on her third mug of coffee. She knew she should make her way to Mrs Clague's, heaven knew her bank account needed the funds, but she couldn't bring herself to leave her apartment – not just yet. There were still a number of neighbours hanging around, no doubt wanting to know the 'skeet', and her thoughts kept returning to the kit bag. How had it got there? Who was Will Taubman? How had he got into her apartment?

He had a key!

Lily heaved a heavy sigh, and shook her head. Mrs Clague would have to wait. Today, she had locks to change.

As it turned out, the locks did not take her long. She managed to get to Mrs Clague's, albeit six hours late, and still had time to do a shop before daylight faded. She was part way through putting the grocery's away when there was a sharp knock to the front door. Lily sighed. Just what she needed, when all she wanted to do was have a quick snack, take a shower and then roll into bed. Hoping it was not one of the neighbours catching up on the gossip, she made her way to the door and pulled it open. On the doorstep stood Juan Cubbon, all smiles, dressed in jeans and sweatshirt.

A wry grin formed on Lily's face, as she eyed his attire. "Social call?"

"Sort of." He leaned forward and tried to peer down the hallway. "You going to invite me in, or are you busy?"

Laughing, Lily opened the door wider. "I was about to make a coffee. I'm guessing you won't say no."

Juan's smile widened, and he stepped through the doorway. "Never one to refuse a pretty lady."

Lily chuckled. Pretty was one thing she had never been called, except by her father, who was long since departed. The heat of embarrassment coloured her face as she made her way to the kitchen. She hoped it would fade by the time she had to face Juan. Keeping her back to him, just in case, she fussed with the kettle and the makings for the coffee, and asked the question she felt sure Juan had called round to answer.

"Did you find out who this Will Taubman is, then?"

Juan cleared his throat before answering. "Not really. The only one with that name in Ramsey is a five-year-old kid. And I hardly think he's going to break in and leave you a pile of dirty clothing. But we did find something in the bag."

Brows arched, Lily tuned and handed Juan his coffee.

"This."

Grabbing his coffee with one hand, he proffered a dirty, dog-eared slip of paper with the other.

Eyes screwed up, Lily leaned forward to gaze at the paper. It had writing on it. Untidy writing, but clearly legible. Reaching out, she grasped the slip and held it to the light.

'Will Taubman', she read. '7 Bark Lane, Ramsey'.

She looked up.

Juan shrugged. "Bark Lane disappeared years ago when they developed South Ramsey. I'm guessing that whoever dumped the stuff used a bag they picked up in one of the charity shops. Along with the clothes." He took a sip of his coffee. "Bloody old-fashioned things, they were. I wouldn't fancy wearing them, that's for sure."

Lily heard the words, but took little notice. She stared at the name and the address. Unconsciously, her hand moved to the heart-shaped pendant nestled against her chest. It was warm to the touch.

"Are you listening to me?"

Lily looked up, met Juan's querying gaze and gave a hesitant smile. "Sorry. I was miles away." Pushing away from the worktop, she said, "Care to move to the lounge?" Then in her best mock upper-class voice, added, "I may even let you have the crate, where you can relax in comfort."

Laughing, she led the way down the hallway, opened the door, and gestured for Juan to precede her. He had no sooner stepped over the threshold than he stopped. Lily heard him sigh, and frowned.

"What is it?"

Moving aside, Juan nodded to the middle of the floor.

The smash of a coffee cup shattered the silence.

Unaware of their impact, a battered pair of mud-splattered boots stood centre-stage, laces pulled, tongues lolling, as though mocking her fear.

★   ★   ★

"For the last time, I ain't been thievin' yer stuff! What makes yer think it's me, anyway? I've enough rubbish of me own without thievin' yours!"

Lily

Arms folded across his barrel chest, Henry's beard bristled in righteous indignation as he glared at Will. They were stood outside Henry's cottage in Chatsworth Terrace, Henry on the recently scrubbed quarry-tile step and Will on the roadway. A stiff breeze attempted to make more of a mess of Henry's wild tangle of hair than it already was, and his face burned with anger.

Will stepped back a pace, out of arm's reach. He was not going to back down until Henry owned up, but did not fancy taking a beating from those brawny arms. He had seen what damage Henry could do when riled.

"Well, who's taking it then?"

The heat of anger faded from Henry's face. His chest heaved in a sigh. Rubbing at his eyes, he shook his head, as though to clear it, then folded his arms over his chest again. "I've no idea, lad. But it ain't me. As I already said, I've enough rubbish of me own without taking yours. It makes no sense, lad."

Honesty shone from Henry's eyes, and Will sagged. He had been sure it was Henry. That would have explained everything. Now, with his denial, Will had no idea who was stealing his gear. The lack of a suspect was worrying. Not that he had anything worth stealing, it was the fact that someone he didn't know had entered *his* property and interfered with *his* belongings.

"I got an idea, lad. Yer can write, can't yer?"

Will nodded.

"Right, this is what we'll do."

★　★　★

It had been two weeks since the appearance of the boots and Lily felt relaxed in her apartment for what felt like the first time since the bag incident. She had changed the locks yet again the day following the appearance of the boots, and that seemed to have done the trick. Even so, Juan had become a regular visitor, both when on duty and when off, and she found herself looking forward to his visits. This morning, though, he had left for a course across, and would not be back for a week, and she knew she would miss him.

Nursing a mug of coffee, she made her way from the kitchen to the lounge, there to watch Border TV on Mr Watterson's decrepit TV – still to be replaced when she had the money to do so – before she left for work. As she entered the room, the fresh, clean smell of newly-laid carpet and paint struck her, causing her to smile, as did the soft, warm feel of the pile on bare feet as she crossed the floor to flick on the TV. At last the place was starting to feel like hers.

A fuzzy, snow-speckled picture sprang to life on the TV and she made her way to the settee to settle down for half an hour before leaving for the day. Freshly cleaned, you could not tell it was second-hand. Along with the armchair she had picked up from the Hospice shop on Waterloo Road, it had been her best buy so far.

Only half-aware of what the newsreader was saying, Lily sipped at her coffee and contemplated the day ahead. It looked like rain, and she did not want to spend the day getting soaked doing outside work.

A piece of paper lay on the floor to the side of the TV and she found her eyes drawn to it. She did not remember dropping it. A thought crossed her mind and she smiled.

Juan!

He must have left her a note before leaving the previous night.

Taking care not to slop her drink, she placed the mug on the small table she had also purchased from the Hospice shop, and rose to grab the paper. Taking it to the window, there to read by better light, she stared at the child-like handwriting, and her eyes narrowed.

Juan had smooth, flowing script, not stilted scrawl that looked like it had been written by a five-year-old. Her frown deepened as she read the words, and her heart faltered.

Stop taking my stuff.
Will Taubman.

Lily felt faint. Her head swam, and she leaned against the window sill for support. The paper floated to the floor as she clutched at her chest.

Will Taubman again. Who was he? Where did he come from? How had he got in? So many questions and so few answers. Stooping, she picked up the spilled paper and ran to the kitchen.

Juan picked up the call after three rings.

"Hello? Whoa! Slow down, Lily. I can't understand what you're saying."

In her fear, and her haste to tell him what had happened, Lily spoke rapidly, her words coming out jumbled and manic. Although she knew it, she could do nothing about it; her need to tell Juan that Will Taubman was back too great.

Eventually, Juan's calming tones worked their magic and Lily, taking deep breaths, managed to tell her tale in a calmer manner. When she finished, Juan said, "You have to leave the apartment, Lily. At least until I get back. This Will guy may be a lunatic and" – he paused – "now I've found you, I don't want to lose you. You understand?"

Shocked by his words, Lily said nothing. She stared out of the kitchen window, but saw nothing. Had he just admitted feelings for her?

"Lily. Lily! Are you there?"

"Umm? Oh, sorry. I was miles away."

"As you should be," Juan responded. The serious tone to

his voice did not go unnoticed. "Listen. I have to go now; they're calling us through. I'll call you later. OK?"

Lily stared at the message on the paper in her hand for a good twenty minutes after Juan had rung off, her mind filled with thoughts of Will Taubman.

Instead of running on fear and emotion, she decided to turn to the part of her that dealt with problems best, and the practical side took control.

Who was he? Well, that was obvious. He was Will Taubman. But *who* was he? What did they know about him?

They knew he lived, claimed to live, at 7 Bark Lane, a lane that no longer existed. That he was a manual worker, judging by the state of the clothing and boots he had deposited in her lounge, and that he thought she was stealing his gear.

What did it mean? Was it someone playing a joke, or something more sinister?

The splatter of raindrops, fat and heavy, on the window broke into her ruminations, and she reached a decision. It was too wet to do her gardening jobs, so she would go to the library and see if she could dig anything up on Bark Lane, and see if a certain Will Taubman used to live there. They were bound to have information on South Ramsey.

The smell of books and polish greeted her as she stepped into the library. Water ran off her boots and coat on to the polished floor as she paused by the entrance, wondering where to start her search. She noticed the puddles beneath her feet, and grimaced an apology at the librarian behind her counter, who returned her gaze with amused understanding.

"Can I help you?"

Lily's boots squeaked as she walked toward the counter, loud and discordant in the quiet. "I'd like to know about old Ramsey," she said, keeping her voice low.

"You'll need our 'local' section," said the librarian. She

pointed over Lily's shoulder. "End of the aisle, turn left, and the local books are on the right."

Nodding her thanks, Lily made her way, as directed, and settled in for some research.

Time passed by without her being aware of it passing. Having commandeered a desk, she had maps of old Ramsey spread out in front of her and also those of modern Ramsey. By photocopying the maps in the library's machine and placing one over the other, taking into account the differing scales, she had come to the conclusion that her apartment block had been built over the site of where Bark Lane used to be. By further correlation, it was also possible that number seven used to be located right where her apartment now stood.

The discovery sent shivers through her body. The prospect of her apartment being haunted was terrifying. Never one to believe in ghosts and things that go bump in the night, she decided to prove that Will Taubman was, indeed, a modern-day lunatic rather than a blast from the past intent on haunting her.

Acquiring copies of census papers for the population of Ramsey for the period when Bark Lane stood proved to be more difficult and time-consuming than searching for the maps, but eventually she had them in front of her. Commencing her search in the 1800s, her forefinger traced the list of people that resided in Ramsey, looking for the name Taubman. Fortunately, the names being in alphabetical order, the search took less time than it did for her to find the census papers.

When looking down the list for 1852, the name Will Taubman glared out of the page at her. Age – twenty-five. Occupation – farmhand. It all fitted with the items that had been left in her apartment.

Lily felt her throat go dry, her eyes glued to the page that held the name Will Taubman. She suddenly felt very warm, and a film of sweat slicked her skin beneath her clothing. Her breathing quickened and she felt faint. She had to get out of the library.

Unaware of the clatter of her chair hitting the floor as she rose, she grabbed her raincoat from where she had placed it on the chair beside her when looking at the maps, and fled into the rain-soaked street. The cries of an angry librarian went unheeded.

By the time Lily got home she was soaked. Too hurried to put on her raincoat, it had flopped around on her arm as she sped along the mostly deserted Parliament Street before cutting through Saint Paul's Square to her apartment. Once inside, she leaned back against her front door for a moment or two to catch her breath, water soaking into the door mat at her feet.

Once her breathing had steadied itself, she pushed herself away from the door and headed to the kitchen. She needed a coffee. Will's message was still on the side where she had left it, her mobile phone lying beside it. Reluctant to go near the paper, she hung her wet coat on the peg to the back of the door before preparing her drink.

The same thought kept going through her head as she waited for the kettle to boil. Her apartment was haunted! It had to be. No one in their right mind would go to the effort of taking on the mantle of a long-dead person just to scare her, would they?

She would have to sell, of course. How could she live in a place where the old occupier refused to leave? What if he turned out to be a poltergeist? She could be hurt, even killed if he decided to turn nasty. Mouldy old clothing and messages were one thing, but injury or death were another.

The kettle clicked off and she filled her mug before moving to the fridge to grab some milk. The fridge was immediately beneath where she had left the message, and her eyes were drawn to it. The child-like writing glared up at her.

> *Stop taking my stuff*
> *Will Taubman*

A thought struck her. If a ghost, if indeed it was a ghost, could write to her, could she not write to it? Tell it to stop bothering her? But what would she say? Keep away, ghost, or my boyfriend will come looking for you?

Unexpectedly, a chuckle escaped her lips, and her eyes flicked to her mobile. She had missed six calls while she was out, and she knew Juan would be at least one of them. She was wrong. All six were from him. His phone was turned off when she tried to call back, so she texted him that she would speak to him later.

Cold from her wet clothing crept into her flesh and Lily decided to wait for the coffee. Moving to the bathroom, she shed her gear and took a shower. The heat from the water succeeded in banishing the cold, and served to calm her nerves. Also, she did her best thinking when in the shower.

She realised that up to now Will Taubman had settled for dumping stuff in her lounge. There had been no attempt to hurt her, and no attempt to cause damage. What if she simply left him a message asking him to stop leaving stuff? Would that work? If he were a ghost, would he take notice? And if he were someone of this time breaking in, would he actually take notice? Of the two, she began to hope that Will Taubman was of the spectral variety rather than some loony trying to scare her.

Both options were scary, but she needed to know what was happening. She could not leave the apartment until she found out, however stupid that might seem. And she knew she could not tell Juan – just yet. He would want her out right away. No, she would have to lie to him and tell him she was fine. At least until she found out more about the mysterious Will Taubman.

"You sure you're OK?" asked Juan.

Lily sighed. It was eight o'clock in the evening and they had been speaking for the past hour, mostly about Lily's problem rather than Juan's course.

"I'm fine. Don't be worrying about me. Concentrate on your course. I'll still be here when you get back."

"I know. It's just ..." His voice faltered. "I'm worried about you, that's all. And I'm too far away to help. I know –" his voice brightened, "I'll get one of the night-shift to keep a check on your place while I'm away. That way, I know you'll be safe."

Lily laughed.

"What's so funny?"

"Nothing. It's just that I never thought I'd have my own police guard at my beck and call."

"Not until I get back, you don't. Seriously, take care and make sure you lock up tonight. I'll get the lads to keep an eye out."

"Thanks, Juan. I'll sleep better knowing the long arm of the law is taking care of me."

Juan snorted. "As long as the only arm of the law around you is mine, I don't care."

Lily giggled. "Goodnight, Juan."

As soon as the phone clicked off, Lily grasped the message she had written on the paper and read it for what seemed like the umpteenth time.

Dear Will.
I am not stealing your stuff; you are dumping it in my front room.
Please stop or I shall have to call the police.
Lily

Like the writing on Will's message, she kept hers in block

capitals in the assumption that anyone who wrote such simple characters would be unlikely to understand her usual untidy, scrawled script – ghost or not!

It took an age for her to drop off to sleep. Having left her note where she had discovered Will's she found herself tossing and turning, wondering whether it would be answered, and worrying whether she actually wanted it answering. If it were a real person who had written the first missive, would he be angry and come looking for her? If it were a ghost, would it turn nasty?

After half an hour of agitation, she rose from the bed, swept the clothes that were hung over a chair onto the floor, and then jammed the chair under the handle of her door. Surveying her handiwork, she decided that the barricade would have to do, no matter how flimsy. At least she would hear the clatter of the chair being moved if anyone tried to get in, which should give her chance to phone the police before beating a hasty retreat through the window.

Before scrambling back into bed she checked once more that her mobile was close to hand and that her path to the window was clear. Satisfied, she pulled the duvet close around her head and again fought for sleep.

The ringing of her mobile woke her. Rudely awakened, she sat upright in the bed, momentarily disoriented. The phone rang again, and she took deep breaths to calm her already frayed nerves. To her surprise, when she answered, her voice remained calm, which was just as well. The caller was Juan, asking if she was all right. After assuring him she was fine and telling him to stop worrying, he reluctantly wished her a good day, but not before letting her know no one had been spotted loitering outside her apartment the previous night.

The news settled Lily's nerves. At least if her note had been answered it ruled out one possibility. A flutter developed in the pit of her stomach. Which would leave the other.

Glancing at the clock she saw that it was eight-thirty, and tossed aside the duvet. It was way past the time she usually rose. Still dressed in her pyjamas, she dragged the chair away from her door, and then walked slowly toward the lounge. For some reason she tiptoed, and with every step her nerves grew more taught. By the time she grasped the handle and pushed the door open they were screaming.

Swallowing the build-up of saliva in her throat, she poked her head around the door jamb. To her relief, the room appeared as she had left it the previous night. The curtains were open, the window locked and there was no sign of anything untoward. She frowned. In fact there was no sign of anything, other than the TV, her settee, chair and table. Her note had gone.

Nerves forgotten, she ran to the spot where she had left it in case it had somehow blown out of view on an invisible breeze, but it was nowhere to be seen. It had been taken. But by whom? And why was there no reply?

Disappointment vied with relief. A part of her wanted there to be a reply now that her note had gone, if only to settle who or what was behind the mysterious goings on. Now she may never know. Then again, perhaps her note had done the trick and whomever it was that was playing silly buggers would pack it all in.

Two days later, that hope was quashed. After rising, Lily, as was her want, took her mug of coffee into the lounge to enjoy a leisurely start to the day, and there it was, nestled on the carpet next to the TV: a piece of paper.

The sight caused her to stop, her heart beating a now too familiar tattoo against her ribcage. Gathering her courage, she urged herself forward, her steps slow and halting, the mug clasped in her hands, to stare down at the untidy script gazing up at her. By squinting, she could just make out what it said.

Lily. Why are you doing this? I live here, not you. So why are you stealing my things? In case you are calling at the wrong house by mistake after your night-time trips, this is 7 Bark Lane and is owned by me, Will Taubman. Please stop bothering me or I will have to alert the watch as to your thievery.

Will

Her thievery? Lily was nonplussed. How could anyone accuse her of thievery when the stuff had been dumped on her floor? Her initial fear at seeing the note vanished, replaced by indignation. Placing the mug on the floor, she grabbed the note and moved over to the window to read it again.

After reading it for a third time she placed it on the sill and gazed out of the window in abstraction. It would seem that she had a ghost. Juan, in his morning call, had again confirmed the lack of any person or persons loitering around her apartment the previous night. So Will had to be a ghost, didn't he?

But a ghost that thought she was stealing his stuff? It didn't make sense. Her hand rose to finger the hearts suspended on their golden chain, a habit she had fallen into when worried, and her thoughts drifted. What if Will were not a ghost, that he was in fact still living and breathing, but in a different time? She'd seen a film about that once, one starring Sandra Bullock and Keanu Reeves, but that was fiction. This was real life. Surely things like that didn't happen for real?

The thought, obscure and totally improbable, stayed with her all day. By the time she finished her gardening jobs she had decided on a plan of action. As soon as she got home she made herself a coffee and then settled down in the lounge to write her letter.

Dear Will. You appear to be mistaken. This apartment is 23 King's Court, not 7 Bark Lane. Bark Lane was pulled down many years ago to make way for this new building. Either you are lying and playing me for an idiot, or you are a ghost with no right to be in my world. Please stop bothering me.
Lily

That night, it took all Lily's self-control not to admit to Juan what had happened, and what she had done. He would only worry if he knew about it and, with any luck, she would have it sorted by the time he arrived home in two days' time. Bidding him goodnight, she showered and retired early, eager to see whether Will would reply to her letter.

Surprisingly, she fell asleep almost immediately, and awoke bright and refreshed to Juan's morning call. Again he confirmed that no one suspicious had been seen outside her apartment, and told her he was looking forward to coming home and seeing her again. On thumbing the end-call button, she realised she was looking forward to seeing him, too. The realisation sent a warm, fuzzy feeling thrumming through her body.

Tossing aside the duvet, she rose and almost ran to the lounge, thrusting open the door to see if there was a piece of paper on the floor. There was, and she skidded to a halt. Would it be the one she'd left last night, or would it be a reply from the ghostly Will?

With eyes fixed on the white sheet, she stepped slowly forward, until she could see the writing more clearly. The writing was Will's. Stooping, she grasped the page and carried it to the window to read it in the light.

Lily. You are the one who is mistaken. 7 Bark Lane is where I live. My house is built of solid stone and there are no plans that I know of to pull it down. I have never heard of a King's Court. I am thinking

*that it is you who are the ghost. One who thieves, and I would like
you to stop.*

The reply had Lily bemused. He thought she was the ghost?
Maybe the Bullock/Reeves scenario was playing out. Maybe
there was a rift – was that what they called it? – in time that
was enabling her and Will to communicate.

Pushing herself away from the window, she decided to prove
to Will that the year she lived in was, in fact, 2008. A copy of
last week's *Manx Independent* was in the kitchen. If she left it
along with another letter he would have to believe she came
from the future. She giggled, wondering how he would take it.
She knew that if she were in his situation she would find it
difficult to believe. The thought had her laugh out loud. She
was in his situation, albeit in reverse.

Placing the paper where she had found Will's letter, she
wrote a message on the cover sheet.

Now do you believe me?

Rising, she looked down at her handiwork and rubbed her
hands together in satisfaction, and said, "Let's see what you
make of that, Will Taubman."

She did not have long to wait. By the time she'd made a
coffee and returned to the lounge to drink it the *Independent*
had gone, replaced by a copy of *Mona's Herald*. The date on
the paper was 29th August 1852 – that day's date, only 152
years earlier – and scrawled at the top were the words, *'Now do
you believe me?'*

Stunned, Lily slumped to the floor, staring at the date and
Will's scrawl. Fiction had become fact. She was communicating
with someone from the past who was still living his life, in the
very spot where she now resided. Suddenly nervous, her gaze
flicked around the room. Was he here now, with her but in a

different time?

After placing her mug on the floor she rose and went to the kitchen to grab her notebook and pen. It was time to find out. Her message was short and to the point.

I believe you.

Placing it where the newspaper had lain, she waited for something to happen. She had no idea what, but excitement had her staring at the slip of paper, willing it to disappear to wherever it went to. And it did. Not suddenly with a pop, but with a gradual dissolution, like a thin sliver of ice melting into the carpet.

Within a matter of moments, in much the same manner, her slip of paper reappeared. Under her words were scrawled Will's.

I also believe you.

Lily clapped her hands in delight. Will was real, not a ghost. Grabbing her pen and another sheet of paper, she asked him a question. The paper took longer to return this time, but Will's words held her spellbound. He had answered her question and posed one of his own.

Grabbing another sheet, she wrote her answer, taking care not to write too modern, and added yet another question of her own. Time flowed by quickly. Before Lily realised, dusk had fallen and her floor was covered in sheets of paper. But she was happy. She had discovered Will was single, two years older than she was, had lived alone since his father had drowned, his mother having died during childbirth, what he did for a living, and what life on the island was like in the 1800s. In turn, she had told him of her life, her dreams, about the purchase of the apartment, her necklace and what life was like the year 2008.

If it were not for the pounding at her front door she would have carried on all night. As it was, startled by the loud hammering, she scrawled a hasty note of apology and placed it on the floor before rising to see who was trying to break her door down. At the doorway to the lounge, she stopped and turned, dismayed at the amount of paper that littered her floor. It would take some clearing up, and sorting, but she intended to keep every piece, as a record of what they chatted about. Closing the door behind her, she smiled. It was like MSN, only without the computer.

Whoever it was outside pounded on the door again.

Annoyed by both the persistence and the interruption, Lily yelled, "I'm not deaf. Give me a moment."

She yanked the door open, intending to give the perpetrator a piece of her mind, but her words were crushed from her body by a fierce embrace.

Lily screamed, and the burly figure jumped back, immediately releasing her, hands rising to cover his ears. Lily's heart raced. She clutched at her chest and half-stumbled backwards, feeling faint.

"What did you go and do that for?" a deep voice asked. The figure belonging to the voice stepped forward, rubbing at its ears. "I think you've gone and deafened me."

The shriek that had been building died in Lily's throat and, eyes narrowed, she flew at the figure, beating small fists into his chest. "Why didn't you call me to say you were coming, you … you, idiot!"

Raising his arms, Juan defended himself against the blows, then reached out and grabbed her flailing arms. "Whoa! Ease up, Lily. What's got into you? I took the last flight back instead of waiting for tomorrow morning's. I thought you'd be pleased to see me."

With her arms still pumping against Juan's grip, Lily met

his amused gaze, and grew more angry. "Because, you idiot –"
She stopped what she was about to say, not ready to admit she
had been communicating with Will. Lashing out, she kicked
Juan in the shin.

Crying out in pain, he released his grip and bent down to
rub at his injured leg. "What did you go and do that for?" he
asked, peering up in bemusement.

"For scaring the hell out of me!" Lily snapped. She folded
her arms across her chest and glared down at him, her foot
beating an angry tattoo on the floor. "Or have you forgotten
there may be a lunatic out there dumping stuff in my lounge?"

Rising, Juan winced. "Oh. Right." Suddenly, he smiled and
held out his arms. "Well, now that you know it's me, how about
that hug?"

His smile was infectious, and Lily found her anger fading.
Stepping forward, she allowed him a momentary hug before
she eased away. "Next time," she warned, "call me before
surprising me."

Juan winked. "But then it wouldn't be a surprise, would
it?"

Pursing her lips, Lily shook her head, and then ushered
him in. There was no answer to that.

Juan stayed for an hour before Lily, feigning tiredness,
managed to shepherd him out, with the promise that she would
go out for dinner with him the following evening. Then, once
he'd left, she leaned back against the door and sighed in relief.
It had been difficult not to admit to her communication with
Will. And every time Juan mentioned the name the more
difficult it became. They had remained in the kitchen the
whole time, Lily claiming the lounge was a mass of ironing
that needed doing and had he called she would have cleaned it
up so they could talk in comfort. By the end of the evening
she was emotionally drained. It felt as though she had been

covering for an extra-marital affair, or at least how she supposed she would feel if she were having one. But she wasn't even married, for heaven's sake. So why did she feel so guilty?

She would have to tell him, of course, but not just yet. Maybe over dinner the following evening. She would see. Hoping that Will had left another message, she headed for the lounge to try and get the papers in some sort of order.

★ ★ ★

"So yer heard nothing back, then?"

Leaning against the wall by the front door, arms folded across his chest, Henry Gale flicked his gaze around the dingy, sparsely furnished room. Will could see the look of disapproval in his eyes, but ignored it. On his wages, what could Henry expect? Luxury and Will Taubman were two things that did not sit well together.

"Not since I told her to stop calling in on her way home and nicking my stuff."

Henry chuckled. "So who'd yer think she is then, this – this Lily woman?"

Will shrugged, and moved across the room to stoop beside the fire. Using a cloth, he took his pot from the spindle and rose. Turning to face Henry, he raised the pot and said, "No idea. Fancy some breakfast?"

Henry shook his head, and levered himself away from the wall and reached for the door latch. "No thanks, lad. I've already eaten. I'd best be off. They spotted a shoal of herring out in the bay and I'd best get out there. Tide's about right and the lads should have the boat about ready by now.

After opening the door, Henry turned to face Will. "You know I lost one of the lads?"

Will nodded, and waited for the expected question.

Henry briefly scanned the room before fixing his gaze on

Will. "You can do better than this, lad. I'll give yer till the end of the week afore I look for a replacement."

Will was still staring at the back of the door long after it had closed on Henry's exit. He knew Henry was right, but the sea was the last place he wanted to earn his living. The farm did not pay much, but he was happy there. And he was needed.

No longer feeling hungry, he placed the pot next to the fire. He had a hard few days ahead of him at Billy's farm, now that harvesting was upon them, and he'd best be away. But before he left he would have to write to Lily and let her know he'd be gone for the best part of a week. Moving to the tall cupboard next to the fire, he opened the door and pulled out the paper with her last message on it. Turning it over, he grabbed a stick of charcoal and wrote his note on the back, then placed the paper on the floor where the others had appeared.

They had been exchanging messages for over a week now and Will found himself looking forward to her notes. At first, he could not believe she was from the future, and was convinced she was a ghost sent to annoy him, but the newspaper and her descriptions of how places he knew and visited looked in the future convinced him. Lily was the closest he had ever been to having a relationship with a woman, and he knew he'd miss her company whilst away working.

Grabbing his pack, he made his way out into the lane, wondering if she would answer his latest question truthfully.

Although mid-morning, there was a chill on the breeze that wasn't present a couple of weeks ago, and Will shivered. Autumn would soon be here, and with it the winds and the rain. His thoughts returned to Henry's offer. It was not the time of year to consider a job on the waves over a job on land. No, Henry would have to find himself another sailor. This one was already taken. Humping his pack on his shoulder, he set out for Billy Teare's farm, little realising that by the time he arrived there, his plans for winter would have to change.

★   ★   ★

I will be away for a week, working on the farm. I will miss you.
What do you look like? I would like to know. Then I can picture
you when we write. Yours truly,
Will

It had been nearly a week since Will had sent the message,
and still Lily had not responded. Mainly because she did not
want to send a photograph of her to an empty house where
anyone could walk in and see it. Will had told her about Henry
Gale, and knew he would not be averse to entering the house
to see if he were in. And seeing as Will had not told Henry
about their exchange of notes, a colour photograph of some
girl from the future would be bound to stir up trouble.

Thinking of which, despite her promise to do so, she still
had not told Juan about Will. Somehow, she could not seem to
find the right moment in which to broach the subject, and the
longer she left it, the harder it became to bring up. Juan, now
that things had stopped appearing in her lounge, assumed it
had been someone playing pranks, and that the police presence
had seen them off, and concentrated his efforts on wooing Lily.
Efforts that were not entirely wasted.

From being a staunch advocate of female independence,
Lily now found herself with two men in her life. One who was
outgoing, loud, gregarious and proud to be seen out with her,
and one who was quiet, reserved and would never be seen with
her. Not in this life, anyway. She knew she would have to tell
each about the other, but not yet. She was enjoying herself too
much.

After placing the photograph on the floor, she checked
everywhere was locked for the night and went to bed. Juan

was on lates, and even though he said he would check on the apartment, she knew he would not call. In fact, she would be lucky if she saw much of him over the next four days. The thought was depressing, but at least she had her notes from Will to look forward to. He should have finished his work on the farm now, if she had read his message correctly.

Every morning for the next two weeks she raced into the lounge, expecting an answer, but her carpet remained bare. And with each day's lack of contact, the more withdrawn she became. Was the rift in time healed, or had something happened to Will that she did not know about?

The not-knowing ate away at her. Even Juan's natural exuberance could not pull her out of her dark mood, and the more he tried the more she withdrew. In the end, after one heated argument too many, he stormed out of the apartment, telling her to call him when she was ready.

Lily winced as the door slammed shut, and sagged against the kitchen worktop, the prickle of unshed tears in her eyes. It was not Juan's fault, so why had she chased him away? Using the back of a sleeve, she dabbed at her eyes. Now she was back to where she'd started; on her own.

Sighing, she levered herself away from the worktop. With any luck, all would be better after a decent night's sleep.

But it wasn't. There was still no return note from Will, and Juan refused to pick up her call. And she knew he was off that day. Staring out of the kitchen window at the rain-lashed roadway outside, the ringing tone in her ear, Lily knew that today was one day she would not spend working. Instead, she would go to the Bean Bar, have a latte, and watch the world go by. After putting on her boots, she grabbed her long coat and stepped out into the rain, head bowed, and headed for St Paul's Square.

The covered walkway sheltered her from the worst of the

elements, but Lily still kept her head bowed as she walked. When passing the bookshop, however, a title grabbed her eye, and she stopped to peer in. In the middle of a display on local authors was a book, *Ramsey From Days Gone By: Paintings by Michael Starkey*. Would there be a painting of Bark Lane, one that would show her where Will lived – used to live?

With there only being one way to find out, Lily bought a copy. Five minutes later she was seated at a table in the Bean Bar, leafing through the pages until she found the one she was looking for. On page 21 was a painting of the lane. Several small cottages flanked a narrow dirt track, barely twelve feet wide, each cottage unique and homely. And to think the lane and cottages once stood where she now lived. And that Will resided in one of them. The thought had her head spinning, and she wondered yet again why Will had not been in touch.

After finishing her coffee she made her way back home. Although the rain had lessened the wind had picked up, and she found herself leaning into the weather to prevent herself being blown backwards. Once home she stripped off her wet clothing and dressed in a baggy jumper and a pair of old trousers before making her way to the lounge to relax in comfort.

She saw it immediately – the paper lying on the floor, and ran over to it, knowing who it would be from. Excitement vied with relief as she grabbed it from the floor, devouring the words that Will had written.

Lily. I am sorry I am late writing you. Billy Teare died and I had to settle the affairs of the farm. It took longer than expected. I now have no job, so will ask Henry if he still wants me. It will mean me being away longer, as fishing is not all that Henry goes to sea for, but it will mean I have money. I will tell you more later. I like the picture you sent. You are very beautiful. May I keep it?
Will

The question caused Lily's lips to twitch into a smile. Shaking her head, she made her way through to the kitchen to pen her reply. When halfway through her note her mobile rang, and Lily grabbed it from the worktop.

"Lily. It's Juan. Can we talk? Over coffee? I ... I've been stupid and ... I miss you. Can we sort this mess out?"

It was an unusually subdued Juan Cubbon that strode up her pathway some twenty minutes later. Even his smile lacked its customary confidence as Lily opened the door to him.

"May I come in?" he asked, on seeing her.

Lily smiled, and moved aside, gesturing toward the lounge with a wave of her hand. "Your coffee awaits, good sir."

Her comment appeared to settle him, and his smile widened to resemble the one she normally associated with him as he stepped into the hallway.

"Lily –"

"Shhh! Not yet, Juan. I have something I need to tell you. Please, go through to the lounge."

His smile faded, and his eyes narrowed at her words, but he did as he was bid and headed for the front of the apartment. Once in the lounge, he halted, and turned to face her.

"What's with all these papers?" A wave of an arm drew Lily's eyes to the piles of Will's notes that she had sorted and stacked on the floor beneath the window.

With a wry smile, she said, "That's what I need to talk to you about."

* * *

"So you mean you have been communicating with someone from 1852? By notes that melt into the carpet and then melt back again?"

Lily nodded. They were sat on the settee, where they had been ensconced for the past two hours, Will's notes piled on the small table and the floor beside them. At first, when she had started her tale, Juan had thought her mad; she could see it in his eyes, but when she had shown him the notes and messages, detailing things that only someone from that era could have known, she could see that he was starting to believe.

Lily reached out and grabbed one of his hands in her own. Meeting his gaze, she said, "I know it sounds unbelievable, but you've seen Will's notes yourself. I'm not mad." She smiled. "So there's no need to ready a room at Ballamona just yet."

Juan shook his head, lips compressed. "I don't doubt you – now. But had you told me this a couple of weeks ago ..." He shook his head again. Then, reaching down, he grabbed the book on Ramsey scenes from the floor. "And you say his house is in a painting in this book?"

Releasing his hand, Lily shrugged. "I like to think so."

Juan flicked through the pages until he reached the one on Bark Lane. "Amazing."

"Juan!"

The urgency of Lily's tone had Juan looking up.

"There. On the floor." She pointed to a spot just in front of the TV, where a sheet of paper had materialised. "It's Will."

Rising, she grabbed it, and read it before handing it to Juan.

My dearest Lily. I must away now for a week or two. Henry has need of me for one of his illicit ventures. It is not something I am proud to be doing, but I have need of the coin. I will write when I return.
Yours in time,
Will

"Who's this Henry?" asked Juan, looking up.

"Henry Gale," Lily answered, settling onto the settee and grabbing the proffered note to read again. "Sometimes a fisherman but mostly a rogue, according to Will. With the farm having gone, he needed a job, and Henry had been pestering him for months to join his crew." Seeing a puzzled scowl on Juan's face, she said, "What's the matter?"

Pursing his lips, Juan shrugged. "Probably nothing, but that name seems familiar. From something I read about once."

Wide-eyed in amazement, Lily said, "So you believe me?"

Juan laughed. "How could I not?"

It took less than an hour after leaving Lily's place for Juan to discover where he had read about Henry Gale, but two days before he dared show her his findings. They were having coffee at the Bean Bar, on Juan's break, when he pulled a sheet of paper from his uniform pocket and handed it to Lily.

"What's this?" she asked, unfolding the paper.

Juan fidgeted on his seat, hands clasped around a mug of coffee. "I think you'd better read it," he said.

As she read, the paper wilted in her hands, and she could feel the colour drain from her face. "We have to tell Will," she murmured, rising from her seat.

Juan grasped an arm and held it firmly.

Lily tried to yank it free, but his grip was too strong. "Let me go," she demanded, unaware of the eyes turned their way. "I have to let him know."

Keeping his voice low, Juan said, "Think, Lily. If you tell him you risk altering the time-line. We have to let it run its course, however unjust or unfair, or risk changing … everything."

Like the paper in her hand, Lily sagged. How could she not tell Will about Henry's, about *his* future, now that she knew? Especially when it meant …"

"Lily!" Juan's grip tightened on her arm again. "You can't tell him. Understand?"

Dumbly, Lily nodded, and rose slowly to her feet. Her smile wan, she said, "I need some time alone. You understand?"

After holding her gaze for a moment, Juan nodded, and gave her arm a gentle squeeze. "You have to think of the now, Lily, not what has already gone."

Lily looked to the floor, unshed tears in her eyes, then turned and left the shop. Instead of heading for her apartment, she carried on down the road the short distance to South Beach. Once there, she sat on the wall and gazed out to sea. Somewhere out there, back in time, Will sailed with Henry, not knowing what his future held. Unfortunately, she did, and could not do anything about it.

As Christmas neared, Lily felt herself slide into depression. Communication with Will had been spasmodic due to his trips out to sea with Henry, but each note contained a warmth and vitality that, by rights, belonged to lovers. And each note reminded her that they did not have long left together. Juan, aware of the reason for her sadness, called round often, and did his best to lighten her mood, but nothing he could do or say could ever brighten the darkness that lay ahead.

It was Christmas Eve when Lily's resolve was tested, and found wanting. A shrivelled rose stem and a message from Will had arrived that morning. In it, he wished Lily a Merry Christmas, promising that he would send her a present upon his return, that Henry had asked him to sail with him, promising him a cargo that would set him up for life. Enough coin to buy his own farm.

Lily knew from Will's writings that a farm was the one thing he had wanted ever since Billy Teare had died, and the one thing he would never live to see should he sail with Henry on this one, last voyage.

Will's message ended with the lines:

If only you were here with me, we could spend our days on the farm together. As it is, I shall cherish your photograph and imagine

you are here, where you belong.
Yours in time,
Will

Not able to sit and wait for Will's demise, Lily penned what she hoped would not be her last message to the past.

My dearest Will.
I too wish I could be there to share your days, but this cannot be. Instead, I would like to think you will enjoy a long and healthy life with someone of your own time and to this end I urge you not to sail with Henry on this trip. My present to you is a long life. Please take heed of my urgings. Do not sail with Henry on this trip. I wish I could tell you more, but I cannot. I risk my future by asking you not to sail, but it is a risk I am willing to take for you. Write back as soon as you are able, if only to ease my mind.
With love,
Lily

Like melting ice, the message disappeared into the carpet, as did the tears that Lily shed.

Christmas Day came and went and the end of the month drew near. Juan, having taken extended holiday leave, refused to leave Lily on her own, and camped out in her apartment. He cooked for her, cleaned for her and took her for long walks to help her overcome a grief so deep that she glided through each day as though it were her last. She'd never received a reply from Will, and knew in her heart that her warning had been too late. That Will was with Henry, and that she would never hear from him again. Subconsciously, she was aware of everything Juan did for her, but was too immersed in her grief to react to his kindness.

On the morning of 28th December Juan opened the curtains to the lounge. Bright, winter sunlight flooded in through the window and illuminated the spot on the floor where Lily left the messages for Will. Only this time it was Lily who occupied the spot. Lying foetal, clothed in her pyjamas, Juan could hear her sobbing.

Quietly, so as not to frighten her, he padded across the room and gently eased his hands under her body and raised her to his chest. She was surprisingly light and he had no difficulty in levering himself upright.

Lily made no effort to escape, and leaned into his chest, her tears felt through the dampening of his t-shirt. With her settled into his arms, he carried her to her bedroom and lay her down on the bed, where once again she curled into a ball. After covering her with the duvet, he went through to the kitchen. He needed a coffee, and the stronger the better.

He had no sooner put the kettle on than a loud knocking at the apartment door had him flinching. Having been too immersed in thoughts of Lily and how he could help her overcome her grief now that the day was at hand, he had not heard the knocking at first, merely been aware of something at the periphery of his mind that was obtrusive and annoying.

Cursing, he walked the short distance down the hallway and opened the door.

"Is there a Lily Brigs that lives here?"

Juan gazed down at the short, scruffy little man who stood on the threshold. Dressed in farmer's dungarees, a pair of mud-splattered green wellington boots and a tattered overcoat that had seen better days, he looked like a tramp.

"And you are?"

"No matter who I am, feller, is there a Lily Brigs that lives here? I have something for her."

"Who is it?"

Juan scowled at the little man, who ducked down to peer around him and up the hallway, before calling over his shoulder. "No one Lily, just someone asking for directions."

The little man grinned. "So she does live here. Thought so." Thrusting a hand into a pocket, he pulled out a tattered envelope and held it out. "This is for her." He peered myopically at Juan. "A present from a friend."

Once Juan had taken it, the little man turned and scurried away.

"Who is it?"

This time Lily's voice came from somewhere closer. On turning, Juan saw her emerge from the bedroom, hair dishevelled, face white, leaning against the door jamb for support. She looked so weak and frail. Concerned in case she fell, Juan stepped forward to wrap an arm around her waist.

"You should be in bed."

Lily's eyes fixed on the faded, crumpled envelope in Juan's hand. "What's that?"

Raising it, Juan stared at the name written on the front, and Lily gasped.

Surging upright from the door jamb, she snatched the envelope from Juan's hands to stare at the name written on the front.

Surprised by the move, Juan placed his hands on her shoulders to steady her shaking, and asked, "What is it, Lily?"

With tears in her eyes, she looked up, then held the envelope for him to see. "It's his writing, Juan."

"Whose?"

"Will's."

Without further explanation, she ran into the lounge, leaned against the window sill, eased open the flap to the envelope and removed what lay inside.

"What is it?"

Lily looked over to where Juan had halted just inside the threshold to the room, and grinned.

"A photograph. My photograph."

In Lily's hand was the colour photograph she had sent through to Will two months previously. The colours were faded, the paper cracked and bent through age, but it was the same photograph, and she could still read the words she had written on the back.

To Will, from Lily.

Only there had been an addition, in Will's child-like handwriting.

I hope you liked my Christmas present. Look in the box beneath the lining. Will.

The necklace warmed, and Lily's hand rose to her chest. It felt like it was on fire. Suddenly knowing which box Will meant, she rushed past a startled Juan and hurtled into her bedroom. On the dresser was the wooden box that housed the necklace.

"A knife, Juan, fetch me a knife!"

Her words were loud and frantic, but she did not care. She had to see what Will had left her.

Not daring to utter a word, Juan returned from the kitchen with a knife. Lily snatched it from his hand and, taking deep breaths, eased the knife's edge inside the box and levered up the red lining. It was difficult to move at first, but once she had one corner raised the whole lining lifted and came free.

In the base of the box lay a black and white photograph. A middle-aged man and his wife gazed out from within the confines of the wooden sides. Dressed in their finery, standing stiff and erect, two young children standing beside them, it had been taken in front of a small farmhouse.

Lily's hands trembled as she reached in to remove the photograph. At first, it would not move, the paper having stuck

317

to the wood, but with gentle persuasion it eventually came free. Lily gazed at the handsome couple and their children for a moment before turning it over. On the back were the words;

To Lily, my guardian angel, forever in my thoughts.
Will

This time, the tears that fell were ones of happiness.

In the kitchen, on the wall where Lily had pinned the report on the demise of the *Brig Lily*, the name of Will Taubman faded from the list of twenty-nine men that had perished at Kittering on 28th December 1852.